You've heard about the critical raves,
but here's what readers are saying online about

The Books of History Chronicles

(Black, Red, White, Showdown, and Saint)

This trilogy is a MUST READ! Suspenseful, insightful, fast-paced, and certainly life-impacting. Ted Dekker is a master of bringing Truth close to home, in a way that causes us the readers to see and feel it in a fresh way.

D. (Pittsburgh, PA)

*Whew, ok I've read all three books in the Circle Trilogy back to back and all I can say is man what a ride. **Ted Dekker has to be one of our generations great story tellers**, this story of Thomas Hunter's fight to save mankind from a terrible virus intended to destroy the world is sure to become a Christian fiction classic much like Lewis's "Narnia" Series and Frank Perretti's "This Present Darkness".*

Todd (Mount Vernon, WA)

*This was the first book by Ted Dekker that I've ever read. It was all I needed to be hooked for life! **Ted Dekker has a way with words and story-telling that not many authors have anymore.** He draws you in and you have to make yourself stop for daily functions such as eating and occasional breathing!*

J. (South Carolina)

I cannot say enough good things about this book and series. It can change how you think. If a book can do that it is an amazing thing. I recommend it without reservation. The Circle Trilogy was my first Ted Dekker book, but it will not be the last.

Teresa (Parkersburg, WV)

I just finished Red, and all I can say is "Wow"! This story just keeps getting better. Is Ted Dekker talented or what? Before I became a Chritian, I used to read secular suspense. **I must say this is better than anything I've read not only in Christian writing, but in fiction period.**

Nicholas (Salt Lake City, UT)

WOW! **Ted Dekker continued to blow my socks off** *in book two of the trilogy Black, Red, and White. The book held my interest, in fact it drew me to continually read to the point that I finished it way faster than most books that I have read(I think my wife was ready to put me out with the dog).*

William (Stouffville, Ontario, Canada)

I am new to Ted Dekker: but I'll be getting further acquainted. The story kept me turning the pages; some of my guesses were prescient and others missed the mark. Captivating! **Where have I been as this author emerged in contemporary mystery fiction?** *A great read!*

Lori (Lake Forest, CA)

It is unbelievable how Ted can take your mind in so many directions at once and then tie all of it together and really put a spiritual meaning to the whole thing. **This is one of my favorite books of all time.**

Franklin (Warner Robins, GA)

Ted Dekker did it again. **He got me wrapped around his fingers** *(or writing I suppose). After months of wait I was not disappointed. This book is one of his best yet.*

Rafa S.

Dekker pulls out all the stops in this tale. I don't want to give too much away, but he really grabs you by the pants and doesn't let go! The blurbs are right, this ranks right up there with King and Koontz, not to be missed!
Matt Gallagher (Mendocino, CA USA)

Cherise (Western North Carolina)

WHITE

teddekker.com

THE CIRCLE TRILOGY

WHITE

The Great Pursuit

TED DEKkER

THOMAS NELSON

Since 1798

NASHVILLE   DALLAS   MEXICO CITY   RIO DE JANEIRO   BEIJING

Published in Nashville, Tennessee, by Thomas Nelson. Thomas Nelson is a trademark of Thomas Nelson, Inc.

Thomas Nelson, Inc. titles may be purchased in bulk for educational, business, fund-raising, or sales promotional use. For information, please e-mail SpecialMarkets@ThomasNelson.com.

This is a work of fiction. Names, characters, places, and incidents either are the product of the author's imagination or are used fictitiously. Any resemblance to actual persons, living or dead, events, organizations, or locales is entirely coincidental.

Library of Congress Cataloging-in-Publication Data

Dekker, Ted, 1962–
    White : the great pursuit / by Ted Dekker.
      p. cm.
    ISBN 978-0-8499-1792-9 (hardcover)
    ISBN 978-1-59554-011-9 (international)
    ISBN 978-1-59554-035-5 (trade paper)
    ISBN 978-1-59554-435-3 (repackage)
    I. Title.
    PS3554.E43W485 2004
    813'.6—dc22

2004010579

Printed in the United States of America
08 09 10 11 RRD 5 4 3

For my children.
May they always remember
what lies behind the veil.

Dear Reader,

Thomas Hunter's story begins in *Black,* Book One of The Circle Trilogy, and continues in *Red,* Book Two. If you've yet to read *Black* and *Red,* I strongly encourage you to start there. *White* is far richer once you've fully experienced Thomas's prior journeys into two realities. There are numerous plot twists that deserve grounding before you plunge into the pages ahead.

Once you've read *Black* and *Red,* you're ready to step into *White.* But be forewarned: nothing will prepare you—or Thomas—for what awaits him in this conclusion to the epic trilogy.

Publisher,
Thomas Nelson Fiction

North Dakota

Finley, population 543. That's what the sign read.

Finley, population 0. That's what the sign could very well read in two weeks, Mike Orear thought.

He stood on the edge of town, hot wind blowing through his hair, fighting a gnawing fear that the gray buildings erected along these vacated streets were tombstones waiting for the dead. The town had bustled with nearly three thousand residents before he'd gone off to school in North Forks and become a football star.

The last time he'd visited, two years earlier, the population had dwindled to under a thousand. Now, just over five hundred. One of countless dying towns scattered across America. But this one was special.

This was the town where his mother, Nancy Orear, lived. His father, Carl, and his only sister, Betsy, too. None of them knew he'd come. They'd talked every day since he'd broken the news of the Raison Strain, but yesterday Mike had come to the terrible conclusion that talking was no longer enough.

He had to see them again. Before they died. And before the march on Washington ramped up.

Mike left his car, slung his jacket over his shoulder, and walked up Central Avenue's sidewalk. He wanted to see without being seen, which, in Finley, was easier done on foot than in a flashy car. But there wasn't a soul in sight. Not one.

He wondered how much they knew about the virus. As much as he did, of course. They were glued to their sets at this moment, waiting for word of a breakthrough, like every other American.

His feet felt numb. Working 24/7 around the studio in Atlanta, he had thought of himself as a crusader on the front lines of this mess, slashing the way to the truth. Stirring the hearts of a million viewers, giving them hope. Breathing life into America. But his drive north along deserted highways awakened him to a new reality.

America was already dying. And the truth was killing them.

The truth that they were about to die, regardless of what the frantic talking heads said. Middle America was too smart to believe that grasping at straws was anything more than just that.

His feet crunched on the dust-blown pavement. Citizens State Bank loomed on his right.

Closed, the sign said. Not a soul.

He'd once held an account at this bank. Saved up his first forty dollars to buy the old blue Schwinn off Toby. And where was Toby today? Last he'd heard, his friend had taken a job in Los Angeles, defying his fear of earthquakes. Today earthquakes were the least of Toby's worries.

The sign in the window of Finley Lounge said it was open—the one establishment probably booming as a result of the crisis. For some the news would go down better with beer.

Mike walked by, unnerved by the thought of going in and meeting someone he might know. He wanted to talk to his mother and his father and Betsy, no one else. In a small inexplicable way, he somehow felt responsible for the virus, though simply letting America in on the dirty little secret that they were all doomed hardly qualified him.

He swallowed and walked on by Roger's Heating. Closed.

Still not a soul on Central or any of the side streets that he could see.

Mike stopped and turned around. So quiet. The wind seemed oblivious to the virus it had breathed into this town. An American flag flapped slowly over the post office, but he doubted any mail was being delivered today.

Somewhere a thousand scientists were searching for a way to break the

Raison Strain's back. Somewhere politicians and heads of states were screaming for answers and scrambling to explain away the inconceivable notion that death was at their doorstep. Somewhere nuclear warheads were flying through the air.

But here in Nowhere, America, better known as Finley, incorporated July 12, 1926, all Mike could hear was the sound of wind. All he could see were vacant streets and a blue sky dotted with puffy white clouds.

He suddenly thought that leaving his car had been a mistake. He should hurry back, jump in, and head to the protest march in Washington, where he was expected by morning.

Instead, Mike turned on his heels and began to run. Past Dave's Auto. On to Lincoln Street. To the end where the old white house his father had bought nearly forty years ago still stood.

He walked up to the door, calming his heavy breathing. No sound, no sign of life. He should at least hear the tube, shouldn't he?

Mike bounded up the steps, yanked the screen door open, and barged into the house.

There on the sofa, facing a muted television, sat his mother, his father, and Betsy, surrounded by scattered dishes, half-empty glasses, and bags of Safeway-brand potato chips. They were dressed in pajamas, hair tangled. Their arms were crossed and their faces hung like sacks from their cheekbones, but the moment they saw him, their eyes widened. If not for this sign of life, Mike might have guessed they were already dead.

"Mikey?" His mother jerked forward and paused, as if trying to decide whether or not she should trust her eyes. "Mike!" She pushed off the sofa and ran toward him, sobbing. Engulfed him in a hug.

He knew then that the march on Washington was the right thing to do. There was no other hope. They were all going to die.

He dropped his head on her shoulder and began to cry.

1

Kara Hunter angled her car through the Johns Hopkins University campus, cell phone plastered against her ear. The world was starting to fall apart, and she knew, deep down where people aren't supposed to know things, that something very important depended on her. Thomas depended on her, and the world depended on Thomas.

The situation was about as clear as an overcast midnight, but there was one star shining on the horizon, and so she kept her eyes on that bright guiding light.

She snugged the cell phone between her ear and shoulder and made a turn using both hands. "Forgive me for sounding desperate, Mr. Gains, but if you won't give me the clearance I need, I'm taking a gun in there."

"I didn't say I wouldn't get it for you," the deputy secretary of state said. She should be talking to the president himself, Kara thought, but he wasn't exactly the most accessible man on the planet these days. Unless, of course, your name was Thomas. "I said I would try. But this is a bit unconventional. Dr. Bancroft may . . . Excuse me." The phone went quiet. She could hear a muffled voice.

Gains came back on, speaking fast. "I'm gonna have to go."

"What is it?"

"It's need to know—"

"I am need to know! I may be the only link you have to Thomas, assuming he's alive! And Monique for that matter, assuming she's alive. Talk to me, for heaven's sake!"

He didn't answer.

"You owe me this, Mr. Secretary. You owe this to the country for not responding to Thomas the first time."

"You keep this to yourself." His tone left her with no doubt about his frustration at having to tell her anything. But of all people he must know that she might be on to something with this experiment of hers.

"Of course."

"We've just had a nuclear exchange," Gains said.

Nuclear?

"More accurately, Israel fired a missile into the ocean off the coast of France, and France has responded in kind. They have an ICBM in the air as we speak. I really have to go."

"Please, sir, call Dr. Bancroft."

"My aide already has."

"Thank you." She snapped the phone closed.

Surely it couldn't end this way! But Thomas had warned that the virus might be only part of the total destruction recorded in the Books of Histories. In fact, they'd discussed the possibility that the apocalypse predicted by the apostle John might be precipitated by the virus. Wasn't Israel featured prominently in John's apocalypse?

She swerved to avoid a lone bicycler, muttered a curse, and pushed the accelerator. Dr. Bancroft was her last hope. Thomas had been missing for nearly three days, and Monique had disappeared yesterday. She had to find out if either was alive—if not here, then in the other reality.

Bancroft was in his lab; she knew that much from a phone call earlier. She also knew that her brother's records were under the control of the government. Classified. Any inquiry about his earlier session with Dr. Bancroft would require authorization beyond the good doctor. With any luck, Gains had given her at least that much.

Kara parked her car and ran down the same steps she'd descended over a week earlier with CIA Director Phil Grant. The blinds on the basement door were drawn. She rapped on the glass.

"Dr. Bancroft!"

The door flew inward almost instantly. A frumpy man with bags under fiery eyes stood before her. "Yes, I will," he said.

"You will? You'll what?"

"Help you. Hurry!" The psychologist pulled her in, leaned out for a quick glance up the concrete stairwell, and closed the door. He hurried toward his desk.

"I've been poring over this data on Thomas for a week now. I've called a dozen colleagues—not idiots, mind you—and not one of them has heard of a silent sleep brain."

"Did the deputy secretary of state—"

"Just talked to them, yes. What's your idea?"

"What do you mean by a 'silent sleep brain'?" she asked.

"My coined term. A brain that doesn't dream while sleeping, like your brother's."

"There has to be some other explanation, right? We know he's dreaming. Or at least aware of another reality while he's sleeping."

"Unless this"—Bancroft indicated the room—"is the dream." He winked.

The doctor was sounding like Thomas now. They'd both gone off the deep end. Then again, what she was about to suggest would make this dream business sound perfectly logical by comparison.

"What's your idea?" he asked again.

She walked to the leather bed Thomas had slept on and faced the professor. The room's lights were low. A computer screen cast a dull glow over his desk. The brain-wave monitor sat dormant to her left.

"Do you still have the blood you drew from Thomas?" she asked.

"Blood?"

"The blood work—do you still have it?"

"That would have gone to our lab for analysis."

"And then where?"

"I doubt it's back."

"If it is—"

"Then it would be in the lab upstairs. Why are you interested in his blood?"

Kara took a deep breath. "Because of something that happened to Monique. She crossed over into Thomas's dreams. The only thing that links the realities other than dreams is blood, a person's life force, as it were. There's something unique about blood in religion, right? Christians believe that without the shedding of blood there is no forgiveness of sins. In this metaphysical reality Thomas has breached, blood also plays a critical role. At least as far as I can tell."

"Go on. What does this have to do with Monique's dreams?"

"Monique fell asleep with an open wound. She was with Thomas, who also had an open wound on his wrist. I know this sounds strange, but Monique told me she thought she crossed into this other reality because her blood was in contact with his when she dreamed. Thomas's blood is the bridge to his dream world."

Bancroft lifted a hand and adjusted his round glasses. "And you think that . . ." He stopped. The conclusion was obvious.

"I want to try."

"But they say that Thomas is dead," Bancroft said.

"For all we know, so is Monique. At least in this reality. The problem is, the world might still depend on those two. We can't afford for them to be dead. I'm not saying I understand exactly how or why this could work, I'm just saying we have to try something. This is the only thing I can think of."

"You want to re-create the environment that allowed Monique to cross over," he stated flatly.

"Under your supervision. Please . . ."

"No need to plead." A glimmer of anticipation lit his eyes. "Believe me, if I hadn't seen Thomas's monitors with my own eyes, I wouldn't be so eager. Besides, I've been tested positive for the virus he predicted from these dreams of his."

The psychologist's willingness didn't really surprise her. He was wacky enough to try it on his own, without her.

"Then we need his blood," she said.

Dr. Myles Bancroft headed toward the door. "We need his blood."

⊸⊶⊷

It took less than ten minutes to hook her up to the electrodes Bancroft would use to measure her brain activity. She didn't care about the whole testing rigmarole—she only wanted to dream with Thomas's blood. True, the notion was about as scientific as snake handling. But lying there with wires attached to her head in a dozen spots made the whole experiment feel surprisingly reasonable.

Bancroft tore off the blood-pressure cuff. "Pretty high. You're going to have to sleep, remember? You haven't told this to your heart yet."

"Then give me a stronger sedative."

"I don't want to go too strong. The pills you took should kick in any moment. Just try to relax."

Kara closed her eyes and tried to empty her mind. The missile that France had fired at Israel had either already landed or was about to. She couldn't imagine how a nuclear detonation in the Middle East would affect the current scenario. Scattered riots had started just this morning, according to the news. They were mostly in Third World countries, but unless a solution surfaced quickly, the West wouldn't be far behind.

They had ten days until the Raison Strain reached full maturity. Symptoms could begin to show among the virus's first contractors, which included her and Thomas, in five days. According to Monique, they had those five days to acquire an antivirus. Maybe six, seven at most. They were all guessing, of course, but Monique had seemed pretty confident that the virus could be reversed if administered within a day or two, maybe three, of first symptoms.

Too many maybes.

Five days. Could she feel any of the symptoms now? She focused on her skin. Nothing. Her joints, fingers, ankles. She moved them all and still felt nothing. Unless the slight tingle she felt on her right calf was a rash.

Now she was imagining.

Her mind suddenly swam. Symptom? No, the drug was beginning to kick in.

"I think it's time," she said.

"One second."

The doctor fiddled with his machine and finally came over. "You're feeling tired. Woozy?"

"Close enough."

"Do you want any local anesthetic?"

She hadn't considered that. "Just make the cut small." She wanted a mark so that if she did wake up in another reality, she would have the proof on her arm.

"Large enough to bleed," Bancroft said.

"Just do it."

Bancroft wet her right forearm with a cotton ball and then carefully pressed a scalpel against her skin. Sharp pain stabbed up her arm and she winced.

"Easy," he said. "Finished."

He picked up a syringe with some of Thomas's blood. The sample was small—they would use nearly half with this experiment of theirs.

"It would have been easier to inject this," he said.

"We don't know if it would work that way. Just do it the way it happened with Monique. We don't have time to mess around."

He lowered the syringe and pushed five or six drops of Thomas's blood onto her arm. It merged with a tiny bubble of her own blood. The doctor smeared the two together with his gloved finger. For a long moment they both stared at the mixed red stain.

Their eyes met. Soft pop music played lightly over the speakers—an instrumental version of "Dancing Queen" by Abba. He'd turned the lights even lower than when she'd first entered.

"I hope this works," she said.

"Go to sleep."

Kara closed her eyes again.

"Should I wake you?"

Thomas had always claimed that an hour sleeping could be a year in a dream. Her crossing to his world would be precipitated by falling asleep here. Her crossing back would be precipitated by dreaming there.

"Wake me up in a hour," she said.

2

Two ceremonies characterized the Circle more than any other: the union and the passing. The union was a wedding ceremony. The passing was a funeral. Both were celebrations.

Tonight, a hundred yards from the camp beside the red pool that had drawn them to this site, Thomas led his tribe in the passing. The tribe consisted of sixty-seven members, including men, women, and children, and they were all here to both mourn and celebrate Elijah's death.

They would mourn because, although Elijah had left no blood relatives, the old man had been a delight. His stories at the night campfires had been faithfully attended by half the tribe. Elijah had a way of making the young children howl with laughter while mesmerizing his older listeners with mystery and intrigue. Only Tanis had told such brilliant tales, they all agreed, and that was before the Crossing, long ago.

There was more about Elijah to like than his stories, of course: his love of children, his fascination with Elyon, his words of comfort in times when the Horde's pursuit became more stressful than any of them could bear.

But they also celebrated Elijah's passing as they would celebrate anyone's passing. Elijah was now in better company. He was with Justin. None of them knew precisely how nor what those such as Rachelle and Elijah were actually doing with Justin, but Thomas's tribe had no doubts whatsoever that their loved ones were with their Creator. And they had enough of a memory of swimming in the intoxicating water of the emerald lake to anticipate rejoining Elyon in such bliss.

They stood in a circle around the woodpile, looking at Elijah's still body in silence. Some of their cheeks were wet with tears; some smiled gently; all were lost in their own memories of the man.

Thomas glanced at the tribe. His family now. Each man, woman, and child carried a blazing torch, ready to light the pyre at the appropriate moment. Most of the people were dressed in the same beige tunics they'd worn earlier in the day, though many had placed desert flowers in their hair and painted their faces with bright colors mixed from powdered chalk and water.

Samuel and Marie stood to his left beside Mikil and Jamous. They'd grown quickly in this past year, practically a man and a woman now. They both wore the same coin-shaped pendants that all members of the Circle wore, usually on a thin thong of leather around their necks, but also as anklets or bracelets as Samuel and Marie did now.

Johan and William had joined the tribe for tomorrow's council meeting and now stood to Thomas's right.

Beyond the Circle, the red pool's dark water glistened with the light of the torches. A hundred fruit trees and palms rose around the oasis. Before the night was done, they would feast on the fruit and dance under its power, but for now they allowed themselves a moment of sorrow.

Thomas and his small band had found their first of twenty-seven red pools amid a small patch of trees, exactly where Justin said they would. In thirteen months, the Circle had led nearly a thousand Scabs into the red waters, where they drowned of their own will and found new life. A thousand. A minuscule number when compared to the two million Scabs who now lived in the dominant forest. Even so, the moment Qurong became aware of the growing movement, he'd organized a campaign to wipe the Circle from the Earth. They had become nomads, making camp in canvas tents near the red pools when possible, and running when not. Mostly running.

Johan had taught them the skills of desert survival: how to plant and harvest desert wheat, how to make thread from the stalks and weave tunics. Bedding, furniture, even their tents were all eerily reminiscent of the Horde way, though notably colored and spiced with Forest Dweller tastes. They ate fruit with their bread and adorned their tents with wild-flowers.

Thomas returned his thoughts to the body of Elijah on the wood. In the end they would all be dead—it was the one certainty for all living creatures. But after their deaths, they each would find a life just barely imagined this side of the colored forest. In many ways he envied the old man.

Thomas lifted his torch high. The others followed his lead.

"We are born of water and of spirit," he cried out.

"Of water and spirit," the tribe repeated. A new energy seemed to rise in the cool night air.

"We burn this body in defiance of death. It holds no power over us. The spirit lives, though the flesh dies. We are born of water and of the spirit!"

A hushed echo of his words swept through the circle.

"Whether we be taken by the sword or by age or by any cause, we are alive still, passing from this world to the next. For this reason we cele-brate Elijah's passing tonight. He is where we all long to be!"

The excitement was now palpable. They'd said their good-byes and paid their respects. Now it was time to relish their victory over death.

Thomas glanced at Samuel and Marie, who were both staring at him. Their own mother, his wife, Rachelle, had been killed thirteen months ago. They'd mourned her passing more than most, only because they'd understood less then than now.

He winked at his children, then shook the torch once overhead. "To life with Justin!"

He rushed the pyre and thrust his torch into the wood. As one, the Circle converged on the woodpile. Those close enough shoved their torches in; the rest threw them.

With a sudden *swoosh,* the fire engulfed Elijah's body.

Immediately a drumbeat rolled through the night. Voices yelled in jubilation and arms were thrust skyward in victory, perhaps exaggerated in hope but true to the spirit of the Circle. Without the belief in what awaited each of them, all other hope was moot.

Elijah had been taken home to the Great Romance. Tonight he was the bride, and his bridegroom, Justin, who was also Elyon, had taken him back into the lake of infinite waters. And more.

To say there wasn't at least some envy among the tribe at a time like this would be a lie.

They danced in a large circle around the roaring fire. Thomas laughed as the celebration took on a life of its own. He watched the Circle, his heart swelling with pride. Then he stepped back from the fire's dancing light and crossed his arms. He faced the dark night where cliffs were silhouetted by a starry sky.

"You see, Justin? We celebrate our passing with the same fervor that you showed us after your own."

An image filled his mind: Justin riding to them on a white horse the day after his drowning, then pulling up, eyes blazing with excitement. He'd run to each of them and grasped their hands. He'd pronounced them the Circle on that day.

The day Rachelle had been killed by the Horde.

"I hope you were right about settling here," a voice said softly at his shoulder.

He faced Johan, who followed his gaze to the cliffs.

"If the Horde is anywhere near, they've seen the fire already," Johan said.

Thomas clasped his shoulder. "You worry too much, my friend. When have we let the threat of a few Scabs distract us from celebrating our sacred love? Besides, there's been no warning from our guard."

"But we have heard that Woref has stepped up his search. I know that man; he's relentless."

"And so is our love for Justin. I'm sick of running."

Johan did not react. "We meet at daybreak?"

"Assuming the Horde hasn't swept us all out to the desert." Thomas winked. "At daybreak."

"You make light now. Soon enough it will be a reality," Johan said. He dipped his head and returned to the revelry.

⸺∞⸺

They sat on flat rocks early the next morning, pondering. At least Thomas, Suzan, and Jeremiah were pondering, silent for the most part. The other members of the council—Johan, William, and Ronin—might also be pondering, but their cranial activity didn't interfere with their mouths.

"Never!" Ronin said. "I can tell you without the slightest reservation that if Justin were standing here today, in this very canyon, he would set you straight. He always insisted that we would be hated! Now you're suggesting that we go out of our way to appease the Horde? Why?"

"How can we influence the Horde if they hate us?" Johan demanded. "Yes, let them hate our beliefs. You have no argument from me there. But does this mean we should go out of our way to antagonize them so that they despise every albino they see?"

The Horde referred to them as albinos because their flesh wasn't scaly and gray like a Scab's skin. Ironic, because they were all darker than the Horde. In fact, nearly half of the Circle, including Suzan, had various shades of chocolate skin. They were the envy of most lighter-skinned albinos because the rich tones differentiated them so dramatically from the white Horde. Some members of the Circle even took to painting their skin brown for the ceremonies. All of them bore the albino name with pride. It meant they were different, and there was nothing they wanted more than to be different from the Horde.

Ronin paced on the sand, red-faced despite the cool air. "You're putting words in my mouth. I've never suggested we antagonize the Horde. But Justin was never for embracing the status quo. If the Horde is the culture, then Justin was counterculture. We lose that understanding and we lose who we are."

"You're not listening, Ronin." Johan sighed with frustration. "For the first six months, Qurong left us alone. He was too busy tearing down trees to make room for his new city. But now the winds have changed. This new campaign led by Woref isn't just a temporary distraction for them. I know Qurong! Worse, I know Woref. That old python once oversaw the Horde's intelligence under my command. At this very moment he's undoubtedly stalking us. He won't stop until every one of us is dead. You think Justin intended to lead us to our deaths?"

"Isn't that why we enter the red pools?" Ronin asked. "To die?" He grabbed the pendant that hung from his neck and held it out. "Doesn't our very history mark us as dead to this world?"

The medallion cradled in his hand had been carved from green jade found in the canyons north of the Southern Forest. Craftsmen inlaid the medallion with polished black slate to represent evil's encroachment on the colored forest. Within the black circle were tied two crossing straps of red-dyed leather, representing Justin's sacrifice in the red pools. Finally, they fixed a white circle hewn from marble where the red leather straps crossed.

"We find life, not death, in the pools," Johan said. "But even there, we might consider a change in our strategies."

Thomas looked at his late wife's brother. This wasn't the boy who'd once innocently bounded about the hills; this was the man who'd embraced a persona named Martyn and become a mighty Scab leader accustomed to having his way. Granted, Johan was no Martyn now, but he was still headstrong, and he was flexing his muscle.

"Think what you will about what Justin would or wouldn't have wanted," Johan said, "but remember that I was with him too."

Light flashed through Ronin's eyes, and for a moment Thomas thought he might remind Johan that he hadn't only been with Justin; he'd betrayed him. Oversaw his drowning. Murdered him.

But Ronin set his jaw and held his tongue.

"I did make my share of mistakes," Johan said, noting the look. "But I think he's forgiven me for that. And I don't think what I'm suggesting now is a mistake. Please, at least consider what I'm saying."

"What are you saying?" Thomas asked. "In the simplest of terms."

Johan stared into his eyes. "I'm saying that we have to make it easier for the enemies of Elyon to find him."

"Yes, but what does that mean?" Ronin demanded. "You're suggesting that the drowning is too difficult? It was Justin's way!"

"Did I say the drowning was too difficult?" Johan glared at Ronin, then closed his eyes and held up a hand. "Forgive me." Eyes open. "I'm saying that I know the Horde better than anyone here. I know their aversions and their passions." He looked to Jeremiah as if for support. The old man averted his eyes. "If we want to embrace them—to love them as Justin does—we have to allow them to identify with us. We must be more tolerant of their ways. We must consider using methods that are more acceptable to them."

"Such as?" Thomas asked.

"Such as opening the Circle to Scabs who haven't drowned."

"They would never be like us without drowning. They can't even eat our fruit without spitting it out."

Thomas spoke of the fruit that grew around the red pools. Although the red water was sweet to drink, it held no known medicinal value. The fruit that grew on the trees around the pools, on the other hand, was medicinal, and some of it was not unlike the fruit from the colored forest. Some fruits could heal; others gave nourishment far beyond a single bite. Some filled a person with an overpowering sense of love and joy—they called this kind woromo, which had quickly become the most valuable among all the fruits. To any Scab who hadn't entered the red pools, this particular fruit tasted bitter.

"That's right; they don't like our fruit," Johan said. "And they can't be like us—that's my point. If they can't be like us, then we might consider being more like them."

Thomas wasn't sure he'd heard right. Johan wouldn't suggest the Circle reverse what Justin had commanded. There had to be sensible nuances to what he was suggesting.

"I know it sounds odd," Johan continued, "but consider the possibilities. If we were to look more like them, smell like them, dress like them, refrain from flaunting our differences, they might be more willing to tolerate us. Maybe even to live among us. We could introduce them to Justin's teachings slowly and win them over."

"And what about the drowning?" Ronin asked.

Johan hesitated, then answered without looking at the man. "Perhaps if they follow Justin in principle, he wouldn't require that they actually drown." He looked at Ronin. "After all, love is a matter of the heart, not the flesh. Why can't someone follow Justin without changing who they are?"

Thomas felt his veins grow cold. Not because the suggestion was so preposterous, but because it made such terrible sense. It would seem that Johan, of all people, having been drawn out of deception as a member of the Horde, would stand firm on the doctrine of drowning. But Johan had made his case to Thomas once already—his suggestion was motivated by compassion for the Horde.

The survival of the thousand who followed Justin depended on being able to flee the Horde at a moment's notice. But the small nomadic communities were growing tired of running for their lives. This teaching from Johan would be embraced by some of them, Thomas had no doubt.

Ronin spit to one side, picked up his leather satchel, and started to walk away. "I will have no part of this. The Justin I knew would never have condoned such blasphemy. He said they would hate us! Are you deaf? Hate us."

"Then go to Justin and ask him what we should do," Johan said. "Please, I mean no offense, Ronin. I'm just trying to make sense of things myself."

William stepped forward and spoke for the first time. "I have another way."

They all faced him, including Ronin, who had stopped.

"Johan is right. We do have a serious problem. But instead of embracing the Horde's ways, it is my contention that we follow Justin by separating ourselves from the Horde as he himself instructed. I would like to take my tribe deep."

This wasn't the first time William had suggested fleeing into the desert, but he'd never made a formal request of it.

"And how can you follow Justin's instruction to lead them to the drowning if you're deep in the desert?" Ronin challenged.

"Others can lead them to the drowning. But think of the women and children. We must protect them!"

"Justin will protect them if he wishes," Ronin said.

Thomas glanced at Johan, then back at William. The Circle's first deep fractures were already starting to show. For more than a year they'd followed Ronin's lead on doctrine, as instructed by Justin, but these new challenges would test his leadership.

What else had Justin told them that day after drawing a circle around them in the sand?

Never break the Circle.

Ronin glared at each of them. "What's happening here? We're already forgetting why we came together? Why our skin is different? We're forgetting the Great Romance between Elyon and his people? That we are his bride?"

"His bride? That's merely a metaphor," William said. "And even so, we are his bride; the Horde is not. So I say we take the bride deep into the desert and hide her from the enemy."

"We are his bride, and whoever follows us out of the Horde will be his bride as well," Ronin said. "How will the Horde ever hear Elyon's call to love unless it's from our own throats?"

"Elyon doesn't need our throats!" William countered. "You think the Creator is so dependent on you?"

"Keep it down. You'll wake the camp," Thomas said, standing. He glanced at Jeremiah and Suzan, who hadn't spoken yet. "We're on a dangerous course here."

No one disagreed.

"Ronin, read this passage for us again. The one about them hating us."

Ronin reached into his satchel and withdrew the Book of History that Justin had given them before his departure. They all knew it quite well, but the teachings it held were at times difficult to understand.

Ronin carefully peeled the cloth off and opened the cover. *The Histories Recorded by His Beloved.* He flipped through dog-eared pages and found the passage. "Here it is. Listen." His voice lowered and he read with an accustomed somber respect. "When the world hates you, remember that it hated me first. If you belonged to the world, it would love you. But you do not belong to the world. I have brought you out of the world, and that is why it hates you."

"Things change with time," Johan said.

"Nothing has changed!" Ronin said, closing the Book. "Following Justin may be easy, but making the decision never is. Are you second-guessing his way?"

"Slow down," Thomas said. "Please! This kind of division will destroy us. We must remember what we know as certain."

He looked at Jeremiah again. "Remind us."

"As certain?"

"Absolute certainty."

The older man reminded Thomas of Elijah. He stroked his long white beard and cleared his throat.

"That Justin is Elyon. That according to the Book of History, Elyon is father, son, and spirit. That Justin left us with a way back to the colored forest through the red pools. That Elyon is wooing his bride. That Justin will soon come back for his bride."

Now Suzan spoke. "And that most of what we know about who Justin really is, we know from the Book through metaphor. He's the light, the vine, the water that gives life." She gestured to the Book of History in Ronin's hand. "His spirit is the wind; he is the bread of life, the shepherd who would leave all for the sake of one."

"True enough," Thomas said. "And when the Book tells us to drink his blood, it means that we should embrace his death. So how can we hide by running deep into the desert, or by putting ash and sulfur on our skin?"

"He also told us to flee to the Southern Forest," William said. "If what you're saying is true, then why didn't he tell us to run back to the Horde? Perhaps because the bride has a responsibility to stay alive."

William did have a point. The dichotomy was reminiscent of the religion Thomas vaguely remembered from his dreams.

"I intend to leave today and lead a hundred into the deep desert," William said. "Johan's right. It'll only be a matter of time before Woref flushes us out. If you expect any mercy from him, you're mistaken. He'd kill us all to save himself the trouble of dragging us back to the city. This is a matter of prudence for me."

Thomas looked down the canyon, toward the entrance to a small enclave where the tribe was slowly waking. A small boy squatted in the sand by the entrance, drawing with his finger. Smoke drifted from a fire around the cliff wall—they were getting ready to cook the morning wheat pancakes. As the smoke rose, it was swept down-canyon by a perpetual breeze, and most of it dissipated before it rose high enough to be seen from any distance. A thin trail of smoke lingered over the funeral pyre beyond towering boulders a hundred meters from the camp.

Thomas took a deep breath, glanced at the pile of large rocks to his right, and was about to tell William to take his expedition when a man stepped around the largest boulder.

Thomas's first thought was that he was hallucinating. Dreaming, as he used to dream before the dreams had vanished. This was no ordinary man standing before him, drilling him with green eyes.

This was . . .

Justin?

Thomas blinked to clear his vision.

What he saw made his whole body seize. Justin was still there, standing in three complete dimensions, as real as any man Thomas had ever faced.

"Hello, Thomas."

Justin's kind eyes flashed, not with reflected light, but with their own brilliance. Thomas thought he should fall to his knees. He was surprised the others hadn't dropped already. They, like him, had been immobilized by Justin's sudden appearance.

"I've been watching you, my friend. What I see makes me proud."

Thomas opened his mouth, but nothing came out.

"I've shared my mind with you," Justin said. "I've given my body for you." His mouth twisted into a grin and he spoke each word clearly. "Now I will show you my heart," he said. "I will show you my love."

Thomas felt each word hit his chest, as if they were soft objects flung through the air, impacting one at a time. Now I will show you my heart. My love.

Thomas turned his head toward the others. They stared at him, not comprehending. Surely they saw! Surely they heard.

"This is for you, Thomas," Justin said. "Only you."

Thomas looked back at—

Justin was gone!

The morning air felt heavy.

"Thomas!"

Thomas turned back toward the camp in time to see Mikil rushing around the cliff. She pulled up and stared at him, face white.

"What is it?" he asked absently, mind still split.

"I'm . . . I think I know something about Kara," she said.

"Kara? Who's Kara?"

But as soon as he asked, he remembered. His sister. From the histories.

3

Woref swung his leg over the stallion and dropped to the sand. Behind him, a hundred of his best soldiers waited on horses that stamped and occasionally snorted in the cool morning air. They'd approached the firelit sky last night, camped at the edge of the Southern Forest, and risen while it was still dark. This could be the day that marked the beginning of the end for the albinos.

The lieutenant who'd first located this camp had never been wrong—once again he hadn't disappointed. Still, they'd been in similar situations a dozen times, the albinos within reach, only to return home empty-handed. The Circle didn't fight, but they had perfected the art of evasion.

Woref stared at the canyons ahead. The blue smoke of burning horse manure was unmistakable. Soren had reported a small oasis south of the camp—roughly a hundred trees around one of the poisonous red pools—but the albinos were too smart to use any wood unless it was already fallen. Instead they used recycled fuel, as a Scab would. They'd adapted to the desert well with Martyn's help. Johan's help.

Woref's dreadlocks hung heavy on his head, and he rolled his neck to clear one from his face. Truth be told, he'd never liked Martyn. His defection was appropriate. Better, it had opened the way for Woref's own promotion. Now he was the hunter and Martyn the prey, along with Thomas. The reward for their heads was a heady prospect.

"Show me their retreat paths," he said.

Soren dropped to one knee and drew in the sand. "The canyon looks like a box, but there are two exits, here and here. One leads to the pool, here; the other to the open desert."

"How many women and children?"

"Twenty or thirty. Roughly half."

"And you're sure that Thomas is among the men?"

"Yes sir. I will stake my life on it."

Woref grunted. "You may regret it. Qurong's losing his patience."

A thousand or so dissidents sworn to nonviolence didn't present a threat to the Horde, but the number of defections from the Horde to the Circle was water on Qurong's flaky skin. He was adamant about pre-empting any deterioration in his power base. Thomas of Hunter had defeated him one too many times in battle to take any chances.

"As are we." Soren dipped his head then added, "Sir."

Woref spit to one side. The whole army knew that Thomas of Hunter's head wasn't the only head at stake here. What they didn't know was that Qurong's own daughter, Chelise, was also at stake.

The supreme leader had long ago promised to allow his daughter to marry once the Horde captured the forests, but he had changed his mind when Thomas escaped. As long as Thomas of Hunter was free to lead a rebellion, Chelise would remain single. At the outset of this campaign, he'd secretly sworn his daughter's hand to Woref, pending the capture of Thomas.

At times Woref wondered if Qurong was only protecting his daughter, who'd made it clear that she wasn't interested in marrying any general, including Woref. Her dismissal only fueled Woref's desire. If Qurong refused him this time, he would kill the leader and take Chelise by force.

"They have no intelligence of our approach?" he asked.

"No sign of it. I can't recall an opportunity as promising as this."

"Send twenty to cover each escape route. Death to the man who alerts them before we are ready. We attack in twenty minutes. Go."

Soren ran back and quietly leveled his orders.

Woref squeezed his fingers into fists and relaxed them. He missed the days when the Forest Guard fought like men. Their fearless leader had turned into a mouse. One loud word and he would scamper for the rocks, where the Horde had little chance of ferreting him out. The albinos were still much quicker than Scabs.

Woref had watched the battle at the Natalga Gap, when Thomas had rained fire down on them with the thunder he called bombs. None had been used since, but that would change once they had Thomas in chains. The battle leading up to that crushing defeat had been the best kind. Thousands had died on both sides. Granted, many more thousands of the Horde than the Forest Guard, but they had Thomas on his heels before the cliffs had crushed the Horde.

Woref had killed eight of the Guard that day. He could still remember each blow, severing flesh and bone. The smell of blood. The cries of pain. The white eyes of terror. Killing. There was no experience that even closely compared.

His orders were to bring Thomas in alive, in part because of information the rogue leader could offer, in part because Qurong meant to make an example of him. But if given the excuse, Woref would kill the man. Thomas was responsible for his loneliness these last thirteen months—these past three years, in fact, ever since Chelise had grown into the woman she was, tempting any whole-blooded man with her leveled chin and long flowing hair and flashing gray eyes. He'd known that she would be his. But he hadn't expected such a delay.

He'd objected bitterly to Qurong's decision to delay her marriage after the drowning of Justin. If Martyn had still been with them, Woref's indiscretion that night might have cost him his life. But in the confusion of such wholesale change, Qurong needed a strong hand to keep the peace. Woref had assumed Martyn's place and performed without fault. There wasn't a Scab alive who didn't fear his name.

"Sir?"

Soren stepped up to him, but Woref didn't acknowledge him. He suppressed a flash of anger. *Did I say come? No, but you came anyway. One day no one will dare approach me without permission.*

"They've gone, as you ordered."

Woref walked back to his horse, lifted his boot into the stirrup, paused to let the pain in his joints pass, then mounted. The albinos claimed not to have any pain. It was a lie.

"Tell the men that we will execute one of them for every albino who escapes," he said.

"And how many of the albinos do we kill?"

"Only as many as it takes to capture Thomas. They're more useful alive."

4

Your sister," Mikil said. "Kara."

Mikil felt her knees weaken. They stood deadlocked, stares unbroken. The others were looking at both of them as if they'd gone crazy.

"I . . ." Thomas finally stammered. "Is that possible? I . . . I haven't dreamed for thirteen months."

She'd awakened in her tent with the certain knowledge that she wasn't entirely herself. Her mind was full of thoughts beyond those she would ordinarily entertain. In fact, she was considering the strange possibility that she was Thomas of Hunter's sister. Kara.

The moment she considered the possibility, her mind seemed to embrace it. The more she embraced it, the more she remembered Thomas's dreams, and more, Rachelle's dreams. As a woman named Monique.

Then she knew the truth. Kara of Hunter had made a connection with her. Details seeped into her mind. Thomas's sister, who'd just fallen asleep in Dr. Bancroft's laboratory, was dreaming as if she were Mikil at this very moment. Mikil's own husband, Jamous, lay asleep beside her. She had no children. She was well liked if a bit stiff-necked on occasion. She was Thomas's "right-hand man."

But she was also privy to Kara's situation in the histories. She had Mikil's memories and Kara's memories at once. She was technically Mikil—that much was obvious—but she was suddenly feeling nearly as much like Kara.

So Kara had joined her brother in his dreams—at least that was how she thought of it. Now Kara stood gaping at a spitting image of her own brother plus about fifteen years. He wore a sleeveless tunic that

accentuated bulging biceps. Below, a short leather skirt that hung midthigh over a well-worn beige tunic. His boots were strapped up high over well-defined calves. The man before her had to be twice as strong as her brother.

"Wow," she said. "You're quite the stud."

Stud? Where had that word come from? Kara.

"A horse?" William said. "You insult him?"

"No, she means something else," Thomas said. "My friends, I would like to introduce you to my sister from my dream world. There, her name is Kara."

William's left eyebrow arched high. "She looks like Mikil to me."

"Yes, but evidently Mikil's brought Kara for a visit."

"Surely you can't be serious," William scoffed.

Mikil grinned. "More serious than you imagine. How else would I know to call him a stud? In the histories it means 'strong,' among other things. Kara's never seen him in this state, and she's surprised by just how strong our Thomas is compared to her brother, who looks the same, less about fifteen years and forty pounds of muscle."

Mikil nearly laughed out loud at the twists in her mind. She felt like both women at once—an exhilarating experience, to say the least.

To Thomas: "Can I speak with you in private? Just a moment."

They stepped to the side and she spoke in a whisper. "You haven't dreamed for thirteen months, you said. Do you know why?"

By his frown, he seemed to be second-guessing his initial conclusion that Kara was dreaming through Mikil. "Where did we grow up?"

"Manila," she said.

"Where does our mother live?"

"New York. Satisfied?"

Slowly a smile crossed his face. "So you're alive, then. The virus didn't kill you?"

"Not yet. We still have ten days to go. You were killed in France by Carlos two, maybe three, days ago. And now Monique's missing as well."

He stared at her, mind grappling with her information.

"Rachelle was killed thirteen months ago by the Horde," he said.

"I know. I'm Mikil. And Kara's sorry . . . terribly sorry."

"So you're saying that thirteen months have passed here but only a couple of days there?" he asked.

"Evidently. And you're saying that you haven't dreamed of Thomas in France in all this time?"

"The last dream I had of Thomas was falling asleep next to Monique."

"Where you were shot by Carlos," Mikil said.

His eyes widened. "Then I was right! I fell from my horse here. I was killed, but Justin healed me through Rachelle."

"But you're not alive in France?" she asked. "When you were brought back before, you came back to life in both realities."

"No. I never died before. I was healed instantly, before I actually died. Both times at the lake. This time I was dead for hours before Rachelle found me."

The exchange stalled.

"By the Hordes who pursue us, what is all this nonsense?" Ronin demanded. They were obviously being overheard.

William grinned. "It's our fearless leader's dream world. Apparently Mikil has joined the game."

Mikil ignored them. "Then you are dead in France, aren't you?"

"I must be."

"But you've only been dead for a couple days. Maybe three."

"So it would seem. And Monique's missing because she died when Rachelle died. She was connected with Rachelle the way you are with Mikil. I haven't dreamed because there's nothing for me to dream."

"And I'm here to bring you back," Mikil said.

Thomas set his jaw. "I can't go back. I don't want to go back. I'm dead there! I'm better off thinking that the histories were a dream."

"I'm no dream. My knowledge of our childhood in the Philippines is nothing like a dream." She shoved out her arm and showed him the cut. "Is this cut a dream? The Raison Strain is only days from showing its first real teeth, France has just fired a nuke at Israel, the world is about to die, and the best I can figure it, you're the only man alive who can stop any of it. Don't tell me it's a dream."

He looked at her skeptically.

"It's been thirteen months—you've lost your edge," she said. "But as you said yourself, you died here when Thomas was killed in France. So now that I'm linked with Mikil, will she also die when the virus kills me in ten days?"

The lights were starting to fire in his mind. She pushed.

"I—Mikil, that is—was wrong to doubt you. The world depends on—"

"Then the world is depending on a dead man," he said.

"This is utter nonsense!" William said. "There are more important matters to deal with than this game. You've lost your mind along with him, Mikil. Now, I would like the blessing of this council to take my tribe deep into the desert to form our own faction of the Circle. That is why I've come, not to reminisce about your dreams."

Mikil and Thomas closed ranks with the group.

"You forget so quickly, William?" Thomas said. "How do you think I made the bombs that blew the Horde back to hell? Was that my magic? No, that was information I learned from the histories."

"Yes, your memories of the Books of Histories, recalled in some trance or dream; I can accept that, however unlikely it sounds. But this nonsense of saving people in history . . . please! It's laughable!"

"You've always doubted me, William. Always. I can see now that you always will. Even Justin talked about the blank Book . . ."

Thomas stopped.

Mikil recalled Justin's words to them in the desert thirteen months earlier. She said what Thomas was thinking. "Justin said the blank Book of History created history. But only in the histories. What could that have meant?"

"We've never known," Thomas said. "Never had a reason to care much about the histories since . . ." He looked at Mikil with wide eyes. "Only a couple of days, you say?"

"Believe me, the histories are real. And if you don't care about them because you've gone and died in France, you should care about them because Kara is still alive."

Thomas studied her. He turned to Ronin. "You have the Book?"

"Which Book?"

"The blank Book. This Book that supposedly only works in the histories."

Ronin hesitated, then pulled out a second Book wrapped in canvas. He extracted it from the packaging. He ran a hand over the cover. The title was embossed in a corroded gold foil. *The Story of History.*

"How would a history book make history?" Mikil asked, walking up next to Thomas.

"You're saying that this Book has power in another dimension that is called 'the histories'?" Jeremiah asked. "How is that possible?"

Thomas hurried toward Ronin, suddenly eager. "May I?"

Ronin handed him the Book.

"Could it be?"

"Nonsense," Jeremiah said.

"You said it yourself," Thomas said. "The analogies and metaphors. The stories," he said, his fingers tracing the title. "They're real. Words become flesh and dwell among us. Isn't that how the Beloved's Book begins?"

Thomas opened the Book. Plain parchment. No words. Thomas's eyes met Mikil's, wide with wonder.

She looked at the Book again. "Do you think . . ." But she couldn't say what she was thinking. How was it possible?

"This is the most outlandish thing I've heard," William said. "You expect us to believe that if you write in that Book, something will actually happen, based on the words alone?"

"Why not?" Thomas said.

"Because the whole notion of the word becoming flesh is a metaphor, as you said. Justin was not some scribbling in a book. You're crossing a line here."

"You're wrong," Thomas told him. Then to Mikil, "Where Kara and I come from, no one is required to dive into a pool of red water and drown to follow Justin. They are simply required to die metaphorically." He looked at Kara. "They take up their crosses, so to speak. Tell them, Kara."

She was making the connections as quickly as he was. Neither of them had been practicing Christians, but they'd grown up with a chaplain for a father. They knew the basics of Christianity well enough.

"'Take up your cross and follow me,' Jesus said. He was executed on a cross, as were many of his followers later. But his followers aren't required to die in that fashion."

"Exactly," Thomas said. "Yet here our following isn't metaphorical at all. The same could be said about evil. There the people don't wear a disease on their skin—it's said to be in their hearts. But look at the Scabs. Their refusal to follow Justin in drowning shows up as a physical disease."

William seemed somewhat stunned by this revelation. He glanced at the others, then back at Thomas. "So now you think this Book, which is from here where metaphors express themselves literally, might do the same in this dream world of yours?"

"Who has a quill?" Thomas demanded. "A marker, anything to write with. Charcoal—"

"Here." Ronin held out a charcoal writing stick with a black point.

Thomas took the crude instrument and stared at it.

"Justin was clear that we should hide this Book," William said. "That it is dangerous. We have to come to some kind of agreement on this."

Thomas paced, Book in one hand, pencil in the other. "And Justin said that the Book only works in the histories—the dream world Kara and I come from. For starters, that confirms the histories are real and can be affected. It also means that the Book should be powerless here."

If what Thomas was saying was true, the Book's power might be quite incredible. "What would you write?" Mikil asked. "I mean, what limits would there be? Surely we can't just wipe out the virus with a few strokes of the pen."

Thomas set the Book on the rock. "You're right. I . . . that seems too simple." The others gathered around, silenced by impossible thoughts.

He looked at the cover again. "*The Story of History.* That means it should be a story, right?"

"As in 'once upon a time'?" Ronin asked. "You're saying that if you wrote, 'Once upon a time there was a rabbit,' then a rabbit would appear in your dreams?"

"Too simple," Mikil said. "And what script should we use?" There was a slight difference between the alphabet used in each reality—the one used here was simpler.

"The script of the histories," Thomas said.

"What do you want to accomplish in this other reality?" Ronin asked. "Your main goal—what is it?"

"There's a virus that will destroy most of humanity . . . you know, the Raison Strain," Thomas said. "The one that ushered in the Great Tribulation as recorded in the Books of Histories. Knowledge of the history has become somewhat vague in the fifteen years since Tanis's Crossing, but we all knew it orally once."

"Yes, of course. The Raison Strain. These were the histories that Tanis was fascinated with." Ronin looked at Mikil. "You're saying that these histories are . . . now? Real now?"

"Haven't you been listening to me?" William said. "That's what I've been saying. I've said that he's only recalling memories, but he seems to think that these dreams of his are real."

"Actually, I'm not sure we know how it works," Mikil said. How could she possibly explain her dual reality at this very moment? "Thomas is the expert here, but I can say whether past or present, the histories are not only real, but we must also be able to affect them."

"But surely you don't think you can change what has been written about as a matter of history," William said.

"We don't know that either," Thomas said. "Without the actual Books of Histories, we don't know what was recorded. As far as we know, the histories record our finding this Book and writing in it today."

That kept them all quiet for a moment.

"Then write a story," Ronin finally said.

William grunted in disgust. "Why should I care about any of this? I care about what is real, here. Like the Horde that pursues us every day. I am going to gather my people and take them deep." He stalked off.

Thomas handed Mikil the pencil. "Your recollection of the writing is fresher than mine. You write."

It was an excuse, she thought, but she reached for the instrument anyway. A slight tremble shook her fingers.

"What should I write?"

"Something simple that we can test," Thomas said. "What is our immediate concern?"

"You," Mikil said. "You're dead in France. And Monique."

"You're suggesting we write them back to life?"

"Why not?" Mikil asked.

"Isn't that a bit complicated? It seems a bit much. Absurd maybe."

"Absurd?" Ronin said. "As opposed to the rest of this, which is supposed to make perfect sense?"

"Write it," Thomas said.

Mikil's hand hovered above the blank page. "Once upon a time, Thomas came back to life?"

"More detail."

"I don't think I can do this. What detail? I don't even know what you were wearing."

"Write this," Thomas said. He glanced at her hand, which hadn't moved. "Ready?"

"Okay." She lowered her hand.

"Thomas Hunter, the man who first learned of the Raison Strain's threat, the same man who was shot in the head—"

"Hold on." Mikil touched the charcoal stick to the page. If she wasn't mistaken, a slight heat rode up her fingers. Then again, her nerves were firing hot. She wrote his words verbatim.

"Okay."

Thomas continued. "The same man who was shot in the head, was killed in France by a bullet to the head. Period. But on the third day he came back to life . . . No, forget that. This instead: But at a time when his body was unattended by any of his enemies, he came back to life. The end."

She lifted the stick. "The end? What about Monique?"

"New paragraph. At about the same time that Thomas Hunter came back to life, Monique de Raison found herself in good health and fully able to continue her search for an antivirus in the United States of America. The end."

Johan sighed. "Honestly, these don't sound like stories to me." He looked in the direction William had gone. "This whole thing seems a bit ridiculous in the face of our predicament. Can I suggest we reach . . ."

Johan stopped. His face lightened a shade. Mikil looked at the others who had honed in on Johan's reaction. He was listening.

Then she heard it. The faint thunder of hooves. On the cliffs.

The Horde!

"Move!" Thomas snapped. "Into the tunnel!"

5

Thomas snatched up the Book and shoved it into his belt as he ran for the tents. Justin had shown his face to him. Then Kara through Mikil. And now the Horde was attacking.

Now I will show you my heart.

In moments they had caught up to William. "Mikil, Johan, get Samuel and Marie into the tunnel with the others! William, the east canyon with me. Five men."

They'd selected this particular wash five days earlier not only for its proximity to the red pool, but because of a hidden passage under two huge boulders in the eastern canyon. The route was almost impossible to see without standing directly in front of it. With any luck the Horde would expect them to take one of the two more obvious escape routes.

How had the Scabs managed to pass their sentries on the cliffs undetected?

The first arrow clipped the rock face on Thomas's left before he reached the tents. He glanced over his shoulder. Mounted archers. Fifty at least.

"Ahead," Mikil shouted. "They've cut off the eastern canyon!"

Cries of alarm sounded throughout the camp. Women ran for their children. The men were already running toward the corral. There was no time to collect dishes or food or clothing. They would do well enough to escape with their lives.

"William?"

"You want only five?" his lieutenant demanded. "The Scabs might not follow us."

They would be the diversion. Under other circumstances he would take at least ten, enough to raise enough dust to draw a pursuit while the others slipped away through the hidden escape route. But Thomas knew that, today, whoever was part of the diversion might not escape.

"Only five," he said. "I have the fire."

He ran to the center of the camp where he was certain to be seen clearly. With any luck they would key in on him. The price on his head was a hundred times that on anyone else's. And Thomas had heard the rumor that Qurong's own daughter, Chelise, whom he had once met deep in the desert, was promised to Woref upon his capture.

The cries quieted quickly. The Circle had been through its share of escapes before. They all knew that screaming was no way to avoid attention. There were enough horses to carry the entire tribe, one adult and one child per horse, with a dozen left over to carry their supplies.

Thomas grabbed the smoldering torch next to the main campfire. Gruff shouting directed the attack overhead. An arrow sliced through the air and thudded into flesh on Thomas's right. He spun.

Alisha, Lucy's mother, was grabbing at a shaft that protruded from her side. Thomas started toward her but pulled up when he saw that Lucy was already running for her mother, gripping one of the fleshy, orange fruits that healed. She reached her mother, dropped the fruit, gripped the shaft with both hands, and pulled hard. Alisha groaned. The arrow slid free.

Then Lucy was squeezing the fruit over the open wound.

Thomas ran to intercept William, who led Suzan and two mounted tribe members. He leaped into the saddle on the run and kicked the horse into a full gallop, leading the others now.

A throaty grunt behind him made him turn his head. It was the old man, Jeremiah. Most of the tribe had already taken their positions under a protective ledge by the stables, but the council had been farthest from the horses when the attack had started. The old man had lagged. A Scab spear had found his back.

In the confusion, no one was running to his aid. If he died, the fruit wouldn't bring him back.

"William, torch!"

He tossed the smoking fire to William, who caught it with one hand and looked back to see the problem.

"Hurry, Thomas. We're cutting this close."

"Light the fires. Go!"

Thomas spun his horse and sprinted for the old man, who lay face-down now. He dropped by Jeremiah, fruit in hand. But he knew before his knee hit the sand that he was too late.

"Jeremiah!" He grabbed the spear, put one foot on the man's back, and yanked it out. The spinal column had been severed in two.

Thomas crushed the fruit in both hands, grunting with anger. Juice poured into the gaping hole.

Nothing. If the man was still alive, the juice would have begun its regeneration immediately.

An arrow slammed into his shoulder.

He stood and faced the direction it had come from. The archers on the nearest cliff stared down at him, momentarily off guard.

"He was once one of you!" he screamed. Without removing his eyes from them, Thomas grabbed the arrow in his shoulder, pulled it out, and threw it on the ground. He shoved the fruit against the wound.

"Now he is dead, as you yourselves are. You hear me? Dead! All of you. You live in death!"

One of them let an arrow fly. Thomas saw that the projectile was wide and let it hiss past without moving. It struck the sand.

Then he moved. Faster than they had expected. Onto his horse and straight toward the eastern canyon.

The first fire was already spewing thick black smoke skyward. William had lit the second on the opposite side of the canyon and was galloping toward the third pile of brush they'd prepared for precisely this eventuality.

Thomas ignored the arrows flying by, leaned over his horse's neck, and plunged into the thick smoke.

━━∞∞━━

Soren raised his hand to give the signal.

"Wait," Woref said.

"The rest will break for the canyon," his lieutenant said. "We should give chase now."

"I said wait."

Soren lowered his hand.

The plan had been to box them in, wound as many as possible from a high angle of attack, and then sweep down to finish them off. Their cursed fruit was powerless against a sickle to the neck. It was a strategy that Martyn himself once would have approved.

Now Martyn was down there among the albinos, trapped with the rest. But suddenly Woref wasn't so sure of the strategy; he hadn't expected the fires.

"They think the smoke will cover them?" Soren said. "The poor fools don't know that we have their escape already covered at the other end."

But this was Thomas they were up against. And Martyn. Neither would think that a bit of smoke would help them escape an enemy that had clearly known their position before the attack.

So why the fires?

"You're certain there are no other routes from this canyon?"

"Not that any of our scouts could find."

Yet there had to be. If he was leading this band of dissidents, which direction would he lead them? Into the desert, naturally. Away from the Horde. Out to the plains where they could simply outrun any pursuit.

"Tell half of the sweep team to cut off the desert to the south," Woref said.

"The south?"

"Do not make me repeat another order."

Soren stood in his stirrups and relayed the order through hand signals. Two mounted scouts, each confirming the message, wheeled their horses around and disappeared.

"The whole tribe will break for the smoke momentarily," Woref said. "I want every archer pouring arrows into the albinos."

"I've already passed the word."

"But why?" Woref muttered to himself. "The smoke will suffocate them if they don't get out quickly."

A whistle echoed through the canyon and, precisely as he'd predicted, nearly fifty head of horses broke from under the ledge of a western canyon wall. Arrows rained down on them. Women clutched their children and rode for the smoke, kicking their mounts for as much speed as the animals could muster.

Multiple hits. They were sitting ducks down there. But they had only fifty yards to run before the smoke swallowed them.

Still, two fell. A horse stumbled and its rider ran on foot. A third clutched an arrow that had struck him in the chest. The one on foot tripped, and three arrows plowed into his back.

Then the albinos were through the gauntlet and into their smoke. Woref's men killed only five. Six, counting the one that the spear had taken earlier. Many more had been shot, but they would survive with the help of their sorcery. This bitter fruit of theirs.

The archers shot a dozen arrows into each of the fallen albinos, then the canyon fell eerily silent.

Woref reined his mount around and trotted along the cliff, eastward, eyes searching for the slightest sign of life beneath the thick smoke. The silence angered him. Surely they wouldn't double back into another onslaught of arrows. There had to be another exit!

Behind him, the sweep team entered the valley, effectively cutting off any attempted retreat.

Thomas had been with the ones who'd lit the fires. Woref's agreement with Qurong was for Thomas. If the parties had split . . .

A cry came from the east. Thomas's group had been sighted.

Woref kicked his horse and galloped up the canyon. He saw them then, five horses raising dust beyond the smoke, speeding directly for his trap.

⸙

Thomas led his contingent from the smoke, praying that every Scab eye was on him. He had surveyed every last inch of this canyon and knew where he would set a trap if he were the Horde commander. Their chances of breaking through that trap were small now. If they'd received warning, they would've had a better chance of sprinting past the mouth of the canyon before the trap had been set.

Two brothers, Cain and Stephen, raced beside Suzan to his right. William brought up the rear.

"Do we fight?" William demanded.

"No."

"We're too late! They'll be waiting."

Yes, they would be.

"We could go back," William said.

"No! We can't endanger the others. Have your fruit ready!"

As soon as he said it, he heard the cry ahead. Thirty mounted men rode into the open, cutting off the mouth of the canyon.

Still they galloped, straight for the waiting Horde.

"Justin, give us strength," Thomas breathed.

The Scabs weren't attacking. No arrows, no cries, just these thirty men on horses, waiting to collect them. There was no way past them.

Thomas reined his mount and held up a hand. "Hold up."

They stopped a hundred yards from the Scabs.

"You're going to let them take us?" William asked. "You know they'll kill us."

"And our alternative is what?"

"Mikil and Johan have had the time they need to get the rest through the gap. We can still make it!"

"They'll have men in the canyon by now," Suzan said. She'd been a latecomer to the Circle, and there wasn't a person Thomas had been so glad to have join them. As the leader of the Forest Guard's scouts, she'd studied the Horde more than most and knew their strategies nearly as well as Johan himself.

"And if we're lucky, they won't find the tunnel," Thomas said.

"Then we have to fight! We can beat them—"

"No killing!" Thomas faced Cain and Stephen. "Are you ready for what this may mean?"

"If you mean death, then I'm ready," Cain said.

"I'd rather die than be taken to their dungeons," Stephen said. "I won't be taken alive."

"And how do you propose to force their hands? If they take us alive, then we will go with them peacefully. No fight, are we clear?"

"I helped them build the dungeons. I—"

"Then you can help us escape from their dungeons."

"There is no escape!"

The brothers had been latecomers as well, and their discovery of life on the other side of the drowning was still fresh in their minds. Both were dark-skinned and had shaved their heads as part of a vow they'd taken. They were adamant about showing as much of their disease-free flesh as was decently possible.

"No fighting," Thomas repeated.

They held stares for a moment. Stephen nodded. "No fighting."

They sat five abreast, facing the Horde. Hooves sounded behind them and Thomas turned to see that the team Suzan had predicted was emerging from the thinning smoke.

"We're buying a whole lot of trouble here," William said.

"No, we're buying Mikil's freedom. The freedom of the Circle."

"Mikil? Don't tell me this has to do with these dreams of yours."

The thought had occurred to him. He wasn't sure what they'd done by writing in the blank Book now in his belt, but either he or Kara had to get back. The lives of six billion people were at stake. Not to mention his own sister's life. If Mikil died, Kara would die.

"If I were concerned only with the histories, I would save myself, wouldn't I? We're doing here nothing less than what Justin himself would undoubtedly do."

There was nothing more to be said. Thomas withdrew the Book from his belt and shoved it into his tunic.

———

Woref rode past his men and studied the standoff in the canyon.

Five.

The other fifty had disappeared.

But among the five was Thomas. If he'd estimated correctly, the others would emerge from these canyons in the south, where his men would deal with them appropriately. His concern was now with these five.

This one.

"Send word: when they find the others, kill them all. I have Thomas of Hunter."

He nudged his horse and rode with his guard to meet the man who was responsible for the grief he'd suffered these past thirteen months. Thomas of Hunter's name was still whispered with awe late at night around a thousand campfires. He was a legend who defied reason. Failing to defeat the Horde with his sword, he'd now taken up the weapon of peace. Qurong would prefer to face a sword any day over this heroic deceit they called the Circle. True, only a thousand had followed Thomas into his madness, but what was a thousand could easily become ten thousand. And then a hundred thousand.

Today he would reduce their number to one.

And today Woref would have his bride.

He stopped ten yards from the albinos. They looked like salamanders with their sickly bare flesh. The breeze brought their scent to him, and he tried his best not to draw it too deep. They smelled of fruit. The same bitter fruit that they used for their sorcery—the variety that grew around the red pools. It was said that they drank the blood of Justin and that they forced their children to do the same. What kind of disease of the mind would push a man to such absurdities?

Two of the prisoners were bald. They looked vaguely familiar. A third was a woman. The mere thought of any man breeding with such a sickly salamander was enough to make him nauseated.

He nudged his horse abreast their leader, Thomas of Hunter. Similarly fashioned medallions hung from each of their necks. He reached down, grasped Thomas's pendant, jerked it free, and held it in his palm. Then he spit on it.

"You are now prisoners of Qurong, supreme leader of the Horde," he said. Then he turned his horse away, overcome by their scent.

"So it would appear," Thomas said.

"Douse them!"

Two of his men rode around the captives and tossed ash on them. The ash contained sulfur and made their stench manageable.

"Where are the others?" Woref asked.

Thomas stared at him, eyes blank.

"Kill the woman," Woref said.

One of the soldiers pulled a sword and approached the black female.

"Killing any of us would be a mistake," Thomas said. "We can't tell you where the others are. We can only tell how they outwitted you, which we will gladly do. But by now they've fled in a direction only they know."

Woref felt a new dislike for this man run deep into his bones. He wondered how smart the rebel would look without lips. But then Qurong wouldn't get the information he needed.

"I know how they escaped," he said. "My scouts missed a break in the cliffs that leads south, into the desert. Your band of rebels is headed into our hands at this very moment."

"Then why do you ask?"

He'd expected a flinch, a pause, anything to indicate the man's surprise at being discovered so easily. Instead, Thomas had delivered this unflinching reprimand.

"You'll pay for your disrespect. I give you my vow. Chain them."

Woref turned his horse around and headed out of the canyon.

Mikil swept the scope across the desert that surrounded the canyon lands.

"Others?" Johan asked.

"No. Just the one group."

Behind them, fifty sets of round white eyes peered from the dark cavern that hid them. They wound their way through the gap and into an adjacent canyon that led them here, to the edge of the southern desert. But they wouldn't break into the open until they were sure that the Horde was gone.

"They'll be in the cave by now," Johan said. "We have to move soon."

"Unless they followed Thomas out of the canyon."

Johan frowned. "Assuming Thomas made it out of the canyon."

She lowered the glass. "Why wouldn't he?"

He glanced back and spoke in a low voice. "I could have sworn I saw Woref on the cliff. They came on us without warning, which means they had already scouted us out. They would have both escape routes covered. I don't see how anyone, even Thomas, could possibly escape without a fight. And we both know that he won't fight."

The revelation stunned her. Not only as Mikil, who feared for the Circle's future without Thomas to lead them, but as Kara, who suddenly feared for her brother's life.

"Then we have to go back!"

"We have the tribe to think about." He took a deep breath. "First the tribe, then Thomas. Assuming he's alive."

She was about to reprimand him for even suggesting such a thing, but then it occurred to her that, as Mikil, she agreed.

She faced the desert. "Then we stay here," she said.

"They'll follow our tracks."

"Not if we block the tunnel. Think about it. They'll never expect us to stay in these canyons. Anywhere but here, right? And they'll never find this cavern. There's a red pool nearby, water, food. I don't want to go deep if they have my brother."

The emotions mixing in Mikil's chest were enough to make her want to scream. She was Mikil, but she was Kara, and as Kara she'd awakened into a firestorm. Surprisingly she'd felt only a little fear, even with the Horde's arrows narrowly missing her head. Mikil had been up against the Scabs a thousand times, most often in hand-to-hand combat.

On the other hand, it wasn't the status quo for the civilians in her charge. They'd lost six in the attack, including Jeremiah. Her heart felt sick.

But there was another emotion pulling at her. The desire to wake up in Dr. Myles Bancroft's laboratory. Thomas had taken the Book—now she wished she'd taken it. There was no telling how many more opportunities they would have to write in it. The thought of those few words she'd written actually having power on Earth made her spine tingle. She had to get back to see if they had worked. Imagine . . .

Johan scratched his chin and looked around. "If we block the tunnel, they'll see that we blocked it."

"Let them. When they can't find us, they'll assume we went deep."

"They'll still look for our trail."

"Then we'll give them one that takes them away from here, further west and into the desert. With the night winds blowing our tracks, they will be lost by morning."

He was silent, thinking.

"I refuse to go deep as long as Thomas's fate is uncertain."

He nodded. "It could work. But we don't block the tunnel at its entrance. It's too late for that anyway." He ran to his horse and swung into the saddle. "We have to hurry."

6

"Kara. Wake up."

She felt her shoulder being shaken.

"That's it, dear. Wake up. You've been sleeping for two good hours."

Kara stared at the frumpy figure at her side. Dr. Myles Bancroft wore a knowing grin. Dabbed a handkerchief on his brow.

"Two hours and not one dream," he said.

The lights were still low. Machines hummed quietly—a computer fan, air conditioning. The faint smell of human sweat mixed with a deodorant.

"Did you dream?" he asked.

"Yes." She pushed herself up. He'd wiped the blood from her arm and applied a small white bandage. "Yes, I did."

"Not according to my instruments, you didn't. And that, my dear, makes this not only a fascinating case, but one that is duplicable. First Thomas and now you. Something is happening with you two."

"It's his blood. Don't ask me how this all got started, but my brother is the gateway between these two realities."

"I doubt very much that there are two realities," he said. "Something is happening in your minds that is certainly beyond ordinary dreams, but I can promise you that your body was here the whole time. You didn't walk through any wardrobe to Narnia or take a trip to another galaxy."

"Semantics, Professor." She slid off the bed. "We don't have time for semantics. We have to find Monique."

Bancroft looked at her with a sheepish grin tempting his face, as if he were working up the courage to ask the delicious question: "So what happened?"

"I woke as Mikil, lieutenant to Thomas of Hunter. She and I wrote in a book that has power to bring life from words, narrowly survived an attack by the Horde, and found safe haven in a cavern after blocking our escape route. I finally fell into an exhausted sleep and woke up here."

Hearing herself summarize, a buzz rode down her neck. She'd played both doubter and believer over the last two weeks with Thomas, and she wasn't sure which was easier.

"No wounds."

"What?"

"You don't have any wounds or anything to prove your experiences like Thomas did."

True.

"Have you heard news?" she asked.

"Not particularly, no." He blinked and looked away. "The world is going to hell, quite literally. The great equalizer that most of us knew would eventually get loose finally has. I just can't believe how fast it's all happening."

"The virus? Equalizing as in it's no respecter of persons. The president is as vulnerable as the homeless bum in the alley. And why are you still so interested in dreams, Doctor? You said you were infected, right? You have ten days to live like the rest of us. Shouldn't you be with your family?"

"My work is my family, dear. I did manage to ingest dangerous levels of alcohol when the whole thing first sank in about a week ago. But I've since decided to spend my last days fussing over my first love."

"Psychology."

"I intend to die in her arms."

"Then let me give you a suggestion from one who's seen beyond her own mind, Doctor. Talk to your priest. There's more to all of this than your eyes can see or your instruments record."

"You're a religious person?" he asked.

"No. But Mikil is."

"Then maybe I should talk to this Mikil of yours."

Kara glanced at the bench where she remembered last seeing Thomas's blood sample. It was gone.

"Don't worry; it's safely stored."

"I . . . I need it."

"Not without a court order. It stays with me. You're welcome here anytime. Which reminds me, Secretary Merton Gains called about an hour ago."

"Gains?" The nuclear crisis! "What did he say?"

"He wanted to know if we had reached any conclusion here."

"What did you tell him? Why didn't you wake me?"

"I had to be sure. Some subjects require an unusual amount of time to enter REM. I woke you as soon as I was confident."

Kara started toward the door, suddenly frantic. She had to find Thomas or Monique, dead or alive. But how? And the blood . . .

She turned back. "Doctor, please, you have to give me his blood. He's my brother! The world is in a crisis here, and I—"

"Gains was quite clear," he said. "We can't afford to lose control. He seemed to suggest that this was a possibility, a threat from the inside."

A mole?

"In the White House?"

"He didn't say. I'm a psychologist, not an intelligence officer."

"Fine. What did you tell him about me?"

"That you weren't dreaming. Which probably means you were experiencing the same thing your brother did. He wants you to call him immediately."

She stared at him, then strode for the desk phone. "Now you tell me."

Bancroft shrugged. "Yes, well, I have a lot on my mind. I'm going to die in ten days, did I tell you?"

<hr />

Bright light stabbed her eyes. Sunlight. Or was it something else? Maybe that light from beyond. Maybe she'd died from the Raison Strain and was now floating above her body, drifting toward the great white light in the sky.

She blinked. There was pressure on her chest, something biting into her collarbone. Her breathing came hard. No pain though.

All of this she realized with her first blink.

Then she realized that she was in an automobile at a precarious angle, hanging from her seat belt. She grabbed the steering wheel to support herself and sucked in a huge gulp of air.

What had happened? Where was she? Panic edged into her mind. If she shifted her weight, the car might fall!

Green foliage was plastered against the windows. A shaft of sunlight shot through a small triangular break in the leaves. She was in a tree?

Monique blinked again and forced her mind to slow down. She remembered some things. She'd been working on the antivirus to the Raison Strain. Her solution had failed. The chances of finding any antivirus other than the one Svensson possessed were nil. She'd been on her way to Washington—an unscheduled trip of desperation. Kara had convinced her that Thomas might still be their only hope, and in the wake of her monumental failure, Monique intended to make the case to the president himself. Then she would go to Johns Hopkins, where Kara was going to attempt to connect with the other reality by using Thomas's blood.

She'd been driving down a side road at night, following the sign that said Gas—2 miles, when her vision suddenly clouded. That was all she could remember.

Monique leaned to her right. The car didn't budge. She leaned farther and peered out the side window. The car was on the ground, not in a tree. Shrubs crowded every side. The hood was wedged under a web of small branches. She must have fallen asleep and driven off the road. There was no sign of blood.

She moved her legs and neck. Still no pain. Not even a headache.

The car was resting at a thirty-degree angle—nothing short of a crane was going to budge it. She tried the door, found it unobstructed, and shoved it open. Released the shoulder harness.

Her purse. It had Merton Gains's card and her identification. She would need money. The black leather purse was on the floor, passenger side. Holding the steering wheel with her left hand, she lowered herself, grabbed the purse, and pulled herself back up.

Monique eased out of the car and started crawling up the slope with the help of the surrounding shrubs. The road was just above her, maybe twenty-five yards, but several large trees blocked a clear view from the air.

How much time had passed?

The trip up the rocky slope did more damage to her than the car wreck. She tore her black slacks and smudged the front of her beige silk blouse with several falls. Her shoes were black flats, but they had slick soles. She kicked them off halfway up the slope, reached back for them, and muttered a curse when one slid ten feet down before stopping. She decided she was better off without them. Her soles had once favored bare earth over shoes anyway.

When she finally clambered over the crest, she found a two-lane road with a solid yellow line down the middle. The sun was directly above—she'd been unconscious all night and half the day?

To her right she could just see the highway. She stared about, still disoriented. Then she turned to her left and walked toward the small red Conoco sign a mile down the road. Or was it two miles? No, the sign had said 2 miles, but as near as she could see, she was halfway between the highway and the station. One mile. She would take her chances with a phone over thumbing a ride.

Almost immediately she regretted having left her shoes. Fifty yards later she decided that she would thumb a ride to the station if at all possible. Assuming there was a ride to be thumbed. The road was deserted. For that matter, the Conoco station could be deserted as well. Last night she'd seen the lights from the highway—a hopeful sign that the station was open. Most she'd encountered along the road were closed.

The hum of a big rig sounded behind her. She glanced over her shoulder. A large fuel truck with a yellow Shell sign on a chrome tank sped down the highway. The sight stopped her. What was a trucker doing driving fuel down the road, knowing that in ten days he would be dead unless the government managed to find a way to stop the Raison Strain? Did the driver really understand what was happening? The reports she'd heard suggested that most Americans were staying at home, glued to the news. The government was paying huge dividends to certain critical companies if they remained open. Mostly utilities, communications, transportation—the essentials.

She assumed that traffic would be limited to people going home to be with their families. But a trucker? Maybe he was going home too.

She headed back off the road, sticking to the grass shoulder. Not a single car drove by during the twenty minutes it took her to reach the Conoco sign.

The station was closed.

"Hello?"

Her voice echoed under the canopy that covered the deserted fuel islands. She walked for the window. "Hello?"

Nothing. She didn't blame them—the last thing she would do with ten days to live is work at a gas station.

The door was locked. No sign of looting. No need to loot when the looters themselves were also infected. Riots would be instigated by thrill seekers determined to take their fear out on others rather than to seize any goods. It would start soon enough.

In fact, now was as good a time as any.

She picked up the small steel drum that read Garbage, drew it back, and swung it with all her strength at the window. The horrendous crash of breaking glass was loud enough to wake the dead. Good. She needed to wake the dead.

Monique waited for a full minute, giving anyone who might have heard plenty of time to note that she wasn't busy looting. Then she picked her way through the broken glass to the black phone on the counter.

Dial tone.

She dug out the card Gains had given her and stared at the number. What if he was the very mole she had warned him of? Maybe she should call the president himself. No, he was in New York today, speaking at the United Nations.

She dialed the number, let the phone ring, and prayed that Gains, mole or not, would answer.

Thomas awoke on his back. The sheet was over his face. Odd. Although the desert night was cool at times, he wasn't one to smother his breathing by burying his head under the covers like some. Covers also impaired hearing. At this moment he couldn't hear his fellow prisoners breathing, though he knew they were sleeping to his right, chained at the ankles with him. He couldn't even hear the sound of the horses near the camp. Nor the Scabs, talking over morning campfires. Nor the campfires themselves.

He yanked the sheet from his face. It was still night. Dark. He still couldn't hear anything other than his own heart, thumping lightly. No stars in the sky, no campfire, no sand dunes. Only this thin rubber mattress under him, and this cold sheet in his fingers.

Thomas's heart skipped a beat. He wasn't in the desert! He was on a mattress in a dark room, and he'd awakened with a sheet over his face.

He moved his feet. No chains. He'd fallen asleep as a prisoner in the desert and woken in the histories. Alive.

He felt the edge of his bed. Cold steel tubes filled his hand. A gurney. Carlos had shot him, when? Three days ago, Kara had said. He hadn't dreamed for thirteen months in the desert because there was no Thomas here to live the dream. They'd brought his body here, why? For examination? To keep the Americans guessing? And where was here?

France.

Thomas eased his legs from under the sheets and swung them to the cold concrete floor. A loud slap echoed in the room and he jumped. Nothing happened. Something had fallen on the floor.

His eyes adjusted to the darkness. A wedge of light shone through the gap at the bottom of the door. He saw the square shape by his foot. Picked it up. A book. He felt its cover and froze.

The blank Book of History, entitled *The Story of History.* His hands trembled. The Book had crossed over with him!

A chill swept over his body. This Book—its story, its words—had brought him back to life. Here he stood, dressed in a torn jumpsuit, barefooted on a concrete floor in France, holding a Book that could make history with a few strokes of the pen.

Justin had called it dangerous and powerful. Now he knew why.

His sole objective was immediately clear. He had to find a pen, a pencil, anything that could mark the Book, and write a new story. One that changed the outcome of the Raison Strain. And while he was at it, one that included his survival.

Thomas paused at the unexpected thought that the Book wasn't unlike the artifacts from Judeo-Christian history. The ark of the covenant with the power to conquer armies. The serpent in the desert with the power to heal. *Say to this mountain, be thou removed and it shall be removed.* Jesus Christ, AD 30. Words becoming flesh, Ronin had said.

There were now officially four things that crossed between the realities. Knowledge, skills, blood, and this Book, these words becoming flesh.

He could just barely see the outline of a door ten feet away. Thomas walked for the door, tested the knob, found it unlocked, and cracked it ever so slightly. The room beyond was also dark, but not black like this one. He could see a table, a couch. Another door edged by light. A fireplace . . .

He knew this room! It was where he and Monique had met Armand Fortier! They'd brought him back to the farmhouse.

Thomas slipped out, still gripping the Book in his right hand. He covered the room quickly, found nothing of benefit, and moved to the opposite door. Unlocked as well. He'd twisted the knob and cracked the door when the sound of echoing footsteps in the hall reached him.

Thomas stood immobilized. Under no circumstances could he allow the Book to fall into their hands. His escape was no longer as important as the Book's safety.

He eased the door shut and ran on his toes for the cell. He slipped into the dark, shut the door, stepped toward the gurney, and shoved the Book under the thin mattress. Then he lay back down and pulled the sheet over his head.

Relax. Breathe. Slow your heart.

The door opened thirty seconds later. Light flooded the room. The footsteps walked across the floor, paused for a few seconds, then retreated. A man coughed, and Thomas knew it was Carlos. He'd come for something. Surely not to check on a dead body.

The room went black.

Thomas waited a full minute before rising again. He walked to the door, flipped the light on, and surveyed the room. Concrete all around. Except for the gurney and one bookshelf, the room was empty. A root cellar at one time, perhaps. They'd probably put his body here because it was cold and they wanted to preserve it for tests.

He decided that the risk of being caught with the Book was too great. He would find something to write with and return.

Thomas checked the adjoining room, found it clear, and stepped out. This time the hall was clear. He hurried past the same window he and Monique had climbed through just a few nights earlier. Sunlight filled the window well. He was about to mount the stairs that climbed to the next floor when a door across the hall caught his attention. A reinforced steel door, out of place in this ancient house.

He stepped across the hall and opened it.

No sound.

He peered inside. Another long hall. Steel walls. They'd built a veritable fortress down here. This hall stretched far beyond the exterior wall and ended at yet another door.

Now he was torn. He could either climb the stairs, which could lead to a guard station for all he knew, or he could examine the door at the end of this hall. Just as likely to find a guard there.

Thomas eased into the hall and walked fast. Voices came to him while he was halfway down, and he paused. But they weren't voices of alarm. He ran the last twenty paces and pulled up at the door. The voices were from the room beyond.

"They've killed half the fish off our coast with these two detonations, but they won't target our cities!"

They were talking about nuclear detonations? Someone had launched nuclear weapons!

"Then you don't know the Israelis. They know we have no intention of delivering the antivirus, and they have nothing to lose."

"They're still principled. They won't take innocents down with them. Please, I beg you, the Negev desert was bad enough. We can't target Tel Aviv. A power play to realign powers is one thing. Detonating nuclear weapons over densely populated targets is another. They're bluffing. They know the world would turn against them if they targeted civilians. As it would turn against us if we did the same."

"You think that world opinion is still an element in this equation? Then you're more naive than I imagined, Henri." So the man protesting was Paul Henri Gaetan, the French president. "The only language that the Israelis understand is brute force."

A third voice spoke. "Give them the antivirus."

Armand Fortier.

"Pardon me, sir, but I thought—"

"The plan must be flexible," Fortier said. "We've shown the world our resolve to use whatever force is required to enforce our terms. We've blown two massive holes in their desert, and they've blown two holes in our ocean. So what? The Israelis are snakes. Utterly unpredictable except in the defense of their land. If we fire again, they will retaliate. Two-thirds of the world's combined nuclear arsenal is presently loaded on ships, steaming to our shores. Now isn't the time to accelerate the conflict."

"You will leave Israel intact?"

"We will give them the antivirus," Fortier repeated. "In exchange for their weapons."

"What proof will you offer them?" President Gaetan again.

"A mutual exchange on the seas, five days from today."

The room went silent for a few moments. The next voice that spoke was one that Thomas recognized at the first word.

"But you will destroy Israel," Carlos Missirian said softly.

"Yes."

"And the Americans?"

"The Americans don't have the Israelis' backbone. They have no choice but to deliver their weapons, regardless of all their noise. We're listening to everything they say. They're acting out of total confusion now, but our contact assures us they won't have a choice but to comply in the end."

"They might demand an open exchange as well," the French president said.

"Then we will call their bluff. I can afford to make Israel wait until the time of our choosing. The United States will no longer play a role in world politics."

Thomas felt his heart pound. He pulled his ear from the door. He'd heard enough.

"And if Israel does launch in ten minutes as they've promised?"

Thomas stopped. A long pause.

"Then we take out Tel Aviv," Fortier said.

———∞———

Thomas sprinted back down the hall toward the root cellar. The plan had changed. He had to get word to the United States before Israel had a chance to launch again. He needed a phone. But in searching for a phone, he might find a pen.

Dangerous, Justin had said. Everything was dangerous now.

Thomas ran for the cell door and twisted the knob. Locked.

Locked? He'd opened it just a few minutes ago from this side. He cranked down on the handle. Heat spread down his neck. He stepped back, panicked. Carlos must have engaged the lock when he left.

Thomas ran his hand through his hair and paced. This wasn't good. He needed a phone!

The meeting was still underway. Thomas sprinted up the stairs, took the steps two at a time, and burst through the door at the top. A single startled guard stared at him. He'd clearly never seen a dead man walking before.

Thomas took him with a foot to his temple, one swift roundhouse kick that landed with a sickening thud. Then a clatter as the man collapsed on the metal folding chair he'd been using.

Thomas didn't bother covering his tracks. No time. He did, however, pluck the nine-millimeter from the man's hand. Short of finding a key to the cell, he would blow the door off its hinges. Noisy but effective.

First the phone.

He passed a window and saw a least a dozen guards milling around the driveway, smoking. They were mostly ranking French military, he noted. Not thugs you'd find in the underground. That would be a concern in a few minutes. Phone—where was the phone?

On the wall, naturally. Black and outdated like most things in the French countryside. He dug in his pocket, relieved to find the card Grant had given him in Washington. On the back, scrawled in pencil, a direct line to the White House.

Thomas snatched up the phone and dialed the long number.

Silence.

For a moment he feared the lines were out. Naturally, the French would monitor all calls. Getting through would be impossible.

The line suddenly clicked. Then hissed for a while. He prayed the call would connect.

"You have reached the White House. Please listen closely, as our menu options have changed. You may press zero at any time to speak to an operator . . ."

Hand trembling. Zero.

A switchboard operator answered after four rings. "White House."

"This is Thomas Hunter. I'm in France and I need to speak to the president immediately."

8

hen you were clearly mistaken," Woref said. "Whatever you think you saw was never there."

Soren shook his head. "I could swear that I saw the albino shift an object under his tunic just before falling asleep. He managed to hide something from us during our initial search."

"But there is no object; you said so yourself. Get some sleep while you can. We raise the army in four hours. Leave me."

Soren bowed. "Yes sir." He left his commander alone in the tent.

They'd made good time and stopped for a few hours' sleep in the dead of night. Tomorrow they would enter the city and receive their reward for Thomas of Hunter's capture.

They had forced the albinos to walk most of the way, carrying their chains, and they had fallen asleep almost immediately, according to Soren. Even if Hunter had managed to conceal a weapon in the folds of his tunic, they had little to fear from him now. The once-mighty warrior was a shell of his former self. He'd not only stripped himself of healthy flesh by dipping in the red pools, but he'd lost his manhood in the process. Hunter was nothing more than a diseased rodent, and his only threat to the Horde was the spread of his disease.

Woref removed the hard leather breastplate and set it on the floor beside his cot. A single lamp spewed black smoke. He ran his hand over his hairy chest, brushed away the flecks of dried skin that had fallen on his apron, and pulled on a nightshirt. The day that he would finally take Chelise into his house as wife had come. The thought made his belly feel light.

He drew back the tent flap and stepped into the cool night. They'd camped in a meadow that sloped away from the forest. From his vantage he could see the entire army, settled for the night, some in hastily erected tents, most around smoldering fire pits. They'd celebrated with ale and meat, both delicacies over the standard rations of fermented water and starch.

The prisoners lay uncovered twenty yards to his right, under the standing guard of six warriors. Woref grunted and headed for the tree line to relieve himself.

A deeper darkness settled over him when he stepped past the first trees. The Horde preferred day over night, mostly due to unfounded tales in which Shataiki lured men into the trees to consume them alive. Until this moment, Woref had never given any such myth a second thought.

But now, with blackness pressing his skin, all those stories crashed through his mind. He stopped and gazed at the trunks ahead. Turned and saw that the camp slept as peacefully as a moment ago.

Woref spit into the leaves and walked deeper, leaving the relative safety of the meadow behind. But not far enough to lose complete sight of the camp.

"Wwrrrreffffffffsssssssss."

He stopped, startled by the sound of his name, whispering through the night. The trees rose like charcoal marks against the dark forest. He had imagined . . .

"Woreffff."

He grabbed the hilt of his short sword and spun back.

Nothing. Trees, yes. A thick forest of trees. But he couldn't see the camp any longer. He'd wandered too deep.

"You're looking the wrong direction, my beast of a man."

The sound came from behind. Woref couldn't remember the last time terror had gripped him in its fist. It wasn't just the darkness, nor the whispering of his name, nor the disappearing of the camp. His horror was primarily motivated by the voice.

He knew this voice!

Gravel sloshing at the bottom of a water pail.

He'd never actually heard the voice of Shataiki before, but he knew now, without looking, that the voice behind him belonged to a creature from the myths.

"No need to be afraid. Turn around and face me. You'll like what you see. I promise you."

Woref kept his hand on his blade, but any thought of drawing it had fled with his common sense. He found himself turning.

The tall batlike creature that stood facing him between two trees not ten feet away looked remarkably similar to the bronze-winged serpent on the Horde's crest. This one, though, was larger than any of the stories claimed.

This was Teeleh.

The bat drilled him with round, pupil-less red eyes. Bulging cherries. His fur was black and his snout ran long to loose lips that hung over yellow-crusted fangs.

The leader of the Shataiki grinned and held a red fruit in his wiry and nimble fingers. "That's right. In the flesh."

Teeleh sank his fangs into the fruit's meat. Juice mixed with saliva dripped to the forest floor. He said the name, speaking through smacking lips.

"Teeleh."

Woref closed his eyes for a moment, sure that if he kept them shut long enough, the vision would vanish.

"Open your eyes!" Teeleh roared.

Hot, sweet breath buffeted Woref's face, and he jerked his eyes open. He reached for the tree on his right to steady himself.

"Are all humans so weak?" the bat demanded.

Had Soren or the others heard Teeleh's cry? They would come . . .

"No. No, I don't think anyone will come running to your aid. And if you think you need their help, then you'll prove me wrong. I've been grooming the wrong man."

Woref's terror began to fade. The bat hadn't attacked him. Hadn't bitten him. Hadn't harmed him in any way.

"Do you know what love is, Woref?"

He hardly heard the question.

"You're real," Woref said.

"Love." The bat took another bite. This time he lifted his snout, opened his mouth wide, let the fruit drop into his throat, and swallowed it with a pool of fluid. When his head lowered, his eyes were closed. They opened slowly. "Will you have some?"

Woref didn't respond.

"You don't mind me saying that you humans make me sick, do you? Even you, the one I've chosen."

The leaves in the trees behind Teeleh rustled, and Woref lifted his face to a sea of red eyes glowing in the darkness. The rustling spread to his left, his right, and behind and seemed to swallow him.

A bat the size of a dog dropped to the ground behind Teeleh. Eyes gleaming, furry skin quivering. Then another, beside him. And another. They fell like rotten fruit.

"My servants," Teeleh said. "It's been awhile since I've allowed them to show themselves. They're quite excited. Ignore them."

The bats kept their distance but stared at him, unblinking.

"Do you love her?" Teeleh asked.

"Chelise?"

"He speaks. Yes, the daughter of Qurong, firstborn among the humans who drank my water. Do you love her?"

"She will be my wife." Woref's throat felt parched, his tongue dry like morst in his mouth.

"That's the idea, I know. But do you love her? Not like I love her—I don't expect you to love her so exquisitely—but as the love of a man goes. Do you feel overpowering emotion for her?"

"Yes." The Shataiki were here to bless his union? That might be a good sign.

"And this love you think you have for her, how can you be sure she will return it?"

"She will. Why wouldn't she?"

"Because she's human. Humans make their own choices about their loyalties. That's what makes them who they are."

"She will love me," Woref said confidently.

"Or?"

He hadn't really considered the matter. "I am a powerful man who will one day rule the Horde. It's a woman's place to serve men like me. I'm not sure you understand who you're talking to."

"I am talking to the man who owes me his life."

Teeleh tossed what was left of his fruit to the ground and wrapped his wide, paper-thin wings around his torso. The Shataiki was taking credit for Woref's rise to power?

"Yes, she will be lured by your power and your strength, but don't assume that she will give you her love. She's deceived like the rest of you, but she seems to be more stubborn than most."

They still hadn't made any move against him. Clearly, the Shataiki, regardless of their fierce reputation, meant him no harm. Teeleh seemed more concerned with his marriage to Chelise than with destroying him.

"I'm not sure what this had to do with you," he said, gaining more confidence.

"It has to do with me because I love her far more than you could ever imagine. I broke Tanis's mind, and now I will have his daughter's heart."

Fear smothered Woref again.

"Do you hear what I'm saying? I will possess her. I will crush her and then I will consume her, and she will be *mine.*"

"I . . . How—"

"Through you."

"You're asking me to kill her? Never! I have waited years to make her mine."

The night grew perfectly quiet. For a long time the bat's red eyes drilled Woref. The Shataiki were growing restless, hopping from branch to branch, hissing and snickering.

"Clearly, you don't understand what love is. I want her heart, not her life. If I wanted to kill her, I would use her father." Teeleh rolled his head and momentarily closed his eyes. "You're as wretched as she is. You're all as blind as bats." He unfolded his wings and stepped forward. "But you will win her love. I don't care if you have to beat it out of her."

Teeleh approached slowly, dragging his wings through dead leaves. Woref's limbs began to tremble. He couldn't move.

"I don't care if you have to club it out of her; you will earn her loyalty and her love. I will not lose her to the albinos. And then you will give her to me."

Where he found the sudden strength to resist, Woref wasn't sure, but a blind rage swept over him. "I could never give her to you. She would never love you!"

"When she loves you, she will love me," Teeleh said. Louder now. "He will try to win her love, but she will come to me. Me!"

And then Teeleh leaned forward so that his snout was only inches from Woref's face. The bat's jaw spread wide so that the only thing Woref could see was a long pink tongue snaking back into the black hole that was the bat's throat. A hot, foul stench smothered him.

Teeleh withdrew, snapped his jaw closed with a loud snap.

"I have shown you my power; now I will show you my heart," he said. "I will show you my love."

Teeleh swept his wing around himself and grinned wickedly. With a parting razor-sharp glare, he leaped into the air, flew into the trees, and was gone. The branches shook as his minions scattered into darkness.

Woref felt hot tears running down his cheeks. He still couldn't move, much less understand.

I will show you my heart. My love.

Then Woref was throwing up.

9

"Follow me," Merton Gains said.

Monique followed him through a short hall to a conference room off the West Wing.

"Kara's in with him. The president's got his hands full with the crisis in the Middle East, and he's got a room full of advisors, but he insisted you come in after hearing Kara. Just tread lightly. They're pretty high-strung in there."

The conference room that Monique walked into was large enough to seat at least twenty people around an oval table. A dozen advisors and military types were seated or standing. A few talked in hushed tones at one side. The rest were staring at three large screens, which tracked the unfolding situation in the Middle East and France.

"Sir, I have Benjamin on the line."

"Put him through," the president said.

The receiver buzzed and he picked it up.

"Hello, Mr. Prime Minister. I hope you have good news for me."

Monique scanned the room for Kara. Their eyes met, and Thomas's sister walked toward her.

"I agree, Isaac, and I don't necessarily blame you for pushing this," the president was saying. "But even in the remotest mountain range, you're bound to have casualties. We don't see how any further escalation will benefit you."

Another pause.

"Naturally. I understand principle." The president sighed. "It's an impossible situation, I agree. But we still have time. Let's not wipe out our cities before we have to."

Kara stopped three feet from Monique, eyes wide. "You disappeared," she said quietly.

"My car ran off the road."

"You were hurt?"

"No. I just blacked out."

"You did?"

Why was this so striking to Kara?

The president had finished his call.

"You were dead," Kara said.

"You mean figuratively. My car slammed into a tree and knocked me out."

"You remember that? Or did you just pass out before the car rolled off the road?"

Kara was right. Monique had no memory of actually flying over the edge. "I passed out first."

"I was there, Monique. With Mikil. I dreamed as Mikil. Rachelle was killed by the Horde thirteen months ago. Because of your unique connection to her, I think you died when she died. You believed that you were Rachelle, right?"

"Rachelle's *dead*?"

"Thirteen months ago."

"But I'm alive. I'm not sure I follow."

"I'll explain later, but I'm pretty sure you were dead."

"And Thomas?"

"Thomas is alive. At least, in the desert he's alive. Rachelle found him dead in the Horde camp and healed him with Justin's power. You know about Justin's power, don't you?"

"Yes. And is Thomas alive here?"

Kara looked deep into her eyes. "You're alive, aren't you?"

"Excuse me," the president said. "You're saying that Monique *died* last night?"

"Sir?"

He held up his hand to silence his chief of staff.

"Monique?"

"Yes, I think she's right. I know it sounds crazy, but if Rachelle was killed in the other reality, I would have died here. We were . . . connected."

"Connected how?"

"Belief. Knowledge." Monique looked at Kara. A small part of her still remembered Thomas's first lieutenant, Mikil, from the short time she'd lived as Rachelle.

"Sir, I think you should take this call," Ron Kreet pressed.

"Who is it?" the president demanded without removing his eyes from Monique.

"He says he's Thomas Hunter."

The president turned around. "Thomas Hunter?"

"I knew it!" Kara whispered. "The Horde didn't kill him!"

"He says he has information critical to the standoff with Israel."

"Put him on speaker."

The chief of staff punched a button and set the receiver in its cradle. "Mr. Hunter, I have the president on the line. You're on a speakerphone. Your sister and Monique de Raison are here as well."

The line remained silent.

"Thomas?" the president said.

"Hello, Mr. President. Monique is alive, then?"

"She's standing right here with Kara."

"The Book works."

"What book?" the president asked.

"I'm sorry, Mr. President. Kara can explain later. Did the others escape?"

"They're safe," Kara said.

"What's this about?" President Blair asked.

"I'm sorry, sir," Thomas said. "I know it isn't making a lot of sense, but you have to listen carefully. The French intend to offer the antivirus to Israel in an open-sea exchange five days from now. The offer is genuine. If Israel calls their bluff and launches another strike, Fortier will retaliate by taking out Tel Aviv."

The president slowly sat. "You're sure about this?"

"Yes sir, I am. I can also tell you that they won't tolerate the existence of a United States postvirus. Can you get me out of here?"

Blair glanced up at a general, who nodded.

"I'll let General Peters give you some coordinates. Are you sure you can make it?"

"No."

Blair paused, then said, "I'm giving the phone to Peters. Godspeed, Thomas. Get back to us."

"Thank you, sir."

The general picked up the phone and talked quickly, feeding Thomas with basic instructions and coordinates for a pickup point fifty miles south of Paris.

"Get the Israeli prime minister on the phone now," the president instructed Kreet. Then to Monique and Kara: "I think I deserve an explanation."

Kara was staring at the floor. She lifted a hand and pulled absently at her hair. "I have to get back and tell Mikil that he's with the Horde."

"You know how to get back?" Monique asked.

"Yes."

———— ⤫ ————

Thomas hung up the phone and took two steps toward the stairs before stopping short. Voices drifted up from the basement.

They were on the stairs!

They would find the guard. Then they would check his cell and find him missing.

He sprinted for the back of the house, through an old kitchen, over a couch in the living room, up to a large window. No guard on the back lawn that he could see. He flipped the latch open.

The window slid up freely. He tumbled to the ground and had the window halfway down when the first alarm came. A loud klaxon that made him jerk.

"Man down!"

Thomas ran for the forest.

———— ⟞∞⟝ ————

Carlos heard the alarm and froze on the bottom step. An intruder? Impossible. They'd evacuated the house only yesterday when the Americans had inserted their special forces in an attempt to locate Thomas. They'd learned of the mission in advance, naturally, and they'd stayed clear long enough for the team to satisfy itself that Monique de Raison's information was simply wrong.

Any intrusion at this point couldn't be part of the American effort. There had been no word. There was always the possibility that their contact had been compromised, but Monique wouldn't have been able to tell them who the contact was, only that they had one. And that was Fortier's mistake, not his.

His radio squawked. "Sir?"

He unclipped the radio from his waist. "Close the perimeter. Cover the exits. Shoot on sight."

He took two steps and stopped. A thought filled his mind. The cut on his neck. The impossible wound from the reality that Thomas claimed to have come from. A bandage now covered the small cut.

Carlos dropped back to the basement and ran toward the back room where the body was kept. The body of Thomas Hunter. He crashed through the first door and inserted his key into the cellar door. He shoved it open and hit the light.

He roared in anger and threw his keys at the wall. They'd taken the body. But how could a team have penetrated his defenses, broken into this room, and taken the body in the space of ten minutes? Less!

Unless this man truly had escaped death before. Unless . . .

But he refused to consider that possibility. Some things pushed a man too far, and the thought of a dead man walking after three days under the sheet was one of them.

Carlos ran from the room, snatching up his radio while he sprinted down the hall.

"Check the windows for footprints. Search the house. Hunter's body is missing. I want him found!"

———∞———

Now he had a serious dilemma. More serious in some ways than any he'd yet faced. Thomas crouched in the forest watching the frenzied search of the house and its perimeter. They'd found the unlatched window and had concentrated their search on that side of the house. All well and good from his perspective on the opposite side of the property. He had escaped cleanly. They had no idea which direction he'd headed. All he had to do now was reach the coordinates in southern France.

But there was still the Book. There was no way he could leave France without the Book. Not because it might prove useful in his hands, but because it could be devastating in the wrong hands. Assuming the Book still worked. They hadn't tested the Book here yet, but surely . . .

The guards had been searching the house under Carlos's direction for half an hour. What were the chances that they wouldn't find the Book? Very slim.

If he waited until the activity in the house settled down, attempted to recover the Book, and headed south within a few hours, he could still make the pickup.

"Anything?" one of the guards yelled.

"Nothing," a man dressed in the uniform of a high-ranking French military officer answered. He stepped into an old Bentley and slammed the door. "Unless you consider an old empty diary with an entry or two something. It must have been lost by an old patient. Found it under the mattress." He stuck the Book out the window. "Beautiful cover though."

The Book? It was right there in the man's hands. The blank Book of History.

The car roared to life. Thomas rose and almost yelled out without thought. He caught himself and dropped back down. Never mind getting caught—anything he did to draw attention to the Book would be a mistake.

The car sped off with Thomas peering hopelessly after it.

The Book was gone.

He stood still, dumbstruck. The officer had no clue what he'd stumbled upon—Thomas's only small consolation.

Thomas spent the next ten minutes considering his predicament before finally concluding that there was no reasonable way to pursue the Book at this time. For the time being it was simply lost.

Unless Carlos . . . Carlos would know the officer.

Carlos. And who could get to Carlos?

Johan. Carlos had connected with Johan once, when Thomas had cut his neck in the amphitheater. Maybe he could get Johan to dream as Carlos . . .

Thomas turned and ran south. He had to sleep and dream. And he would, but he had only twenty-four hours to reach a helicopter that would transfer him to an aircraft carrier in the Atlantic. They were waiting for him in Washington.

10

Chelise of Qurong stood on the balcony of her father's palace and stared at the procession winding its way up the muddy street. They'd captured more of the albino dissidents. Why the people found this a reason for such celebration, she couldn't understand, but they lined the street ten deep, peering and taunting and laughing as if it were a circus rather than a prelude to an execution. She understood their natural fascination with the albinos—they looked more like animals than humans with their shiny hair and smooth skin. Like jackals that had been shaved of their fur. There was a rumor that they might not even be human any longer.

The beast Woref had caught these jackals. He was parading the fruits of his hunt for all the women to see. She wasn't sure how to feel about that. He was uncouth, but not necessarily in a way that was intolerable. So she'd told herself a hundred times since learning his eyes were for her.

She'd never marry him, of course. Father would never allow his only daughter to fall into such hands.

Then again, marriage to such a powerful man who exemplified all that was truly honorable about being human might not be such a bad thing. Every man had his tender side. Surely she could find his. Surely she could tame even this monster. The task might even be a pleasurable one.

Chelise lifted her eyes to the city. Nearly a million people now lived in this crowded forest, though "forest" no longer accurately described the great prize the Horde had overtaken thirteen months ago. At least not here by the lake. Twenty thousand square huts made of stone and mud stretched several miles back from the edge of the lake. The castle stood five stories and was required to be the highest structure in Qurong's domain.

The morning wail still drifted from the temple, where the priests were spouting their nonsense about the Great Romance while the faithful bathed in pain.

She would never speak those thoughts aloud, of course. But she knew that Ciphus and Qurong had fashioned their religion from agreements motivated by political concerns more than by faith. They kept the name and many of the practices of the Forest Dwellers' Great Romance, but they incorporated many Horde practices as well. There was something for everyone in this religion of theirs.

Not that it mattered. She doubted there ever had been such a being called Elyon in the first place.

The lake's muddy waters were considered holy. The faithful were required to bathe in the lake at least once every week, a prospect that had initially terrified most of the Horde. Bathing was a painful experience traditionally associated with punishment, not cleansing.

The fact that Ciphus had drained the red water within a week of Justin's drowning and redirected the spring waters into its basin hardly helped—pain was pain, and no Scab relished the ritual. But as Ciphus said, religion must have its share of pain to prompt faith. And bathing in these muddy waters had none of the red waters' adverse effects. In fact, the bathing ritual was currently in vogue among the upper class. Cleanliness was to be embraced, not shunned, Ciphus said, and this was one teaching that Chelise was beginning to embrace.

She bathed once a day now.

"Excuse me, mistress, but Qurong calls for you."

Chelise faced her maidservant, Elison, a petite woman with long black hair knotted around yellow flowers. Daffodils. Adorning oneself with flowers was the one Forest Dweller practice that Chelise enjoyed adopting more than perhaps any other. They'd never had such a luxury in the desert. As of late, flowers were becoming more difficult to find near the city.

"Did he say why he wants to see me?" Chelise asked.

"Only that he has a gift for you."

"Did he say what kind of gift?"

"No, mistress." Elison grinned. "But I don't think it's fruit or flowers."

Chelise felt her pulse surge. "The villa?"

They all knew that Qurong was building a villa for her in the large walled compound referred to as the royal garden, three miles outside the city. She hadn't seen the villa yet, as Qurong kept the section where it was being built cordoned off. But she'd been to the compound many times, usually to the library to write or to read the Books collected over the past fifteen years. The sprawling gardens and orchards were kept by a staff of twenty servants. Not a blade of grass was out of place. Elyon himself would live here, they said, such was its beauty.

And Chelise would live there too, beside the library where she would sequester herself and write into the night. Maybe even one day discover the key to reading the Books of Histories.

"Perhaps." Her maidservant winked.

Chelise ran into her room. "Quickly, help me dress. What should I wear?"

"I would say that a white gown—"

"With red flowers! Is he waiting?"

"He will meet you in the courtyard in a few minutes."

"A few minutes? Then we have to hurry!"

The palace had been built from wood with flattened reeds for walls and pounded bark for floors—a luxury reserved only for the upper class. The Forest People had built their homes in the same manner, and Qurong had promised that they would all live in such magnificent homes soon enough. Their simple mud dwellings were only temporary, a necessity mandated by the need to build so many houses in a short period of time.

She discarded her simple bedclothes and took the long bleached tunic that Elison had retrieved from her closet. The gown was woven from thread that the Forest People had perfected—smooth and silky, unlike the rough burlap the Horde had made from the woven stalks of desert wheat. The costs of the campaigns against the forests had been staggering, but Qurong had been right about the benefits of conquering them.

"The flowers . . ."

Elison laughed. "The villa won't be going anywhere. Take your time. Sometimes it's best to make a man wait, even if he is the supreme leader."

"You know men so well?"

Elison didn't respond, and Chelise knew that her comment had stung. Maidservants were forbidden to marry.

She sat in front of the resin mirror and picked up a brush. "I will let you marry, Elison. I've told you, the day that I marry, you'll be free to find your own man."

Elison dipped her head and left the room to fetch the flowers.

The mirror's resin had been poured over a flat black stone that reflected her features as a pool of dark water would. She dipped the bristles of her brush into a small bowl of oil and began working out the flakes that speckled her dark hair—an unending task that most women avoided by wearing a hood.

And when will Qurong allow you to marry, Chelise?

When he finds a suitable man for you. This is the burden of royalty. You can't just marry the first handsome man who walks by this castle.

Chelise decided to forget the brushing and settle for the hood after all. She dabbed her fingers into a large bowl of white morst powder and patted her face and neck where she'd already applied paste. The regular variety of the powdery paste soothed skin by drying any lingering moisture such as sweat, but it tended to flake with the skin. This new variety, developed by her father's alchemist, consisted of two separate applications: a clear thin salve, then a white morst powder that contained ground herbs, effectively minimizing the flaking. It might be fine for the common woman to walk around with loose flakes of skin hanging from her tunic, but it wasn't fitting for royalty.

Elison returned with red roses.

"Roses?"

"I also have tuhan flowers," Elison said.

Chelise took the roses and smiled.

They descended the stairs ten minutes later and hurried toward the courtyard. They crossed an atrium that rose all five stories and featured a large fruit tree at its center. Sweet fruit—not the bitter rot that the desert tribes preferred—was the one spoil of the forest that all of the people gorged themselves on. Chelise stopped before the arching entrance to the courtyard, faced Elison, and opened her hands, palms up. "Okay?"

"You're stunning."

"Thank you."

She turned and kissed the base of a tall bronze statue of Elyon—a winged serpent on a pole. "I feel religious today," she said softly, and walked into the courtyard.

Qurong stood in a black tunic beside Woref, who was dressed in full battle gear. Behind them were the albinos under guard.

The sight snatched away any thought of the villa. Chelise stopped, confused. Qurong meant to give her some albinos as a gift? No, that couldn't possibly be it. His gift was to show off his little victory.

Qurong saw her, spread his arms, and smiled wide. "My daughter arrives. A vision of beauty to grace her father's pride."

What was he saying? He rarely spoke in such lofty terms.

"Good morning, Father. I'm told you have a gift."

He laughed. "And I do. But first I want to show you something." Qurong glanced at Woref, who was staring at her directly. "Show her, Woref."

The general dipped his head, stepped to one side, and stood tall like a peacock. For all his fearful reputation, he demeaned himself with this display of pride. Did he think she would tremble with respect at his capturing a few albinos? He should have wiped out the whole band of jackals by now.

She looked at the poor victims. These few were a mockery of his . . .

Something about the albino on the left stopped her. He looked vaguely familiar. Impossible, of course—the only albinos she'd ever seen were the ones dragged in as prisoners these past few months. A couple dozen at most. This man wasn't one of them. Then what was it? His green eyes seemed to look through her. Unnerving. She averted her stare.

The prisoners' hands were bound behind them, and their ankles were shackled. Other than simple loin skirts, they were all naked except for one—a woman. They'd been covered in ash, but their sweat had washed most of it away, revealing broad vertical swaths of fleshy skin.

"You don't know who you're looking at, do you, my dear?"

"What is this?" a voice demanded behind her. Mother had come in. "How dare you bring these filthy creatures into my house?"

"Watch your tongue, wife," Qurong snapped. It was no secret that Patricia ruled the castle, but Qurong wouldn't tolerate brazenness in front of his men.

Patricia stopped beside Chelise and eyed her husband. "Please remove these albinos from my house."

"Thank you for coming, my dear. Your house will be disease-free soon enough. First, please, both of you, look closely and tell me what you see."

Chelise glanced at her mother, who held Qurong with a glare. Her eyes were as white as the moon, but today the moon was on fire.

"For the sake of Elyon, woman! It won't kill you! Look at them!"

Her mother finally obeyed.

Something strange was happening with this ceremonious display, but Chelise was at a loss. They were simply five albinos in chains, headed for the dungeons and then for a drowning. Why would her father take such pride?

She guessed it the moment Qurong spoke.

"You see, even the great Thomas of Hunter is nothing but one more albino in chains."

Thomas of Hunter!

"Which one?" Patricia asked.

But Chelise already knew which one. The once-great commander of the feared Forest Guard was the man who was staring at her. She blinked and looked away again. He looked at her as if he recognized her.

"Take them away," Chelise said.

"So you've captured their leader," her mother said. "This is good news, but their presence in our house is offensive. I'm sure you'll find plenty of commoners to cheer your victory."

Qurong's jaw muscles flexed. Mother was pushing him too far. "It isn't the commoner's victory," he snapped. "It's yours. And it's your daughter's."

Hers? A smile returned to Qurong's face.

"Our daughter's?" Patricia asked.

Now Qurong's eyes were on Chelise. "Yes, our daughter's. Today I am announcing the marriage of my only daughter."

Her mother gasped.

It took a moment for the words to sink in. She felt Elison's hand take her elbow. But what did her marriage have to do with these albinos?

"I am to be married?"

"Yes, my love."

"Well, that is good news indeed," her mother said.

Chelise felt a momentary surge of panic. "Married to whom?"

"To the man who captured him, of course." Qurong stepped to his left and put a hand on his general's shoulder. "To Woref, commander of my armies."

Woref!

Chelise felt the breath leave her lungs. The general's hands hung loosely by his sides—big, thick hands with gnarled fingers. He was twice her size. He lifted a hand and pulled back his hood to reveal his head. Long dread-locks fell over his shoulders. There could be no mistake about it: this man was part beast.

But he was also Woref, mightiest man in the Horde, next to her father. And even now his gray eyes looked at her hungrily. Desire. This mighty man wanted her as his wife.

Whatever reservation she struggled with was more than compensated for by her mother, who rushed over to the general and bent to one knee. She took his hand and kissed it.

"My daughter is yours, my lord."

She stood as quickly and kissed her husband on the cheek. "You have made me a very happy woman."

Qurong chuckled.

"Well," her mother said, facing Chelise. "Aren't you going to say something?"

Chelise was still too stunned to speak.

Her maidservant squeezed her elbow. "It is a most excellent choice," Elison whispered.

Her compassionate voice filled Chelise with courage. She lowered her head and knelt to one knee. "I am honored to accept this gift, great Qurong of the Horde. You have made me a very happy woman."

With those words her apprehension fled. An excitement she'd never known before flooded her veins. She was going to marry the mightiest man on the earth. She would be the envy of every woman who still possessed the fire to love. She was about to find new life.

She heard him coming toward her. She opened her eyes but dared not lift her head. His muddy battle boots stopped three feet from her. Then one knee. He was kneeling!

Woref's hand touched her chin and lifted her face gently. She stared into his gray eyes. A tremble swept through her bones. Was this terror or desire?

Woref leaned forward and kissed her forehead. He spoke softly, but she couldn't mistake the great emotion in his voice. "You are mine. Forever, you are mine," he said. Then he stood.

The courtyard had fallen completely silent. Now her mother sniffed. She'd never heard the sound from Patricia before.

"When will they marry?" Mother asked.

"In three days," Qurong said. "On the same day that we drown Thomas of Hunter."

11

Thomas had recognized her the moment she stepped into the courtyard. This was Chelise, the daughter of Qurong, whom he'd once
met in the desert after the disease had taken him. He'd persuaded her that
he was an assassin, and she'd treated him kindly before sending him on his
way with a horse. He'd barely made it back to the lake to bathe. He would
never forget the pain of that bathing.

He would never forget the kindness of this woman who stared at
him with flat gray eyes. She didn't recognize him.

Now he'd just learned that she was being given in marriage to the vilest
Scab he'd yet met. Woref. He wasn't sure if she wanted Woref or loathed
him, but she'd reacted with enough passion to bring a lump to his throat.

Both Chelise and her mother had used liberal amounts of the morst
to cover their faces and smooth out the cracks in their skin. This wasn't
done for comfort alone, he thought. Not nearly so much would have sufficed. The powder they used actually covered their skin. In its own way,
the Horde's upper class seemed to be distancing itself from the disease. At
least the royal women did.

If not for Woref's armor and Qurong's cloak, both which incorporated heavy use of polished bronze buttons, trims, and a winged serpent
plate on their chests, both men would have been indistinguishable from
any other Scab. They wore their hair long, in knotted dreadlocks, and
cracked skin hung in small flakes off their cheeks and noses. They too used
morst, but the lightly powdered variety that served the practical purpose
of keeping the skin dry, if not smooth.

Seeing the best of the Horde in such close proximity, Thomas was reminded why his people had such an aversion to Scabs. The disease that Justin had drowned to heal was disturbing in the least. Even looking at the disease for too long was frowned upon among some tribes.

Yet Thomas couldn't tear his eyes from Chelise, and at first he didn't know why. Then he understood—he pitied her. This woman who had once treated him with such kindness wanted to be free from the disease, he was sure of it. Or was he simply imposing his will on hers?

When Qurong had announced her marriage, Thomas found himself silently begging her to scream her objections. For a moment he thought she might. Then she'd fallen to her knee and expressed her pleasure, and Thomas's heart had fallen like a rock.

Was she so blind? He felt smothered by empathy.

Qurong had just said something, but Thomas had missed it. The room was quiet. Chelise was looking at him again. Their eyes locked.

Do you recognize me? He willed her to see. *Elyon once sent you to save my life. I am the man who called himself an assassin in front of your tent.*

What had Qurong said that brought this silence?

"Well, then, we have three days to prepare," Qurong's wife said. "Not exactly ample time to prepare a wedding, but considering the occasion, I would say that sooner is better than later." She took her daughter's arm and bowed to her husband and Woref. "My lords." Then she led Chelise from the courtyard.

Three days.

Qurong spoke to Woref: "Take them to the dungeon. Apart from you, no one but Ciphus or myself is to speak to them."

Woref dipped his head. "Sir."

Qurong stepped up to Thomas and eyed him carefully. He lifted his hand and squeezed Thomas's cheeks. "Three days. I'm tempted to finish you now, but I intend to make you speak first." He released his cheeks and absently wiped his fingers on his tunic.

"I will speak now," Thomas said.

Qurong glanced at Woref, then back, grinning. "So easily? I expected the mighty warrior to be more reticent."

"What do you want to know?"

His candor seemed to put the leader off.

"Tell me the locations of your tribes."

"They've moved. I don't know where they are."

Qurong looked at Woref.

"I'm afraid it's true, sir. The tribes move when contact is made."

"You run like a pack of dogs," Qurong said. "The great warriors have turned into frightened pups."

"The bravery of my people is greater than any man who wields a sword," Thomas said. "We could kill your warriors easily enough, but this isn't the way of Justin."

"Justin is dead, you fool!"

"Is he? The Horde is dead."

"Do I look dead?" Qurong slapped him on the cheek. "Did a dead man just strike you?"

Thomas didn't respond. This man was going to drown him in three days—not enough time for Mikil to mount a rescue, not with her duty to protect the tribe first. He had his dreams. If there was any way to turn the tables here, it would come from his dreams.

"Ciphus says you've lost your minds. I see now that he's right. Take them to the dungeons."

He turned away. A guard grabbed Thomas's arm and pulled him around.

"And, Woref," Qurong said, turning back. "Feed him the rhambutan."

He knew?

"We don't want these dreams Martyn spoke about interfering with our plans. If he refuses to eat, kill one of the other prisoners."

⸻

Woref led them from the castle back into the street. Thomas stared, still taken aback by the changes.

He'd grown accustomed to the scent of sulfur during the long trip through the desert, but the stink had nearly overpowered him while they were still two miles from the Horde city. Thousands of trees had been cleared to make room for a city that looked more like a garbage pile than a place humans were expected to live. It reminded Thomas of images from the histories, slums in India, only made of mud rather than rusted tin shanties. Flies had infested the place, drawn by the stink.

Thousands of Scabs had lined the road, giving the war party a wide berth. Some mocked in high-pitched tones; some stood with folded arms; all stared with bland eyes. There was no way to tell which ones had once been Forest People. Thomas didn't recognize a single face.

If Thomas wasn't mistaken, Qurong had built his castle on the very spot that his own house had once been built. The wooden structures that had been homes for the Forest People still stood, but they had fallen into disrepair, and the yards had gone to waste.

"Move!"

They marched toward the lake. The homes once occupied by Ciphus and his council were now bordered by twin statues of the winged serpent. Teeleh.

"The lake . . ."

A guard struck William on the head, silencing him.

They'd crested the shore. The red water was gone, replaced by murky liquid. Hundreds of Scabs were sponge bathing along the shore. So this was Ciphus's Great Romance.

Thomas walked against the rattling of his shackles, dumb with disbelief. They'd heard rumors, of course, but to actually see the devastation to their once-sacred home came as a shock. The gazebos that surrounded the lake had been converted into guard towers. And on the opposite shore, a new temple.

A Thrall!

It looked nearly identical to the one that had once stood in the colored forest. The domed ceiling didn't glow, and the steps were muddy from a steady flow of traffic, but it was a clear reconstruction of the Thrall that had stood at the center of the village before Tanis had crossed.

"Take them to the deepest chamber," Woref said. He spit to one side.

"They speak to no one other than myself and the high priest. If they escape, I will personally see to the drowning of the entire temple guard."

He turned and left them without another glance.

They were marched toward the amphitheater where they'd judged and sentenced Justin. But there was no amphitheater now. It had been filled in. No, not filled in, Thomas realized. Covered. They were being marched to an entrance that led into the dungeons where the amphitheater once stood.

Thomas glanced at Cain and Stephen, who had helped with this construction before drowning in the red waters. They both stared ahead, eyes glazed.

"Elyon's strength," Thomas said softly.

The guards either didn't hear him or didn't mind him invoking the common greeting. They themselves now referred to Teeleh as Elyon, though they didn't seem to notice the incongruity of the practice.

The dungeons were dark and smelled of mildew. The albinos were herded down a long flight of stone steps, along a wet corridor, and pushed into a twenty-by-twenty cell with bronze bars. A single shaft of light, roughly a foot square, filtered through an air vent in the ceiling.

The gate crashed shut. The guards ran a thick bolt into the wall, locked it down with a key, and left them.

Something dripped nearby—a single drop every four or five seconds. Water, muddy or pure, would be a welcome taste now. A distant clang of the outer gate echoed down the stairs.

Thomas sank to his haunches along one wall, and the others followed suit. They'd been on their feet since being wakened in the desert for the last leg of their march.

For a long minute no one spoke. William broke the silence.

"Well, we've done it now. This is our tomb." There was no levity in his voice. No one bothered to challenge him.

The outer door clanged again. Boots clomped down the stairs. They could hear any such approach, not that knowing when the executioner entered the dungeon would be any consolation.

A new guard came into view and shoved a container through the bars. "Water," he said. He pointed at Thomas. "Drink it."

Thomas glanced at the others then walked over and picked up the pitcher. He knew by the smell that they'd mixed rhambutan juice with the water, but he had no choice. It went down cool and sweet.

Satisfied, the guard retreated without waiting for the others to drink. They drained the entire pitcher before the outer gate closed.

Once again they sat in silence.

"Any ideas?" Thomas asked.

"We won't dream now," William said.

"Right."

"Which means you can't go to this other world of yours and retrieve any information that might help us out. Like you did when we made the black powder."

"That's right. I'm stuck here. I could spend a month in this dungeon while only minutes or hours pass there."

"And what's happening there?" he asked. William was starting to believe, Thomas saw.

"I'm sleeping on an airplane after barely making a helicopter pickup south of Paris."

The explanation earned him a blank stare.

"You know the daughter of Qurong," Suzan said. "She was the one who gave you a horse once."

His mind was drawn back to Chelise. She was facing her own kind of execution without even knowing it. Why was this a concern of Suzan's?

"You're thinking something?"

"No. Only that she seemed to be taken with you."

William scoffed. "With his death, you mean. She's a Scab!"

"She's also a woman," Suzan said.

"So is her mother. The old witch is worse than Qurong."

"Let her speak," Thomas said. To Suzan: "She's a woman; what of it?"

"She might think differently than her father. Not about us, mind you. But she may be more reasoned than Qurong."

"Reasoned about what?" William asked. "She would just as soon see us dead as her father would."

"Reasoned about the Books of Histories."

Thomas blinked in the dim light. "The Books of Histories?"

"The Horde still has them, right?"

"As far as we know."

"And you have special knowledge concerning the histories."

"I don't see—"

"Didn't you say that she was fascinated by the histories when you met her in the desert?"

Thomas suddenly saw where she was going. He stood slowly.

"If you could win an audience with her," Suzan continued, "and persuade her that you can show her how to read the histories, she might have the influence to delay our execution. Or at least yours."

"But how would I win an audience with her?"

"This is lunacy," William said. "The Horde can't even read the Books of History!"

"We don't know that they can't be taught." Thomas said. "Suzan may be on to something."

"And what would delaying our execution accomplish?" William objected.

"Are you going to argue with everything?" Thomas demanded. "We aren't exactly brimming with alternatives here. Give her a chance."

He turned back to Suzan. "On the other hand, he does have a point. I doubt a Scab can be taught to read the Books of Histories. They can't decipher the truth in them."

"Did the blank Book work?" she asked.

The Book had crossed over into the other reality. When it disappeared, Thomas had offered no explanation to his comrades. "Yes. Yes, as a matter of fact it did."

"Are there more blank Books?"

He hadn't considered the possibility. "I don't know."

"You may not be able to get an audience with Chelise, but Ciphus will see you," Suzan said. "Make him promises concerning the power of the blank Books."

"They don't work in this reality."

"Promises, Thomas. Only promises."

Then Thomas saw the entire plan clearly. He spun to Cain. "How do I get the attention of a guard?"

12

Five fully armed Scabs led Thomas into the Thrall through a back entrance. The entire structure was built with the original Thrall in mind. Without the option of colored wood, Ciphus had used mud and then covered the mud with dyed thatch work—Horde handiwork. The large circular floor in the domed auditorium was green, again dyed thatch work instead of the glowing resin once shaped by the hands of innocent men. Hundreds of worshipers lay prostrate around the circumference, with only their heads and hands in the green circle.

It was as if they were paying homage to this green lake.

The primary departure from the original Thrall was the large statue of the winged serpent, which stood on top of the dome. A smaller replica hung from its crest inside.

This was Teeleh's Thrall.

Thomas was pushed past the auditorium into a hall and then into a side office, where a single hooded man stood with his back to the door, staring out of a small window. The door closed behind Thomas.

He stood in chains before a large wooden slab, a desk of sorts, bordered on each side with bronze statues of the winged serpent. Candles blazed from two large candlesticks, spewing their oily smoke to the ceiling.

The man turned slowly. Thomas's first thought was that Ciphus had become a ghost. The powder on his face was as white as the robe he wore, and his eyes only a shade darker.

The high priest stared at him like a cat, emotionless, arms folded into draping sleeves that hid his hands.

"Hello, Thomas."

Thomas dipped his head slightly. "Ciphus. It's good to see you, old friend."

For a long time the high priest just looked at him, and Thomas refused to speak again. He would play and win this purposeful game.

Ciphus stepped to a tall flask on his desk and gripped its narrow neck with his long white fingers. He was wearing the same powder as Chelise and her mother had worn, Thomas guessed. The cracked skin was still visible beneath, but not in the same scaly fashion that characterized the scabies.

The priest poured a green liquid into a chalice. "Drink?"

"No, thank you."

"You sure? It's fruit juice."

"We have fruit, Ciphus. Have you tasted it?"

"Your bitter seeds? Your preference for that should be the first indicator that you've lost your senses. The birds and the animals eat bitter seeds eagerly. So do you." He took a sip of the fruit juice.

"Do the seeds eaten by animals also heal them?" Thomas asked.

"No. But animals don't practice sorcery. Which is the one clear indication that you're not truly animals either. So then, what are you, Thomas? You're clearly no longer human; one look at your flesh is proof enough. And you're not really an animal like they all say. Then what are you? Hmm? Other than enemies of Elyon?"

"We are the followers of Justin, who is Elyon."

"Please, not in here," Ciphus said with lips drawn. "We are in his temple; I will not have you utter such blasphemy here." He set the glass down carefully. "You requested an audience. I assume that you intend to beg for your life. You defy me and my council when you have your sword, and now you beg at my feet when I have you in chains, is that it?"

"You don't have me in chains. Qurong does."

"And where is Justin now? I would have thought he would come riding in on a white horse to draw a protective line in the sand for you."

"You can't go on pretending that nothing happened when you killed him, Ciphus."

"Martyn killed him!" Ciphus snapped. "Your precious Johan killed him!"

"And you allowed him to. Johan has found new life. You still live in your death."

"You're wrong. Justin's death *proves* that you're wrong. Only a simpleton could ever be convinced that Elyon would die. Or *could* die, for that matter. You live in this silly condition of yours because of your own foolishness in following Justin's charade. It is Teeleh's judgment against you."

"Teeleh's judgment?"

"Don't try your trickery on me," Ciphus snapped. "Elyon has judged you."

"You said Teeleh's judgment."

"I would never even speak that name in the holy place. Don't put words in my mouth."

He hadn't heard himself. He wasn't only blind to the truth; he was deaf. A man to be pitied, not hated.

"Justin's alive, Ciphus. One day, sooner or later, you'll see that. He will not rest until his bride returns to him."

"What nonsense are you talking about now? What bride?"

"That is what he calls us. You. Any who would embrace his invitation to the Great Romance."

"By drowning? How absurd!"

"By dying to this disease that hangs off your skin and blinds your eyes. By finding a new life with him."

Ciphus frowned and paced along his desk, hands behind his back.

"How did you turn the lake brown?" Thomas asked.

"We drained the defiled water and filled the lake from the spring. We had to get back to the Great Romance; I'm sure you understand. The people went two weeks without bathing, and it was only by the grace of Elyon that he didn't punish us for our indiscretion. An indiscretion that was yours, may I remind you."

"So you're all back to normal here. Bathing away a disease that remains."

"The disease is in the mind, not the skin, you fool. It manifests itself in the cult of yours. What do you call it? The Circle?"

"It represents the circle of marriage."

"So you are married to Elyon?"

"In a manner of speaking, yes."

"And what manner is that?"

"In the same way that he is a lion or a lamb or a boy or Justin."

Ciphus closed his eyes and took a deep breath. "Elyon, give me strength. I can see that you will insist on dying. I had hoped I could help you see sense, Thomas. I really had. The supreme leader listens to me, you know. I may have been able to turn him."

"And you still may."

"Not now. Not with your stubborn heart."

"I'm not suggesting you turn him for my sake," Thomas said. "For yours."

"Hmm? Is that right? I, arguably the most powerful man alive, need your help? How benevolent of you."

"Yes. In all of this building with mud and dabbling in your new lake, you may have missed a point."

Ciphus stared at him. "Go ahead."

"You are not the most powerful man in the world, though arguably you should be. Unfortunately, you are simply a pawn of Qurong's."

"Nonsense!"

"He tolerates you as matter of expedience. His motives are purely political."

"This talk will win you an execution!"

"I've already won an execution. Surely you see what I'm saying, Ciphus. I just came from Qurong's castle. He has no shred of interest in the Great Romance. He knows that making his people subject to a higher power will only strengthen his power over them. He is using you to put a hold on his people."

"There always has been a tension between politics and religion, hasn't there?" Ciphus said. "When you were in your right mind, did the people follow you, or did they follow me?"

"We followed Elyon. The Great Romance was always first! And now you've let that monster in the castle make a fool of you by putting you underneath him."

Ciphus froze halfway through Thomas's point, perhaps as much in fear of being overheard as because of any chord it struck in him. Thomas had to walk a thin line.

"No?" he pushed. "Then consider this: when you decided to allow Justin's execution, I was powerless to stop you. Your word was above mine. But if you now tell Qurong that the council has decided his castle must be torn down, would he do it? I think he might tear down your Thrall instead."

"This is the talk of fools. It is a great privilege for me to serve the people—"

"You mean Qurong. You are the slave of Qurong, Ciphus. Even your blind eyes can see that."

The priest slammed his fist on the table. "And you think that can be changed?" he shouted.

"Good," Thomas breathed. "Then you do see it. Elyon won't be the toy of any man, not even Qurong. How dare you allow him to make the Great Romance his tool? He's reduced your great religion to nothing more than shackles to harness the will of his people. It makes a mockery of Elyon. And of you."

"Enough!" Ciphus had regained control of himself. He set his jaw and folded his arms. "This is pointless. I think our time is over."

"Yes," Thomas said.

Ciphus looked momentarily off guard by Thomas's quick agreement. He dipped his head. "Then you will—"

"Yes, I may have a way to change the imbalance of power between you and Qurong."

The priest's eyes skittered to the door. He blinked rapidly. "You should leave before you earn my drowning as well."

"Exactly. Qurong would drown the high priest for simple words against him. He has it backward. You should have the power to drown him for words against the Great Romance."

Ciphus wasn't ready to capitulate. He knew how dangerous this talk was, because he knew that Thomas spoke the truth. Ciphus *did* serve Qurong. He needed to see the way out before hinting at any agreement.

"The Books of History have a power that is beyond Qurong," Thomas said in a soft voice. "These holy Books may restore the power of the Great Romance to its rightful place. Politically speaking. And with it, you."

A wry smile twisted Ciphus's lips. "Then you don't know, do you? The Books of History, which you were so desperate to find, aren't even legible. Your ploy here has failed."

"You're wrong. They are legible, and I can read them."

"Is that right? Have you ever seen even one of the Books?"

"Yes. And I can read it as if I myself had written it."

The smile faded.

"I also know there are blank Books. They contain a power that would change everything. And I know how to use them."

"How did you know about the blank Books?"

Thomas had guessed that there were more; now he knew. "I know more than you can possibly guess. My interest in the Books of Histories isn't as frivolous as you think. Now they may save both of our lives."

Ciphus picked up his chalice and drank. "You don't realize how bold these statements are."

"I have nothing to lose. And with what I will propose, neither do you."

He emptied the glass and set it down, refusing to make eye contact. "Which is?"

"That you take me to the Books of Histories and let me prove their power."

"Qurong would never allow it. And even if he did, how do I know you wouldn't use this power against me?"

"The Books are truth. I can't use the truth against the truth. You represent truth, don't you? Have I harmed even one man since Justin's death? I am a trustworthy man, Ciphus, mad or not."

The priest eyed him cautiously. "Qurong won't allow it."

"I think he would if the request was properly phrased. It's a matter of the Great Romance. But do you need his permission?"

A light crossed the priest's eyes. He paced, stroking his chin.

"You're sure you can read the Books."

"I'm sure. And I'm sure that you have nothing to lose by testing me. If I'm wrong, you will simply return me to the dungeon. If I can't demonstrate the power, you will do the same. But if I'm right, we will change history together."

"And why would you want to change history with me?"

"I don't necessarily. I want to live. That is my price. If I'm right, you will ensure the survival of me and my friends."

Thomas knew that Ciphus probably couldn't or wouldn't ensure any such thing. He also knew that there was probably no power to show Ciphus. Using one of the blank Books might change things in the other reality—good reason for this plan in and of itself—but the Books would prove powerless here.

No matter. These weren't his primary objectives. He was following another thread. A very thin thread, granted, but a thread.

"Even if I'm wrong about the power, the ability to read the Books of History will give a new power by itself."

"So you can show me how to read them?"

Thomas smiled. "You haven't been listening. You have no idea what you have in your hands, do you? I am your path to the power that's justly yours."

Ciphus picked up his glass, drained the last of the fruit juice, set it down firmly, and walked toward the door. "Then we go."

"Now?"

"What better time? You're right; I don't need Qurong's permission. I have access to the library. I will say that I'm taking you there to extract a full confession from you in writing and to interrogate you on several writings we've found from your Circle."

"I will only show you what I know on one condition."

"Yes, I know. Your life. First the Books."

"No, one other condition. I insist that a third party be present."

"What on earth for?"

"My protection. I want a party to witness our agreement. Someone who's disconnected from your own authority yet has enough authority to corroborate."

"Impossible! It would be tantamount to telling Qurong that I'm working against him!"

"Then choose someone who wants to see the Books of Histories unveiled as much as you do. Surely there's someone Qurong respects enough to listen to in the event you turn against me, yet who doesn't pose a threat to you."

"I don't see it. If you show another person this power, what value is it to me?"

"I won't show them the power. I'll only demonstrate that I can read the Books. This will be enough for them. How about his wife?"

"Patricia. She would just as soon shove a knife into my belly as bathe in the lake."

"Then who is taken with the histories?"

"The librarian, Christoph. But he's hardly better. I don't see the value of this absurd demand. If I'm to trust you, then you'll have to trust me."

"You have reason to trust me. My actions have never undermined you. I, on the other hand, have enough reason to question you."

Ciphus strode deliberately back to his desk. "Then we have no agreement."

"Surely there's someone in the royal court who has enough interest in the histories to bend the rules a bit."

"The royal court is a very small community. There's his wife and his daughter and . . ." Ciphus faced him. "His daughter's quite taken with the histories."

"The one who's to marry Woref? Chelise. Fine, I don't care who it is as long as she is impartial and has a love for the Books. There's no risk to you. We won't tell her that you intend to overthrow her father, only that you've agreed to make my case to Qurong if I can indeed reveal the knowledge contained in the Books. Out of respect to Qurong, you refuse to bother him with the matter until you've verified that I have something to offer."

"No more talk of overthrowing!" Ciphus whispered harshly. "I said no such thing! It's strictly as you said—I'm following up this matter with full intentions of bringing it to Qurong's attention if it has any merits."

"Of course. And you may send Chelise out of the room when it comes time for me to show you the power of the Books."

Ciphus frowned. "Guards!" he called.

"Agreed?" Thomas asked.

"I'll speak with her."

The door opened a few moments later and two guards walked in.

"Return the prisoner to the dungeons."

13

T he arrangement was simple, though a bit suspicious to Thomas. Chelise had agreed to wait for them in the inner library at dusk after the librarian had left for the day. Why so late? Thomas wanted to know. Because Chelise often outlasted Christoph in the library, Ciphus said.

Ciphus used his own mounted guard to transport Thomas in chains through several miles of forest to an expansive walled retreat that was surprisingly beautiful. Stunning, in fact. The moment they passed the main gate, he wondered if he hadn't awakened in his dreams, surrounded by a botanical garden in southern France.

But no, he was sleeping in a plane above the Atlantic. This royal garden was very real.

The entire complex was nestled in a large meadow that Thomas remembered well. The botanical garden hedged in by manicured shrubs was new, but the orchard had been here before. Stone paths wound perfect circles around six large lawns, a different fruit tree centered in each one. The orchard was also circular, as was the botanical garden.

This was Qurong's circle, Thomas thought. At the center stood a two-story structure made of fine wood. Three other buildings—homes, by the looks of them—had been built in each corner of the retreat. A fourth was cordoned off behind the garden.

"The villa that Qurong will give Woref and his daughter as a wedding present," Ciphus said. "She doesn't know yet."

"And that's the library?" Thomas asked, nodding at the large building they were approaching.

"Yes."

It looked far too large for any library, much less one built to hold the Horde's Books. Clearly, whatever it housed was more precious to Qurong than the Great Romance. Ciphus could surely see that much now. Maybe for the first time.

They entered through large double doors into an atrium, empty except for an ornately carved black desk and yet one more of the bronze statues of Teeleh.

"Wait here," Ciphus told his guard.

"What about these?" Thomas held out his shackled arms.

Ciphus hesitated. "Free his arms. Leave the leg chains."

Thomas rubbed his wrists. "Thank you."

"Don't thank me yet. After you."

He followed Thomas into a two-story room that looked old despite its relatively new construction. Ten large desks covered the floor, each with its own lamp stand. The walls were lined with shelves, each filled with scrolls and bound books. Two staircases rose to the second floor, where Thomas could see similar bookcases behind a wooden railing.

He looked around, awed by the woodwork. This was the doing of Forest People. Even the books . . .

"May I?" he asked, stepping toward a bookcase.

Ciphus didn't answer.

He withdrew a bound book from one of the shelves. It was the kind he'd taught the Circle's scribes to use from his memories of the histories. Pounded bark bound around reams of crudely formed paper. He opened the book. The script was an elementary cursive form.

"These are our own histories, created by the scribes," Ciphus said. "Qurong is quite taken with history. Everything is carefully recorded, even the most mundane details. During the day every desk is occupied by historians. We have our own temple scribes to record the history of Elyon since the Second Age."

"The Second Age?"

"The Great Romance since our time as one."

"Then you acknowledge that it's changed."

"Everything changes," Ciphus said.

Thomas looked around the room. "The building is larger than this one room. What's in the rest?"

Ciphus indicated a door on the far side. "Chelise is waiting."

Thomas walked around the desks, put his hand on a large brass handle, and pushed the door open. Several torches lit a large room lined with book-cases, floor to ceiling. Thousands of books.

Thomas released the door and stepped in. The cases rose twenty feet and were serviced by a ladder. No ornate desks or candlesticks here, just books, many more than Thomas had imagined.

Leather-bound books.

The Books of Histories?

"These . . . what are these?"

"The Books of Histories, of course."

"This many? I . . . I had no idea there were so many! These are all Books of Histories?"

"Not exactly an encouraging admission from the man who claims to know all there is about the books," a voice said quietly on his right.

Thomas turned. Chelise stood behind a large desk, on which she'd opened one of the Books. She stepped around the desk and walked toward them, black robe flowing around her ankles. She'd left her hood back, revealing long, dark, shiny hair. The contrast between her white face and so much black was quite startling.

"Did you think my father carried all of the Books with him wher-ever he went?"

Her eyes searched his, and for a moment he thought she might have recognized him from the desert.

She faced Ciphus. "I don't have all night. Either this albino knows something or he doesn't. We can establish that much in a few minutes."

"Matters of the histories are never established flippantly," Ciphus said. "I told you an hour."

"Spare me the eloquence, Priest. Can he read them or not?" She turned to Thomas. "Show us."

Thomas was still too stunned to think straight. He knew that this might be his only opportunity to spend any time with the Books. What were the chances of finding the particular Books that dealt with the Great Deception and the Raison Strain?

"How many are there?"

"Many," Chelise said. "Many thousands."

Thomas walked farther into the room. Torchlight cast a wavering yellow glow over the leather spines. "Are they categorized?"

"How can we categorize what we can't read?" Ciphus asked.

"You can't even read the titles?"

"How can we? They aren't in our tongue."

But they *were* in the common tongue. He looked at a Book on the nearest shelf. *The Histories According to the Second of Five.* What that meant he had no clue, but he could read the words easily enough. They'd all heard that the Horde couldn't read the Books of Histories, but this seemed a bit ridiculous. Were their minds so deceived? And now Ciphus was among them.

"Did you think that the record of everything that has ever happened would be found in two or three Books?" Chelise asked.

"No. I just didn't expect this many." He had to find what he could about the Raison Strain. "Do you know if they are in any order? I would like to look at the one that deals with the Great Deception."

"No, there is no order," Ciphus said. "They were put in place by men who don't read. I thought we'd established that."

"Where did Qurong find them?"

Neither answered.

He looked at Chelise. "You don't know? How could he come into possession of so many Books without a record of where he found them?"

"He says that Elyon showed them to him."

"Elyon? Or was it Teeleh?"

"When I was younger he said Teeleh. Now he says Elyon. I don't know which, and frankly, I don't care. I'm interested in what they say, not where they came from."

"What they say can only be understood by first understanding where they came from. Who wrote them."

"This is your great secret?" Ciphus asked. "You're going to tell us that the only way to read these Books is through your understanding of Elyon? Then don't waste our time."

"Did I say that Elyon wrote them?"

"Do you know who wrote them?" Chelise asked.

He'd sparked some interest in her. *Speak carefully, Thomas. You can't afford to turn Ciphus against you.*

"Where are the blank Books?"

"The blank Books?" Chelise glanced at Ciphus. "I don't care about the blank Books. I can read empty pages as well as you."

Ciphus averted his eyes.

"Then show me the Book you have open," Thomas said.

She let her eyes linger on him, then walked gracefully toward the desk. He followed with Ciphus at his side.

Only he knew that this woman held his fate in her hands. He had to find a way to win her trust. But watching her step lightly across the wood floor, he felt a sliver of hope. Suzan had seen something in her eyes, and he was quite sure he'd seen it too. A longing for the truth, maybe.

Chelise rounded the desk and lowered her hand to the open page. Her eyes studied the page briefly, then rose to meet his. How many times had she looked longingly at these Books, wondering what mysteries they held?

"I leave this one open," she said.

"Why this one?"

"It's the first Book I looked at when I was a child."

Thomas glanced down at the open page. English script. He could read the writing perfectly well. They couldn't know that, except for *The Histories Recorded by His Beloved* and the one Book he'd opened in Qurong's tent, this was the first Book of History he'd read as well.

"And if I can read this Book—if I can tell you what it says—what will you give me?"

"Nothing."

"My death is Woref's wedding gift to you. Wouldn't you think that the life of the man who can read these Books to you would be more of a gift than his death?"

She blinked.

"I'll have no part in this!" Ciphus said. "You said nothing—"

"It's okay, Ciphus," Chelise said. "I think I can speak for myself. Your life is meaningless to me. Even if you can read this Book, which you haven't shown me, you would be useless to me. I couldn't stand to stay in the same room with you long enough to hear you read or learn to read. Years of curiosity have brought me here tonight, but this will be the only time."

The air seemed to have been sucked out of the room. Thomas wasn't sure why her words crushed him, only that they did. He'd faced death before. Although her words were the death sentence to this foolish plan of his, the pain he felt wasn't about his own death. It was about her rejection of him.

"Ciphus has promised me life," he said.

"I said that I would present your case. It will be Qurong who determines your fate, not Chelise. You're a fool for thinking otherwise."

It was at least a lingering hope, but the words fell flat.

He nodded and walked around the desk.

⁂

Chelise knew that her words had cut him, and she found it rather surprising. What could he possibly have expected? He knew that he was an albino. He knew that his defiance of her father would earn him a death sentence, and yet he persisted in the defiance.

If Ciphus had not been present, she might have said the same thing with less of a bite. Although it was true, the thought of being alone with any albino for long made her nervous. Even nauseated.

She watched him walk around the desk, crestfallen. To think that this man had once defied the great Martyn and even Woref. He looked anything but the warrior now. His arms were strong and his chest well muscled, but his eyes were green and his skin . . .

What would it be like to touch skin so smooth?

She dismissed the thought and stepped aside to give him room. He could have taken the Book from the other side of the desk just as easily. Instead he walked closer to her.

She was being too sensitive. He undoubtedly hated her more than she hated him. And if he didn't, he was a fool for misunderstanding her revulsion of his disease.

Thomas reached his hand to the page and followed the words at the top. The writing was foreign to her, but he read aloud as if he'd been reading this language all of his life.

"Kevin walked down the road slowly, drawn to the large oak at the end of the street," he read. "He was quite sure that his heart was breaking, and the knowledge that his mother would never have to work again did nothing to help heal the wound."

He lifted his hand, but his eyes scanned on, reading.

"What does it mean?" Chelise asked.

"It's a story about a boy named Kevin."

"Not the histories?"

"Yes. Yes, it's the history of Kevin's life, written in story form."

"In story form?" Ciphus said. "We don't write histories in story form. This is childish."

"Then maybe you should think like a child to understand," Thomas said. "The boy's just lost his father, and the life insurance is meaningless to him."

Chelise wasn't sure what he meant by life insurance, but the story spoke to her. Something about the simplicity perhaps, the emotion, even the way that the albino had read it had electrified her.

"What's the rest?"

"The rest?" Thomas was turning pages. "It would take me hours to read you the rest."

"How do we know that you're not just fabricating this story?" Ciphus demanded.

"You'll have to learn to read them yourself. Or you, Chelise. What if I could teach you?"

"How?"

"By becoming your servant. I might be able to teach you to read them. All of them. What greater humiliation could Qurong heap upon me, his greatest enemy, than to chain me to a desk and force me to translate the Books? Killing me is too easy."

"Enough!" Ciphus snapped. "You've made your point and it's useless. Please, if you don't mind, I insist that you leave us. I won't have him spouting his lies anymore. Qurong would never approve."

Chelise stilled a tremble in her hands and bowed her head. "I will leave, then."

Ciphus calmed his voice. "But before you do, could you kindly show me where the blank Books have gone to. They aren't on the shelf where I last saw them."

"Of course." She walked to the bookcase where the volumes were kept. She'd seen them just three days earlier.

"This way. I don't know what you could possibly want with Books that have . . ."

She stopped halfway across the room. The bookcase was empty. From floor to ceiling, where hundreds of Books had once rested collecting dust, only empty shelves stood.

"They . . ." She looked around quickly. "They're gone."

"What do you mean, gone? They can't just disappear."

"Then they've been moved. But I just saw them a few days ago. I didn't think anyone had been in here since."

Thomas looked stricken. "How many were there?"

"Hundreds. Maybe a thousand."

"And they're just . . . gone?"

"Where could anyone hide so many Books?" Ciphus asked.

They were both reacting oddly. What was it about these blank Books?

"What does this mean?" Ciphus asked Thomas.

"Without the Books, it means nothing," the albino said.

Ciphus glared at him. "Then you will die in three days."

14

"I really don't care if we only have four *hours*, Ms. Sumner. We don't slow down at this point." He was addressing her on the speakerphone.

"I understand, Mr. President."

The president had allowed Kara to stay in the White House, where she'd observed the chaos from as close as she dared, which was mostly in the halls and on the perimeter. Until Thomas's plane arrived in a few hours, she was out of her league.

The president had asked her to come in with Monique an hour earlier while they hammered through the antivirus issue for the hundredth time. They'd been on the phone with Theresa Sumner for the last ten minutes. None of her news was good. Par for the course—*none* of the news Kara had heard over the past twenty-four hours, since the phone call from Thomas, had been good. Defense, intelligence, health, interior, homeland security, you name it—they all were crawling the walls.

To make matters worse, Senate Majority Leader Dwight Olsen was reportedly behind a protest outside the White House. At last report over fifty thousand campers had vowed to wait the White House out in a silent vigil. It had turned into a spiritual gathering of the strangest kind. A sea of somber faces and shaved heads and robes and those who wanted shaved heads and robes.

They'd burned candles and sung soft songs last night. The swelling crowd was flanked by several hundred reporters who'd managed to put aside the normal clamor for this silent waiting of theirs. *Give us some news, Mr. President. Tell us the truth.*

Front and center was the grand master of ceremonies, the CNN anchor who'd first broken the story. Mike Orear. With less than ten days to go, he'd become a prophet in the eyes of half the country. His gentle voice and stern face had become the face of hope to all whose religion was the news, and to many more who would never admit such a thing.

Reporters called it a vigil for all men and women of all races and religions to pray to their God and appeal to the president of the United States, but anyone watching for more than an hour knew it was simply a protest. The crowd was predicted to swell to over two hundred thousand by tonight. By tomorrow, a million. It was turning into nothing less than a final, desperate pilgrimage. To the headwaters of the peoples' troubles and hopes.

To the White House, where at this very moment the president and his government were running on fumes, trying to put out a thousand fires and turn over a thousand stones, desperate to head off disaster and find that elusive solution.

At least that was how Kara saw it.

She looked around at the ragged men in whose hands the world had been forced to put their trust. Secretary of Defense Grant Myers was still bleary-eyed over the nuclear exchange between Israel and France. They'd persuaded Israel not to launch and to play along with France's offer for an open-sea exchange, but the Israeli prime minister was taking a whipping in his own cabinet for that decision. None of them knew Thomas, Kara thought. The recommendation to play ball with France was precipitated by information from Thomas Hunter.

Phil Grant, director of the CIA, listened intently, slowly massaging the loose skin on his forehead. Another headache, perhaps. Within ten minutes he would get up and take more aspirin. She wasn't sure what to make of Phil Grant.

The chief of staff handled most of the communication coming to and going from the president, a steady flow of interruptions that Blair handled with a split mind, it seemed. The rest gathered there were key aides.

Kara couldn't imagine a man better suited to deal with a crisis of this magnitude than Robert Blair. How many people could juggle so many issues, maintain their overall composure, and also remain completely human? Not many. She didn't think any president could truly shed the political skin that earned him the office, but Blair seemed to have. He was genuine to the bone.

President Blair stood and spoke to Kara. "I need Monique with Thomas, at least long enough for us to flesh this thing out. She'll be at your full disposal the minute she's free. Jacques de Raison is on a flight from Bangkok now with several hundred promising samples, as you know. I need those samples in the right hands. As it turns out, I can't think of anyone more qualified to coordinate this than you. Do you disagree?"

"No, Mr. President. But I'm exhausted." Her voice sounded as if it were in a drum. "And to be perfectly honest, I don't share your optimism. I've spoken to Mr. de Raison about the samples, and they would require a month to analyze—"

"I don't care if you need a year to analyze them! I need it done in five days!"

The president's outburst was uncharacteristic but not surprising. Not even startling.

He closed his eyes and took a calming breath. "I'm sorry. If you think someone else is better qualified to handle this, tell me now."

"No sir. Forgive me. It might help to have Monique here."

President Blair glanced at Monique. "I understand."

Monique had been shuttled to the Genetrix Laboratories in Baltimore yesterday and flown back this morning to continue working with Theresa through a dedicated communications link. Nearly every laboratory with a genetics or drug-related research facility had been connected to Genetrix Laboratories after the Centers for Disease Control and the World Health Organization's facilities had proven inadequate. A staff of twenty-five screeners with PhDs in related fields scoured thousands of incoming threads and passed on any that fit the primary model that Raison Pharmaceutical had established to ferret out an antivirus.

Although her backdoor antivirus proved to be insufficient, Monique had brought one critical piece of information back with her: the gene manipulations she'd designed when creating the Raison Vaccine were at least one part of the antivirus. She'd explained the entire scenario to the president minutes ago. Valborg Svensson never would have kept her alive as long as he did unless he needed the information she gave him—namely, the genetic manipulations that completed his antivirus.

Blair rolled his neck and paced. "So am I to understand by your earlier statements that even if we do find an antivirus in the next five days, manufacturing enough and distributing it may be a problem?"

"Monique?" Theresa said, deferring.

"That depends on the nature of the antivirus, but you do understand that people will die. Even if we found the answer today, some will die. Isolated individuals, for example, who have wandered into the wilderness to find peace."

"I understand. But let's take a broader scenario. Our best estimates are that the first catastrophic symptoms of the Raison Strain could manifest in as few as five days, correct?"

"Yes sir."

"But we may have as many as ten days. And the rollout of the disease will take a few days—not everyone was infected in the first days."

"A week for complete rollout—that's correct."

"So we may have over two weeks before some people show symptoms."

"We may. But the incubation period is likely shorter. We may begin to see symptoms in as few as three days in Bangkok and the other gateway cities."

"And we have how long until people begin to die?"

"Best estimate, forty-eight hours from the onset of symptoms. But it's only an educated—"

He held up his hand. "Of course. All of this is." He faced Monique directly. "If we were to receive the antivirus from Armand Fortier in five days, assuming that's the onset of first symptoms, could we manufacture and distribute it quickly enough to save most of our people?"

"It depends—"

"No, Monique, I don't want 'It depends.' I want your best estimate."

She set her elbows on the table and laced her fingers together. "Six billion syringes—"

"We have twenty-eight plants in seven countries manufacturing syringes around the clock. The World Health Organization will supply the syringes it requests in the event you come through."

"Millions who live in Third World countries won't have immediate access to those syringes."

"They were also the last to be infected. We'll have every plane that can fly loaded with the antivirus within an hour of it rolling off the line. We have worked out a detailed distribution plan that will deliver an antivirus in a syringe to most of the world within one week. It'll be a race—I know that—but I want to know who will win that race."

She took a deep breath. "It's possible that a fast-acting antivirus could reverse the virus if administered within forty-eight hours of the first symptoms."

"So if we start with the gateway cities, like New York and Bangkok, and flood the market with an antivirus five days from now, we would have a chance of saving most."

"Assuming the virus waits five days, yes. Most."

"Ninety percent?"

"That would be most, yes."

"Ms. Sumner?"

"I would concur," she said over the speakerphone.

The president walked to the end of the room, hands grasped behind his back. He looked up at a television that showed a riot in progress in Jakarta, triggered by the news that the supposedly contained outbreak in Java hadn't really been contained at all.

"We are holding the world together by a string," President Blair said. "Our ships are scheduled to hand over most of our nuclear arsenal in three days' time. Our only hope of getting the antivirus from the New Allegiance is to disarm ourselves and open ourselves to nuclear holocaust. Even then,

I don't believe that France intends to deal with us, or the Israelis for that matter, straight. They will give what they have to the Russians, the Chinese, but not to us."

He faced them. "We cannot afford to deal with Fortier. Our only real hope rests in you."

His position seemed extreme to Kara, but she no longer trusted her own judgment of extremity. For all she knew, their only hope didn't rest in Monique or Theresa or anyone from the scientific community, but in Thomas. There had to be a reason that all of this was happening.

"Join me when Thomas arrives," the president said. "You may leave."

They left without a word. Ron Kreet was telling the president that he had a call with the Russian premier in two minutes.

"Doesn't sound promising," Kara said to Monique as they walked the hall.

"It never was. I can't imagine this being solved from this end."

This end? "Thomas?"

Monique nodded. "I'm not saying it makes sense to me, but yes. You were there, Kara. It's real, isn't it? I mean, it felt so real when I dreamed of it."

"As real as this. It's like Thomas is a window into another dimension. He lives in both, and our eyes are opened through his blood."

"But I felt more like Rachelle when I was there. Monique to me was only a dream."

"This can't be a dream," Kara said, looking around. "Can it?"

She didn't answer. She didn't need to—they both knew that they weren't going to figure it out now.

"Do you think of him?" Kara asked.

"All the time," Monique said.

Kara glanced at her watch. "He's probably still sleeping. That means he's with the Horde right now. If he's not dreaming with the Horde, there's no telling how many days will pass before he wakes up."

"In that reality."

"Yes."

"How would he not dream?"

"The Horde may know about the rhambutan fruit."

Monique blinked. "Then we should wake him now! What if the Horde executes him?"

"It doesn't matter if we wake him. The time that passes there is dependent on his dreaming there, not his waking here. Trust me, it took me two weeks to wrap my mind around that one. A week could pass with the Horde in the next few minutes of his dreaming on the plane."

They turned into a small cafeteria.

"He'll be here soon enough," Kara said. "Let's hope he has some answers."

15

Woref stood before Qurong in the council chamber, listening to the old man fume about the missing Books of Histories. The librarian, Christoph, had reported them missing this morning. The scribes had turned the library inside out looking for them, but not a sign.

"How could a thousand volumes just vanish into thin air?" Qurong raged. "I want them found. I don't care if you have to search every house in the city."

"I will, your highness. But I have other matters now."

"What other matters? Your matters are more pressing than mine?"

The old fool couldn't hold a thought for more than a few minutes. His obsession with these Books was interfering with far more important matters; surely he knew that.

An image of Teeleh flashed through Woref's mind and he clenched his jaw. He'd decided to deny the beast. He would possess Chelise, yes. And he would love her as he knew how to love. She would be his, and if she resisted his advance, he would use whatever form of persuasion seemed fitting at the time. But Teeleh spoke of love as if it were a crushing force. The thought made him ill.

"I have a wedding tomorrow."

"And your wedding takes precedence over my books? You expect me to attend the wedding of my own daughter in this state?"

"No sir. Never." The realization that Qurong might put off the wedding over such a trivial matter sent a shaft of anger through Woref's heart.

Qurong paced and grunted. "This takes priority. Nothing happens until we find the Books."

"Sir, may I suggest that your wife might not look kindly on the post-ponement—"

"My wife will do as I say. It's you, Woref. Your inflamed passion compromises your own loyalty to your king. You've been hounding my daughter for years now, and when I finally give her to you, you immediately question my authority! I should call the whole thing off."

Woref suppressed his fury. *I will take your daughter. And then I will take your kingdom.*

Teeleh's words whispered in his memory. *I will make her mine.*

"You have my undying loyalty, my king. I will suspend our search for the remaining albinos and personally see to your Books."

Instead of expressing the appropriate apprehension at Woref's suggestion that they pause their campaign, Qurong agreed.

"Good. Turn every stone. Dismissed." He picked up his goblet and walked away, leaving Woref in a mild state of shock.

Qurong stopped by the door as if something had suddenly occurred to him. "You wish to marry my daughter? Then start with her. No one knows the library like she does." He turned around and eyed Woref carefully. "We'll see if you have the skills required to tame a wench. She's in her bedroom."

Woref trembled with rage. How could a father speak in such a way about the woman who would be his? Such a precious, unspoiled bride, at this very moment resting in her bedroom while her own father slandered her.

Teeleh, yes. But her father!

Woref put his hand on the table to calm himself. The day he ran a dagger through Qurong's belly would come sooner than anyone could possibly guess.

You are angry because Qurong is Teeleh's servant, and now you know that you are as well.

He ground his molars and grunted. Yes, it was true, and he despised himself for it.

Woref stepped across the room, entered the atrium, and gazed at the stairs that rose from floor to floor, up to the fifth where Chelise's room waited in silence. He glanced around, saw that he was alone, and hurried toward the stairs.

Desire swelled in his belly. He wouldn't touch Chelise, naturally. In that way he wasn't like Qurong at all. And he would never harm her. Not even Qurong beat his wife. It wasn't becoming of royalty, he had once said. Either way, Woref could never hurt his tender bride.

Then again . . .

No. He only wanted to see her. To gaze upon her face, knowing that tomorrow she would be his. He'd never been on the fifth floor, much less her bedroom. But now Qurong had given him permission. The Books. He couldn't forget to ask about the Books.

He climbed quickly, afraid that at any moment the wife would come out and demand that he leave. It would be like Patricia. She too would have to be silenced one day. Perhaps he'd take her as his second wife. There was a woman he'd enjoy beating.

But not the daughter. Never Chelise.

He stood before her door and knocked gently.

"Come."

He pushed the door open. She sat on her bed with her maidservant. Their eyes flared with surprise.

"Excuse me." He bowed his head. "I'm afraid that Qurong insisted I speak to you immediately."

"Then you would send a servant up to fetch me," Chelise said.

"He insisted I come. It's a matter of grave importance." He looked at the servant. "Leave us."

The woman looked at Chelise and then left when she didn't object.

Woref closed the door and stared at his bride, who now stood by her bed. Her skin was white and beautiful. Not as white as when she had the morst on, but he preferred it this way. The scent of untreated skin stirred him in a way that only a true warrior would understand. Her eyes were white, like twin moons. Her mouth was round and her body slender in the long flowing robe.

He'd never seen such a beautiful creature as she.

"What is it?" she demanded.

He approached her, careful not to look too eager. "Qurong is concerned about some Books that have gone missing from the library," he said. "He thought that you might be able to help us find them."

"Which books?"

"The blank Books of Histories."

"They're gone?"

"All of them."

"How's that possible? There are so many!"

Woref stepped closer. He could smell her breath now, the musky scent of love.

"Please don't come any closer," she said.

He stopped, surprised by her demand. "I meant no disrespect."

"I took none. But we aren't yet married."

"You're mine by betrothal. We will be married."

"Tomorrow." The tone of her voice irritated him. It was as if she was insisting on tomorrow instead of today. As if she might be looking forward to enjoying one last day separated from him. She didn't crave him as he craved her?

He shifted on his feet. "Yes, of course."

"What do I have to do with this?" she demanded.

His irritation grew. He spoke quickly to cover his embarrassment. "Your father seems to think that you may know something about the Books. You've spent more time in the library than even he."

"I have no clue what could have happened to the Books. I don't see why he sent you to interrogate me about his business. Men are not permitted on this floor. Mother wouldn't approve."

"I don't think you understand the significance of this to the supreme leader. And I don't see what your mother's opinion of my coming here has to do with your taking exception. You have been given to me, not to her."

"Tell my father that I know nothing about the Books, and I'll tell my mother that you disapprove of her rules."

"Her rules will mean nothing tomorrow. We'll live by my rules. Our rules."

She smiled. "You may have won my hand, Woref. I have no argument. But you'll have to win my heart as well. You could start by learning that I am my mother's daughter. You may leave now."

Woref wasn't sure he'd heard her correctly. Was she taunting him? Tempting him? Begging to be subdued?

"The situation is more serious than you may realize." He would test her by stepping closer to her. "Qurong will postpone our wedding until the Books are found."

She smiled again. This time it was a tempting smile, he was sure of it. His mind felt dizzy with desire. He took another step, close enough to touch her.

"Postponing our wedding might be wise. It would give you time to learn respect for a woman's desires."

Black flooded Woref's vision. How dare she conspire with Qurong to withhold what was his! She stood mocking him with this smile, perfectly at ease with denying him.

He swung his hand without thinking. It slammed into her cheek with a loud smack. She gasped and flew backward onto the bed.

"Never!" he roared.

⸺◦∞◦⸺

The shock of being hit was greater than the pain. Chelise knew that she'd been toying with his emotions, but no more so than she'd done a hundred times before with other men. She'd actually found Woref's presence in her room exhilarating. Naturally it would never do to play into his hands—what kind of signal would that send? He would think of her as nothing more than a doll that he could throw around at his whim until he tired of her completely. Mother had told her the same thing just last night.

Chelise spun to him, aghast. Woref was trembling from head to foot.

"Never!" he roared.

She was too stunned to think straight. He had hit her!

Realization of what he had just done suddenly dawned on Woref's face. He glanced back at the door, and when he faced her again, his eyes were lit by fear.

"What have I done?" He reached out for her. "My precious—"

"Get away from me!" she screamed, slapping his hand aside. She scrambled across the bed and stood on the opposite side. "Don't come near me!"

He walked quickly around the bed, panicked. "No, no, I didn't mean to hurt you."

"Back!"

He dropped to one knee. "I beg you, forgive me!"

"Stop begging! Get on your feet!"

He rose.

"How dare you strike me! You expect me to marry a bull? I was toying with you!"

His awful mistake was finally and terribly setting in. He gripped his head in both hands and paced at the bottom of the bed. Her sudden power over him wasn't lost on her. Her jaw ached. She could never marry this man until they set some things straight between them, but on balance he had just given her his greatest gift. He'd bared his weakness.

"How can I marry a man like you?" she demanded.

"Anything," he said, spinning back. "I swear I will give you anything."

"You'll give me anything today, and then take my life in a fit of rage tomorrow? Do I look like a fool?"

"No, my dear. I swear, never again. My honor as this land's greatest general is in your hands."

"One word to my mother and you would lose it all."

"And spend eternity suffering for one moment's fear of losing you. I can't bear the thought of delaying our wedding, even a single day."

She turned her back on him and stared out the window, surprised by the satisfaction she felt at seeing him grovel. Stripped of his rank, he was a mere man, driven by passion and fear. Perhaps wickeder than most. But still unraveled by his desire for one woman.

She would use this to her advantage. The fact was, she had more on her mind today than her wedding tomorrow. Thoughts of the Books of Histories had filled her dreams and awakened her early. Her desire to understand the mysteries hidden in their pages was greater than any desire she'd known.

Chelise faced Woref, who had recovered from his begging and was regarding her with something that looked more like contempt than remorse.

"Hmm. You will give me whatever I want?"

"Whatever is in my power. I must have your love. Anything."

"Then you'll tell my father that the wedding must be delayed until the blank Books are found—we both insist."

His face darkened.

"It's the price for your lack of control. If you want to earn my love, you can start by showing me that you're a man who can receive as well as give punishment."

He dipped his head. "As you wish."

"And I will also require a gift from you as well."

"Yes, of course. Anything."

"I want a new servant."

"I'll give you ten."

"Not just any servant. I want the albino. Thomas of Hunter."

She might have thrown water in his face. "That's impossible."

"Is it? Unusual, yes. Disagreeable, certainly. But I've heard that this man is able to read the Books of Histories. You intend to execute the one man who can fulfill a dream of mine by revealing the Books to me? His death would not only be an affront to me, but it would be far too honorable for him. Better to keep him chained to a desk as a slave. The people would celebrate you for it."

She'd made the decision impulsively, just now, motivated by spite as much as by what Thomas might offer her. For all she knew, he was only pretending to read from the Books to extend his life.

"Qurong would never allow an albino to live in his castle," he said, with less conviction than he should have.

"He won't live in this castle. He'll live at the royal garden. In the basement of the library, under my supervision. If he can read the Books, my father will agree."

Woref didn't like the idea, but she'd effectively cut his feet off at the ankles. There was a certain logic to the whole idea.

"Ciphus won't agree."

"Ciphus is no fool. He will see my reasoning." *And what about you, Woref? Are you a fool?*

She continued before he could dwell on her insinuation. "Consider it an early wedding present. I am requesting Thomas of Hunter in chains, a much more fitting present for me than his head on a platter."

He only stared at her.

"You said 'anything.' Thomas of Hunter frightens you?"

A look of utter contempt crossed his face. She'd gone too far. He turned and walked from the room.

16

The dungeon might very well have been the cleanest part of the entire city. They'd discussed it at length and decided that, because of the smell that seeped from every living Scab, this hole deep in the ground was one of the best places for them to be. The musty earthen scent of dirt and rocks was preferable. In fact, downright heavenly, Cain said.

"I knew it," Suzan said, pacing by one wall.

"The question is whether they will execute us," William said.

Thomas looked at his companions, sickened that their fate wasn't decided yet. "I'll do everything in my power to get us out."

"And what power is that?" William asked.

They had been told not five minutes ago by a temple guard. "It appears that death is too honorable for you," the guard said with a smirk. "The mighty warrior is now a slave, is that it? Better to lick the toes of his conqueror than end it all with a sword." He chuckled. "They collect you in ten minutes. Say good-bye to your friends."

"Where am I going?" Thomas demanded.

"Wherever Qurong wishes. To the royal library today. It seems he needs a translator."

"And us?" William asked.

"You're a gift for the wedding." He smiled and turned his back to leave. "Unfortunately, the wedding has been delayed," he mumbled. Then he left.

Now they waited.

"The same power he used to win her loyalty," Suzan said to William.

"Don't be so sure. She's a lying serpent as sure as we are salamanders in her eyes!" William spit to the side. "I would rather die than serve at Qurong's table."

"I don't think it's his table," Suzan said. "It is his daughter's table. Thomas's ploy worked. The Books of Histories may save our necks before this is done."

"His daughter's table would be worse! There is nothing as revolting as a Scab woman."

"I have to agree with William," Cain said. "I would much rather serve at Qurong's table than his wife's, or his daughter's. Better to face the sword of a warrior than the lying tongue of these women."

"You mean rotten tongues, don't you? You can smell them coming—"

"Stop it!" Thomas said. "You're making me nauseated. It's not their fault that they stink."

"If they would choose the drowning, they wouldn't smell; how can you say it's not their fault?"

"Okay, so it is their fault. But they hardly know better. These are the people Justin is courting."

"We're his bride," William said. "Not these whores."

Thomas was taken aback by his use of the word. It had once been a common expression for him, but not since the drowning.

"We would be most grateful if you could convince this whore"— Suzan glanced at William as she said it—"to spare our lives. Do you have a plan?"

Thomas walked to the corner of the cell and turned. "I guess you could call it that. If I can avoid the rhambutan juice, I will dream. If I dream, I will wake in the histories and tell my sister how to rescue us."

"Your sister, Kara, who was also Mikil at the council meeting," William said with a raised eyebrow. "You're placing our lives in the hands of a character in your dreams?"

"No, in Mikil's," Thomas said. "Unless you have a better plan."

They stared at him in silence. That was it; there were no more plans.

"Well, Thomas of Hunter," Cain finally said, "I for one place my trust in you." He moved forward and grasped Thomas's forearms to form a circle between them, the common greeting. "It makes no sense to me, but you've always led us down the right path. Elyon's strength."

"Elyon's strength."

Thomas repeated the grasp with each.

"Be careful, my friend," William said. "Don't let the disease tempt your mind. If I were Teeleh, I would see no greater victory than luring the great Thomas of Hunter onto Tanis's path."

Thomas clasped his arms. They had never seen any from the Circle catch the disease again after drowning—they weren't even sure if such a thing was possible. But some of the words from *The Histories Recorded by His Beloved* suggested it was possible. *If you remain in me, I will remain in you,* the Book said. They still didn't know precisely what this meant but believed the opposite was also true. William's warning was a good one.

"Elyon's strength."

"Elyon's strength."

⸻ ∞ ⸻

"Where is he now?" Woref demanded.

"Locked in the basement," Ciphus said. "As agreed."

Qurong stood at the top of the steps that led into the royal bath. They'd built the bathhouse at the base of the Thrall, set apart from the prying eyes of the commoners. Only the royal family, the generals and their wives, and the priests were permitted to bathe in the stone house.

"And Chelise?"

"It was your own recommendation," Qurong said, facing his general. "Now you're fretting like a woman?"

Woref dipped his head. "I'm only interested in protecting what is mine."

"My daughter is yours? I don't remember a wedding. What I do remember is that there won't be one until the Books are found."

"Of course. But this man is no ordinary man. I don't trust him."

"Nor I. Which is why I wanted him dead. Although I must admit, this idea of yours is growing on me." He smiled wryly.

Qurong opened his robe and let it fall to the ground. Steam from the hot rocks the servants had set inside the pool rose around the perimeter. He hated the bathing, not only because of the stinging pain, but because it reminded him of capital punishment. Drowning. The Great Romance was a brilliant way to keep the people in their place, but there should be an exception for royalty.

"I am only concerned for your daughter's safety, my lord."

"She has her guard. The albino is under lock and key. If I didn't know better, I would say that you're jealous, Woref."

"Please, don't insult me, my lord."

Qurong walked down the steps and onto the bathing platform. He dipped his foot in the water, then withdrew it. This dreaded practice would be the death of him.

"What of you, Ciphus? What do you say?"

"I say what I said earlier. To keep your captive on a leash takes a stronger hand than killing him."

"Then you agree that he requires a stronger hand."

The high priest cleared his throat. "The albinos don't believe in the sword, if that's what you mean. Even Thomas of Hunter wouldn't harm your daughter. But he may try to escape."

"Is there a way to escape from the library?"

"You would have to ask Woref."

"Well then, Woref?"

"There's always a way to escape."

"Without violence?"

He hesitated.

"Well?"

"No, not that I can think of."

"Then what's your worry? You haven't found the Books. I would concern myself with that."

"Then I would request that as soon as I have married your daughter, you allow me to kill Thomas of Hunter," Woref said.

"I thought that was the understanding."

Woref glanced at Ciphus, who spoke. "Actually, I believe Thomas was meant to serve indefinitely, as long as he proves useful in translating the Books of Histories. It is a task of great benefit to the Great Romance."

"I'm not interested in a translation made by my enemy. It would be untrustworthy. If he can teach Chelise to read the Books, I will let him finish his task before killing him. Otherwise he will die."

The priest frowned. "Chelise is under the assumption—"

"I don't care what my daughter thinks! This is my decision to make. Woref is right. This albino is not to be trusted! Whatever agreement they made when he struck her is none of my concern."

Yes, I do know more than you think, Woref.

"Thomas of Hunter will be my slave until he's no longer useful," Qurong continued. "Then I will kill him myself. Now, if you will kindly both leave me, I have the terrible duty to bathe in this stink hole for a moment."

They bowed, stepped back, and turned to leave.

"Ciphus."

"Yes, my lord."

"I would like you to arrange public display of my slave. A parade or a ceremony where the people see him firmly under my foot."

"An excellent idea," Woref said.

"How much time would you need?" Qurong asked.

Ciphus answered slowly. "Perhaps two days."

"Not tomorrow?"

"Yes, tomorrow, if you want to rush it."

Qurong turned to the pool. "Two days then."

17

Thomas spent the first night alone in the cold, dark cell below the library, praying for Elyon to show himself. A sign, a messenger of hope, a piece of fruit that would open his eyes. A dream.

But he hadn't dreamed. Not of Kara, not of anything.

He hadn't seen a soul since being ushered into the library's basement and locked in the windowless cell. Surely if Chelise had been so eager to uncover the mysteries of the Books, she would have come that first night and demanded he read more.

Maybe the reading was a thin abstraction for her. Or maybe it was Qurong who wanted to hear him read. Or Perhaps Ciphus had arranged it, eager for another chance to be shown the power Thomas had promised.

They'd been in the Horde city three days. Would Mikil have mounted a rescue? No, not if she followed their agreement. Not so long ago the Forest Guard would have stormed in with swords drawn, killed a few hundred Scabs, and freed them or died trying. But without weapons the task was far too dangerous. They all knew that.

Thomas rested his head against the stone wall and lifted his hand in front of his face. If he used his imagination, he could see it. Or could he? Like his dreams, there but beyond normal sight. Like the Shataiki bats that lived in the trees. Like Justin. Without the proper illumination they were all out of sight. It didn't mean they weren't there.

The door suddenly eased open. He scrambled to his feet.

Two temple guards dressed in hooded black robes stood in the doorway, broad swords drawn. "Out. Step carefully."

He walked into the basement's dim light. They marched him up the stairs and down a corridor that paralleled the main library where the scribes worked. He could see the royal garden through a row of windows. Other than the sound of birds chirping outside, the only sound was their feet on the wooden floor.

One of the guards unlocked a door with a large key. "Wait inside."

Thomas entered the large storeroom where the Books of Histories were kept. The door closed. Locked.

Four tall torches added to the light that streamed in through two skylights. They'd left him alone with the Books. He didn't know how long he had, but he had an opportunity here. If he could only find a Book that recorded what had happened during the Great Deception. Any Book that discussed the Raison Strain.

Thomas hurried to the nearest shelf and pulled out the first Book. *The Histories as Recorded by Ezekiel.*

Ezekiel? The prophet Ezekiel?

Heart hammering, Thomas opened the Book. If he wasn't mistaken, this was the prophet Ezekiel. The sentences sounded biblical, at least as he recalled biblical from his dreams.

He replaced the Book and tried another. This one was about someone named Artimus—a name that meant nothing to him. And if he was right, unrelated in any way to the Book of Ezekiel beside it. There was no order to the Books.

There were thousands of Books! He ran for the ladder, pushed it to the far end, and climbed to the top shelf. There was only one way to do this—a methodical search, from top to bottom, Book by Book. And he would have to go by the titles alone. There were way too many Books to inspect each carefully.

He pulled out the farthest to his right. Cyrus. No.

Next.

Alexander. No.

Next. No.

He quickened his pace, pulling out Books, scanning their covers, slamming them back in when they struck no chord. The sound of each volume hitting the back wall echoed with a soft thud. No. No. No.

"Quite frantic, are we?"

Thomas twisted on the ladder. The Book in his hands flew free, sailed through the air, and fell two stories to the wood floor. It landed near her feet with a loud bang.

She didn't move. Her round gray eyes studied him as if she couldn't decide whether he was an amusement or a distraction. A faint smile formed on her mouth.

"I didn't mean to interrupt the great warrior."

Thomas started to climb down. "I'm sorry. I was just looking for a Book."

"Oh? Which Book?"

"I don't know. One that I hoped would ring a bell."

"I've never heard of a Book ringing a bell."

He stepped off the ladder and faced her. "An expression we use in the histories."

"You mean in the Books of Histories. You said *in* the histories."

"Yes."

She picked up the fallen Book. "Did you find it?"

"Find what?"

"The Book."

"No." He looked at the shelves. "And I'm not sure I can."

"Well, I'm afraid I can't help you. I hardly can tell one Book from another."

So here she was, his master. He was relieved it was her and not Ciphus or Qurong. This slender woman had a powerful tongue—she'd proven that much. But she was also genuinely interested in the Books for what they could teach her, not for how they might give her power. Her motives seemed pure. Or at least purer than the others. In some ways she reminded Thomas of Rachelle.

She wore a green robe with a hood. Silk. Before taking the forests, the Horde had been limited to their coarse fabrics woven from thread rolled out of desert wheat stalks.

"Do you like it?"

"I'm sorry?"

"My dress. You were looking at it."

"It's beautiful."

She walked slowly around him. "And me?"

His heart skipped a beat. He couldn't dare tell her what he really thought, that her breath was foul and her skin sickly and her eyes dead. He had to win this woman's favor for his plan to work. He had to dream. It was the only way he could see out of this.

"I'm only an albino," he said. "What does it matter what I think?"

"True. But even an albino must have a heart. You're given to strange beliefs and this cult of yours, but surely the great warrior whose name once struck terror in all of the Horde can still react to a woman."

If he didn't know better, he would say that there was a hint of seduction in her voice.

How would Elyon see her?

He answered with as much conviction as he could muster. "You're beautiful."

"Really? I would have thought you'd find me repelling. Does a fish find a bird attractive? I think you're lying."

"Beauty is beauty, fish or fowl."

She stopped her pacing, ten feet from him. "I'm not asking if I'm beautiful. I'm asking if you find me beautiful."

He couldn't stoop to this deception any longer. "Then to be perfectly honest, I see both beauty in you and some things that aren't so beautiful."

"Such as?"

"Such as your skin. Your eyes. Your scent."

She looked at him for a few moments, expressionless. He'd wounded her. Pity stabbed his heart.

"I'm sorry, I was only trying to—"

"I was asking because I wanted to be sure that you found no attraction in me," she said. "If you had found any beauty in me, I would have kept my distance."

She turned and walked toward the desk. "Naturally, you must keep your distance from me anyway. I find you as repelling as you find me."

"I didn't say you repelled me. Only the disease does that."

This wasn't a good start. "How long will we be together here?" he asked.

"That depends on how long I can stand you."

"Then please, I beg your forgiveness. I didn't mean to offend you."

"You think an albino can offend me so easily?"

"You don't understand. I'm sure that beneath the disease you're a stunning woman. Breathtaking. If I could see you as Elyon sees you . . ."

She turned to him. "I bathe in Elyon's lake nearly every day. He has nothing to do with this. I think it would be better if we change the subject. You're here to teach me to read these Books. You're my slave; keep it in mind."

"I am your most humble servant," he said, dipping his head.

Chelise walked gracefully to the bookshelf and ran her fingers along the spines of several Books. She pulled one out, looked at it, then put it back and went down the row. What did it matter which Book if she couldn't read?

"I used to spend hours looking through these Books when I was a child," she said softly. "I was lost in a hope that I would eventually find one that I could read. A few words even. When I was older, a man once told me that some of them were written in English. If I could only find those, I would be happy."

"A man named Roland," he said.

Chelise turned. "How did you know?"

"I knew Roland. He met you in the desert and you gave him a horse. You saved his life, he said."

"Roland, the assassin. Is he now an albino as well?"

"Yes. Yes, he is."

Thomas followed her along the shelf, running his fingers along the Books. "And there is more. All of the Books are written in English."

She laughed. "Then you know less than you think. How many of these Books have you actually read?"

"I think it's time for our lesson. Pick one."

She looked at him, then the Books.

"Any of them. It doesn't matter."

She pulled a thick black Book from the shelf and carefully ran her palm over its cover.

"May I see it?" he asked, reaching out a hand.

She walked to Thomas and gave him the Book. He could have walked to the desk; it certainly would have been natural to read such a big Book on the desk. But he had ulterior motives now.

He opened the Book in both arms and scanned the page. A Book about some history in Africa. She started to turn for the desk.

"Here, let me show you something," he said.

She looked at the Book.

"Come here. Let me show you." He let half the Book fall and drew his finger along the words on the half he held. She drew close to him, inches from his body.

"Do you see this word?"

"Yes," she said.

He adjusted his grip. "Can you help me with this?"

She reached out and lifted the end that had fallen. Now they stood side by side, each holding one cover of the Book. Her shoulder touched his lightly. A strong waft of her perfume—the smell of roses—filled his nostrils. It didn't cover the odor of her skin entirely, but her scent was surprisingly tolerable.

"Put your finger on this word, as I'm doing."

She hesitated.

"Please. It's part of the way the Books are read."

Chelise put her finger below the first word on her side.

The room suddenly darkened. Thomas glanced up and saw that a cloud had dimmed the sunlight. He lowered his eyes. Wavering orange flames from the torches lit the page. Chelise had her hand on it, waiting for him.

By this light her hand was nearly flesh-toned. The disease was mostly covered by morst, and what he saw by the torch's glow took him completely off guard.

This was a woman's hand. Delicate and gentle, resting lightly on the page with one finger extended as he'd requested. Her fingernails were painted red, neatly manicured.

The sight immobilized him. Time stilled. A terrible empathy rose through his throat. This was how Justin saw her, without her disease.

She removed her hand. "What are you doing?"

"Nothing. I . . ." He looked into her eyes. He'd never been so close to any Scab before. Less than a foot separated her face from his. She was quite beautiful. Her eyes looked hazel and her cheeks blushed with a sweet rose color. It was a trick of the light—he knew that—but for a moment her disease was gone in his eyes.

"I was just noticing what a good student you would make," Thomas said.

"How so?"

"The tools of the trade. Gentle fingers. Clear eyes. Now if we can only work on your mind, you may read this Book yet."

The clouds passed over and the room brightened. Thomas returned his eyes to the page. "You see this word?"

"Yes."

"You know . . ." He glanced at the desk. "Maybe the desk would be better."

She followed him to the desk where he took up the lesson again, this time leaning over by her side as she sat.

"This word is 'the.' You see it?"

"No. It looks nothing like 'the' to me."

"What does it look like?"

"Like squiggly lines."

"But to me it reads 'the.' I can assure you this is a *t* and an *h* and an *e*. My eyes see it as plain as day."

"That's impossible." She looked up at him with wide eyes. "You're saying that this mess of lines is English? Then why can't I see it?"

Thomas straightened. The fact of the matter was that the disease robbed her of the ability to understand pure truth, and the Books of Histories contained only truth. As much as her eyes were gray, her mind was deceived. But if he simply told her that now, she might never agree to see him again.

"I'm not sure you're ready for that lesson yet. We have to start here, with a simple understanding and trust."

"Then this is sorcery? You read with magic?"

"No. But it is a power beyond either of us."

Thomas stood and walked around the desk. "I think that today we should start with a reading. We should familiarize your mind with these words, so that when I am ready to unravel them, you are familiar with the way they read."

"You will read to me?"

"If you would like me to."

"Yes." She stood eagerly. "If I have you to read them to me, why should I read them?"

"Because you won't have me forever. But tomorrow we'll start the lesson in earnest. Now if you could help me find this one Book I was looking for."

"No, please, this one." She lifted the black Book they'd just been reading.

"I was thinking of another."

"Which?"

"I don't know where it is."

"Then read this one. Please."

He reluctantly took the Book and sat behind the desk.

———— ⚬⚬⚬ ————

She walked while he read from the desk. He was an excellent reader, really. His tone was gentle and full of intonation, yet strong when the story called for it.

Chelise looked at the towering bookshelves and lost herself in the tale he was reading. Then another, and another.

"Should I stop?"

"No. Please. Can you read more?"

"Yes."

And he read.

His voice soon sounded nearly magical. He was the kind she could trust, she decided. A good man who was unfortunately an albino.

How many times had she wanted to read what she was now hearing? It was a special day. She leaned against a bookcase and set her head back. The sun was straight overhead. Midday. If these words were steps, she was sure she could climb all the way to heaven.

She chuckled and sat down on the floor. The reading paused momentarily then started again. *Read on, my servant. Read on.*

He read on.

How could simple words carry such weight? It was as if they were working their magic at this very moment. Reaching into her mind and sending her on a journey that few had ever taken. To lands faraway, full of mystery. To lakes and clouds, swimming, diving, flying.

She lay down on a window seat and rolled to one side, lost in other worlds. It didn't seem to matter which story he was telling; they were all powerful.

The one he was reading now was about a betrayal. Tears flooded her eyes and her heart beat heavily, but she knew it would be all right, because she knew that in the end the kind of power that was in these Books would never let her down.

Still, the story he was reading was dreadful. A prince had lost his only love and searched the kingdom only to find that she been forced to marry a cruel man.

She faced the ceiling and began to sob. The reader stalled, and when he restarted, she realized that he was crying too. Her new servant was weeping as he read.

Or was she only hearing that in her mind?

The story changed. The bride found a way to escape the cruel beast with the help of her prince.

Chelise began to laugh. She drew her legs up and spread her arms and laughed at the ceiling.

It was only after some time that she realized hers was the only voice in the room. She stopped and sat up, disoriented. What was happening? Thomas sat at the desk staring at her. Tears stained his cheeks.

And she was on the floor.

She scrambled to her feet and brushed the dust from her robe. "What's going on?" she asked. "I . . . what happened?"

"I can't see the page," he said.

They'd *both* been crying. She hadn't imagined it after all. She glanced at the door—still shut. What if someone had come in while she was in this awful state? She would never be able to explain. She wasn't even sure what had happened herself.

Chelise faced him. "The story did that?"

"It seems the power of truth is quite shocking to your mind." He seemed as surprised as she.

"My mind. Not yours?"

"I've been shocked plenty of times. Try drowning and you'll know what shocking is."

She straightened her sleeves, suddenly embarrassed. But the power! The joy, the mystery. She couldn't help but grin. Could she tell anyone about this? No. It could be very dangerous.

She cleared her throat and took a deep breath. "That will have to be all for now."

He stood. "We'll meet tomorrow?"

Honestly, she didn't know how to proceed. It was a frightening experience. Intoxicating. "We'll see. I think so, if I can find the time."

"Maybe we could read again tonight," he said, rounding the desk.

"No, that would never do. You're my servant, not my librarian."

"Then could you give me a torch for my cell? There's no light."

"No light? I insisted you have light."

Woref.

"And they're making me drink the rhambutan juice on threat of my friends' lives. If I drink the juice, I can't dream, and I must dream."

"Now you're going too far. I'll get you light and good food, but this dream business isn't my concern."

She walked for the door, half of her mind still trapped in the heavens.

"And my friends, they will live?"

She turned at the door. "I'm sure that can be arranged. Yes, of course. Anything else? The keys to your cell perhaps?"

He smiled.

18

Thomas wasn't sure what had happened to him in the library that first day with Chelise, but he found that, try as he did, he couldn't remove her from his mind.

Her heart had been opened to a sliver of the truth; he knew that much. She'd heard the story from history—the unadulterated truth—and she'd become intoxicated by it. Another person might have heard the same thing and listened with vague interest. This much he understood. What was much less in focus was his own reaction to her.

In some strange way, his own eyes had been opened to her. She had heard the truth, perhaps for the first time, but he had seen a truth he'd never seen before. The truth was Chelise. As Elyon saw her.

He spent only an hour with her the next morning, and she seemed guarded. Afraid, even. She walked as he read again, but this time she stopped every few minutes to ask him what the story was about. What time period it had been written in. Who wrote it.

He finally closed the Book and crossed the room to where she'd pulled out a second volume.

"What is it?" she asked.

"You're distracted."

She closed the Book. "Woref is ranting and raving like a lunatic. He's turning the city inside out looking for the blank Books. It's an inquisition."

Thomas was quite sure they wouldn't find them, but he didn't say so.

"That's not what I mean. What did I read yesterday?" he asked.

"A story."

"What story? Tell me the story I was reading when you cried."

Her eyes looked away, distant.

"It was too much for you?"

"You were reading a story about a princess who was taken captive by an evil man."

The story he'd read had been a simple accounting of history, hardly the drama she remembered. Yet she'd heard this in it?

Her eyes misted and she bit her lower lip. He found himself wanting to comfort her. She stood in the sunlight from the window above them, face white with morst, eyes gray and dead. A revolting image once. But now . . .

"That was the truth behind the words I read," he said. "Not what I read. You opened your mind to the truth."

"Then you shouldn't read the Books to me anymore."

"Why not? It's what you've always searched for."

"Not your truth! I've never searched for the ways of an albino! Do you know who I am?"

"You're Chelise, the daughter of Qurong. And who am I?"

"You're my servant. A slave. An albino!"

"And do you think there is any truth in this albino?"

She refused to look at him. They stood in an awkward silence. She finally pushed the Book into his hands and walked toward the door. "There is a tour of the city planned for this afternoon. Qurong wants to show the people his prisoners. You will ride in chains behind us. They will mock you. That is my truth."

Chelise left him without a backward glance.

———⊗———

As promised, Qurong dragged his prisoners through the city that afternoon. The royal family rode three abreast on black steeds, followed by Woref and Ciphus. Then Thomas, on foot and chained—each arm to a Scab warrior on each side. William, Suzan, Cain, and Stephen followed behind with their own guard. An army of a thousand warriors in full battle dress, armed with sickles, brought up the rear.

The horns announced their coming and the streets were lined with hundreds of thousands of disease-ridden Scabs.

Thomas saw the true squalor of the Horde on every side. A baby crawling on the muddy earth between the mother's feet, screaming to be heard above the din of insults that had become a steady roar. Thomas was certain the children cried as much from the pain of the disease as from any other discomfort.

The guards parted occasionally to allow youth to hurl spoiled fruit at them. What little grass had grown on the yard along the parade route was quickly trampled into mud. Several huts collapsed under the weight of spectators.

There seemed to be a particular infection spreading among a sizable portion of the population. Red sores on their necks, raw and bleeding. Thomas plodded on, afraid to look at them, much less care for them.

The parade lasted about an hour, and not once did Chelise turn a kind eye to him or show any hint of misgiving. She rode erect, with no emotion at all. She was right: this was her truth.

He spent the night in his cell, too nauseated to eat. But he still couldn't wash her image from his mind. He begged Elyon for her understanding, her heart, her mind, her soul. He finally cried himself to sleep.

He did not dream.

—⚬⚬⚬—

Chelise rode to the royal garden the next morning, as soon as she felt she could get away without the prying eyes of the court on her. She was flirting with a dangerous game. Even the smallest kindness shown to Thomas could drive a wedge between her and Qurong. Her father loved her; she was sure of that. But his love was conditioned by his people's ways. Hundreds of thousands of men had died in battle trying to defeat Thomas of Hunter. Aiding him in any way would be seen as treason. Qurong could never accept treason, especially not in his own court.

And Woref . . . She shuddered to think what Woref would do if he even suspected the small kindness she harbored for Thomas of Hunter.

She'd settled another matter last night with her maidservant, Elison.

"Why are you so upset over this, Chelise?" Elison had asked. "I would think parading your new slave on a chain would suit you. Thomas of Hunter, of all men! Qurong is calling him his slave, but the word on the street is that it was your idea."

"How did that get out? Do the walls have ears here?"

"I think Ciphus said something. The point is, the people love you for it. The princess towing about the mighty warrior in chains."

"No man should be insulted in that way. Especially a great warrior. The people are like ravenous dogs! Did you see the look in their eyes?"

"Please, my lady," Elison said. "Don't misunderstand the situation here. Thomas of Hunter is the man responsible for widowing one out of every ten women in this city."

"He's great, but not that great."

"The Forest Guard then. Under his command."

"The Forest Guard no longer exists. They don't even carry swords—what kind of enemy is that?"

Elison looked at her, dumb.

"Don't play ignorant with me, Elison. If I can't trust you, then who can I trust?"

"Of course."

She turned to her servant, took her hand, and led her to the window seat. "Tell me that you would rather die than betray me. Swear it to me."

"But, my lady, you know my loyalty."

"Then swear it!"

"I swear it! What is this talk of betrayal?"

"I sympathize with him, Elison. Some people might consider that treason."

"I don't understand. If you were to say something more scandalous, some service you required of him as your slave, I might understand that. But sympathy? He's an albino."

"And he has more knowledge than Ciphus and Qurong put together!" Chelise said. Elison's eyes widened. "You see why I insisted you swear?

To kill Thomas of Hunter would be to take the greatest mind. He may be the only one who can read the Books of Histories."

Her servant looked at her with dawning. "You . . . you like him."

"Maybe I do. But he's an albino, and I find albinos repulsive." She looked out the window at the rising moon. "Strange that we call them albinos when we are whiter than they are. We even cover our skin to make it smooth like theirs."

Elison stood in shock.

"Sit."

She sat.

"You're forgetting yourself. I would think you should sympathize with Thomas yourself. You're both in servitude. He's a very kind man, Elison. The kindest I've met, I would say. I simply sympathize with Thomas the way I might sympathize with a condemned lamb. Surely you can find it in yourself to understand that."

"Yes. Yes, I suppose I can," she said, eyes still wide. "Have you . . . touched his skin?"

Chelise laughed. "*Now* who is scandalous? You're trying to make me ill? I have no attraction to him as a man, thank Elyon for that, or I might be in a real bind. Can you imagine Woref's reaction?"

"Loving an albino would be treason. Punishable by death," her maid-servant said.

"Yes, it would."

She'd risen then, confident in her simple analysis. It was the first time she'd thought about her use of the morst as a way of becoming more albino. Just a coincidence, of course. Fashion was something that changed, and at the moment this new morst that happened to cover their scaly flesh distinguished women of royalty from commoners. In the years to come, it might be a blue paint.

Chelise passed through the royal garden's main gate and turned to Claudus, the senior guard who'd grown up as the cook's son. "Good morning, Claudus."

"Morning, my lady. Beautiful morning."

"Anyone pass this morning?"

"The scribes. No one else."

"Has my slave bathed as I instructed?"

"Yes, and wasn't he filthy! We gave him a clean robe as well. He's waiting inside with the Books."

"Good. I should have asked that you powder him as well." She nudged her horse and then thought she'd better clarify her statement. "I can hardly stand being near him."

"Shall we powder him?"

"No. No, I'm not that weak. Thank you, Claudus."

"Of course, my lady."

She headed toward the library, eager to be among the Books again. With Thomas. In all honesty the thought of powdering him felt profane to her. She didn't want him to be like her. Now there was a scandal.

Chelise tied her horse at the back entrance and slipped into the library, chiding herself for sneaking like a schoolgirl. They all knew she was here, doing precisely what they expected her to do. Qurong had insisted on having the Books read to him after her first lesson, but she'd stalled him. She claimed she wanted to surprise him by reading the Books to him herself. Thomas was her slave—the least they could do was let her spend a few days learning to read before robbing her of her gift.

She also convinced him that the other prisoners might be able to read the Books as well. They should be kept alive for the time.

Chelise unlocked the door, put her hand on the knob, took a deep breath, and stepped into the large storage room.

At first she thought he hadn't been brought yet. Then she saw him, on the ladder high above, searching madly through the Books again. He looked like a child caught stealing a wheat cake from the jar.

"Still looking for your secret Book?" she asked.

He descended quickly and stood with his arms by his sides, twenty feet from her. The long black robe made him look noble. With the hood pulled up and a little morst properly applied, he would look like one of them.

"Good morning, my lady."

"Good morning."

"I have a confession," he said.

She walked to his right, hands clasped behind her back. "Oh?"

"I found the parade yesterday appalling."

She knew he was probing, but she didn't care. "I'm sorry about that. My confession is that I found it appalling as well."

Her statement robbed him of words, she thought.

"No decent man should have to suffer that," she said.

"I agree."

"Good. Then we're in agreement. Today I would like to learn to read."

"I have another confession," he said.

"Two confessions. I'm not sure I can match you."

"I can't get you off my mind," he said.

Now his statement robbed *her* of words. Heat spread down the nape of her neck. He was saying too much. Surely he realized that she could only do so much for him. Light, food, a bath, clothing. But she had her limitations.

"I will never be your savior, Thomas. You do realize that, don't you?"

"I don't think of you as my savior. I think of you as a woman, loved and cherished by Elyon."

"You're saying too much. We should start the lesson now."

He looked away, embarrassed. "Of course. I didn't mean that I had feelings for you. Not as a woman like that. I just . . ."

"You just what? Do you have an albino wife?"

"She was killed by your people when we made our first escape from the red lake. Our children are with my tribe now. Samuel and Marie."

She wasn't sure what to make of that. She'd never heard that Thomas of Hunter had lost his wife. Or had children, for that matter.

"How old are they?"

"Samuel thinks he's twenty, though he's only thirteen. Marie is nearly fifteen."

Thomas walked to the shelf and pulled out a Book. "I think it's important that you realize that your teacher respects you. As a student. As a woman who has ears to hear. I meant nothing else. Shall we begin?"

They spent an hour with the Book, carefully going over the letters that he insisted were English. They weren't, of course, but she began to associate certain marks with specific letters. She felt as if she was learning a new alphabet.

He worked with her with measured reason at first, gently explaining and rehearsing each letter. But as the hour passed, his passion for the task grew and became contagious. He explained with increasing enthusiasm and the movement of his arms became more exaggerated.

They worked closely, she on the chair behind the desk, he over her shoulder, when he wasn't pacing the floor in front of her. He had a habit of pressing the tips of his fingers together as he walked, and she found herself wondering how many swords those fingers had held over the years. How many throats had they slit in battle? How many women had they loved?

She would guess only one. His late wife.

They laughed and they argued over fine points, and gradually she became more comfortable with his proximity to her. With her proximity to his side, bumping her shoulder when he hurried in to point at a letter she'd missed; to his finger, accidentally touching her own; to his hand, gently tapping her back when she got it right.

His breath on her cheek when he was too passionate about a particular point to realize he was speaking loudly, so close.

She was no fool, of course. Thomas was no buffoon. In his own measured way, he was trying to draw her in. Disarming her. Winning her trust. Perhaps even her admiration.

And she was allowing him to do it. Was it so wrong to bump the shoulder of an albino? Did the guards not touch his skin when they shackled him?

Three hours had passed when Thomas decided that a test was finally in order.

"Okay," he said, clapping his hands. "Read the whole paragraph, beginning to end."

"The whole thing?" She felt positively giddy.

"Of course! Read what you've written."

She focused on the words and began to read.

"The woman was give the sword man if running . . ." She stopped. It made no sense to her.

"That's not what you've written," he said. "Please, in order, exactly as you wrote it."

"I am reading it exactly as I wrote it!"

He frowned. "Then try again."

"What's wrong? Why does it sound so mixed up?"

"Please, try again. From the top. Follow with your finger as I showed you."

She started again, pointing to each word as she read. "The woman running if horse . . ."

Chelise looked up at him, horrified. "What's this nonsense coming from my mouth? I can't read it!"

His face lightened a shade. He stepped forward, took the paper she'd written on. His eye ran across the page. "You're not reading what's on the page," he said. "You're mixing the words."

Chelise felt hope drain from her like flour from a broken clay jar. "Then I won't be able to learn. What good is it if I can write the alphabet and form the words if they don't make any sense?"

He set the paper down and paced.

Chelise felt crushed. She would never be able to read these mysteries. Was she so stupid as that? Her throat suddenly felt tight.

Thomas faced her. "I'm sorry, Chelise. It's not your writing or your reading. It's your heart. It's the disease. As long as you have the disease, you'll never be able to read from the Books of Histories."

She suddenly felt furious with him. "You knew this? How dare you toy with me!"

"No! Yes, I suspected that the disease might keep you from hearing, but the other day you did hear the truth behind the story. I thought you might be able to learn."

"I have no disease! You're the albino, not me!" Tears sprang into her eyes.

Thomas looked stricken. He hurried around the desk and knelt beside her. "I'm so sorry. Please, we can fix this!"

Chelise placed her forehead in one hand. She took a deep breath and calmed herself. She didn't understand his sorcery, but she doubted her ignorance was his fault.

Thomas put a hand on her shoulder. "I can help you. I can teach you to read the Books of Histories, I swear. I will. Do you hear me? I will."

"What's the meaning of this?"

Woref's voice echoed through the room like the crack of a whip.

Chelise instinctively gasped and sat up. Woref glared at them from the doorway. She'd left the door unlocked?

The general walked into the room. Thomas withdrew his hand and stood back.

"How dare you touch her?" Woref raged.

Chelise stood. "My lord, he was only instructing me on this passage. He did only what I demanded. How dare you suggest anything else?"

"It makes no difference what you instructed him. No man, certainly no albino, has the right to touch what is mine! Get away from her."

Thomas eased away. "The rules of these holy Books supersede the rules of man," he said. "Are you saying your authority is greater than the Great Romance?"

"I should cut out your tongue and feed it to Elyon."

Woref had lost his reason, Chelise thought. "Then we'll let Qurong decide by whose authority we live," she said. "Yours or Elyon's."

Woref scowled at her, then at Thomas. "I don't see why any instruction would require his comforting."

"Comforting?" Chelise smiled wryly. "You think I would allow this pathetic albino to comfort me? We were playacting. It's a part of breaking the code required to understand that what I can see now is clearly beyond your mind." *Easy, Chelise.*

She stepped closer to him and winked. "But then I'm not fascinated by a man's mind. It's your strength and courage I find exhilarating. If you were a feeble scribe, I would never consent to our marriage."

She walked up to him and drew her finger over his shoulder, stepping behind him. "I expected nothing less than this tirade. You flatter me. But you did misunderstand, my lord. Now tell me why you've come."

He wasn't buying her toying wholeheartedly, but she'd effectively cut him off.

"I have changed my mind about the blank Books," he said, still stern. "They have vanished. My men have searched every possible hiding place for such a large collection, and they can't be found. I think the sorcery of this albino is to blame. They disappeared about the same time he arrived."

"I have no sorcery," Thomas said.

Woref dismissed the claim. "I demand that you convince your father to withdraw his request that I find the Books before we are married."

"You've talked to him about this?"

"I have. He's obsessed with these blank Books."

"And I understand why," Chelise said. "The blank Books make the collection complete. Surely you can find them."

"As I said, they no longer exist. I won't delay my possession of you over this nonsense!"

"Then make my father see the light."

"He will only concede on the albinos," Woref said. "I need you to help him see the light in regard to the Books. I can assure you that I'll make it up to you."

"How has he conceded on the albinos?" Chelise asked.

"He's agreed to kill the other four tomorrow. He said that you thought they should be kept alive, but I've convinced him otherwise. One living albino is bad enough."

She glanced at Thomas and saw the fear cross his face. But she had to choose her battles.

"Fine. Let me think about how to persuade Qurong to forget about the blank Books. Now if you'll excuse us, we are in the middle of a lesson."

Woref stared at Thomas for a few seconds, spit upon the floor, and walked from the room without closing the door.

"I beg you, Chelise, you can't let them die!" Thomas whispered.

She hurried to the door and closed it. "It's out of my hands. How would it look for me to beg for their lives?"

Thomas paced, frenzied.

"We're on dangerous ground here. Not only you, but now me. I know Woref's kind, and I promise you that one day I'll pay for what he just saw. You have to be more careful. Please, keep your distance."

He suddenly stopped and faced her. "I can dream now!"

"What are you talking about?"

"I've been drinking the rhambutan juice because Woref has been holding my friends' lives over my head. He's just removed that threat! I'll refuse to eat the fruit and dream tonight. But they may try to force me. Can you stop them?"

She didn't respond. Why this business of dreams was so terribly important to him, she didn't know. But he was right; Woref had undermined his own threat.

He rushed over to her and grabbed her hand. "Please, I beg you. And you can't say a word about this!" He kissed her hand. "Please, not a word!"

"I . . ." He was still holding her hand. "This isn't keeping your distance."

Thomas released her and stepped back. "Forgive me. I didn't mean that. I lost my mind."

"Clearly."

"But you'll help me?"

"I can't help you. But I don't see the harm in a few dreams." And then she added something that shocked even her. "As long as you promise to dream about me."

19

The helicopter sat down on the White House lawn with a *thump* that pounded through Kara's head. Thomas was on that helicopter. Her brother, who had traveled to hell and back in the last three weeks. Or was it four weeks now?

The rotors wound down slowly. The door opened and Thomas emerged into the afternoon sun. He stepped onto the grass, ducked his head, and hurried toward them.

"Hey, Thomas." She closed the gap between them and met him by the line of secret service agents, which had doubled since news of the crisis had flooded the airwaves.

Thomas took her in his arms and hugged her. "Hey, sis."

"You're alive," she said.

"And kicking."

He turned to Monique, who waited with a sheepish smile. "Monique."

She took his hand and kissed his cheek. "Hello, Thomas."

"How's it feel?" he asked.

He was asking her about waking from the dead, Kara thought.

"You tell me," she said.

"Like waking from a dream."

"Been doing a lot of that lately, from what I understand."

"More than I care. Although I have to say, I think I'm on to something this time."

Merton Gains stepped forward, hand extended. "Good to have you back. The president's expecting you."

The situation room was buzzing when Thomas stepped in, followed by Kara and Monique. President Blair saw him and excused himself from a conversation with the secretary of state. He approached with a tired smile and stuck out his hand.

"The cat has nine lives after all."

"Two, actually." Thomas glanced around the room and lowered his voice. "What I have to say has to be said in private, sir. I'm not sure who we can trust."

"And I can't work in a vacuum," the president said. "Not this late in the game."

"Please, sir, just hear me out. Then you can decide who needs to know. You were told they have someone on the inside?"

"Yes. Okay, wait for me in my office. Give me a minute. Merton, please show them into the Oval Office and leave them."

"Right away, sir."

Blair took his chief of staff aside and spoke quietly.

"This way," Gains said. They followed him silently through several halls bustling with activity. Into the Oval Office.

They stood in the stately office, surrounded by silence.

"The Book crossed over with me, Kara."

"The blank Book? What do you mean 'crossed over'?"

"When I woke up on the gurney in the basement of Fortier's complex, it was with me. It's the only object that's ever crossed between the realities. Skills, blood, and knowledge—and now this Book. And if I'm right, the rest of the blank Books may have followed somehow."

"The Books are knowledge," Kara said. "Knowledge crosses. This is incredible!"

"No, this isn't incredible. I lost the Book. It was taken by one of the guards, who has no clue what it can do. How much time do we have with the virus?"

"Five days. Maybe less, maybe more. Ten before it's all over."

"Then I guess the Book will have to wait."

The door suddenly opened and the president walked in alone.

"Sorry, I got hung up." He walked to his desk and picked up a warm Pepsi can, then ushered them to the sofas.

"Okay, Thomas. You're on."

"This office is clean?"

"Swept for bugs this morning."

"By whom? Sorry, never mind. I can't decide which world I'm in."

Blair nodded. "Talk to me."

"Okay." Thomas took a deep breath and sat on the edge of the couch. "Follow me closely. I understand the immediate crisis between Israel and France has been defused."

"For the time being. But things could get bad anytime. In three days we lose our nuclear arsenal."

"We're going to need the Israelis."

"How so?" the president asked.

He decided to hold back. "What would you say if I told you I may have a way to put a man in their inner circle?"

"You mean next to Fortier?"

"Close enough to smell his breath."

"I would say we should have done that two weeks ago. Who?"

"Carlos Missirian."

"He's with them. I don't understand."

"I think we may be able to get inside of Carlos's head. I'll need Johan for that. They've shared a connection once before; I think Johan could do it again. But he'll need to dream while in contact with my blood."

"I'm not sure I know this Johan."

"Johan is . . . connected with Carlos?" Kara asked.

"You're saying that if Johan dreamed using you as a gateway, he would wake up as Carlos!" Monique said.

"Yes."

"It could work!"

The president held up his hand. "Excuse me. Maybe you could be a little clearer here."

"It's the way our dreams work," Thomas said. "All three of us have dreamed. We know someone in the other world who could get to Carlos."

"Is that all? I'm surprised I didn't think of it."

"Please, we're running out of time, Mr. President."

Blair lifted both hands. "Fine. I'll try anything at this point. How do we get to this Johan?"

"Well, actually, we have a problem there. I'm being held captive at the moment. We have to get Johan to me, which is where Kara comes in." He looked at his sister. "Come back with me. As Mikil. You and Johan have to break us out of the city—the others are scheduled for execution tomorrow."

She stared, lost in the suggestion. "Break you out without fighting?"

"I have an idea. It'll be tricky, but with Johan's help you should have a decent chance."

"You can't fight?" Monique asked. "You should go in there and do whatever's necessary. Kill the lot if you have to!"

"No," Thomas said. "That's not the way the Circle works now."

The president sat back and crossed his legs. "If we weren't facing extinction, I might be calling security at this point."

All three looked at him. Thomas turned back to Kara. "You have to get me out. If Mikil is still near the Southern Forest, a day's ride south, it may already be too late. But I can't think of any alternatives."

A thick black leather-bound book lay on the end table to Thomas's right. A Bible. His dream of the Circle spun dizzily through his head.

"But you're not scheduled for execution, right?" Kara asked.

"No," he said. "Does the phrase 'bread of life' mean anything to you?"

They were silent, not expecting the odd question. Thomas looked at Kara. "The bread of life. The light of the world. Two of a dozen metaphors we use in the Circle to talk about Justin."

"The bread of life," Kara said. "Sounds like a phrase Dad would have used when he was a chaplain."

"From the Gospels," the president said.

Thomas reached for the Bible and lifted it slowly. The Gospels. Was it possible? The air felt thick. Words spoken by his father years earlier wove through his mind. He'd never paid much attention to them, but they spoke softly from the back of his memory, like whispers of the dead.

Or of the living?

He cracked the book open and thumbed through the latter half. Found the Gospels. The Gospel of John.

Thomas read the first line and felt the strength leave his arms. Here in his hands he held a copy of the one book Justin had left them.

The Histories Recorded by His Beloved.

Kara had walked up and was staring at the book. "The Book of Histories?"

Thomas closed the Bible and set it down. "One of them."

"That's one of the Books?" Monique asked. "How is that possible?"

"Everything that happens here is recorded in the Books of Histories," Thomas said. "Everything."

But it was more than that, wasn't it? This was the one book that Justin had left them with. The Circle's dogma was largely based on this book.

President Blair cleared his throat. "Assuming you get to Carlos, what's the plan?"

Yes, the plan.

20

The crowd was swelling exponentially, but not nearly fast enough for Phil Grant. The plan had been simple enough, and the senate majority leader had come through, but time was running out, and now Thomas Hunter had pulled this dream stunt of his again.

Phil walked across the lawn with his radio in hand, dabbing his sweaty forehead with a handkerchief. A line of tan APCs had been stationed every fifty yards to form a large perimeter around the White House grounds. Regular army. A full division had been assigned to Washington. Several tanks sat on the driveway, hatches open and operators sitting on their turrets. Their presence here had been tolerated only because the nation was preoccupied with worse matters. The National Guard had taken to the streets of the nation's fifty largest cities, spanning from New York to Los Angeles. No incidents of fatal conflict. Yet.

A thousand sets of eyes followed Phil as he walked. The protesters stood behind the fence, a good hundred yards off, but their glares pointed even at that distance. The people were a combination of I-told-you-so end-of-the worlders, antigovernment activists, and a surprising number of regular citizens who had connected with Mike Orear and decided that adopting a cause—no matter how practical—was better than sitting at home waiting to die.

Dwight Olsen kept up with Phil's even stride. Phil looked at the opposition leader. The man was oblivious to the real game here, but his hatred for the president had made him an easy pawn.

"We're down to the wire," Phil said. "Tomorrow at the latest. If you can't pull this off, the president's going to try something stupid. You understand that, right?"

"You've said that before, but you know I can't force this. I can't imagine the president starting a war. He and I may not see eye to eye, but he's not a fool."

"That's the point; we can't let him start a war. It's too late for that. Our whole purpose here is to prevent a war."

They approached the front lines of the protest. Mike Orear walked toward them, looking haggard. Dozens of well-known politicians were involved in getting out the protest, but the world's eyes were focused on this one man.

Phil had slipped the suggestion to Theresa on the flight back from Bangkok, and she'd listened intently. They had to give the people a heads-up, and the only way to do it without breaking the president's confidence was to bring in someone who might make the decision to go public on his own. Someone like her boyfriend, who had broad media access. If she hadn't taken the bait so quickly, Phil would have used any of several other leads he had working. The trick had been to hold back the news long enough to let Fortier secure his grip on France. When the news finally broke, they needed it to break big.

Orear grinned and ran a hand through his already-disheveled hair. "Impressed?"

"Mike, I'd like you to meet Phil Grant, director of the CIA," Dwight Olsen said.

They shook hands. "Quite a show you're putting on, Mike."

"It's all the people, not me. I'm sure it's an inconvenience for all you political jocks, but the world is obviously way beyond considerations of convenience, isn't it?"

Phil glanced at Olsen. "Well, that's just the thing, Mike," the senator said. "We're not so sure your vigil is such an inconvenience after all."

Mike gave him a blank stare.

"In fact, after a careful analysis, we've concluded that it just might be the only thing that has any chance of shifting the balance in this game."

"You mean forcing the president to come clean."

Phil grinned. He took Mike's arm and directed him away from the security lines. "Not exactly. Can I count on your complete confidence?"

Olsen walked beside them.

"It depends."

"That's not good enough," Phil said. "This is beyond any one man now; surely you understand that. The decisions made in the next few days will determine the fate of hundreds of millions."

"Then you're talking about changing the president's mind."

Bingo.

"We're running out of time."

"And the public doesn't have a clue what's really going on," Mike said. "That's the whole point of this vigil, isn't it? The public's right to know. And how do you suggest we change what we don't know?"

"I'll tell you what the president's planning," Phil said. "But I need your complete confidence; I'm sure you understand that."

"Fine. If I think you're shooting straight with me, you'll have my confidence. But don't think I won't tell the people what they deserve to know. I won't betray their trust."

"I'm not talking of betraying the people. I'm talking about serving them. You may have more power than anyone else in the country now. We need you to use that power."

Mike stopped. "Spare me the political pap."

"Then I guess I'll just have to trust you, Mike. I hope I'm not making a mistake."

The CNN anchor just looked at him. He was the perfect man, Phil thought. He really believed in this nonsense of his.

"The president is planning to start a nuclear war. He's convinced that France won't deliver the antivirus as promised, and he's decided as a matter of principle to go down in flames. If he doesn't comply with the demands we've received, this country will cease to exist."

"But you don't think he's right."

"No, we don't. Most of his inner circle is against him. We have intelligence that leads us to believe the French will come through with the antivirus in time. Under no circumstance can we allow the president to pull his trigger."

Mike Orear looked at the White House. "So the president doesn't trust the French. And you do."

"Essentially, yes."

"And if you're wrong?"

Dwight Olsen stepped in. "If the president starts a war, we don't have a chance of finding the antivirus, plain and simple. If he doesn't, we have a chance."

"I take it our scientists aren't as close to creating an antivirus as we've been led to believe."

"No."

"You sick . . ." The muscles on Mike's jawline flexed with frustration. "So this vigil of ours is nothing more than our own funeral procession."

"Not necessarily," Phil said, wiping a bead of sweat from his temple. "By tomorrow you'll have over a million people involved. An army. With the right encouragement, this army might be able to change the president's mind."

"The vigil is fine, Mike," Olsen said. "But we're running out of time. Leak the word that a nuclear war might be imminent. We need the president to understand that the people don't want war. And we need the French to see our good faith. It's a last-ditch effort, but it's the only one we've got."

"You want me to start a riot."

"Not necessarily. A riot sends mixed signals of chaos."

"What do you expect these people to do? March on the White House?"

Phil caught Olsen's quick glance. "I'm open to suggestions. But we're going to die here." He let frustration flood his voice, all of it genuine. "This isn't some massive game show you're putting on for the people! You either do what we need you to do, or you don't. But I want to know which it will be. Now."

Mike frowned. He glanced back at the security lines and the peaceful, candlelit demonstration of the "army" beyond. A man in a white robe was performing an ungainly dance, whether motivated by religion or drugs, Phil couldn't tell. A shirtless child leaned against the railing, staring across the lawn at them. He would be leaving this mess in two days; that was the agreement. In time to reach France and take the antivirus before it was too late.

"Okay," Mike said. "I'm in."

They lay side by side in Bancroft's dim laboratory, ready to sleep and dream. Above them, thirty armed guards the president had called in from the special forces formed a perimeter around the stone building on Johns Hopkins's otherwise vacated campus. The good doctor had been home when they reached him, but he'd scrambled back to his lab to perform yet one more incredible experiment on his willing subjects. His only real purpose here was to put them to sleep in tandem, but he insisted on hooking up the electrodes to their heads and laying them out like two Frankensteins in his dungeon of discovery.

On the chopper ride, Thomas had spent fifteen minutes on a secure line with the president, laying out his plan with the Israelis. Blair had quickly agreed to the bold steps he'd outlined. Their greatest challenge was to plan and execute the operation without the French catching any scent of it. Problem was, they didn't know who the French were working with. They might never. The president was more reluctant to agree to no joint chiefs, no FBI, no CIA, no regular military mechanism.

The communication with the Israelis would be handled by Merton Gains, in person. He was the only one Thomas was sure they could trust.

"So then," Dr. Bancroft said, approaching with a syringe in hand. "Are we ready to dream?"

Thomas glanced at Kara. His sister's hand was bound to his own with gauze and tape. The good doctor had made small incisions at the bases of their thumbs and done the honors.

"Three miles to the east, exactly as I showed you." Thomas said. "You have to get there tonight if possible."

She blew out some air. "I'll try, Thomas. Believe me, I'll try."

21

Mikil woke with a start and stared into black space. It was only the second time Kara had crossed over, but because of her past dealings with Thomas's dreams, she knew immediately what was happening.

She was Mikil. For all practical purposes, she was also Kara. Either way, Johan and Jamous were asleep beside her.

Mikil jumped to her feet. "Wake up!"

They jumped. Both of them grabbed at their hips, rolled, scrambled, and came up in a crouch, Johan gripping a knife and Jamous holding a rock. Thirteen months of nonviolence hadn't tempered their instincts for defense.

"What is it?" Johan demanded, blinking away his sleep.

"I'm dreaming," Mikil said. "Break camp. We have to go."

Jamous scanned the forest around them. "Scabs?" he whispered.

"You're not dreaming," Johan stated. "You're awake. Go back to sleep and dream some more. You gave me a heart attack!"

"No, Kara is dreaming!" She scooped up her roll and bound it quickly.

They'd secured a new camp for the tribe, and after more discussion than she would have thought reasonable given the urgency of Thomas's predicament, they'd agreed as a council to send three of their most qualified warriors on a surveillance mission that could be turned into a rescue attempt if the situation warranted.

Five nights had passed since the Horde had taken their comrades. Five nights! And with each passing night, her certainty that Thomas was dead increased. Times like these tempted her to consider embracing William's doctrine to either take up the sword or flee deep into the desert. Even

Justin had swung his sword and fought the Horde once. He'd been Elyon then as well, right? So then Elyon had once used the sword. Why not again now, to rescue the man who would lead his Circle?

She threw the bedroll on her horse, hooked it into place, and spun back to the two men who were staring at her in dumb silence. "Now. We have to leave now! Are you hearing me? Thomas is alive, and he's just told Kara how to get to him. He's in the basement of the library three miles east of the Horde city. The others are scheduled to be executed tomorrow."

"Thomas told you all of this?" Jamous asked.

"We don't have time!" Mikil swung onto her horse. "I'll explain on the way." She kicked her mount and headed north through a large field, ignoring Jamous's call demanding she hold up.

They would catch her soon enough. The sun would rise in less than three hours, and she had no desire to approach the city in broad daylight.

Johan caught her first, pounding down from behind on his large black steed. "Be reasonable, Mikil! Slow! At least slow enough for us to come to grips with this."

They came to the forest's edge and Johan eased to a trot beside her. "This library where he's kept," Johan said. "He told you how to break him out?"

She ducked to avoid a low branch. The trees were sparse here, but to the east the forest would slow them. She urged her horse forward.

"He gave me some ideas and told me that you would know what to do with them. You lived with the Horde long enough to understand them better than most."

Johan didn't respond.

"And he told me some other things about you, Johan." She glanced at him in the dim light. "We need you to dream as well. Evidently you're connected to a man named Carlos who needs to see the light."

"It's enough for now to talk about freeing Thomas based on a dream," he said. "How much of the healing fruit do we have?"

"Two each," Jamous said. "You're expecting a fight?"

"Do you think Thomas would forgive us if we healed a few of them after putting them down?"

Mikil looked at Johan. "Wounding a Scab and then healing them? I don't know." As long as they didn't kill . . . "Why not? That's your recommendation?"

"How can I recommend anything without knowing what Thomas told you in this dream of yours?"

"He told me precisely where he was being kept. He gave me the lay of the land, and he said that there was a woman who had unfettered access to him. He suggested I impersonate that woman."

"And which woman is this?"

"Chelise, the daughter of Qurong."

They both looked at her as if she'd gone mad.

"How much time do we have?" Mikil demanded.

"Turn around; let me see you by the moonlight," Johan ordered.

She obliged him. "How much?"

"Less than an hour," Jamous said.

"Then this will have to do!" Mikil looked at the compound's wall, just fifty yards to their right.

Jamous spit to one side. "It'll never work."

"Then give us a better idea," Mikil said. "How do I look?"

Donning the Scabs' traditional robes wasn't unusual—they often wore the cloaks when they ventured deep into the forest. But Mikil had never applied this white clay to her face and hands. Thomas had suggested she become a Scab princess for the night, and Johan had insisted on a heavy layer of the closest substitute for morst that he could find. White clay.

"Like the princess herself," Johan said.

"Except in the eyes and the voice."

"Every disguise has its limitations. Just do exactly like I said."

Jamous was right; the plan was madness. The only thing worse would be to try it in daylight.

"Remember," Mikil said, "the library is in the center of the garden. He said four guards, two outside and then two in the basement."

"We have it," Johan assured her. "Give us five minutes before you draw them out. And you should raise the pitch of your voice slightly. Chelise is as . . . direct as you. Don't try to sound too soft. Walk straight and—"

"Keep my head up, I know. You don't think I know what a snotty princess looks like."

"I wouldn't say she's snotty. Bold. Refined."

"Please. The words 'Scab' and 'refined' aren't possibly reconcilable."

"Just keep your wits about you," Jamous said. "They may not be refined, but they can swing their blades well enough."

If Mikil died, Kara would die in Dr. Bancroft's laboratory as well, Thomas had said. Strange. But Mikil was used to danger.

"Go."

Jamous hesitated, then clasped Mikil's arms to form the customary circle. "Elyon's strength."

"Elyon's strength."

The men vanished into the night. Mikil ran to the tall pole fence and scaled the tree they'd selected. The royal garden, Thomas had called it. The moon was half full—she could just see the outline of shrubs and bushes placed carefully around fruit trees. The large spired building a hundred yards into the complex was clearer. The library.

No sign of a guard on this side of the garden. Mikil grabbed the sharp cones on two adjacent poles, slung both legs over the fence, and dropped to the ground ten feet below. Her robe was black—if she walked with white face down, she would be invisible enough. She hurried through the garden, surprised by the care that the Horde had put into trimming the hedges and shrubs. Flowers blossomed on all sides. Even the fruit trees had been properly pruned.

She pulled behind a large nanka tree thirty yards from the library's front door, where two guards slouched against the wall. Strange how she felt no anger toward them since her drowning. She couldn't say she felt any compassion for them, as some did, but she regarded her lack of fury mercy enough. The fact that she'd been complicit in condemning Justin only made her anger toward the deception that blinded them more acute.

She had not been surprised to realize that her anger was directed at the disease, not the Horde. She had no compassion for the disease. The difference between her and some of the others—William, for example—was that when she saw two diseased guards, she saw mostly the disease; William would have seen only the guards.

Mikil blinked away her thoughts. It was time for her to practice a little deception of her own. She had to assume that Johan and Jamous were in place.

She lowered her head and walked directly toward the wide path that led to the library. Twenty-five yards. Gravel materialized under her feet—surely they'd seen her by now. She took a deep breath, stood as tall as she gracefully could, lifted her chin as a princess might, and strode directly for the two guards.

The guard on the left suddenly stood and coughed. The other heard him, saw Mikil, and quickly straightened. They were speechless. *Not too many visitors this time of night, is that it, you sacks of scales?*

She stopped near the bottom of the steps. "Open the door," she commanded quietly.

"Who are you?" the one on the right asked.

"Don't be a fool. You can't recognize Qurong's daughter at night?"

He hesitated and glanced at his comrade. "Why are you wearing—"

"Come here!" Mikil jabbed her finger at the ground. "Get down here, both of you! How dare you question my choice of clothing? I want you to see my face up close so that you never again question who it is that commands you! Move!"

She wasn't sure she sounded like a princess, but the guards descended the stairs cautiously.

"I intend to let this indiscretion go, but if you move like mud, I may change my mind."

They hurried forward.

Two shadows flew from each corner of the building, and Mikil raised her voice to cover any sound they might make.

"Now the fact of the matter is that I'm not Qurong's daughter, but know that I'm here on her behalf. She's told me where to find the albino so that I can rescue him. She's in love with our dear Thomas, you see."

The guards stopped on the bottom step just as Johan and Jamous sailed onto the steps behind and clubbed them each at the base of their necks. They grunted and fell in tandem.

They dragged the guards from the stairs and lay them in the grass. "Any damage?" Mikil asked.

"They'll survive."

Thomas would object, but he would eventually see reason. And though these two might jeopardize the rescue, they would live anyway. That was a kind of nonviolence in itself. The bit about the princess's love for Thomas was absurd—something to give them a laugh later. If Mikil was lucky, it might even land the dear princess in a spot of trouble.

"Let's go."

Johan and Jamous entered the library quietly with Mikil right behind. The door to the stairwell was precisely where Thomas had told her it would be.

"This one. I'll call them up." She waited for Jamous and Johan to stand in the shadows on either side of the door, then cracked it open. Torchlight glowed from below.

She nodded at Jamous, threw the door open, and took a step down. "Who's awake down here? I need the help of two guards immediately!"

Her voice echoed back at her. There might have been a sound, but she wasn't sure.

"Are you asleep? I don't have all night! The Books have been found, and Woref demands your assistance immediately!"

Now the sound of clad feet slapped the flat stones below. She spun around just as two guards came into view, both wielding torches.

"Hurry, hurry!" She walked into the foyer as their boots clumped up the steps.

These two were taken by Jamous and Johan with even less incident than the ones outside. It had been too easy. Then again, the right intelligence was often the key to victory in any battle.

Mikil fumbled at one guard's belt for keys, found them, snatched a torch from Jamous, and descended the stairs as quickly as her long robe would allow. A corridor carved from stone led to a door on the left.

"Thomas?"

"Here! Mikil? The door, quickly!"

She inserted the key and unlocked the door. It swung in and her torch illuminated Thomas, standing in a long black robe nearly identical to hers. He saw her face and froze. She had expected him to bound past her and take immediate charge. Instead he seemed oddly stunned by her.

"Relax. Contrary to my ghostly appearance, I'm not an apparition."

"Mikil?"

"This isn't what you expected? Don't tell me, my beauty stuns you?" She smiled.

He seemed to shake himself free. He ran to her and grasped her arms. "Thank Elyon. The others?"

"I have Jamous and Johan. We haven't gone for the others yet."

Thomas sprang for the stairs. "Then we have to hurry!"

She had to warn him. "We had to use a little force, Thomas."

He barged into the foyer and pulled up. Two bodies lay in a heap. He looked from them to Johan, then to Mikil who stepped around him.

"Just a bump, Thomas. If you want, we could feed them some fruit," Mikil said.

Thomas ran to the door and glanced up at the sky. A faint glow was teasing the eastern horizon.

"No time."

22

Thomas ran behind them with the dread knowledge that they would be too late. There was no way four albinos could go unnoticed once the city began to wake.

"Speed, not stealth," he said, passing Mikil. "We don't have time to slip in. We ride hard and we snatch them fast."

"And let them hang eight instead of four today?" Johan said. "We have to think this through."

"I've done nothing but think it through," Thomas said. "There's no other way in the time we have."

"And you intend to do this without force?"

"We'll do what we have to."

They catapulted themselves over the fence and mounted the horses. Thomas rode in tandem with Johan, but they would need five more mounts if they hoped to outrun the Horde.

Thomas led them to the stables, where they collected the horses.

"Saddles?" Mikil whispered.

"Bridles only. We can ride bareback."

It had taken them fifteen minutes, and the sky was gray. They were too late! Riding farther into the city now would be suicide.

And leaving was as good as condemning the others to death.

Thomas swung onto one of the horses and grunted with frustration. So close. The palace rose to their left. Chelise slept there. Something about this escape felt more like an execution to him. Nothing seemed right. They would either be caught and executed as Johan suggested, or they would escape only to meet another terrible fate.

"What is it?" Johan demanded.

"Nothing."

"This isn't 'nothing' on your face! What do you know that we don't?"

"Nothing! I know that you might be right about being caught. I only need one with me. Mikil and Jamous, meet us at the waterfalls in thirty minutes."

"I didn't come to run," Mikil said. "And I have the disguise."

"You're married." He kicked his horse.

"The waterfalls," Johan said. "Hurry."

"Then take this. I don't need it."

Mikil stripped off the robe and tossed it to Johan.

Thomas and Johan rode with two extra horses each, a fast trot, directly for the lake now just half a mile ahead of them. Johan pulled the robe on as he rode.

"She's right about one thing," Johan said. "Anyone who sees our faces will know we are albinos."

"Then our only hope is to hit them before they have a chance to think any albinos would be mad enough to crash through their city. Do you have a knife?"

"You're planning on using it?"

Was he? "Planning, no. I have no plan."

"That's unlike you."

They rode on, straight toward the dungeons now. Their horses' hooves were muted by the soft, muddy earth. Wood smoke drifted through the morning air from a fire in one of the huts to their left. A rooster crowed. The castle still stood in silence, now behind them.

"Mikil tells me that you need me to dream with you," Johan said quietly. "Something about a Carlos."

He'd nearly forgotten.

"Is that a reason to live?"

"Maybe."

Of course it was. But he didn't have the patience to think through this dreaming at the moment. Here, surrounded by the Horde city, something was gnawing at his mind, making him uneasy, and he couldn't understand what it was.

You don't want to be freed, Thomas.

No, that wasn't it. He would do anything in his power to be freed from these animals. Even if it meant hurting a few of them.

A surge of hatred swept through him, and he shivered. What kind of beast would threaten to kill what Elyon had died to save?

Where is your love for them, Thomas?

"I can't pretend to know what's happened to you, Thomas, but you're not the same man I last saw."

"No? Perhaps living here among your old friends has made me mad."

Johan wouldn't dignify his cut.

"Forgive me," Thomas said. "I love you like a brother."

"I may use my weapon?" Johan asked.

"Use your conscience."

Johan nodded at a group of warriors stretching by what looked like a barracks directly ahead. "I doubt my conscience will help against them."

Thomas hadn't seen them. Several watched them curiously. Even with hoods pulled low, the Scabs would know the truth soon enough. Their faces, their eyes, their scent. They were albino, and there was no way to hide it.

"You have the fruit?"

"Two pieces."

"When I go, ride hard."

"That's your plan?"

"That's my plan." One of the Scabs was suddenly walking toward the road as if to cut them off. "Ride, brother. Ride."

He kicked his horse hard. "Hiyaa!"

The steed bolted. Both horses in tow snorted at the sudden yank on their bits. They galloped straight toward the startled Scab, who scurried out of the way.

Thomas and Johan were past the barracks and at full speed before the first voice cried out. "Thieves! Horse thieves!"

Better than albinos. Thomas forced his horse off the street onto the lakeshore and pointed it straight for the dungeons.

There were two guards on duty at the entrance. By their expressions Thomas guessed that neither had ever defended the establishment against a prison break. The guard on the left had his sword only halfway out of its scabbard when Thomas dropped from his horse and shoved it back in.

He swung his elbow into the man's temple with enough force to drop him where he stood.

The second guard had time to withdraw his sword and draw it back before Thomas could take him out with a swift boot heel to his chin. Like old times, quick and brutal.

He snatched the keys from the first guard's belt. "I need thirty seconds!"

"I'm not sure we have thirty seconds," Johan said.

A group of unmounted warriors were lumbering up the path. They'd been caught on foot, but they realized now that stealing horses wasn't the intent of the two riders who'd blown past them.

"Do what you have to," Thomas said. Then he plunged down the steps, three at a time. There was still something wrong gnawing at his gut, but he felt new clarity. They should take a torch to the whole city.

He sprinted down the narrow corridor. "William!" He'd forgotten to grab one of the torches from the wall, and now he was paying for his haste. There were rumors that some of the Horde still kept some of their earliest prisoners alive somewhere in this dungeon, but Thomas wouldn't have the time to look for them.

He called into the dark. "William! Which one?"

"Thomas?"

Farther down. He ran past a row of cells and slammed into the bars of the sixth one. William and Suzan stood, dazed. Cain and Stephen were pushing themselves up on either side.

"We have two dozen Scabs closing in," he panted. He shoved the key into the lock and turned hard. The latch released with a loud clank.

"Are there others?"

"Probably."

"Run! Horses are waiting."

Thomas ran without a backward glance. They would help each other. He felt a surprising compulsion to engage the Scabs who bore down on Johan. A year ago, two of them could have taken on two dozen and at least held them at bay. He could taste the longing to tear into them like copper on his tongue. Blood lust.

Thomas took the stairs in long strides, lungs burning from his burst of activity. The voices of yelling Scabs reached him when he was only halfway up.

"Hold them!"

A voice cried out in pain. Johan?

Thomas tore from the dungeon into the light and slid to a stop.

The sight stalled his heart. Twenty sword-wielding Scabs had formed a semicircle around the entrance. Johan stood with his hood pulled back, bleeding badly from a deep wound on his right arm. The Horde was momentarily stunned by the sight of their old general, Martyn, staring them down.

The scene brought back images of a day thirteen months earlier. They had been gathered around Justin then, but in Thomas's eyes this scene was hardly different. They had killing in mind.

Something snapped on his horizon. Red. He scooped up the fallen sword from the second guard he'd knocked out earlier and swung it in a circle over his head. "Back!" He threw back his hood. "You don't recognize Thomas of Hunter? Back!"

The ferocity in his voice unnerved even him. He clung to the grip with trembling hands, desperate to tear into the Scabs. Johan was staring at him. The Horde was staring at him. He had a familiar power at hand, and he suddenly knew that he would use it.

Here and now, he would swing a blade in anger for the first time in thirteen months. What did it matter? They were all dead anyway.

The Scabs held their swords out cautiously. But they didn't back up as he'd ordered.

William and the others spilled from the dungeon behind him.

"Are you deaf?" Thomas cried. "Take up the other sword, Johan."

Johan didn't move. "Thomas—"

"Pick up the sword!"

You've lost yourself, Thomas.

He rushed the Scabs, screaming. His blade flashed. Struck flesh. Sliced.

Then it was free and he was leaning into his second swing. The sword cut cleanly through one of their arms. Blood flooded the warrior's sleeve.

The attack had been so quick, so forceful, that none of the rest had time to react. They were guards, not warriors. They knew Thomas only by the countless stories of his incalculable strength and bravery.

Thomas stood panting, sword ready to take off the first head that flinched. These animals who wallowed in their sickness deserved nothing less than death. These disease-ridden Shataiki had refused the love of Justin.

They were to blame for Chelise's deception.

Thomas felt his chest tighten with a terrible anguish. He clenched his eyes and screamed, full-throated, at the sky. A wail joined him—the second man he'd cut was on his knees clutching his arm.

Thomas spun to Johan. "The fruit."

Johan reached into his pocket and pulled out a fruit that resembled a peach. "Use this," he said to the Scab, tossing the fruit.

Immediately the Scabs stepped back in fear, leaving the wounded man with the fruit by his right knee.

Thomas dropped his sword and lunched forward. "For Elyon's sake, it's not sorcery, man!" He grabbed up the fruit and squeezed it so the juice ran between his fingers. "It's his gift!"

He grabbed the man's sleeve and yanked hard. The seam ripped at the shoulder and the long sleeve tore free, baring a scaly arm, severed below the elbow. The bone and the muscle were cut.

The Scab began to whimper in fear.

Thomas reached for the arm, but the man slapped him away.

His earlier rage welled up again. He slapped the man on the cheek. "Don't be a fool!" He knew that he was doing this all wrong, that everything about this escape had gone very wrong. But he was committed now.

Thomas gripped the man's arm with one hand and squeezed the fruit over his wound. Juice splashed into the cut.

Sizzled.

A thin tendril of smoke rose from the parted flesh. The healing was working.

Thomas stood and tossed the fruit at the first man he'd cut. "Use it!"

He turned his back on the Horde. The others were staring at him with something like shock or wonder; he wasn't sure which. He marched to his horse and swung up. "Ride."

He was sure the Horde would rush them, but they didn't. They were staring in horror at the man he'd given the fruit to. His arm was now half healed and hissing still. William broke toward a horse. Suzan, Cain, and Stephen rolled onto three others.

"If you think Qurong's power is something to fear or love, then remember what you've seen here today," Thomas said. "This time I give you fruit to heal your wounds. If you pursue us, you may not be so fortunate."

With that he whirled his horse around and galloped toward the forest, stunned, confused, sickened.

What had he done?

23

Nothing," Qurong demanded.

"They run better than they fight," Woref said. He stood on the castle's flat roof with the supreme leader, staring south over the trees. But Woref wasn't seeing trees. He wasn't even staring south. His eyes were turned inward and he was seeing the black beast that had steadily dug its way into his belly over the last few days.

He had known this beast called hatred, but never quite so intimately. He suspected it had something to do with his encounter with Teeleh, but he'd given up trying to understand the meeting. In fact, he was half-convinced the whole thing had happened in his dreams. There wasn't a real monster crawling around his innards, but the knot in his chest and the heat that flashed through his veins were no less real. He was now desperate for Chelise for his own reasons, and they had nothing to do with any nightmare of Teeleh.

He would possess her at all cost, to her or to himself. If he couldn't possess the daughter's love, how could he possess the kingdom?

"That doesn't answer my question," Qurong said. "Do we have a sighting of them or not?"

"No."

The supreme leader rested his hands on the rail that ran along the roof. He stood very still, dressed in a black robe, the withdrawn hood showing his thick dreadlocks.

"You executed the guards as I instructed?"

"Yes."

"The one who was healed by their sorcery?"

"He died quickly enough. A second guard tried to use the fruit, but it didn't work."

"And this is important why?" Qurong asked. He turned and looked Woref in the eye. "I'm interested in the albinos, not a few guards you failed to place properly."

They'd already covered Woref's responsibility in this catastrophe. The fact that Qurong would bring it up again, not two hours later, showed his weakness.

"I have accepted full responsibility. While you steam, they run."

Qurong grunted and looked back to the forest, perhaps surprised at his boldness. Woref kept his eyes to the south. When the time came for him to take his place as supreme ruler, he would burn this forest to the ground and start over. Nothing here attracted him any longer.

He swallowed bile. Other than Chelise, of course. And in some ways he craved the mother as much as the daughter. If he didn't one day kill Patricia, he would marry her as well. But it was the prospect of possessing them, not their pretty faces, that brought the knot to his gut.

He shivered.

"I'm not sure you realize what has happened here," Qurong said. "Two days ago I paraded Thomas through the streets to celebrate my victory over his insurrection. Today he makes a fool of me by escaping. If you think that you will survive Thomas, you are mistaken."

"You give him too much credit," Woref said.

"It took you thirteen months to bring him in, and now he's slipped out of your clutches again!"

"Has he? Know your enemy, we say. I think I'm beginning to understand this enemy."

"Yes. I understand that he outwits you at every turn."

"And what if I were to tell you that I knew his weakness?"

Qurong crossed his arms and turned away from the forest view. "He's an albino! We know his weakness! And it hasn't helped us."

"What price are you willing to pay to bring him back?" Woref asked.

"I'm willing to let you live!"

"And what consequence to the person who aided the albino's escape?"

"Anything but a drowning would mock me," Qurong said.

"No grace whatsoever?"

"None."

"And will you be gracious to your daughter?"

"What does she have to do with this?" Qurong demanded.

"Everything!" Woref shouted. His face burned with heat. "She is everything to me, and you've fed her to that wolf!"

Qurong's eyes flashed with anger. "Remember yourself! Your duty to me as general supersedes any lust you have for my daughter. How dare you speak of her at a time like this!"

"He has escaped with her help," Woref said. He might have slapped the supreme leader. "Don't be a fool."

"She instructed the guards not to force the rhambutan fruit down his throat as I ordered."

"And this is helping him? You're blinded by jealousy of a warrior in chains."

"He's not in chains now. That's the point, isn't it? He's free because he dreamed and found a way to use his sorcery to guide Martyn in, exactly as Martyn once said Thomas of Hunter could. He dreamed because he didn't eat the fruit. Chelise is complicit, I tell you!"

"Mark my word, Woref, if even one guard suggests this is untrue, I'll drown you myself!"

"We executed the guards an hour ago."

Qurong strode to the door that led below and jerked it open. "Bring Chelise to me at once!" He slammed the door. "Then I'll let you accuse her yourself. How dare you accuse my blood of favoring an albino?"

"You don't think I'm distressed? I haven't slept since I saw them—"

"Not another word!"

"I can prove myself."

Qurong was reacting as Woref himself might have had he not seen. The thought of anyone, much less one's royal flesh and blood, conspiring with their enemy was hardly manageable.

The door pushed open and Chelise stepped out. "I just heard that you allowed my teacher to escape!" she snapped, looking directly at Woref. "Is that true?"

"Did I?" he said. Woref felt his control growing thin. She insulted him by thinking he wouldn't know what happened under his command. "Or did you?"

She looked at Qurong. "You're going to let this man suggest that I helped the albinos escape?"

"It doesn't matter if I'm going to allow it. He's already done it."

"And you believe him? The albino wanted to dream so that he could better read the Books, which in part depend on dreaming. Naturally, I let him dream. Is this a crime?"

She knew! It was the only reason she would have for confessing this so quickly! She was trying to sound innocent, but the whore in her was showing clearly enough.

"You instructed the guards not to make him eat the fruit?" Qurong asked.

"Yes. He's my servant, and I thought it would assist him in his duties."

"And would those duties include holding your hand and whispering tenderly in your ear?" Woref demanded.

She seemed to pale, even with the morst on her face. "How dare you?"

"You deny it?" Qurong asked.

"Of course she'll deny it! But I know what I saw with my own eyes when I found them in the library, alone. If it had been anyone other than my own woman, I would have killed both of them."

Qurong was beyond himself. "Is this true, Chelise?"

"That I have fallen in love with an albino? How utterly preposterous! Thomas is a reasonable teacher who can read the Books of Histories, but it's no reason to call me a whore!" She looked at the supreme leader. "Father, I demand you withdraw your consent for me to marry this man immediately. I'll have nothing to do with him until he withdraws his slander and apologizes."

Woref's head swam in fury. He'd never been treated with such disdain. Perhaps he'd misjudged this woman after all. She might be harder to break than he'd first imagined.

And this is why you are so desperate for her.

"Then you deny any favor for Thomas of Hunter," Qurong said.

"The fact that my father has to ask such a question makes me wonder who he's been listening to."

"A yes or no would do, child!"

"Of course I don't favor the albino."

For a long moment the roof was silent.

"Leave us," Qurong said.

Chelise glared at Woref and left.

"You said you can prove this connection between them?" Qurong demanded.

"Yes, my lord. I can."

"You've put yourself in a dangerous position, you do realize?"

"Dangerous only if I'm wrong. I'm not."

Qurong sighed. "Then tell me how."

"If I'm right, then I want your word that Chelise will be mine with no restrictions."

The leader lifted an eyebrow. "She will be yours when you marry. What else could you want?"

I want to teach her who her master is, Woref wanted to say. *I want to break a bone or two so that she never forgets who I am.*

Instead he bowed his head. "I want her hand in marriage without any further restrictions."

Qurong faced the railing and looked south again. "Agreed. Your plan?"

"We still have the albino we took captive two months ago in the deep dungeons. Set him free to find the albinos with a message that if Thomas doesn't turn himself in within three days' time, Qurong, supreme leader of the Horde, will drown his daughter, Chelise, for treason against the throne."

Qurong glanced at him, but only for a moment. "Thomas of Hunter would never be such a fool. Even if he was, I could never drown my own daughter."

"You won't have to. If I'm right, Thomas will return. That will be my proof."

"You're not thinking straight. He would never risk his life for a woman he hardly knows."

"Unless she has seduced him."

The supreme leader glared.

"Then test me," Woref said.

"And if he doesn't come?"

"Then you will sign her death over to me. I will take her as a wife and forgive her in my own way. If I betray my word, then you may kill me yourself."

Qurong looked thoughtful for the first time since Woref had made the suggestion. "So even if you're wrong, you end up with my daughter? What's at stake for you?"

"My honor! If I'm wrong, my honor will be restored by my marriage to Chelise. If I'm right, my honor will be restored by the death of Thomas."

"What if Thomas never receives the message?"

"We'll send one warrior with the albino to return with his answer. At the same time we will conduct the single largest hunt for the tribe that escaped us in the Southern Forest. The tribe is without Thomas and Martyn and other leaders and will be vulnerable."

"Unless Thomas returns to them."

"He won't. Not if I'm right."

Qurong mulled the plan over in his mind, but the lights were already flashing in his eyes.

"They were touching when you saw them in the library?"

Woref spit over the railing. "I saw them."

Qurong grunted. "She always was headstrong. We will keep this quiet. You have your agreement. I'm not sure whether to pray that you're right or that you're wrong. Either way you seem to win."

"I've lost already," Woref said. "I saw what no man should ever have to see."

———⚬❧⚬———

The route they'd been forced to travel had slowed them through the day. Not so long ago, sight of the desert had always filled Thomas with an uneasiness. This was where battles were fought and men killed. This was where the enemy lived. Justin's drowning had reversed their roles, and the desert had become their home.

But as Thomas led the group of eight out of the forest along the lip of the same canyon where they'd once trapped and slaughtered forty thousand of the Horde, he felt the same underlying dread he'd once felt leaving the trees.

He stopped his horse by a catapult that had been torched by the Horde. This was the first time since the great battle of the Natalga Gap that he'd revisited the scene. Tufts of grass now grew on the ledge where black powder had blasted huge chunks of the cliff into the canyon below, crushing Scabs like ants.

Johan nudged his mount to the lip and gazed at the canyon floor. He hadn't led the Horde army that day, but their attack had been his plan.

Thomas eased up next to him. The rubble was still piled high. Birds and animals had long ago picked the dead clean where they could dislodge the battle armor. From this vantage point, the remains of the Horde army looked like a dumping ground for armory, scattered by strong winds and faded by the sun.

"Thank goodness the Horde hasn't figured out how to make black powder," Johan said.

"They've been trying. They know the ingredients, but besides me, only William and Mikil know the proportions. Give them a few more months—they'll stumble on it eventually."

The others had pulled close to the lip and were peering over. Thomas looked back at the forest, nearly a mile behind them now. It appeared dark in the sinking sun, an appropriate contrast to the red canyon lands that butted up against it. The black Horde holed up in their prison while the Circle roamed free in their sea of red.

But something deep in the black forest called to him. An image of Chelise drifted through his mind. Her white face and gray eyes, gazing longingly at the Books of Histories. He had only shrugged when the others questioned him about his prolonged silence during the flight from the Horde city—he wasn't sure why he felt so miserable himself. They were thinking he was sober over his use of force, and he had half-convinced himself that they were right.

Still, he knew it was more. He knew it was Chelise.

Thomas turned his horse from the canyon and walked it slowly along the rocky plateau. The others talked quietly, reminiscing, but another horse followed him—Mikil probably. Kara. They had work to do.

"So there's no doubting now, Kara," he said. "Which is more real to you? Here or there?"

"I wouldn't know." He turned. It was Suzan. She glanced at the forest.

"I thought you were Mikil."

"You're distracted. It's more than the escape, isn't it?"

"Why would you say that?"

"Because I was the one who suggested it in the first place. I think it worked."

"It was a good plan. Maybe I should give you command over one of our divisions." He grinned. But he knew she wasn't talking about the plan.

"I'm not talking about keeping us alive. I'm talking about winning the trust of Chelise."

"Yes, well, that was good too."

"I think maybe she won your trust as well."

He looked at Suzan in the waning light. Her darker skin was smooth and rich. He knew several who'd courted her without success. She was both cautious and wise. There was no fooling her. Suzan would make any man a stunning wife.

"Maybe," he said.

"I want you to know that I don't think it's a bad thing."

"Trust is one thing, Suzan," he said quietly, not entirely sure why he was telling her this. "Anything more smacks of sacrilege. I would never go there. You understand that, don't you?"

She waited for a moment. "Of course."

"Justin calls the Horde, and so we do as well. You could call it love. But an albino such as myself and a Horde woman . . ."

"Impossible."

"Disgusting."

"I don't know how you put up with the smell in the library for three days," she agreed.

"It was horrible."

"Horrible."

"Where are we camping?" Mikil asked, trotting up behind.

"In the canyon," Thomas said. "In one of the protected alcoves, away from the bodies. The Horde will steer clear of their dead."

"Then we should go. We have to bring Johan up to speed and get back."

No campfire. No warm clothes. No bedrolls other than the three brought by Mikil, Jamous, and Johan. Only sand.

Thomas shivered and tried to focus on the next task at hand. Johan.

They sat in a circle of eight, but the conversation was among the three who spoke of dreams. The others listened with a mixture of fascination and, he suspected, some incredulity. The fact that Mikil had known precisely where Thomas was kept them all from expressing their lingering reservation.

It was rather like the drowning—only the experience itself could ultimately turn one into a believer.

Johan stood and paced the perimeter. "Let me summarize this for you, Mikil, so that you can hear just how . . . unique it is. You're saying that if I cut myself and Thomas cuts himself, and we fall asleep with our blood mixed, that I will share his dreams."

"Not his dreams," Mikil said. "His dream world."

"Whatever. His dream world, then. I will hopefully wake up as a man named Carlos because he's made some connection with me earlier, and he thinks he may be me."

"Something like that," Thomas said. "We're not saying we know how it works exactly. But you know that Kara and Mikil had the same experience. For all we know, all of us could have the same experience. For some reason, I am the link to another reality. Another dimension. I'm the only gateway that we know of. If I don't dream, no one dreams. Only life, skill, and knowledge are transferable. Which is what happened to the blank Book."

"It disappeared into your dream world because Mikil wrote in it," Johan said.

"Yes. And if I'm right, the rest of the blank Books went with it."

"You saw them there?"

"No, only the one that I can be sure of. It's a hunch."

Johan sighed.

"Please, Johan," Mikil said. "Our future may depend on you. You have to do this."

"I'm not saying I won't. If you insist, I'd let you use a pint of my blood. But that doesn't mean I have to believe."

"You will believe, trust me," Thomas said. "Now sit. There's more."

Johan glanced around at the others, then seated himself.

They had to be careful what they told Johan about the situation in Washington. He might accidentally plant knowledge in Carlos's mind. And they couldn't risk tipping their hand in the event Carlos refused to play along.

Thomas leaned forward. "When you wake as Carlos, you will be disoriented. Confused. Distracted by what's happening to you. But you have to pay attention and come back with as much information as you can about the virus, Svensson, Fortier—anything and everything to do with their plans. Above all, the antivirus. Remember that."

"Who are these people?"

Thomas waved a hand. "Forget that. The minute you're Carlos, you'll know who they are. But when you wake up back here, you may forget details you knew as Carlos. So concentrate on the antivirus. Are you clear?"

"The antivirus."

"And while you're there, see if he knows who has the blank Book of History. One of his guards took it. Clear?"

"The blank Book of History."

"Good. In addition, there are two primary pieces of information we need you to plant in Carlos's mind. Our objective is to turn him, but short of that we need him to believe two things."

"Okay. I think I can handle two things."

24

For a moment that stretched long into the next, Carlos lay in the attic. Far below was the basement from which Thomas (and Monique) had escaped only days ago, after telling Carlos that he was connected to another man beyond this world—the one who was bleeding from his neck. That was him, Johan.

Carlos touched his neck. Wet. He pulled his fingers back. Sweat, not blood.

Of course there's no blood, Johan thought. That was thirteen months ago. But here in this world it was only a week ago. *I'm in the dream that Thomas told me about! Does Carlos realize that I'm here?* Johan sat up.

Carlos knew immediately that something had changed, but he couldn't define that change. He felt unnerved. He was sweating. A distant voice warned him of danger, but he couldn't hear the voice. Intuition.

Or was it more? His mother's whispers of mysticism had come alive to him these last few weeks. Thomas Hunter had found a way to tap the unseen. He'd lain dead on the cot for two days before apparently throwing off the sheet and climbing the stairs to the main level. True, a doctor hadn't confirmed his death, as Fortier had pointed out. There were stranger examples of near death. But Carlos dismissed the Frenchman's agnostic analysis. Hunter had been dead.

He looked around the room. And now he was here?

———∞∞∞———

No, Johan thought. *It's not Carlos; it's me. And although I know his thoughts, he doesn't necessarily know mine, at least not yet. Carlos isn't the one dreaming. I am. It's just like Thomas said it would be.*

Why Carlos? Because Carlos believed that there was a unique connection between them, although not enough belief to wake Carlos up to the fact that Johan was present, as in the case of Mikil and Kara.

And the man had a week-old cut on his neck to prove it. The same cut that Johan had received from Thomas thirteen months ago in the amphitheater when Justin had exposed him. Mind-bending. But real. As real as Thomas and Mikil had promised it would be.

He was in the histories at this very moment. How, he couldn't imagine—some kind of time warp or spatial distortion, whatever Mikil could possibly mean by that. More importantly, according to Thomas, he could affect history by depositing thoughts into Carlos's mind and by learning his intentions. Two things, Thomas had insisted. Convince him of these two things, learn what you can, and then get out.

———∞∞∞———

Carlos had a sense of déjà vu. Something familiar resided in his mind, but he couldn't shake it loose to examine it properly. He stood and walked to the dresser. He mopped his face with a handkerchief. His breathing felt ragged and his face hot.

This is how you will feel when Fortier slips poison in your drink after he's used you like an animal—sooner than you think.

The thought caught him off guard. Naturally, he had some reason to distrust Fortier. Hunter had suggested as much himself. The moment Carlos had the antivirus, he would take the necessary steps to protect himself. He'd already told Fortier that Hunter had claimed a coup would come on the heels of the virus. They couldn't possibly know that the coup would be orchestrated by Carlos himself. But he was powerless until he had the antivirus.

Now he was thinking that waiting so long might be a problem.

Why will Fortier let anyone even capable of a coup live long enough to conduct it? You have a day, maybe two; then he will snuff you out.

A chill flashed down his spine as the thought worked its way into his mind, not because this simple suggestion was new or even surprising, but because he suddenly knew it was true. Fortier might even do away with Svensson. His grip on this newfound power would last only as long as opportunity to strike back eluded his many new enemies. Fortier would isolate himself for protection. He would burn his bridges behind him.

It was all just a theory, of course, but Carlos was suddenly sure he'd stumbled onto something he could no longer ignore.

A day's stubble darkened his chin. He splashed cologne in his hands and patted his cheeks. A shower would have been part of his normal morning routine. This wasn't a desert camp in Syria.

Another thought occurred to him: he had to meet Fortier. Now. Immediately.

Exactly why, he wasn't so sure.

Yes, he was sure. He had to test the man. Feel him out without sounding obvious. Fortier was leaving for the city this morning.

Carlos stepped to the closet, pulled a beige silk shirt off the hanger, and slipped into it. He lifted the radio from his dresser.

"Perimeter check."

A slight pause. Static.

Then the guards in place around the compound started calling off their status. "One clear." "Two clear." "Three clear." "Four clear" . . . The check ended at eleven.

Satisfied, Carlos checked his reflection one last time in the mirror and exited the loft. Three flights to the basement. Down the long hall. He entered the security code, heard the bolts disengage, and stepped into the large secure room.

A conference table ringed by ten white chairs sat on rich green carpet. The monitors along the south wall were fed by a dozen antennas, only one of which was located on this building. Most were many miles away. Fortier had spared no expense in cloaking the compound's signature. It no longer mattered—the facility was already compromised by Monique and now Thomas. This was Fortier's last visit.

No sign of the Frenchman.

An intercom behind Carlos came to life. "Carlos, please join me in the map room."

He knew. He always knew.

And he might even take care of you now.

Carlos shrugged off the thought and walked to the third door on his left. Why did this Frenchman unnerve him so easily? He was simply one man, and he possessed half the killing skills Carlos did.

Which guard took the Book?

What on earth was that? What book? Had a guard taken the log book—if so, he couldn't remember being told about it.

He shook his head and stepped into the room, closing the door behind him. There were three others in the room besides Fortier. Military strategists. As Carlos understood it, they would all be gone today.

Fortier turned from a wall of maps that showed the exact location of each nuclear power's arsenal, inbound to France. Several had already off-loaded—the Chinese and the Russians were nearly intact on French soil now. The British and the Israelis had followed the United States' lead by offering their arsenals in exchange for the antivirus. There was to be a massive showdown on the Atlantic off France's coast. But the terms of the exchange only ensured that Fortier would get what he wanted.

The weapons.

"Please leave us," Fortier said to the others.

They glanced at Carlos and left the room without comment.

"Carlos," Fortier said, wearing a slight grin. He clasped his hands behind his back and faced the maps. "So close, yet so far."

"I would say you have them in a corner, sir," Carlos said.

"Perhaps. Have you ever known the Israelis to allow themselves into a corner?"

From the beginning, the destruction of Israel had been Carlos's primary concern. Fortier looked back.

"I don't think they are allowing anything, sir. They are being forced. And in a week it won't matter."

"Because in a week we will wipe them out, regardless of what happens in this exchange," Fortier said. "Is that what you mean?"

"Assuming that we take their weapons, yes."

"And what if we don't take their weapons? What if they're bluffing?"

"Then we call their bluff and destroy them anyway. We have the weapons to do that."

"We do. In fact, as of this moment we have the largest land-based arsenal in the world. Most of the United States' arsenal is on the ocean. But from a purely military perspective, our position is still weak."

"You're forgetting the antivirus."

"I'm setting the antivirus aside, and I'm saying that without it our position is strong, but not strong enough. The United States' submarine fleet alone could still do substantial damage. We're still setting up the tactical missiles from China. Russia has 160 intercontinental missiles under my command pointed at North America and their allies. On balance we are in the perfect position to finish the match in precisely the fashion we intended."

"But you have reservations," Carlos said.

Fortier paced and drew a deep breath. "I spent nine hours yesterday in conferences with the highest-level delegates for Russia, China, India, and Pakistan. They've all embraced our plans, eager to play their part in a changed world. There have been challenges, naturally, but in the end their response is better than I could have hoped for."

Something bothered Carlos about the man's tone. Sweat glistened on his forehead; he seemed more circumspect than normal. Perhaps even nervous.

"But I don't trust the Americans," Fortier said. "I don't trust the Israelis. I don't trust the Russians, and I don't trust the Chinese. In fact, I don't trust any of them. Do you?"

"I'm not sure you are required to trust them," Carlos said.

"Trust is always required. One hidden weapon could take out half of Paris."

"Then, no, I don't trust them."

"Good." Fortier lifted a large black book from the top of a file cabinet and slid it onto the table in front of Carlos. He'd never seen it.

"What is this?"

Fortier frowned. "This is the new plan," he said.

This could be good and this could be bad—Carlos wasn't yet sure which. He reached for the book.

"Page one only," Fortier said.

Carlos left the book on the table, lifted the cover, and turned the first page. A list of names ran down the page. His was the fourth down. Missirian, Carlos. The rest of the page contained at least another hundred names, listed as his own, surname first.

"I'm not sure I understand," he said, looking up.

"Our list of survivors. One hundred million in all, by family. We have no doubt as to their loyalties based on family ties and history, and we have precise plans on how to distribute the antivirus to them. The list took five years to compile. There will be some bad apples, of course, but we will deal with them easily enough once the rest are gone."

Carlos felt the blood drain from his face. Fortier had no intention of giving the anti-virus to any nation. Only these would survive.

"Whether your name remains on this list is entirely up to you, of course," the Frenchman said. "But my decision is final."

He wasn't sure what to say. Why was Fortier telling him this? Unless he intended to trust him after all. Or was he telling him to earn Carlos's loyalty so that he could ultimately eliminate him with ease?

"This isn't . . ." Carlos stopped. Pointing out the obvious would do him no favors. Fortier was going to wipe out most of Islam—it could hardly be Allah's will.

"You're concerned with Islam," Fortier said. "I assure you that the book contains the names of your most respected imams."

"And they agree with your plan?"

"They will be given that opportunity."

Yes, of course. "It's prudent. Bold. It solves everything."

Fortier studied him, then finally smiled. "I hoped you would see it that way."

"And the exchange?" Carlos asked.

"Still critical. We aren't out of the woods yet. There's always the possibility that they will find an antivirus in time. Once we have their weapons, their destruction is ensured."

Carlos paced to the end of the table. "You do realize how dangerous this list is. How many know?"

"Ten, including you. None of them have the antivirus yet."

A stray thought suddenly flashed through Carlos's mind. Svensson was key to the antivirus—he'd undoubtedly ensured his survival by manipulating the antivirus in a way only he knew. He'd claimed as much two weeks earlier, and Carlos didn't doubt him. If Svensson was killed, the antivirus would die with him. Though they already had stockpiles of the remedy, surely Svensson had developed a plan for this contingency as well.

Take Svensson.

That was the thought.

Until the antivirus was widely distributed, Svensson might be the more powerful of the pair. Controlling him meant controlling more than Carlos could imagine.

"You will remain here until after the exchange has been completed," Fortier continued. "We need full pressure to bear on the American president through these riots. It is now your highest priority. After the exchange I want this facility leveled."

"And the assassinations?"

"As planned, depending on how well they behave."

———

Armand Fortier watched the door close behind the man from Cyprus and wondered if he had made a mistake by showing him the list. But he needed the man's full cooperation these last few days, and there was no better way than engendering his complete trust. Killing him now, before they had control of the nuclear arsenals, was too risky. Who knew what self-protective measures Carlos had in place even now?

His cell phone vibrated in his pocket. He slipped it out and glanced at the number. A paging code.

Fortier walked to a red phone on the wall and began the tedious process of making an overseas call through secure channels. He'd talked to the man only once before, and the conversation had lasted less than ten seconds. The CIA director had proven invaluable and earned his life. Little did he know . . .

The call finally connected.

"Grant."

"Speak quickly."

Pause.

"I have reason to believe that my contact has been compromised."

Contact? Carlos.

"The man from Cyprus."

"Yes," the American said.

"You're certain?"

"No. But they're trying to reach him."

"How?"

"Through Hunter's dreams."

Dreams. The one unanticipated element in all of this. Fortier still wasn't sure he believed the nonsense. There were alternative explanations that, however unlikely themselves, made more sense than this mystical pap.

"Operations as normal," Fortier said.

"Yes sir."

"He must not learn that you suspect him."

"Understood."

⁂

"What time is it?"

"Almost six," Dr. Bancroft said. "PM."

They'd slept about three hours.

Kara sat up and glanced at their arms, which were still taped together. She looked at Thomas. "We did it."

"So far so good. We're alive and free."

"And Johan is dreaming."

"Hopefully."

Bancroft reached across Thomas and carefully unwound the tape from their arms. "Johan is dreaming," he said. "Tell me this is good news for us. Here, I mean."

"It's as good as it gets for now. What Carlos does is now up to him." Thomas swung his feet to the floor and took a moist antiseptic towelette from the doctor.

"Incredible," Kara said. "I mean, this is absolutely incredible!"

"It gets more real each time. Three or four times and you don't know which is really real."

"Honestly, if I didn't know better, I'd say that this is the dream," she said.

"It might be," Thomas replied.

"I've always wondered what it would be like to live in a dream," Dr. Bancroft said with a shallow smile.

"Until you understand that there are other realities beyond this one and actually experience one of them, this is as real as it gets, Doctor. My father used to say we fight not against the things of this world, but against . . . I can't place the exact quote, but it was spiritual. Trust me, Doctor, you're not living in a dream."

He rubbed an itch under his arm. Bancroft followed his fingers, then looked in his eyes.

"Just a rash," Thomas said. "Probably something I picked up in Indonesia."

He stood and walked toward the desk phone. "Do you mind stepping out for a moment, Doctor? I have a call to make."

Dr. Myles Bancroft left reluctantly, but he left. Thomas dialed the White House and waited while they patched him through. The president was sleeping, but he'd left instruction to wake him when Thomas called.

"Thomas. You dreamed?" His voice sounded worn.

"I dreamed, sir."

"And Johan?"

"If you don't mind, in person. The line may be clear, but—"

"Of course. The chopper's already there on standby."

Thomas nodded. "Things are moving forward?" Meaning was Gains on his way to Israel?

"Yes. But we're down to two days—"

"Excuse me, sir, but not on the phone."

"We may have another problem. The demonstrations are starting to look ugly."

"Bring in the army."

"I already have. It's not my safety that concerns me. It's public sentiment. If this goes badly, my hand may be forced."

"I need more time."

"And I need to find out what's happening—"

"As soon as I dream again, I'll know," Thomas said.

The president was silent. He was extending himself on Thomas's behalf. If his gamble to play the cards as Thomas had suggested failed, several billion people would lose their lives.

Then again, what choice did he really have?

"Get here as quickly as you can," the president said and hung up.

25

Thomas walked in slow circles around Johan, mining his friend for information about Carlos. But this first experience had been so shocking that most of the information was pushed aside by the raw experience of living vicariously through another mind.

They'd been at it for half an hour. Apart from Johan's insistence that Carlos knew nothing about the blank Book and his repeated exclamations about how incredible the dream had been, they'd concluded nothing. With each passing minute Johan's memory was deteriorating.

"Yes, yes, I know," Thomas said. "Indescribable. But what I need to find out is whether Fortier intends to go through with the exchange, antivirus for weapons, as agreed."

"No."

"No? You said—"

"I mean yes," Johan said. "The exchange, yes, but the antivirus you receive won't be effective. I think. Does it make any sense?"

"Yes. You're sure?"

"Quite." Johan blinked. "So at this very moment you, this other Thomas, are sleeping in this palace called the White House? You are dreaming of yourself. But Carlos isn't dreaming about me. I'm real."

"And so am I." Thomas waved him off. "Don't try to figure it out. Tell me about Carlos's plans. Do you think he can be turned?"

"Maybe. He was responsive to my suggestions. Immediately, in fact. Especially if he were to come here as me, like you suggest. He's already given to mystical ideas. And there was something about a book of names. The Frenchman is planning something no one expects."

"He is? And you wait this long to tell me? What?"

"It just occurred to me. And I'm not sure what. Something with the people he plans to give the antivirus to. It's not what everyone thinks. Fewer."

"I knew it!" Thomas spit. "He's bluffing! That's it, isn't it?"

"I think so, yes. Svensson is the key. I don't know why, but Carlos was thinking of him."

"I don't remember Rachelle ever being this forgetful when she dreamed," Thomas said.

"My expertise is battle, not dreams."

"You're every bit as smart as she was. You're just distracted by your own enthusiasm. Like a kid who's lost his mind over a ride."

Johan smiled. "It was a wild ride! I never would have believed if I hadn't experienced it myself. I want to go back again."

"Just remember, now that you have no doubts about your connection to Carlos, his fate may very well be yours. We have to be very careful. If Carlos slips and shows his hand, they'll deal . . ."

The clopping of hooves on the rocks turned his attention. Four horses trotted around the corner. Cain and Stephen. An albino Thomas didn't recognize. And a Scab.

A Scab?

"We found them on top of the cliffs," Cain said, pulling his horse up. "Qurong sends them with a message."

Thomas immediately abandoned all thoughts of Johan and Carlos. The Scab was dressed in a warrior's leathers, but he carried no weapon.

"This is Simion," Cain said, referring to the albino. He dropped from his mount. "He was taken captive several months ago and has been held in the lower dungeons."

Thomas hurried to the thin man and helped him from his horse. He clasped the man's arms in a greeting. "Thank Elyon. We didn't know where to find you. Are there others?" He turned to Johan. "Some fruit and water, quickly."

Simion beamed. He was missing a tooth, and Thomas knew that a boot or a fist had probably taken it out. "Sit, sit." He helped the man sit. "Are there others?"

"Only me," Simion said softly.

Thomas looked at the Scab, who was glancing about furtively. "Help our guest off his horse and give him some fruit."

"Dismount," William ordered.

The Scab stepped down tentatively. "I am unarmed," he said. "My only purpose is to take your response back to my commander, Woref."

"And what is Woref's question?" Thomas asked.

The Scab looked at Simion, who stood unsteadily.

"Qurong has issued a decree," he said.

Mikil stepped in and offered the man her hand. He waved it off.

"Qurong has declared that unless Thomas of Hunter returns to his captivity within three days, he will drown his daughter, Chelise, for treason."

No one spoke. Thomas's mind spun. Chelise was no more guilty of treason than . . .

She'd allowed him to dream.

He faced Johan. "Would he drown his own daughter?"

"I can assure you that he will," the Scab insisted.

Johan frowned. "What matter of treason is this?"

"He wouldn't say," Simion said. "Only that Thomas of Hunter would know."

They looked at him. "She allowed me to dream," he said absently. "Surely no man, not even Qurong, would kill his own daughter for allowing a prisoner to dream."

"No," Johan said. "I agree; there must be more. This is Woref's doing."

"But why would they think such an absurd demand would be of any concern to us?" William demanded.

Immediately Thomas knew.

"Cain. Stephen. Keep our guests company," he ordered. He caught Suzan's stare. "I call a council."

"For what?" William demanded. "This is a simple matter."

"Then our meeting will be short. A woman's life is at stake. We won't dismiss the matter without proper consideration."

He turned his back on them and walked down the canyon, around a bend, and to a patch of bare sand shaded by the towering cliffs. Conflicting emotions collided in his chest.

He ran a hand through his hair and paced. He had no call to feel so concerned for this one woman. Chelise. A woman he hardly knew. A woman who had thumbed her nose at the tribes and was complicit in the hunt for them. Qurong's own daughter! The others would never understand.

"If I didn't know better," William said behind him, "I would say you had feelings for this woman."

Thomas faced them. They stood in a rough circle around him, Johan, William, Mikil, Jamous, and Suzan.

"My feelings for her are no different than Justin's feelings for you, William," he said. "She is his creation as much as you are."

William looked at a loss. "You're actually considering Qurong's demand?"

"What's the use of a council if we don't discuss our options?" Thomas shouted. "You've made a decision already—that isn't our way."

They stood in the echo of his voice.

"He's right," Suzan said. "A woman's life is at stake."

"A Scab's life."

"Suzan is right," Mikil said. "Although I tend to agree with William about the life of a Scab, we should hear Thomas out. We were all Scabs once."

She sat. The others followed. It was long ago decided that sitting was the preferred posture if any argument was likely to break out.

"Elyon, we ask for your mind," Mikil said in the traditional manner. "Let us see as you see."

"So be it," the rest agreed in unison.

William took a settling breath. "Forgive me for my impulsive response. I am impatient to return to the tribe. They are vulnerable without us." He took a deep breath. "You're right, Mikil. We were once Scabs ourselves. But risking Thomas's life for the daughter of Qurong, who will continue to live in defiance of Elyon, is not only unwise but may be immoral."

"Perhaps Thomas should explain himself first," Suzan said.

They looked at him expectantly. And what was he supposed to say? *I think I may have fallen in love with a Scab princess?* The suddenness of the thought shocked him. No. He should say nothing at all about love.

"I want it to be clear that I haven't fallen in love with a Scab princess." He cleared his throat. "But I will admit that she gained my trust while I was with her in the library."

"Trust?" Johan said. "I wouldn't trust any daughter of Qurong's."

"Then call it empathy," Thomas snapped back. "I can't explain how I feel, only that I do. She doesn't deserve her own deception."

"Yet it is hers," Mikil said. "We're all free to make a choice, and she's made hers."

"That doesn't mean she can't choose differently. She's a person, like any one of us!"

His statement rang too loudly for the small canyon.

"No, Thomas, she's not like any one of us," William said. "She's a Scab. I never would have believed I would hear these words coming from you. Your emotions are clouding your judgment. Get ahold of yourself, man!"

"And what about Justin's emotions?" Suzan asked. "Wasn't it his love that led to his own drowning?"

Several spoke at once, and their words were a jumbled mess to Thomas. Like his own feelings. He wasn't sure how he felt. Emotions weren't trustworthy; they all knew that. On the other hand, Suzan asked a good question. How would Justin see this?

He held up his hand for silence. They quieted. "If Ronin were here, we would defer to his judgment. I admit, the thought of this woman's death sickens me, but I will defer to the judgment of this council. I have no argument except for my own emotions, which I've expressed. William, explain your doctrine."

William dipped his head. "Thank you. I have three points that will guide us. One, as to Suzan's question about Justin's emotions, it is said that Elyon is lovesick over his bride. This we all know. We also know that we, the Circle, are his bride. He told us as much in the desert. The Horde is not his bride."

He glanced around, received no objection, and continued.

"Two, the disease, which can only be washed clean by the drowning, is an offense to Elyon. Some say that anything a Scab touches is unclean, though I wouldn't go so far. But a Scab is certainly unclean. To embrace such a wretched creature who has embraced filth is to embrace the filth itself."

"Justin embraced me when I was a Scab," Johan said.

"That was before the drowning was available. In fact, that is why he provided the drowning, so that we could cure the disease. You're saying it makes no difference if we're clean or not? He would never have gone to such lengths if it made no difference."

There was some logic to William's argument, but it didn't sit well with Thomas. He didn't trust himself to speak.

"He hates the disease," Suzan said, "but not the man or woman beneath it."

"Is that why the Book states that he will burn any branch that does not remain in him and bear fruit?" William demanded. "I am the vine, you are the branches, but see what happens to those branches that are fruitless."

That shut them up.

"And finally, if this is not enough, consider Elyon's anger toward those who refuse him. Would you trade yourself for Teeleh, Thomas? Or for a Shataiki? Are the Scabs less deceived than they are? I would say to give yourself to or for any Scab woman is no less offensive than embracing the Shataiki and would invoke Elyon's anger."

The argument was so offensive that none of them seemed able to engage it properly. Instead of finding any encouragement to do what he now knew must be done, Thomas felt his desperation deepen. He could feel his pulse in his ears.

"You all know that I disagree with William," Johan said. "At the last council I argued that we should embrace the Horde by becoming more like them. But this is different. The Circle needs you, Thomas. Your tribe needs you. Many more of the Horde will come to the Circle through your leadership than this one woman."

Thomas looked at the others. Mikil remained quiet, as did Jamous. Not even Suzan objected to Johan's statement.

"This is the council's decision?"

No one spoke.

He stood. "So be it."

Thomas walked from them, rounded the corner, and marched toward the waiting Scab.

"Thomas!" Mikil ran to catch up. "Thomas, please, she's a Scab, for heaven's sake," she whispered. "Let it go."

"I am letting it go!" he snapped.

He stopped in front of the Scab. "Go tell your general that Thomas of Hunter will no more agree to his ridiculous terms than he will drink his own blood." The least he could do for Chelise was to send a clear message to Qurong that he despised his daughter. "And tell Qurong that what he does with his daughter is his business. Now leave us."

The Scab hesitated, then mounted quickly, turned his horse around, and trotted up the canyon.

26

They left the valley in single file and headed across the desert toward the Southern Forest. Thomas's sullen mood had smothered the group. Mikil and Johan had tried to lighten his disposition with talk of the dreams, but he quickly reminded them that there was little hope of surviving in the dreams more than a week. He might be better off eating the rhambutan fruit every night for the rest of his life and forgetting the histories even existed. They finally left him to sulk on his own.

William led and Thomas brought up the rear, behind Suzan, who had consoled him with a kind smile. The horses plodded up the sandy dunes with no more than an occasional snort to clear dust from their nostrils.

With each step Thomas felt his heart sink deeper into his gut. Try as he might, he couldn't lift his own spirits. There was no reason to these emotions he battled. None at all. He told himself this much a hundred times over.

She's a Scab covered by disease, Thomas. Her breath smells like sulfur, and her mind is clouded by deception. She would more likely order your death than drown in a red pool.

Then why this inexorable attraction to her? Surely he didn't love her as a man loved a woman. How could he love any woman after losing Rachelle only thirteen months ago? How could any woman, much less this diseased whore, replace Rachelle?

The file was moving faster than he was, but rather than urging his mount to catch them, he slowed even more. Their decision to sentence Chelise to her death had separated them from him.

It's your shame that holds you back. Or is it protest?

Either way, falling behind seemed appropriate. They glanced back but let him have his space. He was soon a full dune behind them.

Only then, when he was out of their sight completely, did he begin to feel at ease. He let images of her fill his mind without regret.

Chelise staring up at him on the ladder, arms folded as he looked frantically through the Books of Histories.

Chelise repeating the words she'd written, wild-eyed with excitement.

Chelise crushed by her inability to put a full sentence together.

Take the disease from her skin and the deception from her mind and what kind of woman would she be? What prince would be worthy of this princess?

"Hello, Thomas."

He jerked up on his horse. But there was no one. He was next to a lone rock formation between two dunes, alone. No sight of the others. The sun was getting to his mind.

"Over here, my old friend."

Thomas twisted around to the sound of the voice. There, on a small rock behind him, stood a bat.

A white bat. A Roush.

"Michal?"

The animal's furry snout smiled wide. "One and the same."

"It's . . . it's really you? I haven't seen . . ." He trailed off.

"You haven't seen a Roush in a long time, yes, I know. That doesn't mean we're not here. I've been watching you. I must say, you've done well. Much better than I guessed publicly before all the others, though I hate to admit it."

Thomas spilled off his horse and ran toward the bat. He wanted to throw his arms around the creature's neck and tell Michal how good it was to see him. Instead he slid to a stop three paces from Michal and gawked like a schoolboy.

"It's . . . You're really here . . ." Thomas finally stammered.

"In the flesh. Although I would prefer that you keep our meeting to yourself."

Thomas sank to his knees, partially out of weakness, partially to match the shorter creature's height. "I'm sorry. I don't know what's happening to me."

"But I do."

Thomas took a deep breath. "Then tell me."

"She's come over you," Michal said.

Thomas stood. How much did Michal know? "Who?"

"Chelise. The princess."

"I empathize with her, if that's what you mean. She's doesn't deserve to die. We spent time together in the library, and she may be a Scab, but she's not what I expected any Scab to be. Surely Elyon can have mercy on even—"

"You call this empathy?" Michal asked. "I would call it love."

"No. No, it's not like that."

"Then perhaps it should be," Michal said.

Thomas stared at the Roush, dumbstruck. "What do you mean? She's a Scab."

"And so were you. But he doesn't see it that way."

"Justin?"

"Justin."

Thomas glanced up the dune at the trail left by the others. "But the doctrine . . ."

"Then you must have your doctrine wrong. Tell me what William said."

Why had Michal chosen this moment to reveal himself? Hope began to swell in Thomas's chest.

"The Circle is his bride. He's lovesick over the Circle."

"True enough, but he's wooing his bride even now," Michal said. "Believe me, if you were to see Justin now, he would be over there by those rocks, pacing with his hands in his hair, desperate to win the love of the Horde. They will be his bride as much as you."

Thomas looked at the rocks and imagined Justin pacing. His heart began to pound.

"What else did William say?" the Roush asked.

"That Elyon's anger toward those who refuse him must be appeased by the drowning before we can embrace them."

Michal frowned. "I would have guessed that after Justin's death you would understand him better. Elyon's anger is directed toward anything that hinders his love. Toward Teeleh and the Shataiki who would deceive and steal that love. Anything that hinders his bride's love, he detests."

"Not the Scab."

"I'm not saying that I understand it—Elyon is beyond my mind. But his love is boundless. Do you know that when you drown, he's made a covenant to forget your disease? He remembers only your love. Even when you stumble as William does now, Justin vows to forget and remembers only William's love, however imperfect it might be. To say that you humans have it made would be an understatement. I would set William straight, to be sure. Elyon is mostly thrilled. Yes, there is a price to pay. Yes, there is a drowning to be done, but he is thrilled with his bride and desperate to woo others into his Circle."

Thomas knew all of this; of course he did! But not quite in such blatant terms.

"If you were to glimpse Justin's love for Chelise, you would wither where you stand," Michal said with a small grin. "This is the Great Romance."

Thomas began to pace. This meant what? That he was right about Chelise being like any other woman, Scab or not? That he was right in wanting to save her? That any love he might feel for Chelise was no different from his love for Rachelle?

But how could he possibly love a Scab in the same way he'd loved Rachelle? No, Michal couldn't possibly mean that.

"Follow your heart, Thomas. Justin's showing you his own."

Justin's words to him returned. He lifted his head and stared out at the desert and let the truth flood his mind. This was beyond him. He did love Chelise. She might not love him, but he couldn't deny the simple fact that he loved her, more than he could remember loving anyone other than Rachelle.

"Thomas!"

He turned to the dune. Suzan stood on the crest looking down at him. She hadn't seen Justin earlier; did she see Michal now?

He spun. The Roush was gone!

"Thomas, the others are waiting," Suzan called.

He stood still, torn for a long moment. Then he knew what he would do. What he must do.

He ran to his horse and leaped onto its back. With a parting glance at Suzan, he whirled his mount around and galloped away from her, toward the forest.

"Thomas! Wait!"

He crested the first dune and plunged down the far side.

"Thomas, wait! I'm with you!"

Suzan was following. He pulled the horse to a stamping halt. She galloped up behind him.

"I'm going back for her."

"Then we're both going back for her," she said.

"I can't ask you to do that."

"You taught me to live for danger. And although no one knows it, I'm a sap for romance."

The dunes behind her were bare. The others would see their tracks and know what had happened. Hopefully they would keep their senses and continue to the tribe, where they were needed.

"Then we have to hurry." He spurred his horse. "We have to get to her before the messenger does."

"You're not going to turn yourself in?"

"I'm going to take her out of there."

They sprinted over the dune. "What if she refuses to go?"

"Then I'll have to persuade her, won't I?" he said with a wide grin.

———⚬❀⚬———

The tracks told the story plainly enough.

"The fool's gone back," William said.

"And Suzan with him," Mikil said.

Johan turned next to the dune. "He doesn't plan on turning himself in, or he wouldn't have allowed Suzan to follow. He's going after Chelise." It was beyond him, this obsession that Thomas had developed for Qurong's daughter. He'd known her as a spirited woman, beautiful among Scabs, but still a Scab, as diseased as any.

He'd argued that the Circle should relax its standards to make it easier for the Horde to turn, but he'd been thinking about the drowning, not love. Now he wondered if he had it backward. Perhaps they should remain rigid on the commitments required to enter the Circle but love the Horde regardless. In many ways what Thomas was doing now would test his own arguments. Would Thomas become a Scab, or would Chelise become an albino?

Or were their conditions irreconcilable?

"We have to stop them!" Mikil said.

"And how would you do that?" William asked. "Follow them all the way back into the dungeons?"

"We wait for them," Johan said. "Here."

"We can't leave the tribe alone so long."

"Then *I* will wait for them."

Mikil looked at her husband. "Jamous?"

"We wait with Johan." He turned to William. "Take Cain and Stephen with you."

William sighed. "I don't like it. The Circle is in trying times, and its leaders are risking their necks for a whore."

"You need some enlightenment, William," Johan snapped. "This is Thomas, the same man who saved your neck a dozen times."

William frowned and guided his mount around. "Then we'll see you at the tribe. Elyon's strength."

Johan nodded. "Elyon's strength."

More!" Thomas insisted. "I want to pass inspection at five paces."

"Then you'll have to grow scales," Suzan said. They'd stolen the morst paste and powder with some clothes after dark, from a house on the city's perimeter. Thomas had his shirt off and was caking the powder on. Suzan rubbed it onto his back. "It'll be dark and you'll have a veiled hood on. I really don't see the need to be so enthusiastic about this stuff."

"The smell!" He turned to her, wide-eyed, like a child. His passion for this mission was infectious. The others would think he'd flipped his lid if they saw the way he'd carried on throughout the day.

He hadn't flipped his lid. He was losing his heart. He might not admit it, but Suzan would recognize these signs with her eyes closed. Thomas of Hunter was going down a road that he had deliberately skirted since Rachelle's death. He was in the early stages of falling crazily in love. Watching him, Suzan felt a yearning for the same.

He was still doing his best to hide his emotions, or perhaps he wasn't really sure what to make of his emotions, but he couldn't help himself. He'd told her what had happened between him and Chelise at the library in far more detail than any man she knew ever would. He talked expressively, with grand arm movements, drawing irrational conclusions about the simplest exchanges.

"Her arms were folded, Suzan," he would say. "Imagine that!"

"I am imagining it. I'm not sure I get the significance."

"Folded! She knows very well that when she stands like that she's striking a seductive pose."

"Arms folded? I'm not sure—"

"It's not the arms. Forget the arms. It's everything about her. You'll see."

Now he was plastering morst on his face, talking of smell. "I want to smell Horde. I've done it before, right into Qurong's bedchamber while he was snoring like a dragon." He grabbed another handful and slapped it against his cheek. The white residue billowed about his head.

"This time it's into her chamber, and I have a feeling she'll be more sensitive than her father. The morst won't cover my albino scent if it's only on my face, now, will it?"

"If I didn't know you better, I'd say you want to become a Scab for more than sneaking into the castle. You're wanting to be like her!"

"Am I? Well, maybe there was a hint of truth to Johan's arguments. I'm becoming a Scab to rescue a Scab from being a Scab."

Suzan laughed. "One look at you and she'll know you're not a Scab. There's no hiding your true colors—that's where Johan's wrong."

He stood and turned in the moonlight. "Agreed. How do I look?"

"Like a Scab." This was a Thomas few had ever seen. To most he was the mighty warrior turned introspective philosopher. But here in the desert he was becoming Thomas the lover. Suzan grinned. She rather liked this hidden side of him.

Thomas leaped for the robe and pulled it over his head.

"Good?" he asked.

"Good. Definitely Scab."

"Well then. I think I'm ready. It'll take me an hour to reach the castle from here, and an hour back. Give me till daybreak. If I'm not back, use your better judgment." He climbed onto his horse.

He was riding into insanity to fetch a woman who, despite his misguided assumptions, did not love him. And Suzan was enabling him because she knew that once Thomas of Hunter put his mind to something, he always saw it through. That and the romance in her own spirit was cheering him on.

All fine and good, but what if he didn't come back? He'd drawn her along with his infectious passion, but what if it all went badly? If Thomas was dead by morning, she would share the blame.

"Be careful, Thomas. It'll be the lake, not the library, if you get caught."

"I know." He gazed north, toward the city. "Am I doing the right thing?"

"Do you love her?"

"Yes."

"Then go get her, Thomas of Hunter. We've said all there is to say."

He smiled and nodded. "Elyon's strength."

"Elyon's strength."

<hr />

Thomas approached the city from the east, around the royal garden, down the less-traveled road that ran directly to the castle. A bright moon had risen overhead. If anyone spoke to him, he would respond with a dipped head. With any luck he wouldn't have to test his impersonation of a Scab.

The castle rose to his right, tall in the moonlight. He let the horse have its head—this was familiar ground for the animal. He could feel the sweat gathering under the robe, mixing with the morst.

What if she won't come, Thomas?

Suzan had asked the question, and in his enthusiasm he'd assured her that Chelise would come. But he wasn't so sure now. In fact, thinking through his task clearly now, he realized that getting into her room would be the easiest part. Getting Chelise out of her own accord might be far more difficult.

The road was still empty. So far so good. It occurred to him that the single greatest advantage he had was the Circle's policy of nonviolence. The Horde had no real enemies to threaten their security. Their defenses weren't built for an assault, and the penalty for simple crimes, such as theft, were so severe that few Scabs ever attempted them. He'd heard that any infraction against the royal house was punishable by death to the perpetrator's entire family.

The guard around the castle surely had been increased since his escape, but they weren't accustomed to the kind of stealth the Circle had perfected. At least that was Thomas's hope. If the weak performance of their guards yesterday was any measure, he had good reason to hope.

He turned into the forest before he came to any guard on the road. He swung his leg back into a reasonable riding position and guided the horse through the trees, toward the stables behind the castle. The mare snorted at the scent of her familiar pen.

"Easy, girl."

He slipped to the ground and tied the animal to a branch. Light from the castle's back rooms filtered through the trees despite the midnight hour. Hopefully they were torches that burned all night.

Twigs crunched underfoot, but no guards detected the noise. Thomas hurried around the stables. Chelise had told him that her bedroom faced the city on the top floor. He'd seen the stairs that led to the roof during the last escape. He hurried to the fence that surrounded the grounds and peered between the poles.

No guard.

This was it. Once over, he was committed. He gripped the top of the pole, took a deep breath, and vaulted.

"Who goes?"

Thomas was still airborne, dropping to the ground like a parachute, when the voice cut through the night air. Close.

He landed on both feet and stared at a guard ten feet to his right. The warrior had been stationed by the fence.

Thomas lowered his head and walked toward the castle as if nothing at all was unusual about a Scab dropping out of the sky.

"Stop! What's the meaning of this?"

Thomas halted and faced the warrior again, mind spinning through options. More accurately, option. Singular.

The guard had to go. Chelise's life depended on it.

He walked toward the guard, head down. Five paces, he thought.

"Stop there!"

Thomas replied in a high pitch. "The general, Woref, told me to meet him here."

"The general?"

"I am his concubine."

"His . . ."

Thomas moved before the man could process his shocking claim. He dove to his right, rolled once, and came up three feet to the guard's right. The man spun, broad blade flashing.

Thomas let his momentum carry him into a roundhouse kick. His foot connected solidly with the man's temple.

One grunt and the man fell like a sack of rocks.

"Forgive me," Thomas whispered. He dropped to his knee, ripped the guard's sleeve at the shoulder, and hog-tied him, hands-to-feet behind his back. He tore off the other sleeve and gagged his mouth tightly.

Thomas ran toward the building and flew up the stairs. He spilled onto the roof and crouched behind the railing. Had he torn his garment? He checked, catching his breath. All intact, as far as he could tell.

Speed was now an issue. The guard would wake soon enough and, even bound, might be able to raise enough of a fuss to draw attention.

Thomas ran toward the only stairwell he could see. He pushed the latch on the door. Locked. He studied the latch. It was forest technology. His own design.

He'd designed the lock to secure a door against strong winds, not thieves. A simple bronze bolt held the entire assembly in place. He pulled the pin free. The latch fell into his hand. He set it down and eased the door open.

Dim light filled a narrow stairwell. He slipped in, closed the door behind him, and stood very still.

No sound. The castle slept.

Thomas eased down the steps, pausing with each creak. They may have used forest technology, but the craftsmanship had been hurried.

At the bottom, a balcony ran the perimeter of the top floor. In front of him, a single torch burned between two doors. If he was right, one led to Chelise's bedroom. Only one way to find out which.

He poked his head over the railing, saw the courtyard below was empty, and hurried toward the first door.

Again locked.

Again his design.

Again he dislodged the bolt.

He stepped into the room and pulled the door shut. An oil lamp cast dim light over a large bed. She was in the bed, asleep! Thomas took in the rest of the room with a glance. Doors that led to another balcony. A large armoire on which the lamp sat. A desk with mirror. Long flowing drapes. Horde royalty.

The moment of truth had arrived. If this wasn't Chelise, he might be forced to hog-tie yet one more Scab.

He crept to the bed and leaned over the form under the blanket. She slept with the sheets over her head? He had to see her face to be sure, but the thought of unveiling her while she slept . . .

The floor creaked behind. Something struck his head. He fell forward onto the sleeping form and scrambled to right himself.

The object struck him again, square on the back. This time he grunted.

It occurred to him them, midgrunt, that the form under him wasn't a body at all. Pillows.

The third blow hit his head, and for a moment he thought he might pass out. He managed to find his voice. "It's me! It's Thomas!"

His assailant stopped long enough for Thomas to roll over. There, in the orange lamplight, stood a fully clothed woman.

"Thomas?"

"Chelise!" He sat up, head throbbing. "What are you doing?"

"What do you mean, what am I doing!" she whispered. "I'm defending myself."

"I'm here to help you, not attack you."

Chelise held an unlit torch in her hands. She glanced at the door. "How did you get in here? You've come to turn yourself in?"

"No. No, I can't do that."

"Why not? Your escape has landed me in a terrible position. I've been expecting that beast to barge in here all night. I was told that you denied Qurong's demand."

So it was all true. She understood that her life was in danger.

"If I turn myself in, they'll kill me. Would you want that?"

She lowered the torch.

Thomas stood and faced her. They looked at each other for the first time since she'd last left him in the library. Her face looked beautiful by the lamp's flame.

Thomas stepped toward her and started to lift his hand to her face, then thought better of it. "I've come to rescue you."

"I don't need rescuing. What I need is for you to turn yourself in to Qurong so that we can put this madness behind us. I should call the guard right now."

Her dismissal sent a shaft of pain through his chest. His face flushed hot. "Then call the guard."

"Keep your voice down. You look ridiculous in that morst."

"You prefer me without it?"

She walked to her desk, set the torch down, and stared into the mirror, which showed nothing in this dim light.

She hadn't called the guard.

"Listen to me, Chelise. You know as well as I do that whatever life you thought you had in this castle is over. Woref will destroy you. If you survive by turning me in, that beast, as you call him, will give you a living death. And if you refuse to cower under his fist, he'll kill you."

"None of this would have happened without you," she shot back. "Without you Woref wouldn't be such a pig, and without you I wouldn't be put in this terrible position to choose."

"Then at least you see that you do have a choice."

"Between what? Between an animal and an albino? What kind of choice is that?"

He ignored the bite in her words. "Then don't choose either of us. Leave this place and negotiate with your father from a position of strength."

The notion stalled her. When she spoke again, the edge in her voice had softened. "If I leave with you, Woref would never forgive me."

"You won't leave with me. I'll take you by force."

She laughed. "By force? As your prisoner. How can I negotiate with Qurong as your prisoner?"

"We'll think of something. I'll tell Qurong that I want Woref in exchange for you. Something like that. And what would Woref do to possess you?"

"Anything."

"Exactly. Anything. You see, by leaving you can force their hands. If you stay, your life will be a mess, even if you turn me in."

A faint smile crossed her face.

"But you have to understand that I have . . ."

How to say this? He suddenly wished he hadn't spoken.

"What?" she demanded.

"That I think I do have feelings for you," Thomas said. "I can see you feel differently, but I wouldn't feel right taking you out of here without being completely honest about my intentions."

This time she didn't laugh. "Which are what? To win my love? Then let me be honest with you. I know how you albinos look at us. You find us repulsive. Our breath smells and our skin sickens you. I don't know what kind of adolescent notion has climbed inside your head, but you and I could never be lovers."

"We could if you drowned."

"Never."

Thomas wondered then if he'd made a terrible mistake. But Michal had told him to follow his heart, and his heart was for this woman. Wasn't it? The thought of leaving her terrified him, so yes. His heart was certainly for this woman.

"I don't mean to hurt you," she was saying. She'd seen his pain. "I'm sorry. But you have your life and I have mine. I'm attracted to men like me. Men with my flesh."

"Okay."

"Then you understand?"

"I understand. I don't accept. I think I've seen more in your eyes."

"Even if there was, I could not act on it." She stared at him without speaking, then walked to her wardrobe.

"What are you doing?" he asked.

"I'm getting what I'll need for a trip to the desert."

"Then you're coming?"

"As long as you agree to bring me back in exchange for a demand of my choosing."

"Yes. Agreed." He suddenly felt antsy again. "You don't need anything. We have to hurry."

"A woman needs what a woman needs," she said, quickly placing several items in a leather bag. "There's a tub of morst and some paste on the dresser."

"Do you really—"

"It's the scented kind I wore in the library. Trust me, you'll be glad I brought it."

Thomas scooped up the small tub. She walked over and opened her bag. They exchanged a long stare, and he could swear that he was right. There was more behind those eyes than she admitted.

Or maybe not.

"Lead the way," she said.

⎯⎯⎯⎯

He'd been called to the castle in the middle of the night, cause for concern even in peaceful times. Considering the events of the last few days, Woref feared the worst.

This was to do with Chelise; he could feel it. He rode his horse down the street at a steady pace, but his blood was boiling already. There was no greater source of problems in the world than women. They loved and they killed, and even in their loving they killed. Man might do better to remove the temptation from the face of the earth. What good was love at such a terrible price?

He dismounted, walked into the foyer, and drew back his hood.

"Woref." Qurong waited just inside the courtyard. "So glad my trusted general could make it."

Woref lowered his head in respect.

"I was just awakened by some very bad news," Qurong said. He was being too coy for this to be anything but horrible news. "One of your guards was found bound by the back fence."

Thievery?

"He said that a man pretending to speak like a woman dropped over the fence, claimed to be your concubine, and knocked him out. A little while later, he returned with another woman and knocked him out again."

"I assure you, sir, he's lying. I have no concubine."

"I don't care about your lies, General! The second woman was my daughter. Chelise is gone!" He said it slowly and with a trembling voice.

"How—"

"The first 'woman' was Thomas, you idiot!"

"Thomas of Hunter," Woref said. "He took her." Or did she go willingly?

"The guard said she was being forced. Thomas told him to relay that his demand would be forthcoming. He will release Chelise when we comply."

She's gone willingly, Woref thought. His face flushed but he didn't show his anger.

"Now it's your life at stake," the supreme leader said. "If one hair on my daughter's head is harmed, I will hold you responsible. You told her she would be drowned, knowing full well that I would never drown her. *You* said it would teach her a lesson, and *you* leaked a word to call Thomas's bluff. Now she's gone."

"We aren't without recourse, my lord. I've received word that my men are closing in on his tribe. He won't have the only bargaining chip."

Qurong looked at him skeptically.

"They're without their leaders," Woref said. "I've sent reinforcements. They can't escape an entire division."

"It's Chelise I want, not a pack of albinos!"

"You will have Chelise. But only if I will have her!"

Qurong scowled. "Find her!"

28

He tried, but he couldn't sleep. And he wouldn't dream, not until he had won her love, he decided. The virus would likely kill him in a few days' time in the other reality, and he couldn't allow that to interfere with this drama unfolding here. He would simply eat the rhambutan fruit every night. A week, a month, whatever it took. When he finally did dream, only hours would have passed where he now slept at the White House.

He leaned against the rock beside Suzan, gazing at Chelise, who slept ten yards from them.

"For goodness' sake, sleep, Thomas," Suzan whispered. "It'll be light soon."

"I'm not tired."

"You will be. And you're bothering me, sitting like that."

"You're jealous?"

"Of her? If you were another man, perhaps—no disrespect, but my heart is taken."

Surprise turned his full attention to Suzan. "Oh? You've never said anything."

"Some things are best kept quiet."

"Who is it?"

"I won't say. But you know him." She propped herself up on her elbow. "I have to say, though, this new Thomas is quite impressive."

"There's nothing new about me."

"I've never known you to lie awake gazing at a sleeping woman who doesn't love you. Or act so interested in who I love. I've always thought you cared more about swinging a sword than wooing a woman."

"Obviously you've never known me. I wooed Rachelle in the colored forest, didn't I?" He looked at the stars. "Those were the days when romance was thick in the air."

"I was too young to remember," she said quietly.

"Not anymore."

"So I take it you're giving in to this impulse," she said. "Wholeheartedly."

Thomas avoided a direct response. "We were born for the Great Romance."

"Of course."

"I am only following my heart."

"Maybe I could show you a few things myself, Sir Poet," Suzan said.

"Then reveal your man to us and let us watch how you court each other."

"Listen to you. You're even speaking like a poet."

He grinned. "Nonsense. I always wax eloquent. My word was once my sword, but now it's this song of love for the fair maiden who lies hither. Or is it thither?"

"I can see I'll have to teach you the finer points of poetry."

His eyes darted over to the sleeping woman, and he lowered his voice. "You want real poetry? Then hear this: I have lost my heart. It is owned by Chelise, this stunning creature who sleeps in peace. When she frowns I see a smile; when she scoffs I hear a laugh. We rode side by side for two hours, picking our way through the dark forest without a single word, but I heard her heart whispering words of love to me every time her horse put its hoof on the ground. I cannot sleep now because love is my sleep, and I've had enough to last a week. She pretends not to love me, because the disease has filled her with shame, but I can see past her eyes into her heart, where she betrays her true desires."

Suzan chuckled. "If even half of that is true, then you are smitten, Thomas of Hunter."

His grin faded and he diverted his eyes. "It is."

Chelise suddenly moved. Turned her head toward them. "Are you two going to talk all night? I'm trying to sleep."

Thomas blinked. "You're awake."

"And you're talking too much. I don't know how albinos court their women, but you might want to consider a little subtlety."

Silence filled the camp.

"She has a point," Suzan finally said.

"I . . . I didn't know you were listening." Chelise was smiling, he could see it in the dark. "Okay, then, I guess it's time to sleep." He lay down, unsure whether he should be embarrassed or thrilled that she'd heard him.

They lay quietly for a long time.

Then Chelise spoke quietly. "Thank you, Thomas. They were kind words."

He swallowed. "You're welcome."

She rolled over. "Just remember our agreement."

Yes, of course. Their agreement. He'd nearly forgotten.

⊶⊷

Chelise and Suzan let Thomas sleep as the sun rose. They'd both risen an hour earlier and decided that they could wait another hour before heading for the desert. The chance of any Scab stumbling upon them in the small canyon where they'd made camp was remote.

Suzan had bathed in a small creek nearby, and Chelise decided that she would bathe as well. She waited until Suzan was finished before cautiously slipping into the water. Although she'd grown accustomed to the ritual bathing in the lake, the cold water stung her skin.

If it weren't for Thomas, she would never bathe in a stream, but she felt compelled to present herself in a manner that wasn't offensive to the albinos. She bore the pain and washed her skin well. Then she carefully applied the scented morst using a small pool as a mirror. She picked several smaller tuhan flowers and placed the sweet-smelling blossoms in her hair. All of this for his sake.

And why, Chelise? Why are you so concerned about pleasing Thomas? She couldn't answer that question. Perhaps because he was so kind to her.

Albino or not, he was a man, and she could hardly ignore this mad affection he'd displayed by rescuing her.

Chelise faced Suzan, trying not to stare at her dark skin. So very different from her own white flesh. The pendant the albinos wore hung from her neck.

"Why do you wear the pendant?" she asked Suzan.

The albino lifted the medallion in her hand and looked at it. "These are the colors of the Circle. Green for the colored forest, then black for the evil that destroyed us all. Then red, you see?" She indicated the two crossing straps of red leather. "Justin's blood. And finally, a white circle."

"And why white?"

Suzan looked into her eyes. "White. We are Justin's bride."

Such an odd way of seeing things. Foolish even. Whoever heard of being the bride of a slain warrior? Of course, they believed he was still alive.

Absurd.

Chelise looked at Thomas. "Should we wake him?"

"I can't believe he's still sleeping." Suzan smiled. "You must have worn him out last night."

"Ha! I think he's wearing me out with all of his enthusiasm."

Suzan cinched down the extra saddle Thomas had brought from the city. "Do you feel anything for him?"

Chelise hadn't expected such a forward question. She didn't know what to say.

"There lies Thomas of Hunter, legend of the Forest Guard, and he's falling in love with you, daughter of his nemesis, Qurong. It's a fairy tale in the making."

"He's an albino," Chelise said.

Suzan put her hand on the saddle and faced her. "That doesn't mean he's too good for you."

"That's not what I meant."

"No, but it's what you feel. It's why you bathed and why you cover your skin for him. For the record, I agree with Thomas. I think you're quite beautiful. And I don't think you have any idea how fortunate you are to have this man love you."

Chelise felt suddenly choked up. She looked at Thomas. There lay the king of the albinos. Or was Justin their king? Despite his attempt to wipe it off, the morst Thomas had applied last night still caked parts of his face.

"It does feel good, though, doesn't it?" Suzan asked.

"What?"

"Being loved."

She hesitated. "Yes." She wasn't sure she'd ever felt so awkward. Was Thomas right in saying that she was covering her shame? And now Suzan had said the same thing. She'd never thought of it in those terms.

"I think you deserve it," Suzan said.

The knot in her throat grew, and she had to swallow to keep from crying. Where the sudden emotion had come from, she didn't know, but it wasn't the first time the albinos had affected her so easily. The lessons in the library with Thomas had been similar.

Chelise decided then, staring off into the forest so that Suzan couldn't see her fighting tears, that she liked albinos.

"Why don't you wake him?" Suzan said. "We should leave."

Chelise walked over to him, glad for the reprieve. "Wake up."

He grunted and rolled his head, still lost to the world. She glanced at Suzan, but the woman was busy saddling another horse.

She bent down and nudged him. "Wake up, Thomas."

He bolted up, looked around, then saw her and came to himself. He stood and brushed his cloak. "What time is it? You let me sleep?"

"You looked tired."

He glanced at Suzan, then studied Chelise. "I'll be right back," he said and hurried in the direction of the creek. This obsession the albinos had with cleanliness was interesting.

Thomas returned ten minutes later, beaming face clean of the morst. "I feel like a new man. No offense, but the stuff makes my skin itch."

"Really? I find it quite soothing."

"It suits you. The white flowers are a perfect complement."

She smiled. "Thank you." Did he really think she was beautiful, or was he patronizing her?

They mounted and headed south away from the city, toward the desert. Thomas led them along a game trail, far from any well-traveled routes.

—————

They rode without speaking for an hour, Suzan bringing up the rear. Chelise finally broke the silence.

"Did you dream well, Thomas?"

"I didn't dream at all. I ate the rhambutan."

"I thought you wanted to dream. I nearly lost my life over your dreaming."

"I've made a vow: no dreams while I'm with you."

She didn't know what he could possibly have in mind, but she didn't press for an explanation.

Thomas brought his horse closer to hers. "Have you decided what we should demand for your return?"

"We could trade me for Woref, like you suggested," she said. "You could turn him into an albino. That would serve the beast."

Thomas chuckled. "Unfortunately, the drowning only works if it's done willingly. Otherwise we would round up Scabs in bunches and shove them under, wouldn't we, Suzan?"

"It's been suggested," she said.

Chelise shuddered. "What an awful death that would be."

"Do I look dead?" Thomas asked. "Alive like you've never known." He stretched out his arm. "When I move my arm, no pain in my joints. And not just because I've grown used to it."

The thought of drowning terrified her. She had grown so accustomed to the pain in her own joints that she simply ignored it most of the time.

"We could demand sanctuary for your Circle," Chelise said.

"You'd do that?"

She shrugged. "Why not?"

"Suzan, I think she's warming up to us."

Just yesterday she would have responded with a cutting remark to set him straight. Any such comment felt silly now. She let it go.

"Maybe we should let my father stew for a day or two," Chelise said. "I am not in a position to blackmail him very often."

"Perfect. Then we'll wait a week."

"A week? I wouldn't know what to do with myself for a week out here."

"You'll ride with us."

"And where, exactly, are we riding?"

"I haven't decided yet," he said. "Away from the Horde. Out of danger. Would you like to visit our Circle?"

"No, no. I couldn't do that. They would be horrified by me! And I by them. Anywhere but one of your tribes."

He smiled. "Then we'll just head south. As long as I'm with you to keep you safe, and you're comfortable, we'll ride."

She couldn't look at him without feeling *un*comfortable. "Sounds fair."

The sun passed overhead and began its descent toward the western horizon. Suzan rode ahead several times to scout out the route, and at times Chelise wondered if Thomas and his lieutenant hadn't planned the lengthy disappearances so that Thomas could be left alone with her. Not that she minded.

He told her stories of his days as commander of the Forest Guard, and she reciprocated with memories of her days in the desert: how they made use of the desert wheat, where they found their water, what it was like to grow up playing with other children who weren't of royal blood.

He seemed especially taken by her stories of the children and asked dozens of questions about how they learned to cope with the disease, as he called it. He really did think of their skin condition as an abnormality. And, of course, it was to him, as his condition was to her. But, as she pointed out, if you took the world as a whole and compared the millions of Scabs with only a thousand albinos, who was abnormal? And who was diseased?

He graciously let the subject go. There was no reconciling their diseases.

"I met you once in the desert," he said with a grin.

"Before? How could you have?"

"Roland."

"Roland? But Roland was from the Horde."

"Roland was Thomas, commander of the Forest Guard, who'd lost his way and contracted the disease. Naturally I was forced to lie to you."

"You were Roland? I had the life of Thomas of Hunter in my hands? I should have slit your throat!"

"Then you would have foregone the pleasure of riding with me today."

"Honestly, I was quite taken with Roland. I remember that."

"If you had to do it over again, would you still slit my throat?" he asked.

She looked at the rolling shoulders of the horse beneath her. "Knowing what I know today, knowing that I would be in a position to blackmail my father, no."

"Even knowing that I would go on to kill many of your warriors in the wars after that day?"

He made a good point. "Then yes, I'm sorry to say that I would have slit your throat."

"Good. I love an honest woman." They shared a smile.

He was so obvious. Thomas of Hunter, this famous warrior who rode beside her, meant to win her love.

By the time they reached the desert, she wasn't sure that she didn't have some feelings for him. He rode ahead to find Suzan once, and she felt surprisingly left out. Lonely. No, more than lonely, yearning for his company. And when he reappeared five minutes later wearing a silly grin, she felt relief.

"Did you miss me?" he asked.

"Oh, I'm sorry. Were you gone?" She immediately wanted to withdraw the tease. This time she did. "I was alone."

When had all of this happened? In the library?

Suzan galloped toward them, waving her arm. Thomas pulled back on his horse. "She's found something."

"The Horde?"

"I don't think so. Come on!" They rode out to meet her.

Suzan reined back, bright-eyed. "Johan is waiting with Mikil and Jamous. They must have sent William ahead with the others."

"Where?"

"They have a camp in a canyon." She pointed. "Two miles."

Thomas looked at Chelise. "Excellent! It's Martyn."

"He's here?"

"In the flesh." Thomas spurred his horse. "Ride!"

Chelise was terrified by this sudden development—Thomas and Suzan were one thing, but the prospect of meeting more of the Circle didn't sit well. And Martyn! Next to Thomas, there was no other name she'd grown to hate more.

She rode.

While Thomas slept in the White House at President Blair's insistence, Kara was following an insistence of her own. She had no desire to sleep, no cause to dream. She'd only wanted one thing, and that was to understand the rash that had appeared under her arm.

Genetrix Laboratories had become Monique's home. She slept on a cot in her office, and she ate what was left of the food in the cafeteria, although they hadn't received a shipment in three days—the catering company had suspended operations. Didn't matter. They had enough nonperishable foods to feed the five hundred technicians and scientists for at least two days. By then they would know if it was time to go home and start saying their good-byes or to hunker down for a last-ditch effort.

Monique examined Kara's arm in silence. Kara watched her eyes—it was too bad that Thomas was so taken with this other woman in Mikil's world. Chelise. The more time Kara spent with Monique, the more she decided the stiff-spined Frenchwoman was softer than she'd initially assumed. She and Thomas might make a good couple. Assuming both survived.

Monique's eyes were no longer on the cut that had attracted her curiosity. She was scanning the rest of her arm.

"What is it?" Kara asked.

"Have you noticed rashes anywhere else? Your stomach or back, maybe?"

Kara stepped away. "It's happening already?"

"On some, yes. No other rashes?"

"No. Not that I've noticed."

On the other hand, now that she thought about it, her skin seemed to itch in a number of places.

"How long have you known?"

"A few hours," Monique said.

Kara turned to her. "You?"

"No."

"I thought we had another week! Who else?"

"There've been a number of reported cases in Bangkok. Theresa Sumner. The entire team who came to meet with Thomas a few weeks ago. Some in the Far East have reported having the rash as long as ten days. Our guess is that this would only occur among those whose systems are actively fighting the virus. The rash is evidence of the body's resistance, though that doesn't mean much."

The revelation wasn't as shocking as she'd thought it might be. In fact, it was a bit of a relief after so much mystery. Like finally knowing that the cancer you had was terminal after all. You were going to die in exactly thirty days. Live and prepare to die.

"How many?"

Monique shrugged. "Several thousand. Our initial estimations of the virus's latency period were only that, estimates. We always knew it could come sooner. Now it appears to have done just that."

They exchanged a long look. What more was there to say? "So unless we go through with this exchange with France and get the antivirus, we're dead," Kara said.

"So it appears."

"The president knows?"

"Not yet. We're running tests. He'll know within the hour."

Kara sighed, dug in her packet, and pulled out a glass vial with a very small sample of blood. Thomas's blood. Her brother had insisted before leaving Johns Hopkins. His reasoning was simple: he was quite sure that he would be going back to France, but he refused to explain why. In the event something happened to him, he wanted Kara and Monique to have some options.

Kara set the vial on the desk.

"Thomas's?" Monique said.

"His idea. You know what would happen if you and I dreamed with this blood?"

Monique stared at her. "Rachelle is dead. You would wake as Mikil. I don't who I would wake as."

"No. But you would wake. And what would happen if you ate the rhambutan fruit when you were there?"

"No dreams."

"What if you ate the rhambutan fruit every day for the rest of your life?"

"Would it matter? If I die here, I die there. Isn't that how it works?"

"Not if dreaming a one-night dream here lasts forty years there. We could live a full life in another reality while waiting for death to take us here."

A small grin crossed Monique's face. Then an incredulous laugh. "Thomas suggested we should do this?"

"No. He said we would know what to do with it. You have a better idea?"

"No. But that doesn't make your idea sane."

"So you won't do it? He mentioned you, no one else."

"Of course I'll do it," Monique said, taking the small vial. "Why not?"

The smile on her face softened. She stared at the blood sample. "Does Thomas have a rash?"

Kara recalled what he'd said about the rash he'd picked up in Indonesia. "Now that you mention it, I think so, yes. Which means he may be among the first."

No reply.

⟨∞⟩

Mike Orear scanned the swelling crowd, too many to count now—estimates put it at nearly a million. It wouldn't take much to redirect their self-reflection into outrage. The frustration in their eyes was undeniable. The words he was about to speak on the air would do nothing less than open the floodgates of rage, directed at the world's best-known symbol of power: the White House.

He'd called Theresa earlier and fished for more on the possibility of an antivirus, but ever since he'd taken this stance as a voice for the people, she'd gone cold. It was a miracle he'd even gotten through to her. When he had confronted her with the accusation that the administration was misleading the people by holding out hope where none existed, she simply sighed and told him she wasn't working twenty-four–hour shifts to please the administration.

Then she'd hung up on him.

This so-called hope of hers had to be paper-thin. Their only real hope lay with the only man who possessed an antivirus that would do anyone any good: Svensson. If the president didn't play ball with France, there was no hope.

Orear scratched his underarm. The rash that had appeared over a week earlier had subsided, but now it was making a comeback. Odd how so few had the rash. Assuming it was connected to the virus, he'd have thought the rash would be widespread. His mother had it. Maybe it was a genetic thing. Maybe a few of them showed symptoms earlier than what the medical community was predicting.

He shoved the thoughts aside and walked to the tent where the CNN cameras awaited his hourly live update. The tent was set on a stage roughly five feet off the ground, enough to give him a clear view of the crowd. Marcy Rawlins was in a heated discussion with one of the cameramen about the mess they were making with the equipment, and he was point-ing out that cleanliness was no longer next to godliness.

A tall bald man with a handlebar mustache paced along the wooden barricade, glaring at Mike. He wore a beige robe with arms that flared at the cuffs. Take him, for instance. This man looked capable of eating the barricade with only a little encouragement. The armed soldiers would be forced to fire their tear gas. They were nearly half a mile from the White

House, which rose stately behind them, but the only way the guards could stop a marching army of angry protesters was to kill a few.

Those deaths would be on Mike's head. He knew that as well as he knew Marcy needed a Valium. But the death of a few might bring hope and possibly life for millions. Not to mention the 543 souls in Finley, North Dakota, where his mother waited for him to do whatever was humanly possible to stop this mess.

"Two minutes, Mike," Nancy Rodriguez said, taking her seat next to him.

"Gotcha."

He'd dispensed with the tie long ago—he was of the people, for the people. And tonight he would push the people.

Sally applied a quick brush of base to soften the glaze on his cheeks, picked at his hair, then moved away without a word. There wasn't that much for a makeup artist to say these days.

His coanchor leaned toward him. "You might as well know," Nancy said. "I just talked to Marcy. This is my last broadcast."

"What?"

"I've got family in Montana, Mike."

"And I have family in North Dakota. What about what we're doing here for those families?"

"I'm not sure what we're doing here. Other than dying with the rest of them."

Mike understood. He felt the same way at times. But he had no choice in the matter. The people had become his family, and his obligations were now to them as well.

"Stick around for a few minutes, and I promise you'll see what we're doing here."

"Let's go, people," Marcy barked. "You ready, Mike?"

He started the report by running though an update on reports from around the world, mostly riots and the like. Nothing about the anti-virus, as he normally did. Just the problems.

The crowd was over a million, he told them. The traffic into

Washington, D.C., had been forced to a halt, and the police were turning people away.

They'd set up loudspeakers every fifty yards for as far as he could see and around the corner all along Constitution Boulevard. His voice rang out to the people. Mike Orear, their savior on the air. At this moment his worldwide audience was nearly a billion people, they estimated. They'd sold the updates sponsorship to Microsoft for a hundred million a pop. If they came through this alive, Microsoft would shine. If not, they would die with the rest. Smart thinking.

Mike took a deep breath. "That's the news, my friends. That's what they want you to know. That's what the whole world now knows. But I've learned something else, and I want you to listen to every word I'm about to speak, because your life may very well hinge on what I say next."

He glanced at Marcy. She was past being surprised by anything he might say. Her eyes watched him expectantly—she was more audience than producer now.

"The hope for discovering an antivirus, despite what we've all been told by the White House these last couple of weeks, is now almost nonexistent."

A blanket of silence settled over Washington as he spoke the words. Every television, every radio, every speaker carried his announcement. He envisioned the living rooms of America stilled except for the beating of hearts. This was the news they had been waiting for. Hoping against.

"In a matter of days, every living man, woman, and child on this planet will begin to display the symptoms of the Raison Strain. Within days, maybe hours, of that, the world as we know it will . . ."

A terrible sound drifted over the crowd, and at first Mike thought that one of the speakers was overloaded with feedback. But it wasn't the loudspeakers. It was the people.

A terrible wail, probably from one of the end-of-the-world groups, now spread like fire.

"Quiet! Please, there's more."

They didn't stop.

"Please!" he shouted, suddenly as furious at them as he was at the White House. "Just shut up! Please!"

The wail fell off. Marcy was staring at him.

"I'm sorry, but this isn't a game we're playing. You have to hear me out!"

"You tell them, Mikie!" someone shouted. A general barrage of approvals.

He lifted his hand. "Hear me out. The fact is, we're all going to die." He paused. Let the noise settle. "Unless . . ."

Now he let them hang on that one word. In moments like these he was most acutely aware of his power. Like the director of the CIA had said, like it or not, he was one of the most powerful people in the country at the moment. He didn't relish the fact, but he couldn't ignore it either.

"Unless we find a way to get the antivirus that already exists into our hands. That's the killer here: an antivirus that already exists could end all of this in two days. Not a single one of us would have to die. But that's not going to happen. It's not going to happen because Robert Blair has refused a deal that would exchange our nuclear arsenal for the antivirus."

Again he paused for effect. They already knew of the terrorists' ultimatum, but it had never been put to them so bluntly, and never in hand with the world health community's failure.

"My friends, I say, give them the weapons. Give us the antivirus. Give us a chance to live. Give our children another day, another week, another month, another year, and let them live to fight!" He shoved his fist into the air.

Immediately a roar broke from the crowd.

"The rules have changed!" he shouted, feeding on the crowd's growing cries. "We are in a fight for our very lives! We can't allow one man to sacrifice our survival over his own inflated notions of principle!"

Mike was breathing hard. Adrenaline coursed through his veins.

He shoved his finger back at the White House. "This travesty must not stand! In a few days you will all die unless they change their minds! I say, fight for your lives! I say, storm the White House! I say, if we're going to die, we die fighting for our right to live!"

His hand was trembling. He had run out of words.

An ominous silence had smothered the crowd. It was one thing to shout protests. It was another to incite a riot. This talk of death was sinking in.

The scream started in the back somewhere, as far as ten blocks back for all he knew.

The crowd moved as if the straps that held them back had been cut. They swelled forward, screaming bloody murder. The bald man with the handlebar mustache was one among a thousand who breached the barricades first.

Then they were running.

The cameraman spun and took in the mob. He stepped back, nearly fell over a cord, but quickly adjusted and kept the feed live.

Mike didn't know what to do. As far as he could see, the crowd was moving. Forward. Toward him.

A machine gun rattled—tracers streaked over the crowd.

The army troops were already on their feet. Warnings squealed over their bullhorns, but they were lost in the crowd's roar.

The first line rushed past the stage.

Marcy was screaming something, but Mike couldn't understand her. They were going to run right through these defenses and overtake the White House. No one could stop this. He had no clue . . .

Whomp!

Screams of terror.

Whomp, whomp!

"Stand back or we will be forced to fire!"

Whomp!

A cloud billowed from a canister that landed twenty feet from the stage.

"Tear gas!" someone cried. As soon as he said it, the sting hit Mike's eyes.

Whomp, whomp, whomp, whomp!

Chopper blades beat hard nearby, close enough to do whatever damage they were ordered to do.

The crowd surged through the clouds of gas. Another machine gun roared. A momentary silence followed.

When the screaming resumed, it sounded very different, and Mike knew that someone had been shot.

"Get up there!" he shouted, spinning.

But the cameraman was already running through the crowd.

The war had started. Gooseflesh ran up his arms.

Mike's War.

⸻

"The answer is no," President Blair snapped. "I stay here, end of story. Find Mike Orear and his crew and bring them in. I want to go on the air as soon as possible."

Phil Grant frowned. "Sir, I strongly urge you to consider the implications—"

"The implications are that unless we tread very carefully over these next two days, none of us has a prayer. I've known that for over two weeks; now the people are understanding that as well. I'm surprised it took them this long to break down the barricades."

By his hesitancy, the director of the CIA wasn't sure about Blair's evenhanded response to the riots. "I'm not sure they're wrong on this, sir," he finally said.

The possibility that Phil Grant might be working with Armand Fortier crossed Blair's mind for the first time. Who better? His mind flashed over the last few years, searching for inconsistencies in the man's performance. To the best of Blair's recollection there had been none. He was seeing ghosts behind everyone who entered his office these days.

Grant pushed his point. "The riots are only an hour old, and there are already six dead bodies out on the lawn, for goodness' sake. The perimeter around the White House may be reestablished, but they're tearing the city apart. The people of this nation want one thing, sir, and that's survival. Give Fortier his weapons. Take the antivirus. Live to fight another day."

Blair turned away deliberately. This was the same argument, nearly word for word, that Dwight Olsen had made fifteen minutes earlier. Dwight's motivations were transparent, but Phil Grant was a different animal. This wasn't like him. He knew the chances of Fortier coming through with the antivirus were next to nil. To show the Frenchman their military teeth and then beg for an antivirus was simply unacceptable. As long as the United States had some leverage, they were in the game. As soon as they gave up that leverage, the game was over.

Grant knew all of this. Blair decided not to remind him.

"I don't trust the French."

"I'm not sure you have a choice anymore," Grant said. "By tomorrow you could have a full-scale civil war on your hands. You represent the people. The people want this trade."

Blair swiveled around. "The people don't know what I know."

Grant blinked. "Which is?"

Easy.

Thomas's insistence that he trust no one, not a soul, ran through his mind. Gains, Thomas had said. Maybe Gains, that's it.

"Which is what you know. Fortier has no acceptable motive for handing over the antivirus when our ships meet his in"—he glanced at his watch—"thirty-six hours now."

Grant studied him, then set the folder in his hands on the coffee table. "I understand your reluctance. I accept it, naturally. Never could trust the French in a pinch." He stood and shoved his hands in his pockets. "This time I don't think we have a choice. Not with these riots spreading. New York and Los Angeles are starting up already. The country will be burning by noon tomorrow."

"That's better than dead in four days."

The intercom chirped. "Sir, I have a private call for you."

Gains. He'd left very specific instructions. Not even the operator knew that it was Gains on the line.

"Thank you, Miriam. Tell her I'll call right back. Hold all my calls for a few minutes."

"Yes sir."

Blair sighed. "Nothing like a mother to love you." He nodded at the door. "Don't worry, Phil, I'm not going to let this country burn by noon. Get some sleep—you look like you could use it."

"Thank you. I just might."

The director left.

Ghosts, Robert. You're seeing ghosts.

He withdrew the small satellite phone from his desk drawer, locked the door to his office, and stepped gingerly into the closet. Full-scale riots were raging throughout the city, the first signs of the Raison virus had visited them early with this rash, the bulk of the world's nuclear arsenal was about to land in the hands of a man likely to use it, and the brave Robert Blair, president of the most powerful country on earth, was huddled in his closet, punching in a number by the green translucent glow of a secure satellite phone.

The call took nearly a full minute to connect.

"Sir?"

"Quickly."

"We have a go. The Israelis have already directed their fleet as demanded by the French."

Blair let out a long, slow breath. Other than Thomas, who'd first suggested this plan, only four others on this side of the ocean knew the details.

"How many of them are in on it?"

"General Ben-Gurion. The prime minister. That's it."

"Where are their ships now?"

"Approaching the Strait of Gibraltar. They'll round Portugal and reach their coordinates in just over thirty hours, as requested by the French."

"Good. I want you on the USS *Nimitz* as soon as possible."

"I land in Spain in three hours and will be chopped tomorrow." Static filled the receiver. "What about Thomas?"

"He's sleeping," Blair said. "Depending on what happens in his dreams . . ." He caught himself, struck by the sound of his words. They were banking on dreams?

Yes, the dreams of the same man who uncovered the Raison Strain. "If all goes well, he'll join you."

No one other than Kara and Monique de Raison understood Thomas as well as Merton Gains. He sensed Blair's awkwardness.

"It's the right thing, sir. Even if Thomas gave us nothing more, what he's given us to this point has been invaluable."

"I'm not sure whether to agree or disagree," Blair said. "He brought this upon us, didn't he?"

"Svensson did."

"Of course. I'm going on air as soon as they can bring in this character Orear, and I'm going to tell the American people that I'm going to work with the French."

"I understand."

"God help us, Merton."

"Yes sir. God help us."

30

Johan watched the three horses galloping into the canyon toward them. Suzan had found them from the cliff above and waved. Now she led, dark hair flowing in the wind. Born to ride. He remembered her repu-tation as the commander of scouts who could find a single grain of desert wheat in any canyon. As Martyn, he'd feared her nearly as much as he feared Thomas. Intelligence was the key to many battles, and Suzan had matched him at every turn.

He'd never imagined he would ever have the pleasure of riding with her. Seeing her approach with such grace, such beauty, made his pulse quicken. Perhaps it was time to express his feelings for her.

Thomas rode behind her. Odd to think of it, but if he was awake here, it meant he was asleep in his other reality.

Beside Thomas, the woman. The daughter of Qurong.

"He actually did it," Mikil said beside him. "Look at her ride."

"Thomas must have taken her by force. The Chelise I knew would never agree to come on her own."

"Love will compel the strongest woman," Jamous said with a wink at Mikil.

Johan chuckled. "Love? I doubt love compels the daughter of Qurong."

"Either way, you're getting what you argued for," Mikil said. "We're about to see just how friendly albinos and Scabs can be together."

"I didn't have this in mind. I was speaking of the drowning. And the more I think about it, the more I think I was wrong."

"Be careful what you hope for."

Suzan slid from her horse, took two quick steps toward them, and then slowed her pace. Or was it two quick steps toward him? Her eyes were certainly on him. Johan wondered if the others noticed.

Thomas and Chelise had slowed to a trot. Suzan veered toward Mikil and grasped her arms. "Elyon's strength. It's good to see you. William?"

"He went on to the tribe with Cain and Stephen."

Thomas rode in beaming from ear to ear. Chelise stopped beside him, peering tentatively from her hood, face white with morst. She'd placed tuhan blossoms in her hair. This, along with the smooth texture of the morst, was new for the Horde.

Thomas swept his arm toward her. "I would like you to meet the princess. My friends, I present Chelise, daughter of Qurong, delight of Thomas."

Mikil's eyes went wide with amusement. Delight? She was a Scab. And did Chelise agree with his sentiment?

Suzan put her hand on Johan's shoulder. "And this, Princess Chelise, is Johan," she announced. Had they spoken about him?

Johan stepped out and bowed his head. "It's good to see you again."

Chelise was speechless. She'd never seen him as an albino. The poor child was frightened.

Thomas dropped to the sand and reached for her hand. She took it and dismounted gracefully. Thomas held her hand and Chelise made no attempt to discourage him. Had any of them ever seen such a sight? An albino man—Thomas, commander of the Guard—tenderly holding the hand of a diseased woman.

Chelise finally released his hand and stepped forward. She bowed. "Johan. It's a pleasure to meet the great general again."

"Actually, the great general is behind you," Johan said. "His name is Thomas, and I am his humble servant." He indicated the others. "This is Mikil—you might remember her as Thomas's second in command—and her husband, Jamous."

Jamous nodded. Mikil stepped forward. "I can see that you and Thomas have become friends." She let a moment linger. "Any friend of Thomas is a friend of mine." She smiled and reached out her hand.

Chelise smiled sheepishly and took it. Welcoming a Scab as Mikil did wasn't such an uncommon sight—the Circle had led many Scabs into the red pools to drown.

Mikil turned around and sighed. She walked up to Jamous, took his face in her hands, and kissed him passionately on the lips. "I'm sorry, the air is practically dripping with romance. I couldn't help myself."

Thomas blushed and tried to set the record straight for the shocked princess. "You'll have to forgive us, but we aren't too shy about romance in the Circle. We believe that the love between us isn't so different from the love between Elyon and his bride. We call it the Great Romance. Maybe you remember that? From the colored forest?"

"I've heard rumors," Chelise said, but the curious look on her face betrayed her ignorance of any such rumors.

They stood in silence.

"Well then!" Thomas clapped his hands together. "The sun is going down, and we would like some meat. We've had nothing but fruit all day. Please tell me you've hunted down some meat, Johan. It's the least a mighty general like yourself could do for a princess." His eyes twinkled. "You do want meat, don't you, Chelise? You told me how much you love a good steak with your wine. We have wine, Johan?"

"Actually, a simple wheat cake would be fine—"

"Nonsense! Tonight we celebrate. Meat and wine!"

"And what are we celebrating?" she asked. She was growing more comfortable already, Johan thought.

"Your rescue, of course. Johan?"

A shy smile crept across Chelise's mouth.

"We have three rabbits, and our water is as sweet as wine. Should we risk a fire?"

"You can't have a proper celebration without a fire. Of course we risk a fire!"

The night was warm and the moon was full, but Thomas hardly noticed. It could be freezing cold and he wouldn't care. A fire burned in his chest, and with each passing hour he'd embraced its warmth.

So he told himself.

But he was acutely aware of his own growing misgiving at the same time. Just as likely, he hardly noticed the cold night because he was flush with confusion. Where might his odd feelings for Chelise lead them? Seeing his friends in the camp only underscored the peculiarity of his strange romance. He'd boldly called her his delight, of course, but he was feeling like a man with last-minute jitters on his wedding day. What right did he have to make such bold statements so soon and in such contrary circumstances?

The rabbits that Johan had killed earlier filled the camp with a mouth-watering scent. The group made small talk and watched them roast over a spit. There were plenty of issues that could have consumed them in heavy discussion, but Mikil was right: something else was in the air, and it made matters of doctrine and strategy seem insignificant by comparison. There was a romantic tension in the air. The aura of improbable if not forbidden love.

Thomas sat cross-legged close to Chelise, who was seated gracefully on the sand. Mikil leaned back in Jamous's arms to Thomas's right. That left Johan and Suzan, the odd couple out. But it appeared they weren't so odd after all. Whatever feelings they'd hidden before weren't hiding so well tonight. If Thomas wasn't mistaken, the man Suzan had spoken of last night was none other than Johan.

"One leg left," Johan said, reaching for the spit. "Anyone?"

Mikil tossed a bone into the fire and wiped her mouth with the back of her hand. "The best rabbit I've had, and I've had a few."

Johan pulled the leg free. "Suzan?"

Firelight danced in her eyes. She smiled. "No, thank you."

The way she said it so tenderly—this wasn't like Suzan, Thomas thought. Why did love change people so? Johan seemed momentarily trapped by her voice.

"Then I think I'll have it," he said, sitting back next to her. He took a bite, but Thomas was sure his mind wasn't on the rabbit.

Chelise watched them, undoubtedly feeling the intoxicant. She stared into the fire, eyes white. "I never realized there was such kindness among the Circle," she said. "I feel honored to be in your company."

A piece of wood cracked in the fire.

"And I never would have guessed that the daughter of Qurong could be so . . . gentle or wise," Mikil said. "The honor is ours."

Thomas wanted to speak his approval of their acceptance, but he held back.

Chelise lifted her eyes. "How can you love those who hunt you down?"

"We *don't* always," Mikil said. "Maybe if we did, things would be different."

Flames licked the night air.

Chelise eased her hood from her head. She was baring herself to them.

"I think your eyes are beautiful," Suzan said.

Chelise looked away from her. "Thank you." Thomas saw her swallow. Her eyes were beautiful, but none of them could possibly see her disease in the same light he did. They were seeing her through eyes of love, because love was in the air, but they were also pitying her. Her skin was riddled with scales, and her mind was twisted by deception.

If only he could make everything right. A knot rose in his throat. *You are beautiful, my love. I would kiss you with a thousand kisses if you let me.*

He glanced up and saw Mikil staring at him. She understood. She had to understand!

Mikil shifted her eyes to Chelise. "It must be a wonderful thing to be such a beautiful princess."

Chelise lowered her head and traced her finger through the sand. Thomas looked away. The sounds of the fire faded. *My love, my dearest love, I am so sorry. It's not what you think.*

"Jamous and I will take a walk," Mikil said. "All this talk of love can't go unanswered."

Thomas heard them stand and leave, but he couldn't look up.

"And so will Johan and I," Suzan said.

They walked into the night.

Chelise continued to trace the sand by her knees, her finger white with morst to cover her shame. The gentle breeze carried the scent of her disease mixed with perfume.

"It's okay—"

"No," she said. "It's not okay. I can't do this." She looked into the black night. "I want you to take me back in the morning."

Her statement took him completely off guard. It was as if she'd flipped a switch that had powered his hopes. She was right. Nothing was right about his juvenile ambition to win her love.

What was he thinking? Thomas suddenly panicked. He did love her, of course. He wasn't a schoolboy tossed about by infatuation. His love had to be real—Michal had essentially said so himself!

But the fact that Chelise was a Scab with no intent to change was real as well. The disparity between these two realities was enough to suddenly and forcefully send Thomas into a tailspin.

"I don't think that's a good idea," he offered lamely.

"I don't belong here."

Thomas stood. Awkward. Terrified by confusion. She was right. That was what stuck him more than anything. This woman, whom he was sure he had fallen in love with, did not—could not—belong with him. He had been chasing the fantasies of an adolescent after all.

"Excuse me," he said. "I'll be right back."

He headed into the night, unaware of where he was going. He had to think. He wanted to hide; he felt ashamed for leaving her. But it was precisely what she wanted.

Thomas rounded a boulder and headed along white sand, deeper into the canyon. *In the morning I will take her back.* His vision blurred with moisture. *I have no choice. It's what she wants. If she can't recognize a gift when she sees one, she hardly deserves it, does she? She should be running to the red pools, but she's talking about going back.*

A tear leaked down his cheek.

"Where are you going?"

Thomas spun toward the voice on his left.

Justin!

Could it be? He stepped back, blinking.

Yes, Justin. He wasn't smiling this time, and his jaw was firm.

"Justin?"

Justin glanced back toward the boulders that hid the camp. "You left her."

"I . . ." Thomas didn't know what to say. Why had he now seen Justin twice in one week? And why was Justin so interested in Chelise?

Justin faced him, green eyes flashing with anger. "How dare you leave her alone! Do you have any idea who she is? I entrusted her to you."

"She's Chelise, daughter of Qurong. I didn't know that you'd entrusted her to me."

"She's the one my father prepared for me! You've left my bride to sob in the sand!" Justin took several paces toward the camp, then turned back, head now in his hands.

Thomas wasn't sure what to make of this display.

Justin lowered his hands. "I told you myself, I would show you my heart. I sent you Michal when you began to doubt, and already you're forgetting. Do I need to show myself to you every day?"

Justin pointed toward the camp. "You should be kissing her feet, not running away."

"I don't understand. She's only one woman—"

"No! She's the one I've chosen to show the Circle my love for them. Through you."

Thomas sank to his knees, horrified by what he was hearing. "I swear I didn't know. I swear I will love her. Forgive me. Please forgive me. I . . ."

"Please, hurry," Justin said. The moonlight showed tears in his eyes. "Her heart is breaking. You have to help her understand. Don't think I am the only one who wants her. My enemy will not rest."

His enemy. Woref? Or Teeleh? Thomas stood clumsily, his feet charged with an urgency to get back to the campfire. "I will! I swear I will."

Justin just stared at him. "She's waiting," he finally said.

The look in Justin's eyes as much as adrenaline pushed Thomas into a sprint. He stopped after five paces and spun back. "What . . ."

But Justin was gone.

Tears ran down Thomas's cheeks. It was too much. He couldn't stop the terrible sorrow that crashed over him. He turned and ran down the canyon, around the boulder, and straight for the campfire.

Chelise looked up, startled. But he was beyond trying to bring reason to what was happening between them.

He dropped to his knees beside her. "I'm sorry. Please, forgive me. I had no right to leave you!"

She looked at him without understanding, without a hint of softening. But now as he stared into her white eyes, he saw something new.

He saw Justin's bride. The one Elyon had chosen for Justin.

Grief swallowed Thomas whole and sobs began to wrack his body. He closed his eyes, lifted his chin, and began to weep.

He put his hand on her knee. Chelise didn't move.

He couldn't process his thoughts with any logic, but he knew that he was weeping for her. For the tragedy that had befallen her. For this disease that separated them.

The night seemed to echo with his sobs. He removed his hand from her knee. For every cry, there was another, as if the Roush had joined in his great lament.

He caught his breath and listened. Not the Roush, Chelise. Chelise was crying. She'd drawn her knees to her chest and was sobbing quietly.

All thoughts of his own sorrow vanished. Her whole body shook. She had one arm over her face, but he could see her mouth open, straining with her sobs. He sat frozen. He began to cry softly—the pain of this sight was worse than his earlier sorrow.

"What have I done? You don't understand. I love you!"

"No!" she moaned loudly.

He scrambled to his knees and reached out for her. But he was afraid to touch her.

"I do love you! I didn't mean . . ."

Chelise shoved herself up and glared at him. "You can't love me!" she shouted. "Look at me!" She slapped her face. "Look at my face! You can never love me!"

Thomas grabbed her hand. "You're wrong." He lifted her hand and kissed it gently.

⎯⎯∞⎯⎯

She was acutely aware of his hand tightly holding hers. His breath washing over her as he declared his insensible love.

The shame of her white flesh had come over her like a slowly moving shadow from the setting sun. She'd been aware of it back in the library, but only as a distant thought. She'd considered it more carefully after hearing Thomas point it out to Suzan last night.

She was diseased. But she told herself that she would rather live diseased than die by drowning.

Then she'd met the albinos and watched them prepare their small feast. Listening to them talk around the campfire, she couldn't shake her desire to be like these people. Life in the castle was like a prison next to the love they shared so easily.

She knew that her skin offended them, no matter what they said. When Suzan had told her that she had beautiful eyes, knowing full well that they believed her eyes were diseased, the last of her self-assurance had fallen to rubble. She realized then that she could never be like these people. Never be like Thomas.

Worse, she realized that he was right when he said that she wanted to be loved by him. She did want to love him.

Yet she could never bring herself to drown. And without the drowning, she could never be truly loved by him. So then, there was no hope.

You hold my hand, Thomas, but could you ever kiss me? Could you ever love me as a woman longs to be loved? How can you love a woman who repulses you?

Thomas had grown quiet. He put his arm around her shoulders and pulled her closer. She let her sobs run dry.

"You are beautiful to me," he said softly.

She couldn't bear the words. But she didn't have the will to resist them, so she let her silence speak for itself.

"Please . . . I'm dying."

You feel sorry that the woman in your arms doesn't have smooth skin? That she sickens you?

Chelise raised her head to voice her thoughts. His face was there, only inches from hers, wet with tears. The fire lit his green eyes. She was breathing on him, but he made no effort to draw back.

This simple realization was so profound, so surprising, that she lost her train of thought. His eyes gazed at her longingly, drawing her in. Such deep, intoxicating eyes. This was Thomas, commander of the Guard, the man who had fallen madly in love with her and risked his life to rescue her from a beast who would have savaged her.

How could he love her?

She closed her eyes. She could never satisfy such a beautiful man. His love was born out of pity, not true attraction. He could never . . .

His finger traced her cheek, effectively stopping her heart.

"Since the first time we were together in the library, I've loved you," he said. He touched her lips with his fingers. "If only you will allow me to love you."

His words washed over her like a fresh, warm breeze. She opened her eyes and knew immediately that he was speaking the truth.

She slowly lifted her hand. Touched his temple, where his skin was the smoothest. Chelise couldn't bear the tension any longer. She put her hand around his neck and pulled his face down. His soft lips smothered hers in a warm, passionate kiss.

She felt a stab of fear, but he pulled her tighter. Then she gave herself up and let him kiss her longer. His mouth was sweet and his tears felt warm on her cheeks.

His hands brushed her hair back and he kissed her nose and her forehead. "Tell me that you love me," he said. "Please."

"I love you," Chelise said.

"And I love you."

He kissed her on the lips again, and Chelise knew then that she did love this man.

She was in love with Thomas of Hunter, commander of the Guard, leader of the Circle who had loved her first.

31

Thomas rose early, filled with an energy he hadn't felt for many months. The sun was smiling on the horizon; canyon larks sang from the cliff; a morning breeze whispered through his hair.

The Great Romance filled his mind. He understood now. This love he felt for Chelise was tantamount to the love that Justin felt for everyone whom he would woo, diseased or not. The realization was dizzying.

Chelise still slept in her bedroll beside him. He'd found his way past her disease and kissed the woman beneath. He'd stepped past the skin of this world and stepped into another, not unlike what he did when he dreamed.

Yes, Chelise was as disease-ridden as ever. Yes, he could taste the bitterness on her breath. Yes, he would give anything to lead her into the red pool and see her forever changed. But he loved her anyway. And he loved her desperately.

He leaned over and kissed her cheek. "Wake up, my love."

Her eyes batted open. He kissed her again. "Did you dream of me?"

She smiled. "As a matter of fact, I did. You?"

"No dreams, remember?"

She sat up and gazed at the others. Johan was stirring. They'd fallen asleep before the others had returned from their walks. Chelise looked unsure. He would settle that soon enough.

He stood and clapped his hands. "Let's go, everybody. We have a long way to go today."

They stirred from their dreams and sat up.

"Where are we going?" Chelise asked.

"To the tribe. If it's okay with you, that is. Or would you rather send a message to your father?"

She pushed herself to her feet and brushed sand from her cloak. "They won't bite my head off?"

"Not if they expect to live the day."

"Then I suppose I could manage."

Only Thomas and Chelise wore the Horde garments—the rest had traded them for the tan tunics worn by the Circle.

They cleaned the camp quickly and prepared to leave. Thomas saddled his horse and walked toward Chelise, who was working with her mount. He spoke loudly enough for all of them to hear.

"I don't know where you found those rabbits, Johan, but I insist you find more like them for our celebration tonight. There was something in the meat."

Mikil looked at him. "And what are we celebrating this time?"

Thomas put his hand on Chelise's neck and drew her close. "Love," he said and kissed her gently on her lips.

The others were as surprised as Chelise.

"Love it is," Johan said, glancing at Suzan.

Thomas winked at Chelise, who smiled sheepishly. It would take her more time to feel at ease in their company, but Thomas would remove any obstacles.

They rode south into the desert. Normally a journey through the hot dunes would be a quiet, plodding affair, but not this one. They settled into three pairs with Johan and Suzan leading. Thomas and Chelise trailed behind Mikil and Jamous. The hours didn't pass slowly enough for them to plumb the depths of their experiences and theories. But with each passing mile Thomas felt his love for the woman who rode beside him grow.

He had a hard time keeping his eyes off her. Fortunately, there were no cliffs to ride off, or he might have. She rode like a warrior, straddling the saddle, and she had a habit of resting one leg at a time across her steed's shoulder. When he pointed out the cleverness of her riding posture, the others just looked at him with blank stares. To Thomas it was brilliant, though he tried it himself without much success.

She also kept her head up as she rode, chin level, like only a princess could, he thought.

Midday they came to the Oasis of Plums, as the Horde had named it. Chelise excused herself and bathed. When she emerged around the plum trees, Thomas had to look twice to be sure it was her. She'd washed her black hair and applied an oil that made it shine. Flowers again, and the scented morst, but she'd also applied a blue powder under her eyebrows and to her lips. She wore gold earrings and a matching band around her neck. She might have stepped out of the histories' ancient Egypt.

Thomas immediately hurried over to her, took her hands, and declared that she was stunning. The others agreed. And this time, he thought, they actually meant it.

That afternoon they rode six abreast and reminisced about the colored forest. The Roush, the fruit, the lake, the tall colored trees. Chelise asked a hundred questions, like a child first learning that the world was round.

Try as they did, they couldn't find rabbits for a feast that night, but Mikil found two large snakes, which they filleted and roasted over the coals. The meat was sweet and satisfying. Chelise and Johan showed them how to dance, Horde-style, and then Suzan led them in a Circle dance. They debated the merits of each and laughed till their sides hurt.

Johan and Mikil urged Thomas to dream, but he insisted that another night without knowing what was happening with Carlos wouldn't hurt any of them. For all he knew, he'd been sleeping for only a few minutes in the other reality, and he wasn't interested in interrupting his romance with Chelise. For that matter, he might consider eating the rhambutan forever and never dreaming of the virus again.

They broke camp the next morning and resumed their journey south. The tribe was camped four hours away—they would arrive before noon.

"You're sure they'll understand?" Chelise asked.

"Of course, they will. You aren't the first."

"This is entirely different. I'm not coming to drown."

Thomas glanced at the others. "They'll get used to the idea. A day may come when you're more comfortable with the drowning."

"No. I'm the daughter of Qurong, princess of the Horde. I have my limits. It's one thing to fall in love with an albino and make friends with the Circle; it's another thing to become an albino."

She could not know how painful her words were. They hadn't spoken of what would become of their love, but they both knew that some things were irreconcilable. The Horde would never accept peace with the Circle, not while Qurong was their leader and Woref led their forces. And Chelise couldn't expect to be princess of the Horde while living with the Circle.

Chelise looked over at him. "I'm sorry. I didn't mean it like that. You know that I love you."

"And you know that I love you." He winked at her. "That's all that matters."

"A rider!" Suzan pulled up.

Thomas followed her gaze to the south. A plume of dust rose from a lone rider charging hard toward them.

"Is he from our tribe?" Mikil asked.

"He must be. The next closest tribe is a hundred miles from here."

Thomas slapped his horse's rump. "Let's go!"

They galloped out to meet the rider.

"It's Cain!" Suzan shouted, leaning low over her mount. "There's trouble."

Cain reined in hard. His eyes were bloodshot. "Thomas . . ." He glanced at Chelise and back. His horse snorted and sidestepped. "The village was attacked. My brother's dead with nine others. They took half of us before we could escape."

"Slowly, man! Who attacked?" But Thomas knew who. "When?"

"The Horde . . . a division, at least, last night. William sent me out to bring back Johan."

"William's in command? Who was taken?"

"Yes, William. The Horde took twenty-four trapped in one of the canyons. Men, women, children. They caught us without mounts in the middle of the night."

Alarm flooded Thomas's veins. "My son and daughter?"

"They're safe."

His heart eased.

"William is still at the camp?"

"A mile east."

Thomas spurred his horse. "Cain, follow as fast as you can." Their horses were fresh, and they would outrun Cain. "Let's ride!"

"Thomas!"

He looked back and saw that Chelise sat on her steed, stricken with fear. "We'll catch you," he called to Mikil. They galloped ahead.

Thomas swung around and drew up beside her. "This changes nothing."

"There's more, Thomas," Cain said.

Thomas reached out and put his hand on Chelise's neck. "You're with me, my love. Nothing will happen to you, I swear it."

She hesitated. The Horde would want to retaliate. She was assuming the same about the tribe, despite all she'd seen.

"Trust me, Chelise."

"Okay."

Thomas glanced at Cain. "What more?"

Cain stared at them, eyes round.

"Well, what?" Thomas demanded, pulling his horse around.

"William will tell you."

He glared at the man. They had no time for this. "Let's go!"

32

They found the tribe's camp first. What was left of it. The canvas tents had been shredded by swords. Pots and pans were scattered, cots smashed, chickens and goats slaughtered and left to rot.

Several large bloodstains marked the spots where some of the ten had been slain. The bodies were probably with William, awaiting cremation, as was their custom.

Thomas led the others through the camp, sickened. At times like these he wondered if their policy of nonviolence was worthless. Hadn't Justin himself once engaged in battle?

He set his jaw and rode slowly, keeping his anger in check. With a single sword he could take down twenty of the Scabs, but that was no longer who he wanted to be.

"Find them, Suzan," he ordered. Cain still hadn't caught up.

She took a trail that led to the cliffs above the canyon and sped east. They trotted through the canyon below her, waiting for her signal.

No one spoke. They each knew every tribe member as part of a family. Now ten of them had been killed and twenty-four taken captive.

He looked at Chelise, who drew her hood around her face and watched him tentatively. He wanted to tell her it was okay, that they would round the next bend to discover that it had all been a mistake.

A whistle cut through the air. "She's found them," Mikil said.

What remained of the tribe was hunkered down in a wash, one mile east, as Cain had said. Thomas saw them while they were still two hundred yards out. He slowed his horse and studied the lay of the land.

They had four escape routes in the event of a second attack, however unlikely it was at this point. From their position, all the surrounding cliffs were in clear view. William had chosen well.

"Thomas." Chelise's voice was small. "What's going to happen?"

He reached out and took her hand as they rode with the others. "Nothing's going to happen. We will mourn our loss and find a new camp. They are with Elyon now."

"And to me?"

"You're with me. They will embrace you. Your enemy's Woref, not the Circle."

William waited for them with Suzan and several men. The survivors, roughly twenty, were gathered behind them, some prostrate in mourning, others seated quietly, a few studying the surrounding cliffs for any sign of trouble.

Samuel and Marie ran out, and Thomas dropped to hug them. They were used to running from the Horde, but their wide eyes betrayed a new fear.

"Thank Elyon."

"I'm afraid, Papa," Marie said.

He held her tight. "No need. We are in Justin's hands." He clasped his son's shoulder. "Thank you for seeing to your sister. You're a strong one, Samuel."

"Yes, Father."

Thomas remounted and nudged his horse on. The tribe seemed relieved to see them. All except for William. He stood his ground like a man receiving a rebellious son. Johan and Mikil dismounted and hurried past William to console those who mourned.

"That's far enough, Thomas," William snapped.

There was trouble here. "It's okay, Chelise," he said quietly, squeezing her hand.

"That's where you're wrong," William said. "I see you've collected your Scab. How considerate of you to bring this trouble on us."

Thomas stopped his horse ten feet from the man. Three others stood behind him, arms folded. Thomas studied William and chose silence.

"The Horde left us a message," William continued. He looked at Chelise and scowled. Thomas fought the impulse to ride his horse through the man.

"Take your eyes off her! This is Chelise, daughter of Qurong, and she is to be my wife." He wasn't sure of the latter, but he felt compelled to say it. To shout if he must.

"We know who she is!" William shouted. "She is the cause of this great tragedy."

"You blame a Scab who leaves the Horde to find the Circle? I thought it was our purpose to save those who needed it."

"She looks scaly enough to me. And it seems that Woref wants his scaly whore back. If she isn't returned to the city within three days' time, he will execute the twenty-four albinos he's taken."

Chelise's hand twitched in his and he held it tight.

"Never! I won't let him lay a hand on her head. Ever!"

"Then you will send twenty-four of our family to their deaths."

"I will go," Chelise said quietly, pulling her hand free. "If Suzan will ride with me to the edge of the city, I'll go now."

Now Thomas panicked. He gripped his head. "No!" He suddenly felt compelled to get her off her horse. There would be no more riding today.

He slid to the ground, took her hand, and reached to help her dismount. She hesitated, then swung down.

Thomas put an arm around her. "Not another word about this!" he scolded William. "Have you no sense about you, man?"

Chelise turned to him. "He's right, Thomas. Woref will kill them. Or he'll kill half of them and demand again. I won't have the blood of these innocent people on my head."

She spoke like a princess, which made him even more desperate. There was a glint of fear in her eyes, but she stood tall.

Thomas spun to William. The whole tribe was now looking at him. "You see? Does this sound like a Scab? She's more honorable than you!"

"She's only agreeing to return to her vomit," William said. "She's not giving her life or anything as noble as you would imagine."

Thomas was furious. "Council! I call a council."

They just stared at him.

"Now! Suzan . . ."

"I'll stay with Chelise," Suzan said, stepping around William. "And I, for one, find this appalling." She took Chelise's arm. "I am with Thomas, whatever he says."

But Chelise wasn't ready to go without her say. "Thomas, I insist—"

"No!" He calmed his voice. "No, my love, no, no. I can't let you go. Never. Not like this."

Then he turned and walked away without giving her the chance to argue.

⸺∞∞⸺

It was their second council in less than a week, and the circumstances were eerily similar. They dispensed with the seated discussion and settled for pacing and arm waving. Only their traditional call to Elyon even marked it as a true council meeting.

"If you had listened to me, none of this would have happened," William said. "Suzan may agree with you, but I'm sure not a single other member does."

"Then none of them has the true sense of Elyon's love," Thomas snapped.

"Who can know his love?"

"Surely you remember, William. All of you! Has it been so long since we watched Justin drown for us?"

"Then let Chelise give herself as Justin did!" William shouted. "Woref may take some flesh from her hide, but he won't kill her. Otherwise he will kill our friends."

"I'm not sure that Thomas is wrong," Johan said.

"Me neither," Mikil agreed.

"Then you're as foolish as he." He shoved a finger in the direction of the camp. "What would you suggest, that we all just lie down and die for this woman?"

Thomas paced and ran both hands through his hair. "No. I suggest that I go in her place."

"He's not asking for you."

"No, but we have three days." The rough form of a plan gathered, and he spoke quickly. "If I ride hard, I can reach the city in a day and offer myself in exchange for the twenty-four."

William seemed taken back. "If Woref wanted you, he would have demanded you."

"Let him object. We have time! If Qurong refuses my offer, then we agree with his demands. But he'll agree because he thinks like a Scab leader. He will find me far more valuable than twenty-four commoners."

"Then he'll kill you," Mikil said.

"Not as long as you have Chelise. Think whatever you want about Qurong, but he cares as much for his daughter as he does my capture. Don't you see?"

William frowned. "Have you considered the possibility that this goes beyond simple negotiation with the Horde?"

"Meaning what?"

"Meaning this trouble started with your infatuation with a Shataiki whore. You're acting like Tanis acted at the crossing. Maybe this is Elyon's way of purging the Circle of this nonsense."

A tremble ran through Thomas's hands. It was all he could do to keep them at his sides.

"You speak once more against Chelise and I'll trade you for the twenty-four," Johan said. "Thomas is right. You've lost your sense of Elyon's love. Perhaps you should try drowning again."

William scowled.

"I'll go with you," Mikil said.

"It will be—"

"I don't care how dangerous it is. You'll need help with this."

"I will go as well," Johan said. "There's also the matter of the dreams."

"Forget the dreams! I'm not sure I trust William with Chelise. I need you to stay here to keep him away from her."

With a parting glance at William, Thomas walked away, ending the council. No need nor time for a formal decision. He'd made up his mind, with or without the council's full agreement.

Chelise hurried toward him as soon as he strode into view. "Please, Thomas. You have to let me go."

He held up a hand to silence her, then took her arm and led her around tall boulders that offered some privacy.

"We've come to a decision."

"And what about my decision?"

He took her shoulders and gazed into her eyes, fearful that she'd abandoned her love for him. She was being noble in this insistence of hers, yes, but she was also agreeing to leave him for Woref. He couldn't bear the thought.

"Listen to me." He took a deep breath. "You know what will happen to you if you go back. Woref will never believe that I forced you to leave. He doesn't have a believing bone in his body. The man lives for deceit, and he expects the same from everyone else. If he doesn't end up killing you, he'll do worse. You know it!"

She searched his eyes. But she wasn't talking, and that was good.

"I have a plan. Now listen carefully—it can work; I know it can. Your father will trade me for the twenty-four and—"

"No! No, you can't do that! This is my problem."

"This is my problem! I can't lose you!"

"He'll kill you!"

"Not if you stay."

"Then he'll brutalize you!"

"I'm too valuable to him. It will buy us time. If you go back, it will be over. Please, I beg you. It's the only way."

A tear ran from her eye, and he wiped it away with his thumb. "Promise me you'll stay, for my sake. I promise we'll find a way."

Chelise remained quiet, fighting her tears. He leaned forward and kissed her forehead. "I can't live without you, my love. I can't."

"I feel lost, Thomas."

He held her, and she cried on his shoulder. "I have found you."

"I'm not like you. I'm a stranger here."

She was right, but he couldn't bring himself to point out the obvious, that unless she drowned she would always be lost. There would be time for that later.

"Then I will be a stranger with you," he said.

She rested her forehead against his chest. Then she kissed his neck and held him tight, crying.

It was her shame again, he thought. She still couldn't understand or accept his love. His heart ached, but he could only hold her and hope that she loved him as much as he loved her.

"You'll stay?"

"Promise me you'll come back for me."

"I promise. I swear it on my life."

33

Mikil and Thomas made it within a few miles of the Horde city before collapsing for badly needed rest. The moment Thomas fell into sleep, he awakened.

Washington, D.C.

He'd slept the night in the White House, but he'd lived . . . Thomas counted them off in his mind, one, two, three, four . . . four days in the desert, rescuing Chelise. To what end? To return to the city alone.

To end up here, in this mess of a world. He was tempted to knock himself out and return to the larger matter at hand. Chelise.

He forced his mind to focus on this world. He'd learned some things about Carlos and the Frenchman, hadn't he? Yes, from Johan.

The reality of the virus swelled in his mind. They were down to a couple of days. Carlos was the key.

He swung his legs to the floor, walked to the door, and stopped short with the sudden realization that he hadn't pulled on his jeans. Wouldn't do to run through the White House in blue-striped boxer shorts.

He dressed, brushed his teeth with a disposable toothbrush he found in the bathroom, and exited the room.

It took him seven minutes to gain a private audience with the president. Chief of Staff Ron Kreet ushered Thomas into a small sitting room adjacent to the Oval Office. "I don't know what you think you can do, and I can't say I'm a big believer in dreams," Kreet said, "but at this point I would take anything." He raised his eyebrow. "You're aware of the riots?"

"What riots?"

"Mike Orear from CNN said some things last night that sparked the crowd. They stormed the grounds. By the time the army had the situation under control, ten people were killed. Another seventeen in cities across the country."

"You're kidding."

"Not exactly a time for jokes. The president has addressed the nation twice since the riots began, both times with Orear. Things are quiet for the moment, relatively speaking. But fires are burning out of control in Southern California."

"What did he tell them?"

Kreet walked to the door and opened it. "He told them that the United States would cooperate fully with France's demands."

The chief of staff hadn't yet closed the door when Robert Blair showed. "Thank you, Ron. I have it from here."

He stepped in and closed the door behind his back. Blair wore a yellow tie with a blue paisley print, loose at an open collar. His hair was disheveled, and large dark rings hung from both eyes.

They stared at each other for a long moment. "Ron told you about the riots?"

"It's just the beginning," Thomas said. "Are we secure in here?"

"I had the room scanned thirty minutes ago."

"And?"

"Microphone in the lampshade."

Thomas nodded. At least the president was taking all of this seriously. "How's the rest of the world holding up?"

Robert Blair sighed and walked to a navy blue wing-backed chair. "I have to sit. Where to begin? Suffice it to say that if we do find a way out of this mess, the damage to the world's economies, cities, infrastructures, militaries—you name it—will take a decade to recover from, best case. Loss of life from collateral damage could reach into the hundreds of thousands if full-scale riots break out after this goes down tomorrow. The virus has started to flex its muscles—you do realize that."

Thomas sat stunned by this last piece of information. "The symptoms, you mean? I thought we had another five days . . . a week."

"Well, we were wrong. Evidently the first symptom is a rash. It'll last a few days with any luck, but the team that went to Bangkok has already been hit." He glanced at Thomas's shirt. "You?"

Thomas felt his side. "Last night . . ." He'd noticed a faint rash after waking in Bancroft's laboratory, but not like Kara. "My sister has definite symptoms of the virus."

"And so does Monique. Gains . . . the whole team that went to Bangkok. There've been thousands of cases reported in Thailand and now in several other gateway ports. It's a matter of hours before we get hit here."

The conclusion of this matter suddenly struck Thomas as inescapable. Until now, the Raison virus had been a blip on a computer screen. Now it was a red dot of rash. In a matter of days it would turn internal organs to liquid.

He stood. "There's no time—"

"Please sit down," Blair said in a tired but resolved voice.

Thomas sat.

"Did it work?"

"In a matter of speaking, yes. Johan dreamed as Carlos. Unfortunately, he couldn't remember as much as I would have hoped."

"But he . . . got into his mind . . ."

"Yes."

"And?" the president pushed.

"And I'm almost certain that Fortier has no intention of giving you an antivirus that works."

"So we were right."

"Johan also seemed to think that the number of people who ended up surviving the virus would be much smaller than anyone imagines. My guess is that Fortier is planning on turning his back on both Russia and China as well as most of the nations who've capitulated at this point."

"Son of a . . ." The president closed his eyes and took a deep breath. "Of course. What else did we expect?"

Thomas stood again. "Which means that I've got to get back to France as soon as possible. Today. Now."

"You really think you have a chance at this?"

"I have to reach Carlos. I know where he was last night; I've been there before. Fly me in at low level while it's dark and I have a shot of getting in. Our best shot at the antivirus is to make Carlos dream with me. If Carlos wakes up in Johan's mind, we'll have a chance of winning him over."

The president slowly ran his hands over his face and then pushed himself up. "Okay. You're right, but this could be the end. We're out of time."

Thomas lowered his voice. "I'm assuming you won't give them the nuclear weapons."

"Not a chance."

"The Israelis—"

"They agreed."

Thomas walked toward the door. "Then get me to France."

The mood at Genetrix Laboratories had shifted visibly in the last twenty-four hours. The end was at hand, and they all knew it.

The researchers couldn't hide the sudden appearance of red spots. The Raison Strain.

They wore long-sleeve shirts and blouses and slacks, but the rash on their necks was starting to show above their collars. Hope for an antivirus was evaporating as the rash spread. Monique herself still showed no rash, but she could feel her skin crawling, ready to break out at any moment.

Thomas had called for Kara, who'd spent only a few minutes with him before he'd been whisked off somewhere. Kara was returning as soon as a chopper became available. She had nowhere else to turn other than New York, where her mother lived, but she didn't want to leave the immediate area for two reasons, she'd said. One, in case Thomas needed her—for what, Monique could no longer imagine, but she was glad for Kara's company, regardless.

The second reason was more obvious.

Monique rose from her desk and walked to the freezer. The small vial of Thomas's blood rested on the top shelf by itself. She took it out and closed the door.

With this blood she and Kara might find life. It seemed absurd, but she'd experienced this particular stripe of absurdity once before, and she would gladly do it again. They would wait until the last moment, of course. After Thomas had finished whatever he was up to, Kara had said. Then they would apply this blood to their own, take some Valium, and dream a dream that lasted for as many years as they could manage.

She sat down at her desk and turned the glass vial in her fingertips. What was so special about this particular blood? Dr. Bancroft had run it through the lab at Johns Hopkins, and it had come back with no unusual traits. No elevated white counts, no unusual levels of trace elements . . . nothing.

Just red blood. Red blood that brought new life.

She absently flicked the tube. A thought occurred to her.

The door opened and Mark Longly stuck his head in. "The reports from the Bangkok lab just came in."

"And?"

"And nothing. Your father wants you to call him after you've looked at them, but I don't see anything."

"Antwerp?"

"Just got off the phone with them. Nothing new. UCLA has isolated a seventh pair in the string they're developing—it reacts in a fashion consistent with the others, but they're at least a week away from knowing what they have."

Monique nodded. "Cross their data with the strand from Antwerp again, see what—"

"Already have." He stared at her blankly. They'd been through a hundred similar conversations in the last week. Always nothing. Or if it was something, it was a something that meant nothing within the time they had.

"No use giving up now," she said.

Mark tried to smile, but it came off twisted. He closed the door.

Monique returned her thoughts to the vial. *You are my salvation.* She stood and walked to the freezer. Before she put herself under whatever power this blood had to offer, she would have a look at it herself.

But for now, she had a virus to defeat.

Or not to defeat.

34

Mikil pressed her blade against the Scab's neck. "Not a sound and you will live."

She'd taken the man from behind, and Thomas knew that she had no intention of cutting him, but she looked as though she might like to.

"Nod your head!"

The man nodded vigorously.

Thomas walked around him and looked into his eyes. They'd crossed the desert in less than a day and then rested five miles from the city before finding their messenger, a lone sentry who'd been posted on the main road leading in from the west. His white face shone in early morning moonlight.

"We aren't going to hurt you, man," Thomas said. He lifted his hands. "See, no sword. Mikil has a blade, but really it's mostly for show. We only need a favor from you. Do we have your attention?"

The guard didn't move.

"What's your name?"

"Albertus," the man whispered.

"Good. If you don't do what we ask, I'll know what to tell Qurong. My name is Thomas of Hunter. You've heard of me?"

"Yes."

"Good. Then you'll go straight to the castle, wake Qurong, and deliver a message. Tell him that I will turn myself in for the twenty-four albinos he's captured. Bring them to the orchard two miles west of the Valley of Tuhan and I will give myself up. Mikil will take the albinos, and Qurong can have me in their place. Do you understand?"

The guard had settled. "You in exchange for the others they brought in."

"Yes. When did they arrive?"

"Last night."

"They are in the dungeons?"

"Yes. And the guard has been increased."

Thomas glanced at Mikil. They'd expected as much. Any attempted rescue would be a different matter this time.

"We'll be watching. Tell Qurong not to think he can outwit us. A fair exchange or nothing. I want them on horses." He nodded at Mikil. "Release him."

Mikil let the man go. He rubbed his neck and stepped away.

"Ride, man."

"If I leave my post—"

"Qurong will give you a reward for this, you fool! You're delivering his enemy. Now ride!"

The guard ran to his horse, mounted quickly, and rode into the night.

"Now what?" Mikil asked.

"Now we wait at the orchard."

The tribe had fallen for his ploy so easily that Woref had delayed his attack for several hours. But the camp slept in perfect peace, unsuspecting of another assault so soon.

His earlier instructions had been very pointed: kill only a few, capture as many as you can, and leave the rest alive with the message. Do not pursue them. Take the captives to the city, but wait for me with a full division.

As he'd hoped, the albinos had assumed that the Horde had taken what they'd come for.

Wrong. So very wrong.

Woref had arrived midday. He knew the tribe would call Thomas of Hunter in immediately. He knew that Chelise would be with Thomas. The fact that Thomas had left to rescue the twenty-four albinos in the city was now of no consequence. Woref would soon have the one prize he desired.

He closed his eyes and rolled his neck. He could almost taste her skin on his tongue now. A coppery taste. Like blood. Blood lust. Teeleh would want to see her tonight, he thought. He wasn't sure how he knew that, but he fully expected the creature to gloat. Woref shivered with anticipation.

Odd how his passions and those of the winged serpent had somehow become one. He was complicit with Teeleh; he accepted that now. But he was serving his own interests. Frankly, he wasn't sure who was serving whom. When he became the supreme leader of the Horde, he would need the kind of power Teeleh could give him.

But first . . .

He opened his eyes and stared into the night. First he would possess the firstborn's daughter. He would possess her and he would ravage her. She would love him. If he had to beat her love from her with his fist, she would love him. He would have to be subtle at first, naturally. Teeleh was as much about subtlety as he was about brute force. Patience. But in the end she would be his and his alone.

Woref turned to the captain. "If a single one of these albinos is killed, I will drown the man who does it. They understand that? Our objective here is to liberate Qurong's daughter. We can't risk killing her with a stray arrow."

"And afterward?"

"I'll decide."

He looked down at the camp again. She was in the third tent from the left. Unless she'd moved during the night, which was unlikely but possible. His men had been known to miss more than he cared to admit.

"They are in position?"

"We have a ring around the camp. There is no possible escape."

"I've heard those words before."

"This time I'm sure."

Woref grunted. "After me."

He dropped over the ledge and approached the line of men who lay in wait along the canyon floor. They'd painted their faces black, and in their dark battle dress they looked like creatures of the night. The Horde rarely attacked at night because of their fear of Shataiki. Odd, all things considered. But the black bats were too busy preying on the minds in the city to wander out into these canyons.

Woref dropped to one knee at the front of the line and studied the tents. Not a stir. All that remained was to draw the noose tight enough to prevent escape.

"Slowly."

He stood and stepped toward the camp. High on his right, the captain gave the signal to the rest of the ring. Cautiously, so that their boots would make little sound on the sand, six hundred warriors closed in on the tribe.

Woref stopped twenty yards from the first tent and raised his hand.

Not a sound. His heart pounded. The warriors on the far side of the camp had taken a signal and stopped with him. Even if the albinos saw them now, their fate was sealed.

The third tent. His white whore was there, sleeping in an albino's tent. Tonight she would learn the meaning of respect. Tonight a whole new world would be opened up to her. His world.

Woref grabbed a tall sickle from the warrior behind him. "Stay," he ordered softly.

He walked deliberately toward the camp, leaving his men behind. When he reached the third tent, he spread his legs, lifted the sickle, and swung it through the edge of the canvas. The blade sliced through the fabric and the center pole as if they were made of paper. He grabbed the collapsing wall and ripped it aside.

There lay a woman, eyes still closed. A Scab. His whore.

Woref reached down, took a fistful of her hair, and jerked her off the ground. She woke with a scream, eyes wide in terror.

"That's it, dear wife. Let the world know your pleasure."

Chelise grabbed at his hands futilely. Her wails shattered the still night. Tent flaps flew open, and albinos stumbled out like rats from their dens.

The Horde army didn't move.

Woref dragged Chelise to the edge of the camp, hauled her up so she could stand, and spun back. The albinos were already in full motion, scurrying for an escape. Let them. They would run into warriors within a few strides.

"No one takes what is mine!" he shouted. "No one!"

"Johan, the eastern route is blocked," a voice cried.

Martyn?

His warriors were still awaiting his signal—to kill or not to kill.

Woref spun Chelise around and clubbed her on the temple with his left hand. Her wails fell quiet and she sagged. He released her hair and let her fall in a pile.

"Martyn!" His voice rang through the canyon. "Martyn steps forward or I will kill every soul."

"We don't need your threats to motivate us," Martyn said, walking in from Woref's left. "You've been threatening us for a year already."

Martyn looked odd without his white eyes and skin. Puny. Sickly.

"This is the mighty general? You look ridiculous, my old friend."

"And you look like you could use a good bath."

Woref wasn't sure what to make of the man. The dark woman they'd taken captive earlier stepped up beside Martyn. His fortune was far greater than he could have hoped for. In one night he would claim his bride and slaughter Johan, leaving Thomas to weep on his own.

"I've reclaimed what is mine, and now I will take pleasure in watching you die."

He lifted his hand.

"My lord, I demand an audience." A tall albino stepped forward. Another one of the five they'd captured a few days earlier. Fear danced in his eyes.

"You're not in a position to demand anything."

"Then I beg. You will thank me."

Woref lowered his hand. "And you are . . . ?"

"William. I am a council member, and I have authority in the Circle."

"What are you up to?" Martyn demanded of the albino.

The one named William lifted his hand to silence Martyn. Interesting. What kind of man would Martyn both object to and respect with his silence?

"Then speak."

"Alone. We aren't people of violence; there's no danger from me."

Woref grabbed Chelise by her arm and dragged her to the line of warriors. "Watch her." The tall albino met him to one side.

"Speak."

William spoke in a low voice. "I can assure you, General, that I argued in the strongest possible terms against this madness. Thomas has endangered the entire Circle, and now we will pay with our lives. You must believe me when I say not all among the Circle are so antagonistic as Thomas."

"You're begging for your life? I have no time for this."

"I'm giving you my motive for delivering Thomas of Hunter to you."

"You can deliver him to me how?"

"I know where he is and where he will be tomorrow. Let us live and I will go with you."

"Your word against the life of Martyn. Am I a fool?"

"You know as well as I do that we're bound by our word in the Circle. Consider my motive. Since the death of his wife, Thomas has been a detriment to us all."

"Then you would betray your own leader?"

"He's betrayed us! If I'm wrong, then you can kill me. Would I give my life for a man I despise?"

Woref considered the man's argument. He had the look of a despairing man, given to deception, perhaps. But who was he betraying?

The tribe was looking at them in silence. Powerless.

"I'll kill Martyn and take you," Woref said.

"No. Then kill us all. Johan is a shadow of the great general you once knew. Let him live out his puny life. Take me and I will deliver Thomas, who's the only threat among the Circle."

"Where is he?"

"Near the city, planning another rescue."

Woref turned toward the captain. "Put this man in chains. The rest live. Keep the army here until morning. Make sure none of them leaves this canyon; I want no pursuit."

He'd come for Chelise. If he could also take Thomas, the last of Qurong's reservations about his general would be gone.

His mind turned toward the unconscious form on the ground. The woman who had brought him so much grief. The one he loved.

His only regret was that he would have to exercise restraint for the time being. Bringing a battered daughter home to her father would not do. But there were always other ways.

He glanced back at the albino and saw that he was staring at Johan. He wasn't sure if it was a look of betrayal or one of regret. They would know soon enough.

∽∞∽

"So soon!" Mikil said, gazing down from her perch in the tree. The sun had just risen when the long line of albinos appeared at the edge of the field with a guard for each. A second row of guards marched into the field on either side.

"What did I tell you?" Thomas said. "Qurong is no fool. He suspects that Chelise will be compelled by my captivity as much as the Circle is. Do you see Woref?"

"No. There's a general, but I don't think it's Woref."

"You'd think he would handle this himself." Thomas looked back at the trees behind them. "The way's clear?"

"There's no way they could have set a trap this soon. Give me ten minutes on them and we're free." Mikil gripped his shoulder. "You're sure about this, Thomas? It's bothering me."

"And you're not bothered by their deaths?" He nodded at the albinos, who now sat on their horses in a long line, waiting for the next move. "Just make sure that nothing happens to Chelise. Without her my life is worthless."

"Johan would hog-tie her himself if he thought she might leave."

"Not like that. If she left me for Woref now, I think I'd rather be dead. And she still has the disease, Mikil. I don't trust her mind."

"But you trust her heart."

"I'm staking my life on her heart."

They'd developed a plan for getting Thomas out—a risky move involving an exchange for Chelise in the desert—but it would require her cooperation.

"Elyon's strength, my friend." He clasped her arm.

"Be careful, Thomas."

"I will."

"If we get through this, I would like to dream with you. Become Kara."

"If Kara lives, I think she would like that."

Thomas lowered himself to one of the horses, took a deep breath, and walked out into the open field beside the apple trees.

"We meet halfway," he yelled.

They saw him and held a brief discussion. The general Mikil had seen called out to him. "Slowly. No tricks. We have men on either side."

Thomas nudged his horse and walked toward the line. The albinos began to move forward.

He passed them on the right, less than twenty yards from three archers who had their bows strung. If he bolted now, they would take him easily. He nodded at the albino closest to him, an older woman named Martha. She looked at him with fear in her eyes.

"I'll be seeing you soon enough, Martha. Be strong."

"Elyon's strength," she said quietly.

And then he was past them and in the hands of the Horde. The tribe members trotted over the field and disappeared into the trees.

"Off the horse!" the general ordered.

Thomas dismounted and let them tie his hands behind his back with a long strap of canvas. "You expect me to walk all the way?"

The general didn't respond. They tied his horse to two others, pushed him back in the saddle, and led him away.

Thomas rode into the Horde city for the second time in two weeks. Once again he saw the squalor caused by the disease. Once again he tried unsuccessfully to ignore the filth and stench of Scabs who screamed insults at him. Once again he approached the dark dungeon that had once been a great amphitheater built for the expression of ideas and freedom. This time they passed the castle without taking him to Qurong. That would come soon enough.

No fewer than a hundred guards surrounded the dungeon, all armed with bows and sickles. These were no army regulars. They were scarred from battle and scowled with bitter hatred.

The dungeon guard led him down the wet steps and along the same corridor he'd walked before. But they passed his old cell and took him down a second flight of stairs to a lower level lit only by torches. They shoved him into a small cell, slammed the gate shut, and left him in total darkness.

Thomas collapsed in the corner, exhausted. There was nothing to do now but wait.

And dream.

35

The only jump Thomas had ever executed was more of a cannon shot than a one-two-three leap, and that one out the back of a military transport that had been cut in half by a missile two weeks earlier. This time he would buddy-jump with Major Scott MacTiernan, Army Ranger.

The French defenses weren't accustomed to engaging enemy aircraft over their soil—the sudden shift in power was only two weeks old, and the military was being coerced. All of this played into the Americans' hands. The C-2A Greyhound cargo plane came off the USS *Nimitz* five hundred miles off the coast of Portugal, and flew south over Spain and then up western France, hugging the land below radar. As soon as they neared the drop point, the pilot pitched the nose up and let the plane claw for the dark skies.

Air defenses painted them at two thousand feet.

"You got ten seconds," the master snapped. They'd estimated the window based on the time it would take the French radar to confirm and respond to the sudden blip on their screens. The parachute was made of a fabric that would give them little if any signature, and even so, they wouldn't be in the air long enough to cause alarm.

"Remember, relax," MacTiernan said, facing the wind over Thomas's shoulder. He checked the straps that lashed Thomas to his chest. "On three."

Thomas fell into the darkness, eyes wide behind the goggles. The aircraft's roar was immediately replaced by the rush of wind beating his ears. He was along for the ride—a very short ride, the major had warned.

MacTiernan pulled the cord. The chute tugged them skyward. MacTiernan guided them in with night vision. The ground was a mixture of black swaths, which Thomas assumed were forest, and slightly lighter fields. They were on top of them, then drifting into a field.

"Watch your legs! Coming up in five. Run with me, baby! Hit the ground running!"

They feathered in for a landing, hit hard, and stumbled forward. Silence.

The parachute flapped once as it folded in on itself and settled to the ground. Thomas shrugged off the harness and checked his gear. Black pants with a knife strapped to one thigh and a nine-millimeter semiautomatic strapped to the other. Canteen, compass, radio with a homing device that could be picked up from Cheyenne Mountain. Black T-shirt, black ski cap, black sweater wrapped around his waist. Night-vision goggles.

The prospect of using a weapon gave him mixed feelings, but he wasn't sure that he was meant to be a pacifist here in this reality. He still wasn't sure what he felt about a whole slew of issues here, particularly religious issues. He wasn't a man of the cloth, for crying out loud. He was a man deeply affected by his dreams of another reality, but in his short few weeks of tripping between the worlds, he hadn't had the time to unravel theology here as he had there. He might never have the time.

"One piece?" MacTiernan was kneeling, penlight on a small map, compass in hand.

"Looks like it," Thomas said. "Where do you put us?"

The major pointed to their right. "One mile that way. I have you on GPS; if you drift left I give you one click. Right, two clicks. You got it?"

"Left one click, right two clicks."

"No other communication unless absolutely necessary. Remember, two hours. We have to clear this sector and make our rendezvous in five hours. We miss the window, we miss the chopper. It's already en route. Missing it would cost us ten hours—this isn't like a fixed wing."

They'd come in on the much faster transport to make the drop tonight, but they wouldn't have the same luxury on the return trip. With any luck they wouldn't need it.

"Two hours." Thomas checked his watch.

"You get in a bind, I come after you. That's the plan."

Thomas didn't bother responding. He was up to much more than this, and much less at once, depending on the reality, depending on the enemy, depending on the day.

He reached the edge of the compound in thirty minutes of careful going. MacTiernan corrected his course only twice. The return trip, assuming there was one, would take only ten minutes. He had an hour and twenty minutes to execute the mission.

The farmhouse sat in the middle of the field, a hundred yards distant. Except for a dull glow from the windows on the first floor, it was dark.

Thomas pulled on the night-vision goggles, squinted at the green light, and then slowly scanned the perimeter. One guard on the north side. Two by the road that snaked into the forest on the far side. Lighter than he would have guessed. Had they already vacated? Their cover here was blown; they knew that. They'd depended on secrecy, not high-tech security for protection, but they'd never planned on one of their corpses coming to life and escaping to tell the world of the location. Their only option would have been to abandon the facility.

He ran in a low crouch, straight toward the basement window that he and Monique had escaped through before. The effectiveness of his mission now depended on speed and surprise.

He squatted with his back to the stone wall and caught his breath. No light from the hallway past the window. No light from the upper floor. That would be his entry point.

Three weeks ago an ascent like the one that dared him now would have been unthinkable. Climbing the stones that formed the fifteen-foot wall would be difficult, but not impossible. Transitioning to the roof that jutted out at least four feet was the problem.

Night goggles still in place, he checked his surroundings, and then, hand by hand, foot by foot, he scaled the wall. The soffit stuck out just above his head. He leaned back and gazed at the gutter, two feet up, four feet back. Or was it five feet back? Missing this leap would end the mission as quickly as a bullet to the head.

He set his feet, thought of how Rachelle would have laughed at the ease of this particular attempt, and sprang backward like an inverted frog.

He'd overestimated the jump. But he arched his back and corrected. Still upside down and flying with good speed, he grasped the gutter, folded at his waist into a pike position, then whipped his legs back to continue their natural arc. He treated the gutter as a high bar, and his momentum carried him up and over like a world-class gymnast.

The gutter creaked and began to give way, but his weight had already shifted. He released, floated over the edge of the roof, and landed on his hands and feet, like a cat.

A shingle came loose, slid over the edge, and fell into the grass below. No other sound. He scrambled to the only dormer on this end of the house and listened beside the window. Still no sound.

The room inside was dark, and with the goggles he could see that it was also vacant, unless someone was crouching behind the boxes. Storage room.

Thomas fumbled for the duct tape he'd brought and ran three long strips down the glass. Then he unwrapped the sweater around his waist, covered the window to muffle sound, and smashed it with his elbow. A crunch but no shattering glass. Good enough.

He shoved the tape roll and sweater in his belt and carefully pushed through the broken glass. Two minutes later he stood in the dark storage room, staring at a dozen stacks of boxes.

Thomas withdrew the gun and cracked the door. Small hall. One other door. Clear.

He stepped out carefully. Only one way to do this.

The first door looked as though it led to a closet. It did.

The second appeared to lead to a larger room. It did. A bedroom. Thomas extended his gun and pushed the door open.

The blinding light hit him then, while he had one foot in and one out, door still swinging.

The goggles! He swept at his face and knocked the contraption from his eyes.

"Hello, Thomas."

Voice to his right. This was Carlos.

"I see you insist on coming for me until I finally kill you for good."

Easy, Thomas. This is what you expected. Play the game.

He dropped his gun and lifted both hands. "We need to talk. It's not what you think."

Carlos held a gun on him at five paces. He still wore a bandage over the cut on his neck. A grin nudged the corner of his mouth. Small red dots peppered his face. So the man hadn't taken the antivirus. Or the antivirus didn't work.

"I watch an armed man climb my roof, sneak through a window wearing night-vision glasses, and am expected to consider the possibility that my judgment of his intentions is false?" Carlos asked. "Don't tell me: you came to save me."

"I came because I know that you met with Armand Fortier yesterday," Thomas said. "He showed you a list of the people he expects to survive the virus. Now you have to ask yourself how in the world I could possibly have this information."

The grin faded. Carlos blinked. "You've tricked me one too many times. This time you will fail."

"And if I do, then you will die. We both know that your name's on that list only as a lure for you and only for the moment. Tell me how I know so much. Tell me how I walk off your gurney after two days without a pulse. Tell me how any of what you've seen me do with your own eyes is possible."

Carlos just stared at him. But his mind was bending—Thomas could see it in his eyes.

"I came here for two reasons. One, I've come with proof. If you let me, I can show you beyond any possible doubt that my dreams are real and that you play a significant role in those dreams. The second reason I've come is to save your life. The simple fact of the matter is that we need you, but you'll do us no good if you're dead. You may hate Americans and Israel and all that, but unless you know what's really going on here, you can't possibly be in a position to make informed decisions."

He said it all in a rush, because he knew that he had to plant these seeds in Carlos's mind before he pulled the trigger. His words seemed to have made an impact. But the man wasn't unnerved as much as he was irritated.

"I don't know what kind of sorcery—"

"We don't have time for this, Carlos. I just came five thousand miles to make contact with you, and what I have to show you may save the Arab world from extermination. What does it take to get your attention? You still have a cut I gave you last time without touching you, for goodness' sake! You have to let me prove myself."

Too much had happened for Carlos to dismiss this as a game of wits. His neck, Thomas's escapes, the knowledge of his conversation with Fortier—all of it unexplained.

"How?"

"By letting you dream with me."

The man's face reddened. "Do you take me as some kind of fool?" His fist clenched. "I cannot accept this! This . . ."

Thomas moved while the man was momentarily distracted by his frustration. Dropped shoulder to his left, single spin, heel to the man's gun hand. Even if Carlos had fired, the bullet would have gone wide.

Fortunately, he didn't even manage that.

His outstretched hand flew wide. Thomas followed with an open palm to the man's solar plexus. Carlos stepped back, shocked. Unable to breathe.

"Sweet dreams." Thomas hit him on the side of the head, and the man dropped.

Working quickly, he pulled out his knife and cut his finger. Then he ran a thin slit along Carlos's forearm. He smeared his own blood along the cut.

"Make him understand, Johan. Please make him understand."

Thomas let the man dream ten minutes before waking him. A minute probably would have sufficed, but he didn't want to take any chances. He shook the man hard, slapped him once on the cheek, and stepped back to the cot, gun extended.

Carlos groaned, went silent, then jerked up with a gasp.

Thomas knew immediately that Carlos had dreamed with Johan. He was far too seasoned to wake in this state of disorientation for any other reason.

"Where were you?" he asked.

Carlos looked at him, glanced at the gun, ignored it, and stared into Thomas's eyes.

"With Johan, I mean. Where were you?"

"In . . . in the forest."

"The forest?"

"Going to the Horde city."

That made no sense. Johan was coming after him? The man had left his post for a mission to rescue Thomas? If he'd done anything to endanger Chelise, Thomas would have his head.

Carlos stared at his gun again. Now the real question. "Do you believe me now? There's another reality beyond this one, and in that reality you and I are on the same side. There's more."

"If I die here, then Johan will die there," Carlos said. He was hardly more than a child who'd just learned the truth.

"And I'm depending on Johan," Thomas said. "I would never let him die. So you see, I *am* here to save your life."

As long as Carlos believed the dream was more than a simple dream, Thomas was sure he would succeed.

They stared at each other for a full minute. It was one thing to believe that another reality existed. It was another thing altogether to change your plans because of that reality.

"If we don't stop Fortier, we will both die," Thomas said. "Along with most of the earth's population. Is this what you had in mind?"

No answer. But his eyes showed no defiance. He was still caught up in the wonder of it all.

"There's only one way to stop Fortier, and that's to take away his teeth."

"The antivirus," Carlos said.

"Yes. The United States must have the antivirus. It's the only force that has a plausible chance of dealing with Fortier." Thomas paused. "Can you get the antivirus?"

"No."

Thomas lowered his gun. "Do you believe that I won't harm you?"

"Yes."

Carlos slowly stood. "I don't know how . . ." He stopped and looked at his hands.

"And you may never know. It doesn't matter. What does matter is that we stop them. You may be our only chance to do that. You're sure that you can't get your hands on the antivirus? It does exist. Please tell me that it exists."

"It exists, but Svensson's protected himself by separating it into two components somehow. He alone controls one, which will be used only at the last moment."

"Then we have to take Svensson. If we control even one component of the antivirus, we will have a bargaining chip. At the moment we have nothing except for the weapons. With any luck we can force Svensson's hand."

"Will you give them the weapons at the exchange?"

It was a moment of truth. If he told Carlos their plans, he might be tipping his hand to the enemy. On the other hand, doing so could earn him the trust he needed. Without the antivirus, all was lost.

"No," he said.

A moment passed between them. Carlos understood what Thomas had just done.

"Does Fortier plan on giving us an antivirus that works?" Thomas asked.

"No." Case settled. They were now together.

Carlos took a very deep breath and tilted his head to the ceiling. "What do you want me to do?"

"Take Svensson. Don't kill him—we have to protect the antivirus. Who's taken it?"

"Only Fortier and Svensson," Carlos said.

"Good. If we go down, so does everyone except those two. I doubt that's Svensson's idea of paradise. He'll be forced to deal."

Carlos nodded. "Maybe. But you have no idea how dangerous this is."

"Dangerous? We're way beyond dangerous, my friend. This history's already been written once, and in that history most of us die. I would say it's more like impossible. But that doesn't mean we don't try. They say with a little faith you can move mountains. That's all I'm asking. Move a mountain. Will you?"

The man from Cyprus frowned deeply. "Clearly, I don't have a choice."

"The fate of the world may very well rest in your hands."

"Not yours?"

"No, my presence would only compromise you. Do you see this?"

"What do you have in mind?"

"Did you hear what Carlos told him?" Fortier demanded into the phone.

"No."

"How long? How could you have allowed this?"

"Forgive me, sir. He slipped past our guard. We don't know how long they were together. By the time we understood what was happening, he was gone."

"You're absolutely sure that it was an American?"

"No, but it was clearly no one we knew."

The phone was silent while Fortier considered the matter.

"Shall we take any action?" the man asked.

"No. Carlos stays there. Under no circumstance is he to leave. Consider the compound his prison, but he must not know. Business as usual. If he tries to leave, kill him."

36

Thomas ducked below the spinning blades over his head and ran from the helicopter. The USS *Nimitz*'s massive tower reached high just ahead. He'd seen the large fleet from the air. Over two hundred ships from the United States alone. Dots on the ocean, each leading a long tail of white foam.

The British fleet was to the north five miles. The Israelis were using mostly freighters—more than thirty, each loaded to the gills with weapons they denied they actually possessed. There was enough nuclear firepower in a five-mile radius of this aircraft carrier to blow up the world fifty times over.

The first sign that not all was normal on deck was the absence of flight crews. The fact was, the *Nimitz* was being run on fumes, with fewer than fifty troops to guide her across the Atlantic.

Thomas hardly recognized Merton Gains. The man wore a white turtleneck and dark glasses, but if he thought they hid the rash on his face, he was fooling only himself. Thomas hurried toward him. The secretary extended his hand. Wind buffeted his hair.

"Thank God you made it. Just in time."

Thomas took his hand. "They've started?"

"Two hours ago. You have a front-row seat on the observation deck if you want it."

"Absolutely."

The senator paused. "You're not as bad as I thought you'd be."

The rash.

"No. I have it under my arms." He wasn't sure what to say. "Are you okay?"

Gains spit to one side and turned toward the door.

Thomas followed Gains out of the wind and to a large room full of electronics he could only guess at. Radar—that he could see. Large screens with hundreds of blips. Among those blips floated the sharpest edge of America's military sword—six full carrier groups, hundreds of ships carrying everything from their most sophisticated attack aircraft to nuclear weapons. A second large wave of ships was on the way with more, but this was Fortier's primary prize.

Gains introduced him to the first officer. "This is Ben Graver. He's going to talk us through the operation."

Ben took his hand without any expression. "Can't say it's a pleasure," he said.

"Neither can I," Thomas said.

"Should be done in another hour."

The plan was simple. Per French demands, each ship was to be anchored at specific coordinates and their crews off-loaded to a single ship from each country. French crews would board the vessels and verify the cargoes, and only then would the antivirus be turned over.

The obvious problem with the exchange was the lack of a guarantee that Fortier would actually deliver the antivirus after confirming his receipt of weapons. His best offer, and the one Thomas had insisted they accept, had been to anchor one ship containing the antivirus with each navy. They could examine the ship but not take control of it until after Fortier's people had taken possession of the weapons.

"The admiral's aboard?" Thomas asked.

"He is."

"I need to speak to him. Now."

Ben eyed him, then picked up a phone. He spoke quietly and set it back in the cradle. "This way."

Admiral Kaufman. Brent Kaufman, personal friend to the president. The tall, gray-haired man with broad shoulders and blue eyes received them and immediately dismissed the first officer.

"Welcome to hell," the admiral said.

"No, hell comes in two days," Thomas said. "This is more like purgatory."

The admiral frowned. He turned to two ranking men in British and Israeli uniforms. "This is General Ben-Gurion for the IDF, and Admiral Roland Bright from the British fleet."

Thomas took their hands in turn. "Does the first officer know what's about to happen?"

"He does," Kaufman said.

"My understanding was that no one except—"

"I don't know how many ships you've been on, son," the admiral said. "But you can't do what the president has ordered me to do without at least a minimal crew. Someone's got to pull the trigger."

He was right. Thomas regretted challenging the man.

"The French aren't going to give us the antivirus," he said.

"What?" Gains said. "That's . . . Then what are we doing?"

"We're playing ball," Thomas said. "We're hoping for one more chance at getting our hands on a solution that works."

The British admiral's face had lightened a shade. "Under no circumstances am I risking this fleet and this cargo without some assurance that we have an even exchange. This was—"

"Excuse me, sir, but this is exactly what we agreed to. If we don't turn the weapons over exactly as agreed, we tip our hands. At this very moment we have a man on the inside closing in on the antivirus."

"Frankly, I'd sign on for blowing the entire country back into the Stone Age," Ben-Gurion said.

"And the antivirus with it?" Thomas said. "I'm not saying our alternatives have anyone jumping for joy here. We're hanging on by a thread, that's it, but at least it's something."

"I can tell you that I will pay dearly for this tomorrow," Ben-Gurion said.

"Tomorrow the world's eyes will be on the mounting dead, not a few missing nuclear weapons. Our play was based on the hope that they would turn over the antivirus, true enough. Now that we know they have no intention of doing so, our plan still has merit. If we turn tail now, Israel will be hit with missiles within the hour."

"Then we wipe them out."

"I realize your mind is on your military, General," Thomas said. "But trust me, the virus makes your army look like plastic toys. Please understand this: you cannot, under any circumstances, fire on Paris or anywhere near Paris. If you inadvertently take out the antivirus, ten days from now this world will have a population of two."

"Two meaning whom?" Gains asked.

"The only two who've already taken the antivirus. Fortier and Svensson. The only chance for survival the rest of us have is giving my man a chance. That means we follow the plan with one change."

The British admiral arched his left eyebrow. "A change?"

"Can we delay the explosives?"

"We control that from here," Kaufman said.

"Then we delay six hours."

"Why?"

"My man needs the time."

"They will retaliate," Ben-Gurion said. "You said so yourself."

"Not if we play our cards right. Not if my man succeeds. Not if we threaten to wipe out Paris."

"I thought you said we couldn't risk compromising the antivirus."

"We can't. But we can call their bluff. If it gets that far, they'll know we have nothing left to lose. They won't run the risk of a final desperate launch on our part. You've held back ten long-range missiles?"

"Yes," Ben-Gurion said.

"There you go. They might doubt our resolve, but they won't doubt yours." He turned to the window and gazed at the battleship on their port side. The menacing guns that jutted over the water were now useless toys in a game with far higher stakes than their manufacturer's wildest imagination.

"I don't know where you learned your strategy, lad," the British admiral said behind him. "But I like it. And as far as I can see, it's our only option."

"Admiral Kaufman?" Thomas asked without turning.

"It might work." He swore. "I don't see an alternative."

"Then let's give them something to think about," Ben-Gurion said. "We're with you."

Thomas turned back to them. "Thank you."

Honestly, it felt good to be commanding men after this thirteen-month hiatus in the other reality. This could be Mikil and Johan and William he was commanding. Thomas wasn't sure what President Blair had told these men to pave the way for their taking suggestions from a twenty-five-year-old, but it had worked.

∽∾

The exchange took an hour longer than anticipated, but by 1600 hours the nuclear arsenals of the United States, Britain, and Israel were in the hands of the French aboard more than three hundred ships that steamed steadily toward their coast.

As payment, the USS *Nimitz* had taken ten large crates filled with canisters of powder that a team of virologists from the World Health Organization quickly confirmed contained an antivirus, though there was no way to verify its authenticity for at least ten hours. Even then, they wouldn't know its true effectiveness. A complete test would take a full day.

In addition to the crates, the aircraft carrier now carried the three thousand crew members who'd been off-loaded from the American fleet.

Thomas had left his radio with Carlos as planned. The arrangement couldn't have been clearer. He had a twelve-hour window. If he succeeded, he would activate the homing beacon. If he hadn't yet succeeded, he would not.

There had been no homing signal.

The six-hour delay had come and gone. Thomas watched the clock on the observation deck, and with each jerk of the minute hand, his hopes dropped a notch.

Come on, Carlos.

Perhaps there was no way to change history after all.

Kaufman walked into the room and removed his hat. His eyes glanced at the clock. "We're in confirmed range five minutes, then we start losing a consistent signal."

Thomas stood. "Then what are you waiting for, Admiral? Send the message, fire the missiles, and drop the ships."

A grin crossed Kaufman's face. "At least we go out in a blaze of glory."

"Maybe."

Thomas watched the plan unfold over the first officer's shoulder at the radar station. The message sent to Fortier was straightforward: *fire one round in retaliation and the next ten will target Paris.* It wasn't worded quite so simply, but the meaning was the same.

The missiles were next. Twenty-six in all, eighteen cruise missiles from batteries outside Lankershim Royal Air Base in England and eight tactical nukes—compliments of the IDF. The targeting was straight-forward and unmistakable: every major command and control facility in and around the deposits of the Russian, Chinese, Pakistani, and Indian nuclear stores in northern France. They couldn't take out the weapons themselves without risking massive detonations that would level civilian populations, but they intended to at least temporarily cripple France's use of their newly acquired arsenal.

Admiral Kaufman gave the order calmly over the intercom. He could just as easily have been telling his wife that he would be home soon.

"Scuttle the ships."

The observation deck quieted. The air felt stuffy. Thomas kept his eyes glued on the sea of bright dots on the radar screen. Each one represented a loaded ship, including six full carrier groups crowded with fighters. The computer displayed them as steady signals, as opposed to signatures that lit with each sweep of the radar.

"Is it working?"

"Give it time," Ben said. "These things don't drop like stones, I don't care how you do it."

For a while nothing happened.

"Confirmed detonations," a voice said over the comm.

Five more minutes, still nothing.

Then the first light winked out.

"Ship down. Israeli freighter, the *Majestic*."

A billion dollars of nuclear weapons was on its way to the bottom.

Then another and another. They began to wink out like expired candles.

"Back to the Stone Age," Ben said quietly.

"There will be plenty more where those came from," Thomas said. "Assuming there's anyone left to build them."

Here in the silence of the aircraft carrier's observation deck, the destruction of the world's nuclear arsenal looked like something on a video game, but a hundred miles away, the ocean was burning with three hundred slowly sinking blazes. The weapons required far more to detonate them than random concussion and heat from conventional explosions. They would sink to the ocean floor intact, awaiting salvage at the earliest possible opportunity.

Assuming that anyone was around to salvage them.

Thomas watched the screen for nearly an hour, mesmerized by the silent vanishing of tiny green lights.

Then the screen went black.

For a moment no one spoke.

Gains stuck his head into the room. "I just talked to the president, Thomas. They're sending a plane to pick you up."

He turned. "Me? Why?"

"Wouldn't say. But they're sending an F-16 with in-flight refueling. He wants you back in a hurry."

"No clue at all?"

"None. But the news is out."

"The media already knows what we did here?"

"No. The news about the virus. The symptoms are widespread in all of the gateway cities." He pushed his sunglasses up on his nose. "It's begun."

"How long do I have?"

"They'll be here in an hour."

Thomas walked toward him. "Then I don't have much time, do I?"

"What are you going to do?"

"Sleep, Mr. Gains. Dream."

37

A door slammed above Thomas, waking him. A faint scream.

He opened his eyes and stared into pitch darkness. For a moment he thought he was on the ship, hearing another round of fire. But the cold, damp floor under him pulled him back to this reality.

In the dungeon.

How long had he slept?

The scream came again, louder now. He sat up and caught his breath. Chelise?

No, that was impossible. Chelise was in the tribe's hands, safe.

Or was she? He was fully awake now. Carlos had said that Johan was coming. Why?

Footsteps sounded overhead. A dim light wavered down the corridor. Boots on the stairs.

Thomas scrambled to his feet, lost his balance, fell against the wall, and pushed himself off. He hurried to the gate and gripped the bars. Torchlight glistened off wet rock walls. They were coming for him.

He saw Woref's familiar face, glowing by the light of a torch he held in his left fist. His right hand grasped the end of a rope. So the time had come. He took a deep breath and stepped back from the bars.

Woref stared in through the bars. He had someone else behind him— another prisoner or a guard.

"The mighty Thomas of Hunter," Woref said. "So clever. So brave. To come all this way for nothing. William is dead."

"William?"

"You remember him. Tall. Green eyes. A weak fool who talks too much.

He convinced me to spare the tribe in exchange for you. I suppose you should be proud of him."

Spare the tribe. What was the man speaking of? Thomas felt the blood leave his extremities.

"Surprised?" Woref said. "Imagine my surprise to find that you'd already given yourself up in exchange for the other albinos. You were sure you'd be safe as long as your whore was with the tribe."

Thomas's mind spun in dizzying circles.

"It appears the fearless commander of the Forest Guard has finally been outwitted." Woref tugged on the rope. Chelise stumbled past him, lips quivering, hands bound. Something sharp, like fingernails or a claw, had drawn three streaks of blood on her right cheek. Her eyes were wide with terror, and the morst on her face was streaked with tears.

Thomas wavered on his feet. He couldn't think straight.

"I thought you'd like to see her before I clean her up and deliver her to her father," Woref said.

Thomas slammed into the bars. "Chelise . . . Oh, my dear . . ." He spoke to Woref. "How dare you hurt the daughter of Qurong!"

Woref's smile faded. "So you still care for her. Did you really think the daughter of Qurong could ever return your pitiful love? No one told you that you're an albino? She belongs to me, you filthy slab of flesh! And I can assure you that whatever doubts she might have entertained toward me have been removed."

The terrible truth of their predicament washed over Thomas. Chelise could barely keep her eyes open. A single glance at her drooping face brought a tremble to his bones. Woref had abused her in ways he couldn't guess.

His rage against Woref faded as he gazed at her. A terrible sorrow swept through his chest. "Chelise. I'm so sorry." Tears blurred his vision. He sank to his knees.

"Forgive me, my love, forgive me," she cried.

She was crying for him! He reached his hand through the bars.

A fist slammed against his arm, numbing it to the shoulder. Woref turned and slugged Chelise in the jaw. She fell back against the wall and groaned.

"Please, don't hurt her!" Thomas's eyes flooded with tears. This wasn't what Woref had expected. Thomas's love for Chelise, yes, but not Chelise's love for him. The general stood trembling from head to foot.

Thomas lunged for the man through the bars. His face collided with cold bronze, but he managed a hand on the general's leather breastplate.

Woref swung another fist—not at Thomas. At Chelise. It struck her in her side and she gasped.

Thomas fell back in horror.

"For your love of my wife, you will die a terrible, painful death," the general said. He grabbed Chelise by the hair and shoved her ahead of him, down the corridor.

She wasn't his wife. She didn't love him. She despised the beast who would enslave her. Thomas knew all of this. But he could do nothing except fall to the stone floor and weep.

Johan watched the twenty-four tribe members ride in single file down the rocky cliff pass. Suzan sat on a lathered horse on his right, and Mikil faced him on her own horse. Nearly two days had passed since the Horde army left them. They'd debated following but knew that whatever Thomas had intended was already done. And now here was proof. He'd traded himself for the twenty-four without knowing that Chelise had been taken.

Mikil had just learned about Chelise herself, and she was furious.

"He left her in your command! You've just signed his death!"

"Give me the right to use a sword and we would have escaped," Johan said. "Woref outwitted us." He frowned and spit to the side. "I should have known."

"It's my fault," Suzan said. "I should have found the army, but they'd taken their prisoners. We honestly thought they were gone."

"It's done," Johan said. "The question is how we help Thomas now."

Mikil grunted and pulled her mount around. The tribe was running out to meet their family. Little did they know.

"As I see it, we have only one choice," Johan said.

"I can tell you that any rescue won't be easy," Mikil said. "The city is braced for us. If Thomas isn't dead already, he's holed up somewhere only Woref knows about."

"Then we die trying," Johan said. "I couldn't live knowing I let this happen."

"I agree," Suzan said. "William is likely in the dungeons as well. Or dead."

"William?" Mikil demanded. "What happened to William?"

Johan told her. They could only assume that he'd agreed to betray Thomas knowing that Thomas was beyond being betrayed. He'd saved the tribe. He was a cantankerous troublemaker, but the Circle blood ran deep.

Mikil set her jaw. "Let me get Jamous. I need to bathe and saddle a fresh horse. Then we leave."

<hr />

Qurong stood over the bed, staring at his daughter, who slept peacefully. She was bruised and there was some bleeding on her scalp and on her cheek, but otherwise she was healthy, the doctor said. Woref had seen to it that she was freshly bathed and covered in morst when he brought her into the castle, draped across his arms.

His wife pulled the covers over Chelise's shoulder. "We let her sleep."

Qurong followed her into the hall. "She's been brutalized!" Patricia whispered harshly. "Any fool can see that!"

"She was in captivity with the albinos. Of course she's been brutalized. But she will be fine. You'll see. She'll probably be up this afternoon, running to the library or something. She's a strong woman, like her mother."

"I'm not so sure this is the work of albinos. Since when do they brutalize their prisoners?"

"Maybe she fell down a cliff, for all we know. Things happen in the desert. Woref thinks she might have fallen off a horse." He came to the stairs and stopped. "She's safe. I have gained my daughter back. Now let me go and see what I can do to keep her safe."

"You would believe a goat that told you what you wanted to hear," Patricia said. "My daughter would never defile herself. I'll speak to them with you."

He started to object but then decided he could use her. What Woref and Ciphus intended to prove, he didn't know, but better two against two.

The chief priest and the commander of the armies waited for them in the dining room as instructed. They stood from the long table when Qurong pushed the door open. Both dipped their heads in respect.

Woref's face had been scratched. Three thin lines of blood seeped through the morst on his cheek. If Qurong wasn't mistaken, he'd been bruised on his eye as well. This all since bringing Chelise in earlier. His commander had been beaten?

"I see you've taken the liberty of eating my fruit," Qurong said.

"We were told . . ."

He waved Ciphus off. "Fine. My house is your house. At least when you're invited."

Patricia walked in and they bowed again, out of respect to Qurong, not to his wife. If she had come alone, they would treat her like any other wife. Patricia had never approved of the custom, but none of her outrage had changed it. Men were honored over women; it had always been so.

"What is this all about?" Patricia demanded.

Woref glanced at Ciphus, who nodded. The snake would always defer, Qurong thought. His backside was his only holy relic, and he would cover it well.

"There are some things that you should know, my lord," Woref said. "I took the liberty of counseling Ciphus before I came to you."

"Yes, of course. Spit it out."

"It's the condition of your daughter. I can tell you after bringing her to safety that she is not herself. I fear she's been bewitched by the Circle. By what manner of torture or brutality, I don't know, but she woke up once screaming terrible lies. Her mind's been tampered with."

"What kind of lies?" Patricia demanded harshly.

"Lies of all kinds. She accused me of capturing her when, of course, it was the albinos who captured her. She said that I struck her and dragged her by the hair, something I wouldn't think of doing to my bride. She thinks the albinos are her friends and we are her enemies."

"Don't be ridiculous," his wife said. "If she said that you slapped her, I would believe her! How many women have you hit before, Woref?"

He looked at Qurong, shocked by her accusation. "That is hardly the point, I assure you. She's been bewitched!" His face flushed. "How dare you accuse me of mistreating the woman I would die for!"

They stared, facing off.

Qurong intervened. "Ciphus, what are your thoughts on this bewitching? Is it possible?"

"The mind is a delicate thing, prone to deception. Yes, I think it is possible. It wouldn't surprise me at all. Give her time and she will come to. Her heart is something else, of course. Sins of the mind are forgivable. Sins of the heart are not."

"I still don't trust you," Patricia said, glaring at Woref. "If you are to have any peace as my son-in-law, you'd better learn how to correct that. And if you ever treat my daughter like you do your other women, I will see you drowned myself."

For a moment Qurong wondered if Woref would lose control of himself. This was what his wife wanted, of course. She would do whatever was necessary to earn the man's indebtedness; then she would use her advantage however she saw fit.

Qurong smiled. "Welcome to the family. And for the record, I agree with my wife. Harm one hair on her head and you *will* drown, Woref." He paused. "But I'm sure you didn't come simply out of concern for Chelise. Exactly why are we here? I would think both of you would be as pleased as I am. We have Thomas, and now that we know how the albinos think, we will leverage him to bring the entire Circle to its knees. Chelise is safe. All is good."

Woref didn't seem able to talk. Ciphus answered for him. "My lord, there is one matter that you should consider. Your daughter's mind is one thing, as I said. But if she has committed treason—"

"I don't want to hear this!" Patricia said, marching past them toward the kitchen. She turned back. "If you dare suggest that my daughter has any feelings for that wretched beast, I'll cut your tongue out. She could never love an albino. Never!"

"Of course not. Because if she did, she would have to pay the price required by law."

"You heard my wife!" Qurong said. "Chelise is incapable of loving an albino! If she did, I would drown her myself. Are you going to continue with this nonsense?"

Ciphus dipped his head. "I'm only doing my duty as your loyal priest, my lord. Just so you remember that no law is above Elyon's law, as all the Horde knows."

"Fine. Are you finished?"

Woref was seething, and Qurong thought it odd. Surely he'd been forthcoming. Neither answered him.

"Then get out! Both of you. I don't want to hear of this again."

They stepped back, bowed, and left the room.

"How dare they?" his wife snapped.

"They dare because they are far more powerful than you may realize," he said. "This religion and this Elyon of his may be a lot of nonsense, but we used it to our benefit to control the people. This on pain of death, that on pain of death . . . the whole system one of threats and rewards dictated by some god we can't see. Ciphus is the only one the people see. His word is nearly as powerful as mine."

"Then it's time you threw him out!"

"So the people could throw me out?"

"You have an army! Squash the people."

"The army are the people! I've put Elyon above me, and they prefer it that way. They feel less captive. They're serving a god, not a man."

He picked up a green pear and took a bite. "Power is always in the balance, my wife. I no longer have the power to upset that balance. Not if it works against me."

38

The guard opened the door that led into the dungeon while Woref was still ten yards from it. Fifty torches blazed in the midnight hour, lighting the perimeter of the compound and path to the single entrance. If the albinos came for Thomas now, they would have to fight their way through three hundred of his best warriors. Even then, there was no way into Thomas's cell. Woref carried the only key, and nothing short of the black powder the Forest Guard had once used would blast the bars free.

He stooped beneath the door's thick lintel and descended the long flight of steps, the guard just behind.

"Wait here," he said, taking the torch. He walked down the narrow corridor, boots loud on the rock floor.

There was a terrible risk in this plan of his, but the moment Chelise had spoken those words—*Forgive me, my love, forgive me*—Woref vowed to change her. Or kill her.

Thomas was no longer his concern. They would use him, destroy him, drown him. None of it would change anything. His bride's love was all that mattered now. His whole purpose for living had focused on this day, he realized. The sum of his life would come down to winning and losing love.

Over time, he could persuade Chelise to submit to him. But as long as she loved Thomas, her affection would be compromised. And if he killed Thomas now, he would only live on in her mind, haunting Woref forever.

He couldn't kill Thomas. Not yet.

But he could use Thomas to secure Chelise's love.

Woref descended the second set of stairs quickly, eagerly. Ciphus had approved the plan for his own reasons, namely, to save Chelise's life. If she publicly rejected Thomas and openly embraced Woref, the matter of her heart would be settled.

Woref heard the prisoner shuffle to his feet. Expecting another glimpse of his dear love, perhaps? *You and your kind are the worst life has to offer. And when I'm finished grinding you under my feet, I'll commit my life to finishing off the rest.*

Thomas was standing in the middle of the cell, peering out expectantly when Woref stopped before the bars. His eyes glanced to Woref's right, then returned when he saw the corridor was empty.

Woref paced, primarily to squash his impulse to throw open the door and kill the man where he stood. He blinked away sweat that leaked into his eyes.

"You and your precious Circle are finished, Thomas. I'm sure you realize that by now."

The albino just looked at him.

"Your problem is that you misunderstand sentiments intended merely for self-gratification. Affection, loyalty, love. Your friends will come to your aid, bound by honor, but they will only find their own deaths. We will use their misguided sense of duty to our advantage."

Still no reaction.

"You can't save your friends, but you can save Chelise."

His eyes moved.

"You do love her. I can see that." Woref felt sickened by his own words, but he pushed on. "And if you love her, I would think you would be interested in saving her life."

"I love her," the albino said. "More than my life."

"I'm not interested in your life!" Woref shouted. He calmed himself. "Do you know the price that she will pay for this heretical sentiment you've dragged out of her? You've sentenced her to death. It's our law."

"Qurong won't kill his own daughter. She'll never admit her love for me openly. And her father will believe her over you."

"Then I will kill her!" Woref said. He was trembling, but he didn't care. Let the jackal know the truth. "Only Elyon himself knows how desperately I need this woman," he said. "If she won't love me, then she won't love any man. I'll rip her tongue out and throw her to the dogs."

Fear slowly crossed the albino's face. "You won't," he said. "You're too consumed with your own life to risk it."

"I will. There are ways to kill that cannot be traced. I can assure you, the death of Chelise will be brutal."

Thomas's mouth turned down and began to twitch. His breathing was shallow.

Woref smiled. "You know that I'm capable of this. You know, in fact, that I would relish it." He could hear both of their breathing now, loud and ragged in the narrow passage. The implications of what he was saying had the albino's mind in a vise. Woref hadn't expected to feel so much pleasure.

"If Chelise still loves you in three days' time, she will die. Only you can save her life. I've arranged for you to spend time with her in the morning. No one will know. I will give you this one opportunity to change her mind and her heart."

His words hung in the air between them. And their meaning had its full intended effect. Tears flooded the albino's eyes and ran down his cheeks. His face knotted. He slowly lifted both hands, gripped his hair, and began to weep silently.

Woref smiled.

There was nothing else to say, but he was transfixed by this sight of such terrible sorrow. The albino loved the woman nearly as much as he himself did. And what could the albino say? Nothing. He was outwitted. Trapped.

He would have to find a way to convince Chelise that he no longer loved her.

"I will be listening and watching. Don't think that you can fool me."

Woref turned and walked from the cell.

The albino's sobbing began when he was halfway down the second corridor.

39

He had been sucked into the darkest, coldest corner of reality and left there to rot. There wasn't a sound except for his own sobs and the long wails that he tried in vain to silence. He couldn't see—not the walls, not the cold stone floor, not his fingers if he put them an inch from his eyes. His body shivered and his mind refused to sleep.

But all of this was like paradise compared to the hell that engulfed Thomas's heart.

He lost his sense of time. There was black and there was cold and there was pain. How could he do what Woref had demanded? He thought about a hundred ways to save Chelise without crushing her love. His love. But not a single one could hold his trust.

With Woref or his conspirators listening, watching, the slightest advance that Thomas might make would result in her death. She wouldn't be told, of course. She would see him and run to him for an embrace, and he would have to push her away. Woref wanted to see her heart crushed by Thomas so that she would receive Woref's love.

Thomas was being forced to make her despise him. It was the only way to save her life.

But what could he do to make her despise him? The answer drained his body of tears.

Now Thomas wanted to do nothing but sleep. Dream. Anything to tear him away from this agony. In all of his fury, Woref had neglected to make him eat the fruit. If only he could die of the virus and never wake again. If only there was a rhambutan fruit in the other reality that he could eat so that he would never have to come back here to crush her heart.

But the more he tried to shut down his mind, the more it revolted in desperation to find one flicker of light. One thread of hope.

There was none.

He finally lay on his back, staring at the dark. For a very, very long time, nothing happened.

And then a sound reached him. The sound of boots.

"Why the back door?" Chelise asked.

"I understand that your father wants no one to disturb you," Ciphus said, opening the door to the library. "I assume he knows that certain people would object."

She stepped into the hall. "I don't understand. Some time alone with the Books of Histories might clear my mind, yes, but I don't see why anyone would object."

"Did I say alone, my dear?"

Thomas? Ciphus wore a knowing grin. Father had arranged for her to see Thomas? No, that would make no sense!

Chelise stopped. "What's happening, Ciphus? I demand to know!"

"I can't say for sure. I was told only to bring you here and ask you to wait with the Books. Your father understands that you will spend the day resting in the library. You're not feeling well enough to do that?"

"I feel fine. It doesn't explain all this secrecy."

"Please, Chelise, this wasn't my doing."

Ciphus opened the door into the large storage room and walked in. Chelise followed. The last time she'd been in here had been with Thomas. The memories soothed her like a warm salve.

Ciphus turned to leave.

"Woref knows I'm here?"

"Woref? I'm guessing he's with your father. Your wedding day does require some planning."

"My mother told me just this morning that I wouldn't marry anyone I didn't approve of. I don't approve of Woref."

"Then maybe that's why your father agreed to your being here. Maybe its the safest place for you. Woref won't take a refusal lightly. Let the peace in this room calm you. You're as safe here as in the castle."

Ciphus left. She'd agreed to come because her mother was driving her frantic, and the servants were gawking at her as if she'd risen from the dead. Her mind was on Thomas, and she couldn't stand walking around the castle thinking of him.

Now she wondered if she'd made a mistake. There were no busybodies peering at her here, but this room with all these Books made her feel empty. Alone.

Chelise crossed to the desk and stared at the Book Thomas had tried to teach her to read. She couldn't read it because it was designed to be read by those whose eyes were opened. She was surprised that she could accept that so easily now.

She had to be careful. Thomas was in the dungeon—the thought made her sick. But she couldn't endanger his life by attempting to secure his release. Woref knew. A shiver ran down her spine and she closed her eyes. Their predicament was hopeless now. The only man who truly loved her was sealed in a tomb, and she had no will to live without him. If Thomas wasn't imprisoned, she would simply run. She would find the Circle and dive into their red pool and find a new life.

But if she ran now, they would kill him. And if they knew how she felt about him, they would kill both of them.

Her head ached. She'd covered her bruises with morst, but the pain from the blows would take a few days to ease. Mother seemed convinced that she'd been abused by the albinos. With Thomas in the dungeon, Chelise wasn't sure what to tell her.

She pulled the chair out and started to sit when the door suddenly opened.

Thomas stepped in.

The door closed behind him. Locked.

The blood drained from her face. They'd brought Thomas here? His face was ashen and his eyes were red, but he wasn't cut or bruised.

She glanced around. The room was empty, of course. And the door was locked.

Tears sprang to her eyes and she hurried toward him. "Thomas!"

He wasn't looking at her. Something was wrong.

"What have they done to you? I'm so sorry—"

"Stay away from me," he said, lifting his hand.

She stopped. "What . . . What do you mean?" She glanced at the door. Someone was listening? "They're listening?"

"How should I know? It doesn't matter. I've been found out."

Chelise walked up to him, took his arm, and whispered quickly. "They're listening, aren't they? Woref's up to something!" He looked so sad, so completely used up. Her heart fell. "Woref took me from the camp. I had nothing to do with it. What on earth do you mean you've been found out?"

His eyes moistened. A single tear leaked from the corner of his left eye and ran down his cheek. She reached a trembling hand to wipe it.

Thomas moved his head away. "Please, if you don't mind, not so close. Your breath."

His words ran through her heart like a sword. He couldn't mean that! They were forcing him!

He stepped away from her and walked to one of the shelves. His steps were uneven, and he looked like he might fall. "I'm sorry, Chelise. They asked me to come here to transcribe the Books. I didn't know you were going to be here, but I can't hide the truth from you any longer."

"What truth?" she demanded. "Ciphus brought me here knowing that you'd be here! They're forcing us—"

"Stop it!" he snapped. "Of course they knew you were here. They brought you because they think it's only fair that I tell you the truth myself. I don't blame them." He faced her, his expression cold. There was a tremble in his voice.

"Do you have any idea how putrid you Scab women smell to us? Did you stop to wonder how we could stand you in our camp for so long?

Did you notice how the others kept disappearing for fresh air? We used you!" He faltered. "We needed the leverage."

"You're lying! You're standing there trembling like a leaf trying to persuade me that you don't love me. But I've seen your eyes and I've felt your heart, and none of this is true!"

For a long moment they just stared at each other, and she was sure he would break down and rush to her.

"Believe what you want. Just keep your distance. I don't want to hurt you any more than I have to. Even a Scab woman deserves some respect." He turned to the shelf and pulled out one of the Books.

Chelise's mind flashed back to their time in this very library just a week ago. To the poetry he'd recited while he thought she was sleeping. To the long days riding together on horseback. To the first time he'd kissed her.

And she knew that he was lying. Why?

Unless . . . What he said did make some sense. But she wouldn't believe it! No man could show the kind of affection he'd shown her while pretending. He'd wept over her.

She didn't know his game, nor why he was being forced to do this, but she decided to play along.

"Fine. You don't love me; I can accept that. I stink to the highest heaven, and you find me repulsive. You're speaking your mind and being plain. That doesn't change the simple fact that I love you, Thomas of Hunter."

She turned her back on him, walked to the desk, and sat. Even from here she could see the tears on his cheek. "Maybe we should start from the beginning. You won my love. Now what should I do to win your love?"

He turned on her, face red. "Nothing! I'm not interested in your love! Leave me. Find a Scab and love him."

"No, I won't go. I don't believe you." She crossed her arms.

"Then you're a fool. You love an albino who you think loves you, but he doesn't. They'll drown you for this misguided, adolescent infatuation with a man who could never love you."

His words were so cutting, so terrible, she wondered if he might be telling the truth after all. And even if he wasn't, he might as well be. Any love they might have shared was now over.

"I still don't believe you," she said. But even as she said it, tears began to stream down her face. She stared at him, suddenly overcome by his words.

What if they are true, Chelise? What if the only love you've ever known turns out to be a false love, and the love you will know is a brutal love that grinds you into the ground? Then there is no true love.

Thomas continued to read the Book in his hands. He was either so crushed by his own words that he couldn't proceed with his charade, or he truly did not care for her and was now disinterested.

Gradually her tears stopped. She wasn't going to leave this room without knowing the full truth. He just read the Book, refusing to look at her.

A thought occurred to her. "If I drowned in one of your red pools and became an albino like you, would you love me then?"

He turned his back to her and leaned against the bookshelf.

"If I didn't smell and I didn't look so pale, could you stand to touch my skin then?"

Nothing.

She slammed her palm on the desk. "Talk to me! Quit pretending you're reading that Book and talk to me! There's a red pool on the north side of the lake, you know. I could run there right now and dive in. Would that change your mind?"

Thomas faced her. He blinked. "There is?"

"Yes, there is. It's all that remains of the original lake. They've covered it with rocks so you can't see it, but I've heard it runs underground. We'd have to remove the rocks. Would that satisfy you?"

For a moment he seemed completely caught off guard. Then he set his jaw. But the tears were flowing again.

She stood and walked toward him. "Please, Thomas. Please, I beg you. I can't believe—"

"Stop it!" he snarled. "Grow up! I don't love you!" His glare was so ferocious that she could hardly recognize him. "I could never love you after using you. You're a spent rag."

Chelise's legs felt weak. He might as well have drilled her with an arrow. She couldn't move.

He slammed the Book on the shelf, walked to the door, and turned the handle. It was locked. He slapped the panel with his palm. "Open this door! Let me out!"

Nothing happened. He hit the door again, then turned back. Chelise felt numb. She still didn't think she could believe him, but she was left with nothing else to believe in.

He walked to the corner, sat on the floor, and lowered his head into his hands. His shoulders shook gently.

Chelise returned to the desk and sat down. *You should leave now,* she told herself.

And go where? To Woref? To the castle where Qurong planned her wedding? To the desert to die? Chelise lay her head down on the desk, closed her eyes, and began to cry.

They remained like that for a long time. Whether his mind was on his own failure in this plot he talked about, or whether it was on her— impossible to tell. It hardly mattered anymore. She was dead either way.

A thump on the wall pulled her from the depths of despondency. She opened her eyes.

Another thump. Then again, *thump, thump.*

She lifted her head. Thomas was standing in the corner, hitting his forehead against the wall.

Thump, thump, thump.

Then harder. And suddenly very hard.

The whole wall shook with the impact of his head, crashing against the wood. She pushed her chair back, alarmed. His teeth were clenched and his face was wet with tears.

He was killing himself?

Thomas suddenly spread his mouth in a roar, drew his head way back, and slammed it against the wall with all of his strength.

The wall shuddered. He collapsed, unconscious.

It was then that Chelise remembered his dreams.

40

Carlos stepped into the dark cell and locked the door behind him. He flipped the light switch on. The gurney Thomas had lain on sat empty. He still couldn't wrap his mind around this situation, but he had decided that Thomas was right: Fortier had no intention of leaving any part of the Muslim world intact.

He walked to the cabinet and unlocked the door. He wasn't sure why Fortier had asked him to monitor the exchange from the remote feeds at the farm, but with each passing hour he grew more nervous. The Frenchman had overemphasized the need for Carlos to stay put. It was tantamount to an order. The exchange was now under way, and Carlos had finally resolved that he could wait no longer. If he was to act against Fortier, it would have to be now.

He withdrew the Uzi and three extra magazines. Two grenades.

He unbuttoned his shirt and jammed two of the clips into his belt. The rash on his belly had spread up to his neck and along his arms. The symptoms of the virus were now spreading beyond the gateway cities. In four days' time there wouldn't be a person alive without the red dots. In a week half the world might be dead.

He buttoned his shirt, grabbed a plastic charge with a detonator, shoved them into his pocket, and closed the cabinet.

If Fortier hadn't ordered him to stay, he might have been able to take Svensson as Thomas had suggested. But if he tipped his hand by leaving against orders, his usefulness would expire. No chance of securing Svensson. The man would go deep.

Carlos walked to the door and slid the safety off.

As soon as he made a play to leave this compound, the Frenchman would take steps to protect the antivirus, but there was one thing Carlos could try. One last desperate act to right some of the wrong he'd brought upon his own people.

He hung the weapon on his shoulder and pulled out his pistol. Working by habit, he screwed the silencer into the barrel and checked the chamber.

The hall was empty.

He walked quickly, eager now to do what he did best. *There is a reason you hired me, Mr. Fortier. I will now show you that reason.*

Carlos headed up the steps. The first guard he saw was a short, thick native of France who hadn't learned to smile. The man saw him and immediately lifted his radio to his mouth. Carlos put a slug through the radio—and through the back of his open throat.

He stepped over the man and walked toward the back door.

The second guard was facing the driveway by the door. The bullet caught him in his temple as he turned. He toppled sideways. Not a sound other than the familiar *phwet* of the gun and the dull smack of slug hitting bone.

But the sound might as well have been a siren to the three trained men by the Jeep. They spun together, rifles ready.

Carlos preferred to leave the compound without giving them a chance to call in his departure. Paris would know that something was wrong when the farm missed their next report in fifteen minutes, but fifteen minutes was a lifetime in situations of this nature. Literally.

He kept the pistol leveled, scanning through the sights. Movement. He shot two of the guards as he ran through the door. Dropped into a roll.

The third guard got off a scream and managed to squeeze the trigger on his automatic weapon before Carlos could bring his gun up.

A hail of bullets smacked the wall above him. Worse, the gun's chattering echoed through the compound with enough volume to wake Paris.

Carlos put two bullets through the guard's chest. The man's finger held the trigger as he fell backwards, stitching shots into the sky. Then the gun was silent.

There was a chance the communications operator in the basement might not have heard, but the guards on the perimeter would have.

He slid into the Jeep, fired the engine, and snatched up his radio. "We have a situation on the south side. I repeat, south side. The Americans are bringing in a small strike force."

He dropped the radio on the seat and floored the accelerator.

"This is Horst on the south side," a voice barked. "I don't see them. You said south side?"

Carlos ignored the question. He only needed enough confusion to slow the two guards at the gate. He roared around the corner and headed straight for them. One had his binoculars trained to the south.

Carlos stopped twenty yards away, threw open his door, and planted one foot on the ground, swinging out. "Any sign?"

"Gunshots—"

Carlos shot the one without the binoculars first. The other heard the silenced gun but couldn't respond quickly enough to save his life.

This is what I can do, Mr. Fortier. This is only part of what I can do.

He ran to the gate, slapped the large red button that opened it, and returned to the Jeep.

When Carlos next glanced at his watch, he saw that exactly two minutes had passed from the time he fired the first shot to the time he exited the long driveway that fed the main road.

Paris was two hours by the primary roads. Five hours by back roads. And Marseilles?

Reaching his destination unscathed would be his greatest challenge. If he managed to make it through, he had an excellent chance of completing his mission.

Armand Fortier looked at the thirteen men seated around the conference table. He had promised these men the world. Dignitaries from Russia,

France, China, and seven other nations. Not one of them would live beyond the week.

"I can assure you this is of no consequence. We knew the Americans and Israelis at least would never turn over their weapons. From the beginning our objective was to pull their teeth, not take over their arsenals. We simply put them in a position where they felt secure doing it."

"And now you'll insist that you also expected them to destroy—"

"Please," he said, exasperated, cutting the Russian off. "No, we did not predict this exact response. To be honest, I expected more. None of it matters. They are in a box. The only weapon that matters now is the virus, and we control that. The game has been played perfectly by all accounts." He stood. "I'm sure you're eager to complete our arrangements for the antivirus. Soon enough, but I am needed elsewhere at the moment. If you need anything over the next few hours, please don't hesitate to ask."

He left them without a backward glance. It was the last time he intended to see any of them.

Fortier walked evenly down the hall. For years he had rehearsed this day. He'd pored over his own graphs and debated possibilities ad infinitum. The outcome had always been certain. He'd always known that if he could get his hands on the right virus, the world would be his to manipulate.

But he'd never actually lived through stakes so high. For the first time he looked at the reports pouring over the television monitors and wondered what he had done.

He'd done what he'd set out to do, of course.

But what had he really done? Over six billion people were infected with a lethal virus that would kill them within the week if his antivirus wasn't distributed within the next forty-eight hours.

His thrill was barely manageable.

He'd read once that Hitler had frequently experienced profound physical reactions to the elation he felt when exercising his power. He'd exterminated six million Jews. Who could have imagined the power that Armand now held in his hand?

God.

But there was no god. For all practical purposes, he was God.

Fortier stepped into a small room at the end of the hall and picked up a black phone.

He was experiencing the exuberance of a god. But with the power came immeasurable responsibility, and it was this that caused him to wonder what he had done. Just as God must have wondered why he'd created humans before sending a flood to wipe them out.

It was a beautiful thing, this power.

Svensson picked up on the first ring. "Yes?"

"Issue the order and meet me in Marseilles."

The distribution of the antivirus was one of the most complex elements of the entire plan. In most cases, those who ingested the antivirus would do so without knowing they had. It had already been administered to a number of key individuals in their drinks or their bread. In most cases, the elect would be called with some mundane excuse to a remote distribution point, where they would unknowingly inhale a localized airborne strain. They would leave destined to survive. The risk of the antivirus landing in the wrong hands would pass in less than twenty-four hours. By then, even if someone got hold of it, he wouldn't have time to manufacture or distribute it.

"No problems?" Svensson said.

"Carlos has turned. He's on his way here."

The phone was silent. They had prepared two installations for this final phase, one in Paris, one in Marseilles on the southern coast of France. No one except the two of them knew about Marseilles. It was now all over but the waiting.

"He's no idiot," Svensson said.

"Neither am I," Fortier said. "Remember, no evidence. Leave the antivirus in the vault."

41

The riots had fallen apart on two counts. The word that the United States had traded its nuclear arsenal for the antivirus and then summarily sent that arsenal to the bottom of the ocean had sent a shock wave across the nation. The news jockeys and political pundits might have spent countless hours dissecting the implications, but another, greater urgency trumped even this stunning bit of news.

The virus had struck.

With a vengeance.

Millions of people in America's urban centers helplessly watched the red spots spread over their bodies. No amount of anger or saber rattling could make these symptoms vanish. Only the antivirus could.

But the antivirus was on its way, Mike Orear insisted. The president had stood on the steps of the Capitol and declared their victory to the world. Hope was not dead. It was being shipped at this very moment, ready to be whisked to the gateway cities, where it would be infused with the blood banks. Within a matter of days, every resident of North America would have the antivirus.

Thomas had followed the news over a secure microwave receiver at twenty thousand feet above the Atlantic. America was holding its collective breath for an antivirus that would not work.

They collected him from the *Nimitz* and streaked back into the sky without offering any answers to his questions. Worse, they declined his request to speak to the president. Not that it mattered—they were in the final throes of a hopeless death anyway. He sat with his hands between his knees, listening to the speculations and calculations and ramifications or possibilities and inconsistencies until he was sure his heart had fallen permanently into his stomach.

The game was over. In both realities.

The fighter settled in for a landing at BWI. Baltimore. Maryland. Johns Hopkins?

They transferred him to a helicopter. Once more he was denied information as to the nature of his sudden recall to the country. Not because they were hiding anything from him—they simply didn't know.

But his guess that they were taking him to Johns Hopkins proved inaccurate. Twenty minutes later the chopper set down on the lawn adjacent to Genetrix Laboratories.

Three lab technicians met the chopper. Two took his arms and hurried toward the entrance. "They're waiting for you inside, sir."

Thomas didn't bother asking.

The moment he stepped into the building, all eyes were on him, from the foyer, through a large room filled with a dozen busy workstations, to the elevator, which they entered and descended. They had heard of him. He was the one who'd brought this virus on them.

Thomas ignored their stares and rode down three floors before stepping out of the elevator into a huge control room.

"Thomas."

He turned to his left. There stood the president of the United States, Robert Blair. Next to him, Monique de Raison, Theresa Sumner from the CDC, and Barbara Kingsley, health secretary.

"Hello, Thomas." He turned around. Kara walked up to him. Sweat glistened on her face, but she smiled bravely. "It's good to see you," she said.

"Kara . . ." He glanced at Monique and Theresa. The rash had covered Theresa's face. Monique's was clear. The president and the health secretary had been infected twelve hours behind them, and their faces were still clear, but the red spots were showing on their necks.

He knew then what they had called him to do. They wanted the dreams. That had to be it. These four wanted to take him up on his suggestion to Kara and Monique that they dream a very long dream using his blood.

"I apologize for the secrecy," Robert Blair said. "But we couldn't risk word of this getting out."

Thomas could hardly bear to look at Kara's face. "How are you feeling?"

"I'm fine."

"Good," he said. He faced the others. "The rash is taking over. Gains is pretty bad, but I . . . You have to hurry."

"You're right," Monique said. "Time is more critical than you can imagine."

"But you don't need me here. I left the blood for you to dream."

None of them moved. They just looked at him.

"What's going on?"

Monique stepped forward, eyes bright. "We've found something, Thomas. It could be very good." Her eyes darted to Kara and back. "And it could also be very bad."

"You . . . you found an antivirus?"

"Not exactly, no."

"You notice that neither Monique nor I have the rash, Thomas?" Kara asked.

"That's good. Right?"

"How's that rash under your arm?" Monique asked.

He instinctively touched his side. "I have it . . ." Now that he thought about it, he hadn't felt the itching for some time. He lifted his shirt up and ran his hand over his skin. No sign of the rash.

"You sure that wasn't a heat rash? I think it was."

Meaning what? He, Monique, and Kara hadn't broken out yet.

"You're virus-free, Thomas."

Monique turned around and pressed a button on a remote in her right hand. The wall opened, revealing a bank of monitors surrounding a large flat screen. The smaller monitors were filled with charts and data that meant nothing to him. But the huge screen in the center was a map of the

world. The twenty-four gateway cities where the virus had initially been
released were marked with red dots. Green circles indicated the hundreds
of labs and medical facilities around the world that were involved in the
search for an antivirus. White crosses marked the massive blood collection
efforts that had been underway since news of the virus went public. Small
crosses spread out from the gateway cites, indicating smaller collection
centers. They had enough blood, he knew that.

But without an antivirus to distribute through the blood, it was useless. "I've run your blood through more tests than I can name in the last
twenty-four hours. They showed nothing unusual." She faced him again.
"Honestly, I can't tell you why I decided to test your blood against the
virus, but I did." She paused.

"And?"

"And it killed the virus. In a matter of minutes."

Thomas blinked. "I'm immune," he said absently.

He felt Kara's arm slip around his. "Not just you. Monique and I have
been in contact with your blood. It killed the virus in both of us."

He looked at the others. Why the long faces? This was good news.

The president forced a smile. "There's more."

A faint suggestion presented itself to him, but he rejected it. Still, the
thought was enough to flush his face.

"Enough with this melodrama. Just get it out. Why am I immune?"

"I think it was the lake," Kara said. "You were healed in Elyon's water.
It changed your blood."

"You were in his lake."

"As Mikil. Not as Kara. Not as me and not in the emerald lake before
it dried up. You were there as yourself, in person. And if it wasn't the lake,
then it was when you were healed by Justin later, after you had the virus.
It's the only thing that makes sense."

Yes, it was.

"However it happened, there's no question that your blood contains
the necessary elements that kill the virus," Monique said.

"And yours?"

She paused. "No. Not like yours."

He wasn't sure he liked where this was going.

"You know what it is about my blood that kills the virus?"

"Not entirely, but enough to duplicate it, yes." She walked to one of the smaller screens. "I isolated various components of your blood, white cells, plasma, platelets, red cells—the virus is reacting to the red cells. I then isolated—"

"I don't care about the science," Thomas said. The suggestion that had dropped into his mind was reasserting itself, and he suddenly had no patience for this presentation of theirs. "Just cut to the bottom line. You need my blood."

She turned around. "Yes. Your red blood cells."

"Something in my red blood cells is acting like an antivirus."

"More like a virus, but yes. When it comes into contact with normal blood, it spreads at an astounding rate, killing the Raison Strain. I've dubbed it the Thomas Strain."

Thomas hesitated only a moment.

"Then take my blood. Do you have time to reproduce enough to distribute as planned?"

"It depends," she said.

"Depends on what?"

She glanced at Barbara Kingsley, who stepped up. "Our plan with the World Health Organization was to collect blood from millions of donors near the gateway cities, categorize and store that blood using every form of refrigeration available, and then prepare it for infusion of the antivirus if and when it was secured. We have the blood, roughly twenty thousand gallons in and around each gateway city."

"I know all of this. Please, depends on what?"

"Forgive me," Barbara said. "I just . . . whether we have enough time to use your blood to effectively infect all of the blood collected depends on how much of your blood we use."

"Infect," Thomas said, trying to ignore the implications. "You mean turn the collected blood into an antivirus."

"Yes," she said. "One of our people put this simulation together." She pointed the remote at the wall and pressed another button. "The effects of the antivirus in your blood have been dyed white so that we can see them. The simulation runs at an exaggerated speed."

Thomas watched as red blood, running like a river across the screen, was suddenly overtaken by a dirty white army of white cells from behind. This was his blood "infecting" the red blood.

He blinked at the sight. A picture from his dreams filled his mind. A hundred thousand of the Horde pouring in the canyons below the Natalga Gap. They had been the disease then. Now his blood would be the cure.

"How much do you need?" Thomas asked.

"It depends on how much of the blood we've collected needs to be infused with—"

"How much of the blood you've collected do you need to save the people who've donated it?" Thomas demanded.

"All of it," Barbara said.

"So then quit dancing around the issue and tell me how much of my blood you need to convert all of it!"

Monique paused.

"Twelve liters," she finally said. "All of it."

"Then what are we waiting for? Hook me up. Take twelve liters. You can do a blood transfusion or something, right?"

Monique hesitated and Thomas knew then that he was going to die.

"We have a time problem."

Kara came to his rescue. "What she's saying, Thomas, is that every hour they delay will cost lives. They've worked it out. The model shows a rough number of ten thousand every hour delayed, increasing exponentially each hour. They need to take as much blood as they can in as short a period of time as they can."

"While giving me a transfusion . . ."

Now it was her turn to hesitate. "The problem with a transfusion is that the new blood would mix with your blood and dilute its effectiveness."

Only an idiot wouldn't understand what they were saying, and part of Thomas resented them for not just spitting it out. Heat spread over his skull. He turned from them and faced a large window that looked into a room equipped with a hospital bed and an IV stand. This was his deathbed he was staring at.

"How do I survive this?" he asked.

"If we slowed the process and took only part of your blood, we have a chance of—"

"You said time was a factor," he said. "That would cost thousands, tens of thousands of lives."

"Yes. But we might be able to save your life."

"Thomas."

He looked at the president.

"I want you to know that I in no way expect you to give all of your blood. They say they can save over five billion people and still have a decent chance of saving you if they slow down the process and take nine pints. They may be able to reproduce your red blood cells at an accelerated rate. The number saved could go up to six billion."

"So we delay several hours, a day, to save my life, and we only lose a billion. Best case. Is that about it?"

They looked at him. That was precisely it.

"I want you to know that this is entirely your choice," the president said. "We can ensure the survival of North America and—"

"No," Thomas said. "He gave me life for this." It all made sense now. Thomas looked at Kara. Her eyes were misty. "History pivots on this sacrifice. You see? I was given life in the lake so that I could pass that life on to you. The fact that it'll take my life is really inconsequential."

He was following in Justin's footsteps. Of course. That was it. He didn't know how everything would work out in these two realities of his, but he did know that his life had been pointed at this moment. This choice.

"Let's do it," he said. "Take it all." He started toward the room with the hospital bed but turned back when they didn't follow. "I will sleep, right? I need to dream. That's all I ask. Let me dream. And Kara. Kara dreams."

Her eyes were round. "Thomas . . ." Words failed her.

He forced his mind back to his last dream. Mixed in with this business of his blood, it felt distant.

"That's my one condition," he said.

They stared, silent.

Thomas took Kara aside and lowered his voice. "You have to dream, Kara. I'm—"

"Thomas, I—"

"No, listen to me." He spoke quickly. "I'm back in the library with Chelise. Woref is trying to force me to deny my love for her. He's threatened to kill her if I don't." Thomas ran a hand through his hair, remembering everything now. "I need you to wake as Mikil and find Qurong. You have to dream before I do—you'll need enough time to get into the Horde city, find her father, and convince him to rescue his daughter from Woref at the library. It'll be dangerous, I won't lie. And if Mikil's killed there, you may die here. But it's the only thing . . ."

How could he ask her to do this?

"Please," he said.

Kara set her jaw, then stepped forward. "Of course I'll do it," she said. She kissed him on the forehead. "It's the least I can do for my brother. For the commander of the Forest Guard."

He was suddenly sure that he was going to cry. She saw it in his eyes and whispered gently, "I love you, Thomas. It's not the end. Justin has more. I know he does."

Thomas tried to answer, but he was choked up.

He cleared his throat. "Then let's do this."

"Thomas . . ." A tear slipped down Monique's cheek. She loved him, he knew. Maybe not as a woman loves a man, but she'd shared enough of Rachelle's love for him to care deeply.

"It's okay, Monique. You'll see. It'll be okay."

"You don't have to do this," Robert Blair said. "You really don't."

"Don't be unreasonable. You wouldn't have called me here if you thought differently. How can you even suggest I think differently?"

They seemed frozen.

Thomas turned and strode toward the waiting room.

Three white-suited surgeons prepped Thomas. Kara had insisted that she dream in the same room as he. They'd sedated her and taped a patch with some of his blood to the same small, scabbed incision that Dr. Bancroft had made on her arm. She turned her head and stared at Thomas, who rested on his back, wondering if he could feel the heparin they'd just injected intravenously. The thrombolytic agent would keep his blood from congealing when it entered the bypass machine.

"I'll see you on the other side, Thomas," Kara said.

He faced her. Monique stood by her bed, arms crossed, fighting emotions that Thomas could only guess at. The president was outside the room on his cell phone. Evidently Phil Grant was missing. Figured.

"Elyon's strength," his sister said.

Thomas offered a weak smile. He could feel the first effects of the drugs.

"It's a passing, Kara. Just a passing." He nodded at the window. "They may not understand what's happening, but you do. You know as Mikil. It's the way of Justin."

"It doesn't feel like that here," she said.

"That's because the Circle doesn't always feel real here. But does that make it any less real? We have *The Histories Recorded by His Beloved*, Kara. The connection is obvious. It's the same here as there; can't you see that?"

She faced the ceiling. "Yes. I can. But even in the Circle there's a sadness at the passing, for those left."

She was right. "If I don't make it, tell them, Kara. Tell them what we both saw."

"I will."

"Did I tell you about the red pool they have hidden behind the lake?" he asked.

She turned to him. "No. Really?"

"Really. Chelise says they drained the lake but they couldn't get rid of all the water, so they covered it up on the north side."

"The red pools," Kara said. "Like blood." Her eyes closed briefly, then opened. The drugs were working.

"I love you, Thomas."

Then her eyes rested shut.

"I love you too, Kara."

He looked up at the bright light above him. Time seemed to slow.

"You'll begin to feel drowsy," one of the doctors said. "We've administered the anesthesia into your IV."

They'd explained that they were using a simple bypass procedure that would pump his blood into the blue machine at his right. He wanted to dream, so they would put him under quickly. He would feel no pain, not even a prick. Once they started, the entire procedure would take less than ten minutes.

The doctors stepped aside, and Robert Blair stepped to the side of his bed. He put his hand on Thomas's shoulder. "I want you to know that not a soul living will have any doubt about who saved their lives," he said. "You're changing history."

"Is that what you think?" Thomas was having a hard time focusing. "Maybe I am. I'm saving some lives. When Justin died, he did much more. If you thank anyone, thank him."

"Justin," the president said. "And who is Justin?"

"Elyon. God."

Blair lifted his eyes and stared out the window. "Believe me, I will never think of God in the same terms again."

"Thomas." A hand touched his other shoulder. He faced Monique. She was trying not to cry but failing.

"None of this was your fault," Thomas said. "It wasn't your vaccine that caused any of this. It was what a man did with your vaccine. Remember that."

"I'll remember," she said softly. He could hardly hear her now. His world was slipping.

"The real virus is evil," he heard himself say. "The disease of . . . of the Horde."

Then he was sleeping.

Dreaming.

———

Monique could not bear to watch the entire procedure. All nice and neat with white gowns and silver instruments and sophisticated machines, but in the end they were simply draining Thomas of his blood until he died.

This was how they slaughtered cows.

Then again, it had been his choice. This man who'd come to her rescue repeatedly and saved her life twice already was now giving the ultimate sacrifice. She knew of no braver man.

The only consolation was his dreaming. If he could dream and eat the rhambutan fruit every night for as long as he lived, he might live out a full life in the other reality before he died here, in the next few minutes. It was possible.

On the other hand, he might die in both realities. This was now in Justin's hands.

Monique told them to call her when it was over and retreated to her office. She locked the door, sat behind her desk, and buried her face in her hands.

Then she wept uncontrollably.

The call came twenty minutes later.

She picked up the phone. "Yes?"

"We're done."

She let a moment pass. "He's dead?"

"Yes. I'm sorry."

"How long did he dream?"

"Maybe twenty minutes."

She took a deep breath. "You know what to do." Thomas's sacrifice would mean nothing without a cup of his blood being delivered to each of the gateway cities within the allowable time frames.

"It's already on the helicopter, headed for the airport where the planes are standing by."

Monique hung up. She glanced at the cooler. A sample of his blood was still in there, enough for her to dream one last time. But he was dead now. She had no right to try something so speculative without understanding its implications.

Or did she?

42

Mikil jerked up from her bedroll, eyes wide in the bright morning sun. Kara!

For a long moment her mind wrestled with the information that Thomas had given her. He was in the library under threat of Chelise's death. He'd just knocked himself out. But how much time was there?

She scrambled to her feet and ran for the horses, yelling at Johan, who had lifted himself on one elbow. They'd traveled all night and collapsed in this cave, just outside the city, at first light.

"Do not move! Wait here. I'll be back."

"Where are you going?" Suzan demanded.

"To the city."

Suzan jumped to her feet. "Then we go with you!" she said.

"No!" Mikil grabbed the reins and swung into her saddle. She pulled her horse around. "I have to do this alone. We can't risk losing anyone else."

"Mikil, please!" Jamous ran for her. "You can't go alone. Let me come."

She leaned over and kissed him on the head, then on his face. "I'll return. I promise, my love. Wait here, I beg you. Wait for me."

She kicked her mount and sped into the trees.

"Mikil!"

"Wait for me!" she cried.

———⟐———

Thomas opened his eyes. He was on the floor of the library. His head throbbed. A hand was on his shoulder. Chelise sat on the floor beside him, crying quietly. How long had he been out? There was no way to tell.

Long enough.

Or maybe not long enough, depending on Mikil.

He closed his eyes and tried to clear his mind. They'd been together for an hour, maybe two, all of it worse than he imagined even lying in the dungeon, fearing the worst. The very sight of her when they'd removed his blindfold and shoved him into the library had made his knees weak.

Chelise. His love. The one woman he would gladly give his life for. This stunning being who was white with disease only because she didn't yet know the truth. But he couldn't see her disease. To him her painted face and gray eyes were the sun and the stars.

He'd done his best for an hour. The words from his mouth felt like acid. But he knew that Woref would take her life if he failed. If she died now, her death would be eternal, and that was something he couldn't bear. His only hope had been to give her the gift of life, so that perhaps one day someone else could lead her to the drowning where she would find her Maker.

Now there was another hope. A thin sliver of light. Mikil. He had to give her time.

But there was also something else now. He was going to die. When they took the last of his blood to save the world from the virus, he would die, there and here. Although an hour there in his dreams could be a month here, it could also be just a few minutes.

He could not die without expressing his true love one last time.

He lay still and let her cry softly, afraid to open his eyes again. It had all begun with a bump on the head. He'd lived a month in one reality, unknowingly releasing a plague and then perhaps undoing that same disease. And he'd lived sixteen years in this reality, where another kind of disease had been loosed and then undone.

Both would end in his death.

None of that mattered now. Only Chelise mattered. From the very beginning it had all been about her. This one woman who must be given the opportunity to dive into a pool of red to trade her white skin for the white gown of a bride. Justin's bride.

He had to give Mikil more time.

⎯⎯⎯⎯⎯⎯

The main library had been cleared of the scribes by Christoph in a simple agreement that would one day give him more authority. The chief librarian was no fool. He knew that in time Woref might have even more power than he had now. Ciphus was another story. The chief priest had agreed to bring Thomas, but he refused to implicate himself in any way. He could play both sides, a snake if ever there was one.

Woref's most trusted lieutenant, Soren, sat by the wall that butted up against the storage room that held the Books of Histories. He occasionally peered through a small slit they'd cut in the wall to give him a clear view of the entire back room from above the fourth shelf of Books.

Woref stood by the opposite window, looking out at the circular orchard in the middle of the royal garden. He had no interest in watching the albino—some things were better left unseen. He was interested only in the conclusion of this matter.

The fury that had raged through his mind after seeing Chelise's response to Thomas in the dungeons had surprised even him. He'd dreamed of Teeleh screaming into his face, fangs wide, throat deep and black. The beast had slashed him with his taloned claw.

Woref woke from the nightmare weeping. Cheek bleeding.

Recalling the event now, his neck went hot and his fingers trembled. He closed his eyes and calmed himself. Black flooded his mind. *You will kill her, Woref. You know that. In the end, even if she loves you, you will strike her too hard or choke her too long, and she will die in your arms. Why not today and be done with it?*

Because we want her love.

"He's waking, my lord."

Woref opened his eyes. He had to give the albino credit. According to Soren, he'd done well, then knocked himself out to spare himself the pain. It had seemed rash to Soren, but Woref understood. He knew Thomas's heart, and he despised him for it.

The woman was another matter. Her love for Thomas ran deeper than he'd imagined. She was a stubborn whore. But he knew that she was crying for herself, not for Thomas.

It was now only a matter of time. Teeleh would have his wench's love.

—— ✺ ——

He couldn't bear lying awake while she cried anymore. Thomas took a deep breath and rolled away from Chelise. She jumped to her feet and stepped back. "Thomas?"

Woref or one of his faithful was still watching, listening. They'd let this go on only because of Thomas's convincing performance thus far.

He looked around, as if dazed. "How much time has passed?" he whispered.

"What?"

He looked at her. Face streaked. Eyes wide. Her question lingered on a parted mouth. Thomas suddenly couldn't trust himself to speak. He would break down, here and now, and cling to her ankles and beg her forgiveness for the way he'd cut her to ribbons with his tongue.

He swallowed and diverted his eyes. "How long was I out?"

She didn't respond right away, which meant she didn't know either. He couldn't do this! He couldn't bear it any longer!

"I don't know, maybe half an hour. Or ten minutes."

"Only ten minutes?" Mikil would need much more time! Then again, if she'd fallen asleep and dreamed only five minutes before he had, she could have spent a whole day here already. In any case, no one had come for them yet. Which could only mean that Mikil had not succeeded. For all he knew, she was dead.

"It could have been an hour," she said. Her tone was sharper now. He glanced at her and saw that she was frowning. Still staring at him, but with more resolution now. There was only so much of this she could take before she began to believe his lies.

"Please," she whispered.

Thomas clasped his hands behind his back and strolled down the line of Books. Please! She'd said please, and she might as well have kissed his lips!

He tried to think of the missing blank Books and the very serious consequences that could follow the Books appearing in the other reality. But he had no room in his heart now for what-ifs. He couldn't tear his mind away from the woman who watched him walk as if he was disinterested in her.

I am interested in you, my love. Look at my face, my hands, the way I walk, the way I breathe. Can't you see past this charade and know that I will always love you?

That would defeat the purpose of his game, wouldn't it?

What if he actually succeeded? What if she turned against him in rage and never loved him again?

His heart began to crash in his chest. He came to the corner and stopped. Tears were filling his eyes again, and he tried to blink them away. He closed his eyes and begged her to forgive him. It was worse than death.

Mikil, where are you? He had to make Woref believe that he was playing his diabolical game. He had to stay strong for her sake. Silence smothered the library. A deep void of death. A sealed tomb filled with . . .

Thomas opened his eyes. There was a sound behind him. A very soft wail. Not like her other sobs. There was an unmistakable sound of finality to her groan.

Terrified, he looked back.

Chelise was lying on the floor, facedown, with her hands extended above her head, weeping.

Thomas was stumbling toward her before he could tell his feet to move. He would not bear this! What had he done?

He fell to his knees, threw his arms over her head, and buried his face in her hair. He tried to speak, but his throat wasn't cooperating.

He tried to be gentle—to pull back and tell her what he desperately wanted to tell her, to stroke her face and wipe her tears, but all he could do was cling to her and cry into her hair. Woref would come. At any moment they would crash through the doors and pull him off of her. He had to tell her!

But he could only shake over her like a leaf.

Stop it, Thomas! You're terrifying her!

Then he lifted his head, sat back on his legs, and wept at the ceiling. "I . . . love . . . you." It came out as hardly more than a whisper.

He sucked in a lungful of air and gazed at the back of her head through his tears. He stroked her hair with his fingertips. "I love you, Chelise, my bride, more than I could possibly love anything else." Her crying had stilled. "I'm so sorry . . . It was a lie, all of it was a lie, so that you would forget about me."

His words rushed out with relief. "I had to drive you away so they wouldn't kill you, but I can't do it. I can't do it; I don't have the strength to see you suffer. Forgive me, forgive me, my love."

Chelise's back rose and fell with her deep breathing. Did she believe him? The thought that she might not dashed through his mind. He dropped on her again, clung to her shoulders, and wept into her back.

"I beg you, forgive me! I didn't mean a word, I swear it."

He was smothering her again!

Thomas pulled back.

Chelise pushed herself to her knees, facing away. Thomas trembled, horrified by the thought that she might not believe him.

She turned slowly and he saw that her mouth was locked in a silent cry. She stared at him through pools of tears. She was regretting? She was . . .

Chelise threw her arms around his shoulders, buried her face in his neck. "I knew you loved me!" she sobbed. She kissed him below his ear and ran her fingers up the nape of his neck and squeezed him as if she were clinging to life. "I love you, my darling! I will always love you."

Thomas was beyond himself. He wrapped his arms around her, giving her only enough space to breathe. "Marry me!" he cried. It was absurd, but he didn't care. He wanted her to hear it. "Marry me!"

She hesitated only a single beat. "I will." She wept over his shoulder. "I will marry you."

The door crashed open and slammed behind Thomas. Boots pounded over the floor. A fist grabbed his hair and yanked him back with such force that he thought his neck might have been broken.

He fell back and Chelise came with him.

Woref snatched a handful of her hair and jerked her off of him. Chelise screamed.

"Leave her!" Thomas tried to rise. "Leave her—" Woref's boot connected with his temple and he fell flat.

He had to get up. He had to stall Woref. He had to kill the man. They were both dead anyway. Thomas pushed himself up. The room was spinning. He blinked and gathered himself. It occurred to him that no one else had come into the room. Whatever Woref planned, he would blame Thomas.

"Qurong . . ." Thomas gasped. "Qurong won't let you . . ."

Woref shoved Chelise against the wall and held her by her neck, hand drawn to hit her. "Now I will kill you," he said. His voice rose. "Do you hear me, you filthy whore? I will pound you until you die," he screamed in rage. "No one defies me! Not the daughter of Qurong, not Qurong himself!"

He swung his hand.

"Stop!"

The door flew inward.

Woref was committed—his open hand slapped Chelise's cheek with the sound of a cracking whip. Her head snapped sideways. But Woref had pulled back his full strength at the last moment. She stared at the doorway with wide eyes.

Thomas followed her stare. There stood Qurong. And Ciphus. And behind them, Mikil, hands bound.

———∞∞∞———

The supreme leader stood with both hands clenched, head bared. The vein at his temple bulged beneath his long, thick dreadlocks.

"Release her."

Woref withdrew his hand from her neck. He swept back a rope of hair that had fallen over his face. "This woman has committed treason by loving an albino," he said. "For that she must die."

Qurong stepped into the room. Thomas stood and looked at Mikil, who was staring at him.

"What is she doing here?" Qurong demanded.

"I brought her to save her life," Woref said. "Ciphus knows."

"I only know that you ordered her here," the chief priest said. "I know nothing else."

"You lie!"

"I'll decide who's lying," Qurong said. He stared at his daughter, lips drawn in a thin line. "How could bringing her here save her life? She was never condemned!"

"She condemned herself by loving the albino." Woref spit on the floor. "I knew and I demanded that the albino retract his love so that she would come to her senses. It was the least I could do for you."

"Then you're a fool," Qurong said bitterly. "You see things that don't exist. Who are you to judge the love of my daughter? My wife is right; you have a death wish for her."

"I can assure you—"

"Silence!" The supreme leader paced in rage. "I don't care what you say, your word is no longer trustworthy."

"Perhaps your daughter should speak for herself," Ciphus said.

They all looked at Chelise. Her eyes glanced around. Stared at Thomas. Then settled on her father.

"Then speak," Qurong said. "But I warn you, we have a law that binds us."

Thomas felt his heart sink. She had to deny her love! If she only denied it, Qurong would give her the benefit of any doubt and let her live. Woref's plot was exposed; she would be safe.

Chelise stared at her father for a long time. She looked at Thomas, and he shook his head barely, so that no one but her would see. *Please, my love. I know the truth. Save yourself.*

She locked onto his eyes and stepped away from the wall. "You want to know the truth, Father? You want to know why this beast you've put in charge of your armies is so outraged?"

She walked toward Thomas and stopped in front of him. "You want to know why this albino bound me and stole me from the castle? Why he would cross the desert for me on foot if he had to? Why he would give his life to save mine?" She paused. "It is because he loves me more than he loves his own breath."

Thomas felt his brows wrinkle in fear for her.

Chelise took his arm, stepped by his side, and faced her father. "And I love him the same."

They were six frozen statues.

"I'm sorry, Father. I can't lie about this."

Thomas saw the same fear he felt for her life pass through Qurong's eyes. "You're being forced . . ."

"I'm not," she said.

"You can't possibly say this! Do you know what this means?"

"It simply means that I love him. And for that love I will pay any price."

The supreme leader's face flushed with fury. He glared at Ciphus.

The priest bowed his head. "Then her fate is sealed, my lord."

Slowly, like the fading sun, Qurong's face changed. The resolve that had served him so well in a hundred battles settled over him. He glanced at Chelise once, then looked at Thomas.

"Forgive me," Thomas said. "I would do anything—"

"Shut up! Against the wall! Both of you."

Thomas and Chelise stepped over to the wall and pressed their backs to the bookcase.

"Release him," he snapped at Chelise. "Move away."

She obeyed.

"So then. The price for the head of my greatest enemy is the death of my own daughter. So be it."

He turned his back on them and stared at the back wall.

"Woref, please join them."

The general seemed not to have heard. "I'm sorry, my lord, what—"

"Join them on the wall."

"I don't see—"

"Now!"

Woref stepped next to Thomas.

"Ciphus."

Ciphus walked over and pulled Woref's sword free before the man could make sense of what was happening.

Qurong faced him. "I sentence you to death for treason against the royal family. You will die with them."

Woref stood aghast. "I don't think you understand, my lord. I've committed no act of treason!"

"You denounced me. You also had every intention of killing my daughter. I told you if you hurt her I would drown you myself, and now I will do that."

"This is an outrage!"

"It is fair," Ciphus said. "It is just."

"Come!" Qurong ordered.

A guard stepped in, followed by a line of others, moving quickly. Twenty filed in and surrounded them.

The supreme leader stepped up to Woref, grabbed the band across his chest that gave him his rank, and ripped it free. "Bind them!" he ordered. "They will drown tonight." He threw the sash on the floor and stepped toward the door.

"What of the other albino?" Ciphus asked. "She came willingly. On your behalf."

Qurong's eyes were sad and his fight was gone. He looked at Mikil. "Release her."

43

Thomas stood in heavy leg chains on the wooden platform that reached out over the muddy lake. A half circle of roughly fifty hooded warriors, each armed with swords and sickles, stood behind the dock. Every third one carried a blazing torch that cut the night with flickering orange light. Ciphus waited to one side with several council members, avoiding eye contact with Thomas. Qurong was evidently on his way.

None of this mattered to Thomas. Only Chelise mattered. He searched the darkness behind the guards for a glimpse of her. Neither she nor Woref had been brought yet.

Conflicting emotions had beat at Thomas as he lay in the black cell. He'd wanted to die; he'd wanted to live.

At any moment he might die as he lay on the bed where they were draining his blood. Part of him begged Elyon to spare him the agony of seeing Chelise drowned by allowing him to die now.

Part of him begged Elyon to let him live another hour, long enough to see his love just one more time. They would die, but in their death they would be together. He couldn't bear the thought of not looking into her eyes again.

He didn't know what they'd done with her after they'd been pulled apart at the library, but his mind hadn't rested in imagining. Was she in her castle, crying on her bed while her mother wept for her life in the courtyard? Was she in the dungeon, thrown to the floor like a used doll? Was she demanding her father reconsider his sentence or screaming at him for abandoning her in favor of this mad religion he'd embraced?

Thomas faced the lake and scanned the barely visible distant shore.

Who was watching from the trees? Mikil and Johan, maybe. But they were powerless without swords. He was amazed to realize he had no fear of this drowning that awaited him. Justin had suffered far worse.

But Chelise . . . dear Chelise, how could she have consigned herself to death with this mad admission of love for him? He didn't care about the honor it brought him. He didn't care that she had stood up for principle or that she'd done what was right. He only cared what happened to her.

She would die. Not just in this life, but if he understood Justin, in whatever life awaited them.

Thomas lifted his eyes to the stars. *Why? How could you do this to such a tender soul? She isn't beautiful to you? Her skin offends you? Then why did you put this ache for her in my heart? This is how you will leave your bride?*

There was a commotion behind him, and he twisted to see if . . .

Thomas caught his breath. She was there. Chelise walked down the bank between four horses that guarded her. She was dressed in a white gown and she held her head steady, giving no sign that she was the victim rather than the administrator of this drowning.

Thomas searched her face to see if she had seen him, but her hood was raised and her eyes were shaded. The guards parted to receive her.

Thomas saw Qurong then, riding nobly on his horse with a large guard. They came down the shore from Thomas's right. There was no sign of Patricia.

Qurong stopped twenty yards up the bank. He would see his own sentence through without any display of weakness. But even from here, Thomas could see the supreme leader's drawn face. He wouldn't be surprised if those were claw marks on his neck from Patricia.

Now Woref was being marched down the bank behind Chelise. But Thomas didn't care about Woref.

Chelise walked past the warriors. The flames lit her face.

She was staring at him.

Thomas felt his remaining strength wane. His face wrinkled in sorrow.

She stepped onto the platform and stopped ten feet from him. Thomas moved toward her without thinking.

"Back!" A fist clubbed his head. The night went fuzzy, but he didn't lose sight of Chelise.

"We are dying for our love!" she said for all to hear. "You'll deny even that? If you are going to drown us, then let us share at least a moment of the love we are dying for!"

The guard glanced at his superior.

"Let her go to him," Qurong said.

Chelise walked toward him slowly, like an angel. Her chains, hidden by the flowing white gown, rattled on the boards. Fresh tears ran from her eyes when she was halfway to him. He stumbled toward her, and they fell into each other's arms.

There was no reason to speak. The tears, the touch, the hot breath on their necks spoke much louder than words.

Shame on the rest! They stood watching a true love that had been condemned by the religion they had the nerve to call the Great Romance.

Here was romance!

Woref stepped onto the platform.

"Enough," Qurong said. "Finish this before I force the rest of you in with them!"

"Put them abreast!" Ciphus ordered.

"You gave your life for me," Chelise whispered in his ear. "Now I will die for you." She sniffed.

"You don't have to!" Thomas said. "It's not too late . . . your father will accept your denial. Please, I know your love, but you have to find a red pool . . ."

Hands pulled her from behind. Her eyes looked into his.

"You're my red pool," she said.

⸙

"We aren't going to make it!" Mikil said. "They're already on the platform. Hurry!"

She'd raced back to the others, knowing that she would need their help if there was any chance to save Thomas. But time was running out.

"We still don't know if this will work," Suzan said. "We still have time to stop the execution. Four of us with swords could scatter them!"

"Not as easily as you think," Johan said. "If they have the sashes of assassins, they won't run like the ones we walked through the other day."

"We can't save him by killing the Scabs," Mikil snapped. "We might as well be Scabs ourselves. Just dig!"

Jamous threw his weight into his sharpened stick. The passage was now four feet deep, and they clawed away at both ends. Close, so close. Any swing and either wall of remaining dirt would be breached. They'd cleared over a hundred medium-size boulders and now worked feverishly with torn hands on the soil that separated the two bodies of water.

Mikil shoved the dirt aside as fast as she could, careful not to be hit by one of their digging sticks. Her husband paused, panting. "Suzan's right. We don't know this will—"

"Just dig! There's nothing that says it takes more than a drop! Is an ocean of blood better than a bucket? One drop of Thomas's blood and I can enter his dream world. I'm telling you that one drop of this will do the same. Now—"

"I'm through!" Johan shouted.

They froze. Had his voice carried across the lake? It no longer mattered. They were running out of time.

"It's flowing!" Johan dropped to his knees and pulled aside clods of dirt. Red water spilled over his fingers and splashed into the bottom of their trench.

"The other side!" Mikil cried. "Break it down!"

———— ❦ ————

"Unhand me!" Woref seethed.

The guards shoved them into position, three abreast across the wide platform. Several tall towers similar to the one they'd used to drown Justin stood to the left of the dock. Evidently Qurong had ordered a method that would spare him from watching his daughter struggling while hanging from her feet, half submerged. The heavy bronze shackles around their ankles would pull them to the bottom where they would drown unseen.

They now stood ten yards from the end of the platform. Chelise looked straight ahead, jaw set. But her show of strength couldn't stop the steady flow of tears down her white cheeks.

Thomas tore his eyes away from her. *Please, Elyon, I beg you. Rescue your bride. Have mercy.*

"Step forward," Ciphus ordered. "Stop at the edge of the platform."

Hands pushed Thomas. He moved ahead without any more encouragement. "Please, Chelise. This water means nothing to me, but I can't bear the thought of your death."

"I couldn't live with myself," she said softly. "And you're wrong. My father would never undo what he's ordered. I don't want him to."

He came to the edge and stopped. "You could save yourself. You could save me. You could keep my heart from breaking."

Woref looked ahead at the forest, eyes now searching with quick movements. "I beg you, I beg you," he whispered. His stoic bravado had been replaced by this odd plea to the forest.

Thomas followed his eyes. This was the same forest in which he'd seen the Shataiki after Justin's death. What did Woref see?

"I beg you, my lord," the general muttered. He was crying out to Teeleh, Thomas thought. Let him.

Thomas followed Chelise's gaze into the dark water ten feet below them. Long poles disappeared into the black depths. How many bodies were entombed down there, bones chained to their anchors?

The guards were binding their hands behind their backs now.

"Please, my love . . ."

"You've drowned before."

"But not in this water."

"Did you know that when you dove in, or did you sink in desperation?"

It had been both. Fear and a sliver of faith. But there was nothing to hope for here. He stared across the lake. Beyond the torch's reach the water was jet-black. Blacker than midnight. Blacker than he remembered.

"Now stand and face the rage of Elyon," Ciphus said behind them. The planks creaked under his feet as he paced. His voice rose. "Let this be a lesson to all who would defy the Great Romance by denouncing those whom Elyon himself has put over this land."

Chelise looked at him. The flames danced in her misty eyes. Her lips trembled. "You are my husband."

"And you are my wife," he whispered.

"Prepare them!" Ciphus said.

A guard behind each of them planted a fist between their shoulder blades and grabbed their hair.

"Pull!"

The guards jerked their hair down so that their heads buckled backward, forcing them to stare at the sky above. Three abreast, hands bound with canvas strips, feet laden by heavy chains, powerless and readied to die.

Mikil dropped to one knee on the right of the trench and stared across the black waters. Jamous knelt beside her; Johan and Suzan followed their lead on the other side.

"Please, Elyon," she whispered. "Mercy. Save him."

She glanced down at her left. The trench was roughly two feet wide and four feet long, and it now flowed with a rich stream of the red water from the red pool they'd found behind them. Thomas had told Kara about it absently, but the moment Qurong had sentenced him and Chelise to death in the library, she'd known that this was their only hope. To find the pool of Elyon's water and dig through the barrier between it and the Horde's lake.

But would it be enough?

The red water looked like a black fan as it spread out into the brown muddy waters. Moving fast. Faster than she would have guessed.

"Please, Justin. Save your bride."

"Thomas!" Chelise's voice was faint, tight. Her throat felt frozen. She'd seen both kinds of drownings before—from the platform and the tower—and if there was any measure of relief in her sentence, it was that Qurong had mercifully chosen the platform. In a fit of outrage, her mother had finally demanded at least that much, and her father had quickly agreed.

"Elyon's strength," Thomas whispered.

"As Elyon has commanded, so now you die," Ciphus cried. "Now die!"

A hand shoved her in the back, and suddenly there was nothing beneath her feet.

None of them made a sound as they fell. Woref hit the water first. Chelise saw his splash from the corner of her eye just before the cold water swallowed her legs, then her chest. Thomas plunged in on her left.

Then she was under.

She fell straight down, pulled by the chains bound to her ankles. She instinctively struggled against the restraints around her wrists—as was the custom, they were only loose bindings hastily tied to prevent an episode at the last moment on the platform. Amazingly they came free, sending a streak of hope through her mind. She opened her eyes.

Black. So black.

She clenched her eyes shut and, in so doing, shut the door on the last of her hope.

Elyon! Take me. Take me as your bride as you have Thomas. Her thoughts were born of panic, not reason. At any moment her feet would land in a pile of bones.

Elyon! Justin, I beg you!

The water around her feet, then her legs, changed from cold to warm. She opened her eyes and looked down in surprise. She'd expected a murky lake bottom below her—black demons clamoring for her in their lust for death.

What she saw was a pool of red light, dim and hazy, but definitely light! She looked left, then right, but there was no sign of Thomas or Woref.

Then Chelise fell into the warm red water. She floated. Serene. Silent. Unearthly and eerie. She could hear the soft thump of her own pulse. Above her, Qurong and Ciphus were watching the water for signs of her death—bubbles—but here in this fluid she was momentarily safe.

And then the moment passed and the reality of her predicament filled her mind. It was warmer and much deeper than she'd expected, and it was red, but she was still going to drown.

Her eyes began to sting, and she blinked in the warm water but received no relief. Her chest felt tight, and for a moment she considered kicking for the surface to take one more gulp of air.

She opened her mouth, felt the warm water on her tongue. Closed it.

Is it Justin's water?

But who would willingly suck in a lungful of water? She'd entered intending to die. She knew that Thomas was right—the disease had ruined her mind! But dying willingly had felt profane.

She hung limp, trying to ignore her lungs, which were starting to burn. But that was just it—she didn't have the luxury of contemplating her decision much longer.

A wave of panic ran through her body, shaking her in its horrible fist with a despair she'd never felt before.

Chelise opened her mouth, then closed her eyes. She began to sob. A final scream filled her mind, forbidding her to take in this water. Thomas had drowned once, but that was Thomas.

Then her air was gone. Chelise stretched her jaw wide and sucked hard like a fish gulping for oxygen.

Pain hit her lungs like a battering ram.

She tried to breathe out. In, out. Her lungs had turned to stone. She was going to die. Her waterlogged body began to sink farther.

She didn't fight the drowning. Thomas had wanted her to follow him in death, and this is what she was doing. There was no life above the surface anyway.

The lack of oxygen ravaged her body for long seconds, and she didn't try to stop death.

Then she did try. With everything in her she tried to reverse this terrible course.

Elyon, I beg you. Take me. You made me; now take me.

Darkness encroached on her mind. Chelise began to scream.

Then it was black.

Nothing.

She was dead. She knew that. But there was something here, beyond life. From the blackness a moan began to fill her ears, replacing her own screams. The moan gained volume and grew to a wail and then a scream.

She knew the voice! She didn't know how she knew it, but this was Elyon. Justin? It was Justin, and he was screaming in pain.

Chelise pressed her hands to her ears and began to scream too, thinking now that this was worse than death. Her body crawled with fire as though every last cell revolted at the sound. And so they should, a voice whispered in her skull. Their Maker was screaming in pain!

A soft, inviting voice suddenly replaced the cry. "Remember me, Chelise," it said. Elyon said. Justin said.

Light lit the edges of her mind. A red light. Chelise opened her eyes, stunned by this sudden turn. The burning in her chest was gone. The water was warmer, and the light below seemed brighter.

She was alive?

She sucked at the red water and pushed it out. Breathing! She was alive!

Chelise cried out in astonishment. She glanced down at her legs and arms. The shackles were gone! She moved her legs. Free. Real. She was here, floating in the lake, not in some other disconnected reality.

And her skin . . . She rubbed it with her thumb. The disease was gone! Thomas had been right! She was an albino. Here in the bowels of this red lake she was now a stunning breed, and the thought of it filled her with a thrill she could hardly fathom.

She spun around, looking for Thomas, but he wasn't here.

Chelise twisted once in the water and thrust her fist above (or was it below?) her head. She dove deep, then looped back and struck for the surface. What would they say?

She had to find Thomas! Justin had changed the water.

The moment her hand hit the cold water above the warm, her lungs began to burn. She tried to breathe but found she couldn't. Then she was through, out of the water.

Three thoughts mushroomed in her while the water was still falling from her face. The first was that she was breaking through the surface at precisely the same time as Thomas on her left. Like two dolphins breaking the surface in coordinated leaps, heads arched back, water streaming off their hair, grinning as wide as the sky.

The second thought was that she could feel the bottom of the lake under her feet. She was standing near the shore.

The third was that she still couldn't breathe.

She came out of the water to her waist, doubled over, and wretched a quart of water from her lungs. The pain left with the water. She gasped once, found she could breathe easily, and turned slowly.

Water and strings of saliva fell from Thomas's grinning mouth. She wasn't sure what had happened to him, but he was alive.

She lifted her arm and stared. Her skin had changed. A dark flesh tone. Deep tan. Smooth like a baby's skin. And she knew without a doubt that her eyes were emerald, like Thomas's.

She was as albino as any albino she'd ever seen.

Only then did it occur to her that Qurong was still seated on his horse less than thirty yards from where she stood. His face was stricken. To her left the guard stared in stunned silence. No sign of Woref. He was undoubtedly drowned.

"Seize them!" Ciphus cried from the platform.

"Leave them!" Qurong ordered.

Chelise walked out of the lake, plowing water noisily with her thighs. Thomas walked beside her—there was no need for words.

In some ways she felt as if she was looking at a whole new world. Not only was she a new person, drowned in magic, but the Scabs she faced were now foreign to her. The disease hung on them like dried dung. But when they understood what Elyon had done for them in this lake, they would flock en masse into the red waters. She would be run over, she thought wryly.

Then she remembered her own resistance to the drowning. She stared at her father, who still looked as though he was staring at something in his nightmares come to life.

"The law states that they must drown!" Ciphus said, walking to the edge of the platform, finger extended.

"They have drowned," Qurong said.

"They are not dead!"

"Does my daughter look like a Scab to you?" Qurong shouted. "If this is not a dead Scab, I don't know what is. She's been drowned and paid her price! You will not lay a hand on her."

Chelise wanted to run up and throw her arms around him. "Father, it's real. The water is red! This is now a red pool."

His eyes jerked to the water behind her. She followed his gaze. The lake looked black, but there was a tinge of red to it.

Ciphus was staring and had now seen it too. "Seal off the lake!" he shouted, spinning to the guard. "No one enters."

"No!" Chelise. "The people must be allowed to drown! Father, tell him."

Qurong looked back out at the water. He scanned the surface. "And Woref?"

"Woref didn't believe," Thomas said.

Her father eyed him. "And how did this water become red?"

"I don't know for sure, but I'm guessing that Mikil and Johan found the red pool you had covered."

Qurong frowned. "Seal the lake," he said.

"Form a perimeter at the top of the shore," Ciphus said. "Not a soul steps on the beach until we have repaired this damage."

Chelise took a step toward Qurong. "Father, you can't allow this!"

He lifted a hand. "Stop there."

"Drown!" she cried. "You have to drown, you and Mother! All of you!"

Her father drew his horse around so that he faced her. "They are free to go," he said. "They and their friends will be given free passage from our forest. No albino is to be hurt before we know the truth of what has happened here."

"Father . . . please, I beg you . . . you know the truth."

"You're my daughter, and because of that I will let you live in peace," he said. "But I have my limits. Leave now, before I change my mind."

He turned his horse and walked up the shore.

Chelise stared after him, torn between the urge to drag him into the lake and the realization that she was no different only a day ago. But there was hope, wasn't there? He was going to consider the matter.

"I'm sorry," Thomas said, putting his hand on her shoulder.

She faced him and her sorrow faded. His skin, just this morning an interesting enigma, was now deliciously brown and smooth. His green eyes shone like the stars. He was truly beautiful.

"Are my eyes . . ."

"Green," he finished. He brushed her cheek with his thumb. "And your skin is dark, the most beautiful I've ever seen."

"I am his bride now?" she asked.

"You are. And mine?"

"I am."

She felt as if she might burst.

He winked and then took her hand. "We should take your father at his word and get out while we can. The Circle will be waiting."

The Circle. She glanced back. Ciphus was glaring at them. Two dozen guards had formed a line by the platform, barring them from following Qurong, who was just now guiding his horse past a hastily formed perimeter guard.

The Circle was waiting. She grinned, suddenly eager to be gone from here and among her new family. To be with her husband.

Thomas of Hunter.

"Then we shouldn't keep them," she said and stepped toward the waiting forest.

44

Marseilles, France.

Carlos had waited three days now, and not a single vehicle had crawled out of the underground facility. But they were there; he would stake his life on it.

Birds chirped on the hillside, oblivious to how close they had come to moving up the food chain three days ago. Here in the country outside of the port, the morning was peaceful and cool. Down in the city there was a scramble to acquire one of the coveted syringes that were now flowing out of Paris. The news was of nothing but the virus. More accurately, the antivirus. The Thomas Strain, they were calling it. The man had reportedly given his life. Carlos wasn't ready to believe that just yet.

There were enough vaccinations to go around, they said, but that didn't stop the panic. The distribution plan was essentially the reverse of their blood-collection efforts. Syringes filled with the Thomas Strain had already flooded the gateway cities. Every refrigerated vehicle in France was now carrying the antivirus to distribution points across the country, where hundreds of thousands waited their turn in long lines.

Meanwhile, Carlos lay in wait with his weapon.

He glanced at his forearm. The red spots had disappeared. He still couldn't make sense of it, but there was only one cause that made any sense. He'd been in contact with Hunter's blood.

The man's funeral was to be held in twenty-four hours. Carlos would use every power at his means to be present. He had to see for himself. And if Hunter was finally dead . . .

The thought knotted his gut and he let it trail off.

If Fortier didn't emerge soon, he would go to the authorities—the French military would like nothing better than to drop a few bunker busters on this site and rid the world of the men who had sullied their reputation. The French president, who'd followed Fortier's demands all too quickly, would probably do it himself to bolster his standing with the people. The world was too distracted by the virus at the moment, but one day Carlos might set them all straight.

The problem with going to the authorities now was that it meant leaving his post long enough for them to make an escape. Unlikely, but he wouldn't put anything beyond Fortier.

So Carlos waited in his hole on the hill.

He'd decided halfway to Paris that the bunker there made no sense. Fortier and Svensson would hole up in Marseilles, where no matter what the outcome of the next few days, they would be safe. With this new plan of theirs to betray so many who'd surrendered their weapons, Paris was full of too many enemies.

Carlos had confirmed that two vehicles had recently driven over the soft ground that led to the hidden bunker below. It could be no one but Fortier and Svensson—no one else knew of its existence. The only reason he knew was because he always knew more than they meant for him to know.

It all made sense in the most apocalyptic way. They had unleashed their weapon and would hunker down until it had done its work before emerging to a new world.

But they hadn't factored in Thomas. Or his dreams.

Carlos reached into his pocket and pulled out another pill. He'd slept once since setting up his post, but it had been early, before the news of the Thomas Strain had broken. He popped the pill in his mouth and swallowed.

He imagined that Fortier and Svensson were down in that hole arguing furiously at this very moment about what had gone wrong. They . . .

The earth on the hill below suddenly moved. Carlos froze. So soon?

Slowly, like a giant whale opening its mouth, the hill opened up. He snatched the antitank missile and sat upright. So they had decided to leave France while the world was still distracted by the crisis. There had been a few massive manhunts before, but none like the one that would surely follow this debacle.

Carlos armed the missile, hefted it onto his shoulder, and aimed it at the entrance. His hands were shaking from the combination of exhaustion and shattered nerves.

The garage door stopped. Open. Then nothing.

He willed the car to emerge. It would be the white Mercedes with armored plating. They would split up later, but they wouldn't risk two cars at this point if only one was armored, which Carlos knew to be the case.

Come on, come on. Come out.

He could practically taste the cordite on his tongue from the anticipated explosion. The missile would tear the car to a thousand pieces.

The nose of the white Mercedes suddenly poked out of the garage.

Steady . . .

Then the body.

Carlos waited until the garage door began to close. One car. Windows tinted so he couldn't tell if they were both inside.

He suddenly couldn't wait another moment. He triggered the missile. A loud *whoosh.* Pressure on his shoulder. Then a streak of exhaust and a waft of hot air on his face.

He willed the missile all the way into the Mercedes. It struck the right front passenger window. For a split second, Carlos saw the legs in the passenger's seat.

That made two occupants.

The detonation shattered the morning air. A ball of fire split the car at its seams. Blew the roof off. Smoke boiled out.

Then it was just roaring fire.

Carlos grabbed his binoculars, adjusted the focus, and studied the flames. He'd seen enough in his time to conclude now that he had just killed two men.

One of them was Armand Fortier. The other was Valborg Svensson.

He lowered the glasses. Unlike Thomas, these two would not be coming back to life.

Kara watched the casket sink below the green turf at Arlington National Cemetery. They were giving Thomas a full military burial with all the honors, and hundreds of people she'd never met were being moved to tears by the event, but to her the whole funeral felt oddly insignificant.

Her brother was alive.

Not here, nor in a way any of these people could possibly understand the way she did. But he was more alive than any of these who wept.

The president stood on her right. Monique on her left. Five days had passed since Thomas's death. They'd wanted to march his casket down Constitution Boulevard while the world watched, but Kara had convinced the president that if Thomas had a say in the matter, he would protest. They'd settled on this more subdued but still nationally broadcast affair.

The seven guns had gone off and three fighters had roared overhead, and Kara had watched it all with mild interest. Her mind was still on Thomas's blood. The blood that Monique still had in storage.

She couldn't get it out of her mind.

Beyond the skin of this world waited another world, as real, perhaps more real. There Thomas was alive and by now surely married to Chelise. He'd died while in the lake, and somehow it had given him life. There was no doubt in her mind that Justin had orchestrated everything.

Justin had allowed Thomas to fall in love with Chelise so that the Circle would know how he felt about them. Kara was sure that if she could see Justin now, he would be racing circles around his bride on a white stallion, thrilled by the beauty of his creation. By the love, however mixed it was, that they had for him.

This was his bride!

And in his eyes her dress was spotless. White.

Someone handed her a shovel. She snapped out of her thoughts. They wanted her to do the honors? She stepped forward, scooped up some dirt, and tossed it into the grave.

Then it was over. She turned her back on the burial. The gathered crowd began to step away.

"I want you to know that I've commissioned a statue for the White House lawn," the president said. "You may think Thomas would object, but this isn't about Thomas anymore. It's about the people. They need a way to express their gratitude. This isn't going to end."

She nodded. The Thomas Strain had smothered the virus in a way that none could have hoped for. There were deaths, but remarkably few. Under two hundred thousand at last count, and most of those the result of people trying to bypass the system. Some riots, a refrigeration truck ambushed, and the like. The Thomas Strain was just now reaching remote destinations around the world—mostly in the Third World, part of South America, China, Africa, where the Raison Strain had been the slowest to infect. The world would never be the same, but it had survived.

If Thomas had been delayed on the aircraft carrier by only three hours, the death toll would have been significantly higher.

The president put his arm on her shoulder. "You okay?"

"Yes." She smiled. "Thank you, sir."

"If there's anything I can do, you let me know."

"I will."

He turned away, and Monique stepped in to replace him.

"So," she said, sighing, "now what?"

"Now I don't know."

"Do you think his blood still works?"

"I don't know. Six billion people now have some of his blood in them, don't they? They're not dreaming."

"They have no reason to dream," Monique said. "Without belief, you don't dream."

Kara walked with Monique. "Or maybe the dreams don't work because he's dead," she said. "'Course, I dreamed once when he was dead."

"Maybe we should find out."

Kara looked into her eyes. "Tempting, isn't it?"

"I've thought about it more than once."

"I don't know. Something tells me that it's changed. I think we should leave it alone for now. It's safe, right?"

"Believe me, no one's touching it."

"There is something else that worries me," Kara said.

"The Book," Monique said without hesitation.

Kara stopped. "That's right. The blank Book of History. Or should I say Books. Thomas seemed to think that they all crossed over. At this very moment there exists at least one Book, last seen in France, which has more power than any of the nuclear weapons Thomas sank."

"Surely it'll show up."

"That's what I'm afraid of."

45

A sunset painted the dusk sky orange over the white desert. Thomas sat on his horse at the lip of a small valley that resembled a perfect crater roughly a hundred yards across. The depression harbored an oasis, and in the center of that oasis a red pool was nestled among large boulders. A ring of fruit trees grew from the rich soil beside the limestone that held this particular pool. Twenty-four torches blazed in a perfect circle around the pool. The rock ledge around the water was roughly fifty yards in diameter, and it kept the pool clean so that, from his perch above the scene, he imagined he could almost see the bottom, though he knew it was at least fifty feet deep.

Tonight Thomas of Hunter would wed once again.

Chelise, who was now being prepared by the older women, would soon walk into the circle of torches and present herself for union with Thomas as was the custom from the colored forest. The four-hundred-odd members of this tribe had been joined by another two thousand from those tribes close enough to make the trek for the occasion. They were gathered on the far slope, beyond the ring of torches.

Thomas's mind went briefly to Rachelle. He missed her, always would. But the pain of her loss had been whitewashed by his love for Chelise. Rachelle not only would approve, but she would insist, he thought.

Ten days had passed since Chelise's drowning. In that time nearly five thousand of the Horde had joined the Circle, urged on by Chelise's passionate voice. If ever there was a prophet in the Circle, it was she. With Qurong's own daughter now among the albinos, the threat from the Horde had all but vanished. At least for the time being. Teeleh wouldn't wait long before taking up his vain pursuit again, but until then Qurong's decree would protect the Circle from any unauthorized attack. Rumor had it Ciphus was being forced to keep his disapproval to himself. He'd drained the lake and was refilling it again. His religion would be back in full swing soon enough.

Suzan and Johan were mounted on black horses next to Thomas. They would be married in two days in a similar ceremony. Mikil and Jamous sat on the other side. They were fools for love, all of them. The Great Romance had swallowed them whole, and this gift of love between couples was a constant reminder of the most extravagant kind.

"How long?" Thomas asked.

"Patience," Mikil said. "Beautifying is a process to be enjoyed."

"And marriage isn't? I don't see how they could possibly add to her beauty."

Suzan chuckled.

Thomas lifted his eyes and looked at the sunset. It was a paradise, he thought. Not like the colored forest, but close enough. With Chelise at his side and Elyon on the horizon of his mind, more than a paradise.

"You still haven't dreamed?" Mikil asked.

The dreams.

"I dream every night," he said. "But not of the histories, no. For sixteen years the only way I could escape the histories was to eat the rhambutan fruit. Now I couldn't dream of the histories if I tried."

"But they did exist," Johan said. "I was there myself."

"Did they? Well, yes, the histories existed. But when we finally get access to the Books in Qurong's library—"

"He's agreed?" Susan asked.

"Eventually we'll get our hands on them. I'm sure the fact that we can read them will play to our favor. But when we have access to the Books, I don't know what we'll find. It happened; I'm sure it happened. But will it all be recorded? I don't know. Either way, I don't live in the histories. I live here."

An unsure smile crossed Suzan's mouth. Thomas looked at the boulder around which Chelise would soon come. What was keeping them?

"You don't believe that it happened, Suzan?" he asked. "Tell her, Johan. Was it real or was it only a dream?"

"If it was a dream, it was the most incredibly real dream I ever had."

"Did I say I didn't believe?" Suzan said. "But let's be honest, Thomas. Not even you know exactly what to believe about these dreams. Mikil has her thoughts about shifts in time; you talk about shifts in dimensions. I'm not saying the dreams didn't happen, Elyon forbid. But they make about as much sense to me as the red pools do to the Horde."

"Exactly!" Thomas said, impressed. "To a Scab the notion of drowning to find new life is absurd. And to all of us, the notion of entering a different dimension through dreams is as absurd. But the lack of understanding doesn't undermine the reality of either experience."

"I must say, the memory is fading," Mikil said. "It hardly feels real anymore. Everything that was so important to Kara seems so distant. What consumed that world hardly matters here."

"No, what happened there helped to define me," Thomas said. Although he had to agree. The human race had faced the threat of extinction, but the drama there was overshadowed by the drama here.

"But I see your point, and I think it was meant to be," he continued. "How can the rise and fall of nations compare to the Great Romance? Think about it. A whole civilization was at stake there, and at first it scared me to death. But by the end, the struggles in this reality seemed far more significant to me. Certainly far more interesting. The battle over flesh and blood cannot compare to the battle for the heart."

He took a deep breath. "On the other hand, the blank Books are gone. That's interesting. And how the Books came into existence in the first place. For that matter, how I bridged these two realities."

Johan faced him, eyes bright. "I have a theory. Why and how Thomas first entered the black forest, we'll never know, because he lost his memory, but what if he managed to fall, hit his head, and bleed at precisely the same moment that he was struck on the head in the other reality? This could have formed a bridge between what can be seen and what can't be seen."

"Then Earth, the other Earth, still exists?" Suzan asked.

"It must," Johan said. "And the blank Books are most likely there."

"Unless you subscribe to Mikil's theory that Elyon used Thomas's dreams to send him to another time," Suzan said. "You see what I mean? They both make sense only if you use liberal amounts of imagination."

"Principalities and powers," Thomas said absently. "We fight not against flesh and blood, but against principalities and powers."

"What?"

"Something I now remember from the other reality. It was no less obvious there how these things worked. They called it the natural dimension and the spiritual dimension."

"Spiritual. As in spirits?" Suzan asked.

"As in the Shataiki here. We can't see them, but our battle is really against them, not the Horde."

"Well, we know the Shataiki are real enough," Johan said. "So why not the dreams?"

A distant rumble like the sound of thunder from the far side of the world drifted over them. Thomas cocked his head. "You hear that?"

They were all listening now. The rumble grew steadily. Thomas's horse snorted and stamped nervously.

"The ground's shaking!" Suzan said. "An earthquake?"

"Too long."

All of their horses were now restless, unusual for beasts trained to stand still in battle.

"Dust!" Mikil cried, pointing to the desert.

They turned as one, just as the first beasts crested the long dunes in the nearby desert. Then more came, thousands, stretching far to the left and to the right.

Thomas's first thought was that the Horde had staged a massive attack. But he immediately dismissed the notion. Johan spoke what was on his mind.

"Roshuim!" he cried.

A thousand, ten thousand—there was no way to count such a large number. The massive white lions that Thomas had last seen around the upper lake when he'd first met the boy poured over the dunes like a rolling fog.

They were split down the middle. There, slightly ahead of the lions, rode a single warrior on a white horse.

Justin.

Johan, Mikil, then Jamous and Suzan slid from their saddles and dropped to one knee. It was their first sighting of him since they'd fled the Horde after his death. The sounds from the crowd opposite them had stilled, but they rose as one and stared to the west.

Thomas had just overcome his shock and started to dismount when Chelise walked out from the boulders below them. She seemed to glide rather than walk. His bride was dressed in a long white tunic that swept the sand behind her. A ring of white tuhan flowers sat delicately on her head.

Thomas froze. Chelise surely heard the approaching thunder, but she couldn't see what he saw from her lower vantage point. She must have assumed it was the pounding of drums or something associated with the ceremony, because her eyes were turned toward him, not the desert.

Her eyes pierced him, and she smiled. Oh, how she smiled.

She reached the circle, faced him, and lifted her chin slightly. The black, red, and white medallion hung from her neck, fastened by a leather thong.

On Thomas's left, the Roshuim lions ran on, led by Justin. It occurred to Thomas that he was still standing in one stirrup. He lowered himself to the ground, stepped forward, and knelt on one knee. Chelise followed his gaze.

The lions split and swept in a wide circle, pouring around them as if this pocket of desert was protected by an unseen force.

Justin, on the other hand, drove his horse straight on, right over the berm that encircled the small valley, directly toward Chelise.

Now she saw.

Justin reined his horse back ten yards from Chelise, who stood in stunned silence. The stallion whinnied and reared high. Justin's eyes flashed as only his could. He dropped the horse to all four, then slid to the sand and took three steps toward her before stopping. He was in a white tunic, with gold armbands and leather boots strapped high. A red sash lay across his chest.

The lions still poured around the valley, giving them all a wide berth, twenty yards behind Thomas.

Justin looked up at Thomas. Then back at Chelise, like a proud father. Or a proud husband?

He strode into the circle, up to Chelise, took her hand, and bent to one knee. Then he kissed her hand and stared into her eyes. Chelise lifted her free hand to her lips and stifled a cry. She might be a strong woman, but what she saw in his eyes would undo the strongest.

Justin stood, released her hand, and stepped back. He placed both hands on his hips, then immediately lifted them to the sky, and faced the stars.

"She's perfect!"

He turned toward the gathered crowd, most of whom had fallen to their knees. "And each one of you, no less! Perfect!"

Justin bounded for his horse, leaped into his saddle, grabbed the reins, and galloped up the slope, directly toward Thomas.

The Roshuim had completed a circle and now faced the valley. The moment Justin cleared the lip, they fell to their bellies in a soft rolling thump and lowered their muzzles to the sand. The sight knotted Thomas's throat, and he wanted to throw himself to the sand and worship as the lions did, but he couldn't tear his eyes from Justin, racing toward him.

"Elyon . . ." Johan whispered.

Justin veered to their right. Then the sound of metal sliding against metal ripped through the still air. Justin pulled his sword free, leaned off his mount, and thrust the blade's tip into the sand.

He wheeled his horse around and rode away from Thomas, hanging low in a full sprint, long hair flowing in the wind, dragging the sword in the sand. The soft cries of joy joined the thudding of his horse's hooves. They all knew what he was doing. They'd all heard the stories.

Justin was drawing his circle.

And he was drawing it around all of them, claiming them all as his bride. The circle was symbolic.

Justin, on the other hand, was not.

He completed the circuit behind Thomas and turned his horse back toward them. Thomas felt compelled to lower his head. Justin's horse walked by, hooves plodding, breathing hard, snorting. Leather creaked.

It stopped at the top of the slope, not ten yards from where Thomas knelt.

For a long moment there was silence. Even those who had been crying on the opposite slope went quiet.

Then the sound of laughter. A low chuckle that grew.

Surprised, Thomas glanced up at Justin. The warrior/lover who was also Elyon had thrown back his head and had begun to laugh with long peals of infectious delight. He thrust both fists into the air and laughed, face skyward, eyes clenched.

Thomas grinned stupidly at the sight.

Then the laughing started to change. Honestly, Thomas wasn't sure if this was laughter or sobbing any longer.

The grin faded from Justin's face. He was weeping.

Justin suddenly lowered his arms, stood up in his stirrups, and cried out so they all could hear him. "The Great Romance!" He glanced to his left and Thomas saw the tears on his cheeks. "From the beginning it was always about the Great Romance."

He sat and turned his stallion so that its side faced the valley.

"It was always about this moment. Even before Tanis crossed the bridge, in ways you can't understand."

Justin scanned the crowd.

"My beloved, you have chosen me. You have been courted by my adversary, and you have chosen me. You have answered my call to the Circle, and today I call you my bride."

For a long time he gazed over the people who filled the valley with the sounds of sniffing and crying. Chelise was kneeling in her own tears now.

Justin turned toward Thomas. He nudged his horse forward.

"Stand up, Thomas."

Thomas stood, legs shaking. He looked up at Justin, but he found it difficult to look into those emerald eyes for more than a few moments.

"No, look into my eyes."

Those wells of creation. Of profound meaning and raw emotion. Thomas wanted to weep. He wanted to laugh. He was in the lake again, breathing an intoxicating power that came from those eyes.

"You have done well, Thomas. Don't let them forget my love or the price I've paid for their love."

I won't, Thomas tried to say. But nothing came out.

Justin looked at the others and nodded at each. "Suzan, Johan. Jamous, Mikil." He let tears run down his cheeks. "My, what a good thing we have done here."

His jaw flexed and his nostrils flared with pride.

"What a very good thing."

Then he pulled his stallion around. "Hiyaa!"

The horse bolted. On cue, the massive ring of Roshuim stood and roared. The ground shook.

Chelise ran from the red pool, up the slope toward Thomas. She pulled up beside him, staring at Justin. Thomas drew her close, and they watched the receding entourage in awed silence.

Justin galloped into the desert, followed by the ranks of white lions on either side. The desert settled back into silence.

For a long time no one spoke.

And then Thomas married Chelise, surrounded by an exuberant, rejoicing Circle still intoxicated by Justin's love.

Epilogue

So then, were you right or were you wrong?" Gabil asked, scanning the titles of Books on the library's top shelf. "It really is a simple question with a simple . . ." He stopped short. "Ah! I've found it!"

He withdrew an old leather-bound book and swooped down toward Michal, who teetered on the edge of the desk, peering at another Book of History he'd withdrawn only minutes ago. A single candle lit the old pages. The Horde library lay in shadows, deserted at this late hour.

"None of this is simple," Michal said. "Patience."

"I thought you said you'd found it," Gabil said, fluttering for a landing beside Michal. He set the Book he'd retrieved on the desk.

"I said I found the section that deals with the Great Deception, not the actual sentence that states the actual date."

"You did tell Thomas of Hunter early in the twenty-first century. I remember that much."

"And if I did, then you agreed," Michal said, scanning the page.

"Did I? You're positive?"

"Did you disagree? You're far too interested in this minor point, Gabil. What difference does the date make in the end? This is a silly exercise."

"I'm interested because the histories couldn't have said early in the twenty-first century. Thomas changed history. The virus didn't ravage the world. So the question is, when does the Great Deception take place? Or does it even?"

Gabil studied the cover of his Book, then opened it to the first page.

This history was taken from the colored forest. He flipped toward the back of the Book.

"Of course the Great Deception takes place," Michal said. "I'm reading the details now, as we speak. You see, right here . . ." The Roush stopped.

"What?" Gabil released the page in his fingers, hopped once, and leaned over to see.

"Give me some room," Michal protested. "This . . . I don't remember anything about . . ."

"I knew it!" Gabil chirped. "Yes, I did. I knew it. It's changed, hasn't it?"

"Well, it's no longer early in the twenty-first century. But we could have been mistaken about that. But these other things . . ."

"Thomas changed history!"

Michal ran his finger down the page. "The Tribulation as recorded by John hasn't changed, but the date . . . and the Great Deception . . ." He returned to where he'd started reading. "I do say, the events leading up to John's prophecy have changed."

"He did change history. He did, he did!" Gabil hopped again, twice, lost his footing, and toppled to the floor. He bounded to his feet and did a little jig of sorts. "Ha! It's fascinating! It's magnicalicious!"

"Please, settle down. That's not even a word."

"Why not?" Gabil said. "If Thomas can change history, I think I have the right to change a few words."

He jumped back up on the desk and resumed his search in the Book that recorded the colored forest's demise.

Michal looked at him, still gripping the page he'd been reading. "So you really think knowing how Thomas entered the black forest will shed any light on—"

"Here!"

Michal jumped. "What is it?"

"I think I've found it! This Book records his story." He flipped forward to the very end, scanning anxiously. "Here, here, it has to be here in this volume."

Michal looked over the pages with interest.

"Give me space," Gabil said.

"Humph." Michal took a tiny step to his right.

Gabil came to the last page and stopped cold. "What is this?"

"What?"

"It's been . . ." He leaned forward. "It's been changed. Erased and written over."

Michal crowded Gabil again. "What's it say?"

The smaller Roush ran his index finger under the words of the last paragraph, which were clearly written in handwriting different from those preceding.

He read aloud.

"Then the man named Thomas found himself in the black forest, where he fell and hit his head and lost his memory. Ha."

Gabil looked up at Michal, taken aback.

"'Ha'?" Michal asked, incredulous. "It says 'ha'? That's it?"

"That's it. Then it's signed."

Gabil looked at the page. *"Billy, Storyteller,"* he read. "Someone named Billy who is a storyteller wrote this."

They stared in silence for a few seconds.

Michal sighed and returned to his Book. "I have to admit, this is . . . fascinating."

"It seems Thomas wasn't the only one who changed history," Gabil said. "Didn't I tell you? Ha!"

"Ha?"

"Ha!" He closed his book and hopped on top of it. "So read. Read this new history that I told you we would find even though you doubted." He lifted his chin and grinned.

Michal eyed his fuzzy friend. "Yes, I guess you did tell me."

Then the Roush took a deep breath and began to read from the Book of Histories.

THE END

COMING
FULL CIRCLE

It's amazing how clear hindsight is. If only our foresight were as clear. If we only had been able to see then what we see now, we could have purchased a hundred thousand shares of Google and become gazillionaires. If only, if only, if only. But every once in a while—for reasons beyond our understanding—we make decisions that might as well have been made with clear foresight even though we had little at the time.

Such was the case with my penning of the Circle Trilogy—*Black, Red,* and *White*—in 2003. I won't lie; much of what's happened since was in my mind way back then. But not everything . . . not by a long shot.

The whole idea for the Circle Trilogy began during a time of meditation when I saw a crystal clear image of a man diving into a lake and breathing the water: not ordinary water, but the essence of God Himself. The man trembled in the folds of intense pleasure.

That was it.

I threw myself into expanding this image into a tale that I called *The Song of Eden* and submitted it to a reputable agency. The story was summarily rejected.

So I retooled and rewrote and resubmitted, this time with an agent who believed in what I was doing. He submitted the new and improved story to a dozen publishers, and they all passed, saying it was too edgy for the intended market.

Over the next few years I went on to publish a handful of novels with Thomas Nelson that quickly gained acclaim. Armed with renewed confidence and Thomas Nelson's full support to write whatever I desired, I returned to *The Song of Eden*, completely overhauled the story, renamed it *Black*, and resubmitted the fresh manuscript as Part One of a trilogy.

I still remember waiting for that *Come to Jesus* phone call all writers either dread or beg for after turning in a manuscript. *What is it: thumbs up or thumbs down? If it's thumbs up tell me, tell me more, and don't stop telling me.*

If it's a thumbs down there has to be a mistake. Reconsider, repent, return, and restate.

In the case of *Black* the call was from then VP of Marketing and now Publisher of Fiction at Thomas Nelson, Allen Arnold. And it was the former kind of call, the kind you live for. But this time Allen took it a step further. "Ted, what do you think about publishing the entire trilogy, all three books, in the space of one calendar year? We'll call it The Year of the Trilogy. Can you do it?"

Intoxicated by the flattery, I made a show of bemoaning the effort he was asking of me, but then gave up the charade and cried out my response. *Yes! Of course!*

Six months later I was still slaving over *Red*, swearing that if I ever made it through the next few months I would never agree to such an absurd notion again.

Little did I know.

My objective in writing *Black, Red,* and *White* was to retell redemptive history by mirroring it in another reality while keeping the reader firmly rooted in our own world. I didn't want to write pure fantasy: rather an amalgamation of thriller and fantasy that incorporated intense pacing with weighty exploration of truth.

But not everyone at Thomas Nelson was as enthusiastic as Allen Arnold. I remember being told by one member of the team that publishing this series could very well sink my career. Why? Because nobody read this kind of story.

The prediction crushed me. But I was growing used to rejection by this point, and rather than folding up my books and going home a defeated storyteller, I went where my heart led me. I began to work on an expansion of the story by plotting out what would eventually become Project Showdown: *Showdown, Saint,* and *Sinner.*

By the time the trilogy was released, we all began to realize that instead of not being read as some had predicted, the Circle Trilogy was striking a chord with a whole new group of readers. A large group at that.

The ideas were larger than me. Thousands wanted to chime in. So we launched The Circle, a virtual gathering place at teddekker.com to discuss the stories. Fifty thousand joined over time, and their thoughts led me to consider an even *further* expansion of the story. After all, plumbing the depths of our own redemptive history isn't a task easily handled by three measly books. Nor six.

And so was born the idea of not three books, not six books, but *ten* books to flesh out the full story. It would be called The Books of History Chronicles. Three series, each dependent upon the others, yet each completely independent. Stories that twist in and out of each other like grapevines before the harvest. You can read any of the three following series first or last, but it is best to read the books within each series in order.

The Circle Trilogy – *Black, Red, White*

The Lost Books – *Chosen, Infidel, Renegade* (May 2008), *Chaos* (May 2008)

Project Showdown – *Showdown, Saint, Sinner* (October 2008)

In addition graphic novels are now available for the Circle Trilogy, with plans for the rest to come out in graphic format in short order.

As I write this short history on The Books of History Chronicles, I have just begun writing the final book of ten, *Sinner,* and the interconnection woven throughout all ten books is amazing to me. I had my plans at the outset; sure I did. But this is no simple linear story your grandmother cuddled up next to the fire to read.

This is a labyrinth of wickedness and destruction and pleasure and, above all, love, because in the end it's all just one big, mind-bending love story, isn't it?

It's as if the books had their own story to tell, and I've come along as the scribe chosen to pen them. A confession: I just learned this year where the worms in *Showdown* actually came from. I should have known, of course, it makes perfect sense. All the signs were there.

I've also learned why Thomas was allowed to cross realities. And why Billy wrote that one innocent little statement that started the whole thing in *Showdown*. My family thinks I've lost my noodles because each night I come bounding out of my dungeon, giddy like a child having discovered one more nugget in this saga of ours. The further you get the better the discoveries become.

Four years have passed since *Black,* the novel that so many within the publishing world said would never work, was published with the full support of Allen Arnold. Today more people are buying the Circle Trilogy on any given day than any other novel I've written before or since.

I once told Allen that I was born to write these chronicles. Admittedly, their writing is only a small part of my life. But if I was born to write them, then in a small, small way you may have been born to read them. We, like the stories themselves, find ourselves interconnected in this wonderful thing called the story of life. You are part of my history and I am a part of yours. And this, my friend is what it means to come full circle.

Welcome to the Books of History.

Welcome to the Circle.

Ted Dekker

It began in a
coffee shop in Denver.

Now it spans two realities,
ten novels, and
three graphic novels

Welcome to
The Circle . . .

THE BOOKS OF

CIRCLE TRILOGY

CIRCLE GRAPHIC NOVELS

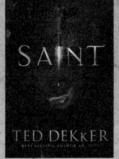

An Excerpt from Chosen

beginnings

O ur story begins in a world totally like our own, yet completely different. What once happened here in our own history seems to be repeating itself thousands of years from now.

But this time the future belongs to those who see opportunity before it becomes obvious. To the young, to the warriors, to the lovers. To those who can follow hidden clues and find a great treasure that will unlock the mysteries of life and wealth.

Thirteen years have passed since the lush, colored forests were turned to desert by Teeleh, the enemy of Elyon and the vilest of all creatures. Evil now rules the land and shows itself as a painful, scaly disease that covers the flesh of the Horde, a people who live in the desert.

The powerful green waters, once precious to Elyon, have

vanished from the earth except in seven small forests surrounding seven small lakes. Those few who have chosen to follow the ways of Elyon now live in these forests, bathing once daily in the powerful waters to cleanse their skin of the disease.

The number of their sworn enemy, the Horde, has grown in thirteen years and, fearing the green waters above all else, these desert dwellers have sworn to wipe all traces of the forests from the earth.

Only the Forest Guard stands in their way. Ten thousand elite fighters against an army of nearly four hundred thousand Horde.

But the Forest Guard is starting to crumble.

11:08PM - DENVER, COLORADO

ONE OF THE BENEFITS OF THE LAST SHIFT AT THE JAVA HUT: FREE CAFFEINE...

SMACK!

HUH?

WHAT THE...?

THAT'S WEIRD...

SMACK!

SOMEBODY'S SHOOTING AT ME!

WAIT A MINUTE...

WHY WOULD SOMEONE BE SHOOTING AT ME?

THAT'S CRAZY.

THOMAS HUNTER!

OK. SO I'M NOT GOING CRAZY.

WHICH MEANS...

SMACK!

...SOMEBODY IS SHOOTING AT ME.

GOTTA FIND COVER FAST...

...AND TRY TO STAY ALIVE IN THE MEANTIME.

CLANG!

NEED TO FIND SOMEWHERE TO HIDE...

NO POINT IN HIDING, HUNTER!

YOU'RE A DEAD MAN!

A NEW YORK ACCENT?

HOW'D THEY FIND ME?

I GUESS A HUNDRED GRAND WAS JUST TOO MUCH TO LET SLIDE.

I ONLY HAVE A FEW SECONDS BEFORE HIS EYES ADJUST.

GOTTA MOVE...

THWIP!

UNGHH

THINK HE JUST GRAZED ME...

NOW, IF YOU JUST COME A LITTLE CLOSER, WE CAN TALK ABOUT THAT HUNDRED GRAND...

SNAP!

FACE TO FACE!

WAIT FOR IT...

SWISH!

CRACK!

THAT'LL GIVE HIM SOMETHING TO CHEW ON.

BUT HE LOOKS LIKE A BIG BOY, I THINK HE'LL NEED...

...SOMETHING MORE TO CONSIDER!

KYA!

NOT BAD FOR AN OUT OF SHAPE BLUE BELT.

IF THEY FOUND OUT WHERE I WORK THEN THEY KNOW WHERE I LIVE.

UNGHHH

HEAD'S THROBBING NOW.

GOTTA GET OFF THE STREETS. KARA'S PLACE SHOULD BE SAFE.

SHE CAN FIX ME UP WHEN SHE FINISHES HER SHIFT AT THE ER.

ANYWAY, SHE'S ALWAYS COMPLAINING HER LITTLE BROTHER DOESN'T VISIT ENOUGH.

LOOKS ALL CLEAR. THINK I'M SAFE. FOR THE MOMENT AT LEAST.

GOOD THING I KNOW WHERE SHE KEEPS HER SPARE KEY.

MAYBE I SHOULD LIE DOWN... JUST FOR A MINUTE.

KARA WILL BE HOME SOON...

... SHE CAN TELL ME...

...IF IT'S SERIOUS...

THE STORY CONTINUES IN
THE CIRCLE TRILOGY GRAPHIC NOVELS

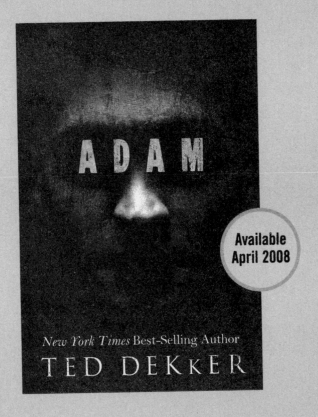